IN THE BLEAK MIDWINTER

JULIA SPENCER-FLEMING

IN THE BLEAK MIDWINTER

THOMAS DUNNE BOOKS ST. MARTIN'S MINOTAUR NEW YORK

THOMAS DUNNE BOOKS.
An imprint of St. Martin's Press.

IN THE BLEAK MIDWINTER. Copyright © 2002 by Julia Spencer-Fleming. All rights reserved. Printed in the United States of America. No part of this book may be used or reproduced in any manner whatsoever without written permission except in the case of brief quotations embodied in critical articles or reviews. For information, address St. Martin's Press, 175 Fifth Avenue, New York, N.Y. 10010.

www.minotaurbooks.com

Designed by Lorelle Graffeo

Hymn on page ix, "In the Bleak Midwinter," from *The Hymnal 1982*, published by The Publishing Co.

Hymn on page 68, "The King Shall Come When Morning Dawns," from *The Hymnal 1982*, published by The Publishing Co.

Library of Congress Cataloging-in-Publication Data

Spencer-Fleming, Julia.
    In the bleak midwinter / Julia Spencer-Fleming.—1st ed.
        p.   cm.
    ISBN 0-312-28847-6
    1. Adirondack Mountains (N.Y.)—Fiction.   2. Episcopal Church—Clergy—Fiction.
3. New York (State)—Fiction.   4. Police chiefs—Fiction.   5. Women clergy—
Fiction.   I. Title.
    PS3619.P645 I5   2002
    813'.6—dc21

                                                            2001051303

10   9   8   7   6   5   4   3

~To Leslie~

WINTER MUST BE COLD FOR THOSE WITH NO WARM MEMORIES.

—DELMER DAVES AND LEO McCARY

ACKNOWLEDGMENTS

Thanks to Ruth Cavin, Julie Sullivan, and every-one at St. Martin's Press for making my first time so much fun, and thanks to Luci Zahray for dis-covering me. This book was immeasurably improved by the critiques of those who read it as a work-in-progress: Adele Hutchinson; my father, John Fleming; Karen Fletcher; Les Smith; and Anne Steele Zembala. I had expert help from the clergy of the Cathedral Church of St. Luke, Port-land, Maine, and from Timothy J. LaMar, for-merly of the U.S. Army Infantry, who took me shooting and explained what it sounds like when you bash in someone's head with a rock. Thanks to my mother, Lois Fleming, my first and best writing instructor, editor, critic, and fan. Finally, thanks to my husband, Ross Hugo-Vidal, who went through everything but a plague of locusts during the writing of this book and lived to tell the tale.

In the Bleak Midwinter

LYRICS BY CHRISTINA GEORGINA ROSSETTI

In the bleak midwinter, frosty wind made moan,
Earth stood hard as iron, water like a stone;
Snow had fallen, snow on snow, snow on snow,
In the bleak midwinter, long ago.

Our God, heaven cannot hold him, nor earth sustain;
Heaven and earth shall flee away when he comes to reign;
In the bleak midwinter a stable place sufficed
The Lord God incarnate, Jesus Christ.

Angels and archangels may have gathered there,
Cherubim and seraphim thronged the air;
But his mother, in her maiden bliss,
Worshiped the beloved with a kiss.

What can I give him, poor as I am?
If I were a shepherd, I would bring a lamb;
If I were a wise man, I would do my part;
Yet what I can I give him: give him my heart.

CHAPTER ONE

It was one hell of a night to throw away a baby. The cold pinched at Russ Van Alstyne's nose and made him jam his hands deep into his coat pockets, grateful that the Washington County Hospital had a police parking spot just a few yards from the ER doors. A flare of red startled him, and he watched as an ambulance backed out of its bay silently, lights flashing. The driver leaned out of his window, craning to see his way between cement rails.

"Kurt! Hey! Anything for me?"

The driver waved at Russ. "Hey, Chief. Nope. Heart attack stabilized and heading for Glens Falls. You heard about the baby?"

"That's why I'm here."

Kurt continued to back out, almost to the end of the parking lot. "Jesum, hard to imagine sumpin' like that here in Millers Kill—" The rest of his commentary was lost as he heeled the ambulance into the road. Russ waved, then pushed open the antiquated double doors to the emergency department.

His glasses fogged up within seconds in the moist heat of the foyer. He pulled off the wire frames and rubbed them with the end of his scarf, mentally cursing the myopia that had finally led him, at forty-eight, to cave in and wear the damn things full time. His stomach ached and his knee was bothering him and for a moment he wished he had taken that security consulting job in Phoenix like his wife had wanted.

"Hey! Chief!" A blurry form in brown approached him. Russ tucked his glasses over his ears and Mark Durkee, one of his three night-shift officers, snapped into focus. As usual, the younger man was spit-and-polished within an inch of his life, making Russ acutely aware of his own non-standard-issue appearance: wrinkled wool pants shoved into salt-stained hunting boots, his oversized tartan muffler clashing with his regulation brown parka. Hell, Mark was probably too young to get a cold neck, even with the back of his head shaved almost bald.

"Hey, Mark," Russ said. "Talk to me."

The officer waved his chief down the drab green hallway toward the emergency room. The place smelled of disinfectant and bodies, with a whiff of cow manure left over by the last farmer who had come in straight from the barn. "Man, it's like something out of an old Bing Crosby movie, Chief. The priest at Saint Alban's found the little guy bundled up at the door of the church. The doctor's checking him out now."

"How's the baby look?"

"Fine, as far as they can tell. He was wrapped up real well, and the doc says he probably wasn't out in the cold more'n a half hour or so." Russ's sore stomach eased up. He'd seen a lot over the years, but nothing shook him as much as an abused child. He'd had one baby-stuffed-in-a-garbage-bag case when he'd been an MP in Germany, and he didn't care to ever see one again.

Mark and Russ nodded to the admissions nurse standing guard between the ER waiting room and the blue-curtained alcove where patients got their first look-see. "Evening, Alta," Russ said. "How's business?" The waiting room, decorated with swags of tired tinsel and a matching silver tree, was empty except for a teenager sprawled over one of the low sofas.

"Slow," the nurse said, buzzing them into the emergency treatment area. "Typical Monday night." The old linoleum floors carried the rattle of gurney wheels and the squeak of rubber-soled shoes.

"Over there," Mark said, pointing. Framed by limp white curtains dangling from ceiling tracks, an athletic-looking woman in gray sweats was leaning on a plastic incubator, writing in a pocket-sized notebook.

"Who the hell's that?" Russ asked. "I swear, if they let a reporter in here before we've cleared the facts I'll—" he strode toward the incubator. "Hey, you," he said.

His challenge brought the woman's chin up, and she snapped her head around, zeroing in on the two policemen. She was plain, no makeup and nondescript dark blond hair scraped back in a ponytail. She had that overbred look he associated with rich women from the north side of town: high cheekbones and a long thin nose that was perfect for looking down at folks. Mark grabbed his arm, grinning. "No, no. That's the priest, Chief." He laughed out loud at the expression on Russ's face. The priest? Christ on a bicycle. She gave Russ a look that said, "Wanna make something of it?" He felt himself coloring. Her eyes were the only exceptional thing about her, true hazel, like granite seen under green water.

"Officer Durkee," she said, her gaze sliding off Russ as if she had already weighed and found him wanting. "Any word yet from the Department of Human Services?" There was the barest trace of a Southern accent in her no-nonsense voice.

"No, ma'am," Mark said, rocking back and forth on his heels. "But I'd expect that. They got a lot of ground to cover around here, and not many people to cover it with." He was still grinning like a greased hyena.

Russ decided the best defense was a good offense. "I'm Russell Van Alstyne, Millers Kill chief of police." He held out his hand. She shook firm, like a guy.

"Clare Fergusson," she said. "I'm the new priest at Saint Alban's. That's the Episcopal Church. At the corner of Elm and Church." There was a faint testiness in her voice. Russ relaxed a fraction. A woman priest. If that didn't beat all.

"I know which it is. There are only four churches in town." He saw the fog creeping along the edges of his glasses again and snatched them off, fishing for a tissue in his pocket. "Can you tell me what happened, um . . ." What was he supposed to call her? "Mother?"

"I go by Reverend, Chief. Ms. is fine, too."

"Oh. Sorry. I never met a woman priest before."

"We're just like the men priests, except we're willing to pull over and ask directions."

A laugh escaped him. Okay. He wasn't going to feel like an unwashed heathen around her.

"I was leaving the church through the kitchen door in the back, which is sunken below street level. There are stairs rising to a little parking area, tucked between the parish hall and the rectory, not big, just room enough for a couple cars. I was going for a run." She looked down and waggled one sneaker-shod foot. Her sweatshirt read ARMY. "The box was on the steps. I thought maybe someone had left off a donation at first, because all I could see were the blankets. When I picked it up, though, I could feel something shifting inside." She looked through the plastic into the incubator, shaking her head. "The poor thing was so still when I unwrapped him I thought he was already dead." She looked up at Russ. "Imagine how troubled and desperate someone would have to be to leave a baby out in the cold like that."

Russ grunted. "Anything else that might give us an idea of who left him there?"

"No. Just the baby, and the blankets, and the note inside."

Russ frowned at Mark. "You didn't tell me about any note," he said.

The officer shrugged, pulling a glassine envelope out of his jacket pocket. "Reverend Fergusson didn't mention it until after I had called you," he explained. He handed Russ the plastic-encased paper.

"That's my fault, yeah," said the priest, not sounding at all apologetic. Russ held the clear envelope at arm's length to get a better view. "I didn't call DHS until I was over here, and I wanted to make sure they knew what the baby's parents intended." She looked over his arm at the note. "I'm sorry, but I handled it without thinking about any fingerprints or anything."

It was an eight-by-eleven sheet of paper ripped from a spiral-bound notebook, the kind that you could get anywhere. The handwriting, in blue ink, was blocky, extremely child-like. Russ guessed that the note's author had held the pen in her left hand to disguise her printing. "This is our baby, Cody," it read. "Please give him to Mr. and Mrs. Burns here at St. Alban's. We both agree they should have him, so there won't be any trouble later on with the adoption. Tell our baby we love him."

Russ lowered the note and met the priest's green-brown eyes. "Kids," he said.

"That would be my guess," she said.

"Who are the Burnses?"

"Geoffrey and Karen Burns."

"The lawyers," Russ said, surprised.

"They're parishioners of St. Alban's. I understand they've been seeking adoption for over two years now. They've been on the Prayers of the People list for the past two weeks, and as I recall, our secretary told me that's a regular thing for them."

"This is something published? Or what?"

"Prayed out loud, every Sunday during the service."

He looked closely at her. "Sounds like at least one of the baby's parents might go to your church."

She looked uncomfortable. "Yeah. Although I'm sure that everyone who knows the Burnses also knows they're looking for a baby."

"Why leave it at St. Alban's then? Why not on the Burnses' doorstep?"

Reverend Fergusson swept her hands open wide.

Russ handed the note back to Mark. "What time did you find the baby?" he asked the priest.

"About . . . nine-thirty, quarter to ten," she said. "There was a welcoming reception from the vestry tonight that finished up around nine. I changed in my office, checked messages, and then headed out. I already gave Officer Durkee the names of the people who were there."

Russ squinted, trying for a mental picture of the area where Elm branched off the curve of Church Street. One of Tick Soley's parking lots was across the street from the church, one light on the corner but nothing further up where the houses started. "What did you say was behind the little parking area?"

"The rectory, where I live. There's a tall hedge, and then my side yard. My driveway is on the other side of the house."

Russ sighed. "The kids—the parents—could have parked in any one of those spots and snuck over to the stairs with the baby. I somehow doubt we're gonna get an eyewitness with a license number and a description of the driver."

The priest tapped the glassine envelope. "Chief Van Alstyne, exactly how hard do you have to look for the parents of this baby?" For the first time Russ let himself take a long look into the portable incubator. The sleeping baby didn't look any different from every other newborn he had ever seen, all fat burnished cheeks and almond-shaped eyes. He wondered how hard up or screwed up or roughed up a girl would have to be to pull a perfect little thing like that out of her body and then leave him in a cardboard box. In the dark. On a night when the windchill hovered at zero degrees.

He looked back at the priest. She was leaning toward him slightly, focusing on him as if he were the only person in the whole hospital. "I don't need to tell you that leaving a baby like that is called endangering a child," he said. She nodded. "And of course, if we can't find the parents, it's going to take longer for DHS to actually get the baby out of foster care and into an adoptive home. But the thing is to find out how voluntary this really was, giving up the baby."

Her mouth opened and then snapped shut. He continued. "When a woman really wants to give up her kid for adoption, she usually gets in touch with an agency, or a lawyer, or somebody, well before the baby is born. These throwaway situations—"

"She didn't throw Cody away. Whoever she is."

"No, she didn't. Which makes me think it's not one of those times when the mother is a druggie or a drunk or a psycho. But it does make me wonder if her boyfriend or her father forced her into it. And if she's not already regretting what she did, but is too scared of us or of him to come forward and reclaim her son."

"I never thought of that," Reverend Fergusson said, biting her lower lip. "Oh dear. Maybe I shouldn't have—"

The emergency room doors opened with a hydraulic pouf. Russ recognized the small, bearded man in the expensive topcoat and the striking brunette woman at his side, but he'd know who they were even if he had never seen them in the Washington County Courthouse before, just from the look on Reverend Fergusson's face.

"We got here as soon as we could," Geoffrey Burns said. His voice was tight. His glance flicked around the treatment area, lighting on the incubator. His wife saw it at the same time.

"Oh . . ." she said, pressing one perfectly manicured hand to her mouth. "Oh. Is that him?"

The priest nodded. She stepped aside, allowing the Burnses a clear view of the sleeping baby. "Oh, Geoff, just look at him . . ." Karen Burns hesitated, as if showing too much eagerness might cause the incubator to vanish.

Her husband stared at the baby for a long moment. "Where's the doctor who's been treating him?" he said. He looked at Russ. "Chief Van Alstyne. I take it the Department of Human Services hasn't seen fit to send anyone over yet."

"Mr. Burns." Russ nodded. "I expect we'll see somebody soon. They're a little overwhelmed over there, you know."

"Oh, don't I just," Geoff Burns said.

"I take it Reverend Fergusson called you about the note that was found with the baby?" Russ glanced pointedly toward the priest, who lifted her chin in response. "You folks know that it's way too early to start thinking of this boy as your own. No matter what the parents wrote."

Karen Burns turned toward him. "Of course, Chief. But we are licensed foster parents without any children in our home right now, and we intend to press DHS to place Cody with us." Mrs. Burns had a voice so perfectly modulated she could have been selling him something on the radio. Russ glanced at Burns, thin and short, and wondered at the attraction. His own wife was one hell of a good-looking woman, but Karen Burns would put her in the shade.

"Under the standard of the best interests of the child, it's preferable that a pre-adoptive child be fostered with the would-be adoptive parents, if there are no natural relatives able to care for the child. Young v. The Department of Social Services."

Russ blinked at the lawyer's aggressively set brows. "I'm not contesting you in court, Mr. Burns," he said. "But we don't know that there aren't any natural relatives. We don't know if the mother gave him up of her own free will or not." He shifted his weight forward, deliberately using his six-foot-three-inches as a visual reminder of his authority here. "Isn't it a little odd for a professional couple like you to be foster parents?"

Karen Burns laid her hand on her husband's arm, cutting off whatever he was about to say. "I work from home as well as from my office, part time. On those times we've had a child in our care, I just cut way back."

"I assure you we're properly licensed and have passed all the state requirements," Burns said, his face tight. "We are fully prepared to make the sacrifices necessary to care for a child. Unlike the biological parents of this boy."

Karen Burns twisted a single gold bangle around her wrist. "Of course you have to look for the parents, Chief Van Alstyne. And I'm sure that anyone who took such care to make sure their baby would be found immediately, and left a note asking us to be his adoptive parents, would only confirm that request."

Her husband spoke almost at the same time. "We intend to file for TPR immediately, on grounds of abandonment and endangerment." There was a pause. The Burnses looked at each other, then at Russ. They both spoke at once.

"I hope you do find her. She undoubtedly needs help and counseling."

"I hope you don't find her, to be frank. It'll be better for the baby all around."

Reverend Fergusson broke the awkward silence. "What's TPR mean?"

"Termination of parental rights," Russ answered. "Usually happens after the court takes a DHS caseworker's recommendation that there's no way the child ought to go back to the parent. Takes months, sometimes years, if DHS is trying to reunite the family." He rubbed his forehead with the palm of his hand. "During which time the kid is in foster care."

"Unless, as in this case, the child is an abandoned infant and the parents can't be found," Geoff Burns said, tapping his finger into his palm in time to his words.

"Uh huh," Russ agreed. "Unless they can't be found."

CHAPTER
TWO

The pediatric resident, bright-eyed and way too young for comfort, entered the treatment area from behind a blue baize curtain. "Oh, hey!" he said. "You must be the Burnses! Your priest here told me about you. Hey, you wanna hold Cody here or what?" He unlatched the top of the incubator and scooped up the baby expertly, placing him in Karen Burns's arms before she had a chance to respond.

"Oh," she said. "Oh." Her husband put his arm around her, turning her away from the others. Russ, rubbing away at the headache building behind his eyebrows, felt the weight of attention on him. He glanced down at Reverend Fergusson, who was looking at him instead of at the would-be-parents. It took him a moment to identify the expression on her face, it had been so long since he'd seen it directed at him. Sympathy.

The resident was trying to give his report to Durkee, who was just as doggedly pointing him in Russ's direction. "Hey," he said, "You're the police chief? Really neat."

"I think so." Over the doctor's shoulder, Russ could see Reverend Fergusson's lips twitch.

"The baby's in real good shape," the doctor said, pulling out several sheets of paper stapled together. "Here's a copy of his tests and the examination results. I place the time of birth within the last two or three days. No drugs in his system, no signs of fetal alcohol syndrome, no signs of abuse. His cord was cut and wrapped inexpertly, but somebody kept it nice and clean. We'll have to wait until he's had a bowel movement, but I'm guessing he's been fed formula."

Russ scanned the report, noting the blood group—AB negative—and the notation that the baby had been bathed at some point in his brief life. "Okay," he said. "Mark, get me the box and the blankets, we'll see if we can get anything from those. I want you to stay here until somebody from DHS arrives, unless you get a squawk." Mark nodded and disappeared into the examination cubby. Russ folded the medical report and tucked it into his jacket pocket.

"Here you go, Chief," Mark said, returning with the box. He passed it to Russ, who examined it without much hope of anything useful. It was sturdy, new-looking, marked with the logo of a Finger Lakes orchard. Lane's IGA and the Grand Union probably had hundreds just like it tossed in their storerooms. The blankets were a mix: an old, well-worn gold polyester thing, a heavy woolen horse blanket in plaid, and what looked like two brand-new flannel baby blankets, the kind his sister had by the dozens. Russ had a sudden image of himself going door-to-door, asking, "Ma'am? Do you recognize any of these blankets? And has anyone in your household given birth lately?"

Reverend Fergusson had gone over to the Burnses and was talking softly to them. Karen Burns said something, looking at her husband, and he nodded. All three of them bent their heads. Russ realized with a shock that they were praying. Openly displayed religion made him as uncomfortable as hell, and it didn't help when the priest signed the cross over both of them and then laid her hands on the baby and blessed him. She really was a priest. Jesus Christ. A woman priest. Were Episcopalians like Catholics? He'd have to ask his mother, she'd know.

When Reverend Fergusson broke away from the Burnses and walked straight toward him, he thought for one guilty moment she must have read his mind and was coming over to give him what for.

"Chief Van Alstyne, will you be leaving soon?" she asked.

"Yeah," he said, warily. Did she want to pray over him, too?

"Ah. Well, Karen and Geoff are going to stay here until after the caseworker arrives, and I, um . . ." She worried her lower lip some, hesitating. "I called an ambulance, you see, 'cause I thought Cody ought to be seen as soon as possible, and I, I don't have . . ."

The light dawned. "Do you need a ride home, Reverend?" Russ said. "I don't want to impose . . ."

"I'd be glad to give you a lift, if you don't mind me stopping by the station to drop this off before we get to your house. I want to make sure our fingerprint guy has it first thing in the morning." He hefted the box.

"I'm not in any hurry," she said. "On the other hand, I did want to get to the rectory sometime tonight, and I understand that the taxis in Millers Kill aren't the quickest to respond to a call . . ."

Russ snorted. "If you're talking about In-Town Taxi, you're right. One car is their whole fleet, and when the driver decides he's done for the day, you're outta luck." He waved good-bye to Mark and gestured for the priest to precede him through the emergency department doors.

" 'Night, Chief," the admitting nurse called.

" 'Night, Alta," he said.

The dry, cold air outside the overheated hospital was like a good stiff drink after a hard day. Russ breathed deeply. He noticed the priest wasn't carrying a coat. "Hey, Reverend, you can't go outside in just sweats this time of year. Where are you from, anyway?"

She looked down at her unseasonable outfit. "It shows, huh? Southern Virginia. And when I was in the army, I managed to never get myself stationed any place where the temperature dipped to below freezing."

"Neat trick," he said. In the army? A woman priest in the army. What next? She parachute out of planes dropping bibles?

"I was a helicopter pilot," she said. "Late of the Eighteenth Airborne Corps. You'd be surprised how often we needed to drop men and gear into overheated climates."

"No, I wouldn't," he said. "I was career army. First in the infantry, then an MP. I retired about four years ago."

"Really?" She stopped in her tracks. "We'll have to compare postings." She looked up at him curiously. "It's just that the way you knew everybody, I assumed you'd lived in Millers Kill all your life."

Russ pulled open the passenger-side door of his cruiser. She slid into the seat, yelping at the chilly vinyl. He crossed to the other side, dropped the box into the backseat, and got behind the wheel. "I was born here, lived here my first eighteen years." He started up the car, turned on the radio, and grabbed the mike. "Ten-fifty, this is Ten-fifty-seven. I'm rolling, en route from the hospital to the station." The radio crackled and Harlene's voice came on the line. "Ten-fifty-seven, this is Ten-fifty. Acknowledged you en route from the hospital to the station. We'll see you soon."

The woman beside him was shivering, her arms clasped around herself, her knees drawn up. "Sorry," he said. "The heater in the old whore takes a long time to warm up." A second after he spoke, he remembered he was talking to a priest. "Oh, Jesus," he said, caught himself, then blurted out, "Christ!" at his own stupidity before he could help it. He hung his head, laughing and groaning at the same time.

"You! Swearing in front of a priest!" She pointed her finger at his chest. "Drop and gimme twenty!" He stared at her, not sure he was hearing right. She smiled slowly, her eyes half-closing. "Gotcha."

Russ shook his head, laughing. "Okay, okay. Sorry." He shifted the cruiser into gear and eased it out of the hospital parking lot onto Burgoyne Avenue. Nearing midnight on a Monday, there was hardly any traffic on the normally busy road.

Reverend Fergusson shifted in her seat, exclaiming briefly when she hit a particularly cold spot. "You were telling me you were born and raised right here . . ."

"Oh, yeah," he sighed. "Probably would have gotten a job at the mill and never left town. But I got out of high school in 'sixty-nine and my number came up in the Instant Loser Lottery. Next thing I knew, it was good-bye New York State, hello Southeast Asia."

He checked the gauge on the heater. "Turned out the army and I made a pretty good match. We went from Vietnam to the Gulf together." He switched the blower to high and the interior began to warm up. "After I retired,"—no need to go into detail about that phase of his life—"I decided the time was right to finally come home. The old chief was retiring, and they needed someone with experience who wanted to live the quiet life up here in Washington county. It's a good outfit, eight officers and four part-timers, and I liked they way everyone worked together. My wife, Linda, loved the idea of us finally settling down somewhere other than a big city or busy post"—well, that was half-true, she *had* wanted him to settle down—"and she likes being so close to my mother and my sister." Now that was a whopper. But it was the party line, and he stuck to it. "So that's how I wound up back in my old home town a quarter-century after I left."

"Does your wife work?"

"Oh, yeah." He swung into the right-hand lane and turned onto Morningside Drive. The lights from the new Wal-Mart turned the night sodium orange. "She has her own business, making custom curtains. It's been more successful than either of us imagined." He slowed, checking out the cars in the parking lot. He didn't like all-night stores, they were targets for trouble. "She's getting into mail orders now, says she wants to make up a whole catalogue. It's great, it's been really just great."

"Sounds like she found her vocation. Good for her. It can be hard for some military families to readjust to civilian life. You two have any kids?"

"No," he said. "What's your story? You came from Virginia originally?"

"Born and bred in a small town outside of Norfolk," she said. "My family owns a charter and commercial air business. I had always thought I wanted to be part of it someday, so after college, I joined the army as a helo jock. The military is still the best way to train for a career as a pilot, you know. And the army was putting on a big push to get female recruits into non-traditional fields. I was the only woman in my unit."

"Must have been tough," he said. Now that he thought about it, she did seem less like a bible-tosser and more like the type to be dropping arms in an LZ.

"At times, yeah. It was good though." Taking his eyes off the road for a second, he could see a one-sided smile flash across her face. "But, as it turned out, I had to put my piloting plans aside when I was called to the priesthood. I went back to Virginia to go to seminary, which was really good for my parents."

Russ didn't want to get into the murky mystical depths of how someone was "called to the priesthood." "How'd you wind up here?" he asked.

"I spent a summer as an assistant curate in the Berkshires. I had never been in this part of the country before, and I just fell in love with it. I started looking for a position somewhere in New England, and when St. Alban's came open, I thought, well, it's only a half-hour drive from Vermont . . ."

"Ah ha," Russ said. "So you haven't experienced a North-country winter yet." The light at the intersection with Radcliff Street turned red, and he pumped his brakes to avoid skidding on the icy spots.

"Therein lies the rub, as they say. My internship ran from May through September, so I was a little unprepared for six inches of snow before the end of November. I've only been here for three weeks, so I'm not exactly acclimated yet. I do have a coat, though. But when I stumbled over the baby, I was on my way out for a run."

He looked at her again. She was obviously fit, but she wasn't a big woman, scarcely up to his shoulder standing. "Just because this is a small city and we look like Bedford Falls from *It's a Wonderful Life*, don't be fooled into thinking bad things can't happen here. They can, and do, so watch where you run if you're out at night alone."

She waved a hand, unconcerned. "I can take care of myself," she said.

"Lemme guess, you know karate, you're trained in the art of self-defense . . ."

"Nothing formal. But the army made sure I could break somebody's arm if I needed to."

The light turned green. He rolled onto Radcliff, causing an ancient Chevy Nova that had been barreling down the street to brake hard in an attempt to get under the thirty-five-mile-an-hour speed limit. "Lemme tell you, Reverend, somebody tries to mug you, they aren't gonna get close enough for you to break their arm. Every ass—uh, jerk on the streets today's got a gun. Even up here. They come up outta New York City, just like the drugs do."

He glanced at her when he made a left turn onto Main. She was studying the peaceful storefronts and frowning, absently rubbing her forearm with one long-fingered hand. "Is that a big problem in Millers Kill? Drugs?" she asked.

Russ sighed. He knew when he was being side-stepped. "Not too bad, no. Alcohol is the number one drug of choice up here, like you'll find in a lot of rural areas. My biggest single crime problem is domestic violence, and nine times out of ten there's alcohol involved."

He pulled the cruiser up in front of the station. "I'll leave the car running for you," he said. "Be back in a minute." He grabbed the box and took off through the icy air, bounding up the stairs two at a time.

There was nobody at the front desk at this hour. Instead, he loped into the dispatch room, where Harlene was just pouring herself a cup of coffee. "Harlene, you good lookin' woman!" he said. Harlene was some ten years his elder, a big, square woman with an uncannily organized mind and a photographic memory of every highway, lane, and dirt road in three counties.

"One of these days, I'm going to slap you with a sexual harassment lawsuit," she said, hefting herself into her chair and curling her headset over her springy gray hair.

"And let Harold know how much fun you're having over here? No way." Her husband Harold had recently retired, and was riding Harlene pretty hard to quit work and stay at home with him. "I'm gonna lock this into evidence," Russ said, waggling the box. "Will you leave a note for Phil to get on it first thing in the morning? Prints, hairs, anything he can come up with."

Harlene peered at the cardboard. "You want him to send it on to the state if nothing pans out?"

"No. No need to spend the money. This is that abandoned baby Mark called in. More likely than not the mother'll surface within a week or so. You know how these things run."

Harlene nodded. The teenager wound up in the hospital with postpartum complications. Or she broke down and told a friend, who told another, until there wasn't any secret anymore.

"Okay, Chief, you got it." She pointed to the coffeemaker. "Just brewed a fresh pot," she said.

"Gotta haul it," Russ said, stuffing the ends of his scarf back into his jacket. "I'm giving the priest who found the baby a ride back to St. Alban's rectory."

"You and a priest." Harlene snorted. "I'd give good money to hear how that conversation goes."

"Actually," Russ said, enjoying his moment as much as Mark had his, "She's very easy to talk to. She's old army, too."

Harlene was gratifyingly surprised. "Well! Didn't know they could *have* women priests." She looked into the middle distance for a moment. "Ask her what she thinks of my sexual harassment suit," she said.

Russ bit back a laugh and grabbed the locker key off the hook on the wall. He clattered downstairs and unlocked the evidence cage, tagging the box and scribbling his entry information in the dog-eared log-book. Within two minutes he was running back upstairs, shouting a good-night to Harlene, and out the front door again.

When he got into the cruiser, Reverend Fergusson jerked her hand away from the radio. "Sorry," she said. "I couldn't resist. I wanted to see if it sounded like it does on all those television shows."

"And?" Russ said, backing the car out of his parking spot.

"And it sounds like the state police have wa-a-a-ay too much time on their hands," she said. "One guy was going on and on about some fishing tournament he'd gone to. It sounded more like *Bassmasters* than *Dragnet*."

They both laughed. "Yeah, well . . ." Russ said. "Mondays are the quietest night of the week. You come cruising with me on Friday, then you'll really hear something."

She pinned him with those clear hazel eyes. "Could I?"

Startled, he almost ran a red light. He looked at her. "Reverend, why on earth would you want to do something like that?" he said.

"Because I want to get a feel for the problems of Millers Kill that I won't get in a vestry reception," she said. "Because I need to figure out what kind of outreach ministry my church ought to be doing, instead of just what my parishioners feel comfortable doing right now. And be-cause," she grinned, a reckless, one-sided grin that made him think she must be mistaken about a priestly calling, "I'm a recovering adrenaline addict. Who hasn't had a fix in a while. Green light."

"Huh." He drove on. "Doesn't your church have a mass or whatever it is on Fridays? I recall seeing cars there in the evening. And besides, I'm out pretty late. Don't you, I dunno, get up early to pray or some-thing?"

She made an amused sound in the back of her throat. "Saturday's a day off for me. At least, it's supposed to be. So I can sleep in. If worse comes to worse, I can double up. Praise God while I'm making pancakes, thank the Lord while I'm doing the week's shopping." She began to sing almost inaudibly, "And He walks with me, and He talks with me . . ."

"Uh-huh. I may not know much about religion, but I can tell when I'm being sold a bill of goods."

"So can I come?"

How do I get myself into these situations? he thought. "Okay, yeah," he said finally. "But you do what I say, when I say it, and if I decide for whatever reason that it's not safe, you get left behind. No arguments."

"Do I strike you as the argumentative type?" she asked. He snorted. Along Church Street, the municipal Christmas decorations had been hung on the lampposts. Same fuzzy plastic candy canes and reindeer that had been there when he was a kid. Same fake greenery around the poles, same fat outdoor bulbs. He wondered where they got replacements from. No way anyone was still making lights like that. He turned onto Elm. The rectory was a pretty Dutch Colonial from the turn of the century.

"Here it is, on the left."

"Nice," Russ said, parking in the drive. "Bet you've got great woodwork in there."

The priest groaned. "I can't tell," she said. "The place is all over boxes, most of 'em completely unlabeled, so I have no idea what's in there. I have some I filled before my last posting to Fort Rucker and haven't unpacked in seven years. They could contain anything from 'eighties-style miniskirts to relics of the True Cross for all I can remember. Somehow, there always seems to be something more interesting to do than unpacking and housecleaning . . ."

He slung his arm over the seat and turned toward her. "You gotta get one of those ladies' committees over to do their thing. Have you set up and sparkling in no time."

"Oh, yeah," she said. "And they'd do a great job, too. But you know, you get the place clean and organized at the start and forever after, whenever one of my parishioners came over for a visit, they'd be thinking, My! She certainly didn't keep this up very well!" She looked up the drive to her house, smiling a little. "Ah, it's just the new-posting blues. A new town, all new faces. It can get . . ."

"Lonely."

"Yeah."

They sat in companionable silence, not in any hurry to end the ride.

The radio squawked. "Ten-fifty-seven, this is Ten-fifty. I've got an accident reported out on Route Thirty-Five, at mile fifteen."

Russ clicked in the mike. "Ten-fifty, this is Ten-fifty-seven. Acknowledged. I'm rolling to Route Thirty-Five, mile fifteen." He spread his hands apologetically. "Duty calls. Good-night, Reverend Fergusson."

"Oh, for heaven's sake, call me Clare." She opened her door and slid out, leaning down to keep him in view.

"Clare," he said. "And you can call me Chief." She laughed loudly. "No, no, call me Russ. After all, if we're going to be partners next Friday . . ."

She nodded. "I'll be there. Russ. Good night, now." She slammed the door. He waited until she had reached her front door and let herself in. Without keys. He made a mental note to get on her about that come Friday. He backed out of her drive and hit his lights, unaccountably smiling all the way to Route Thirty-Five.

The girl unlocked the deadbolt and turned the latch. It was cold in the kitchen, but then again, she had been desperately cold all night long. A light had been left on for her in the hall. She walked to the stairs and tried to remember what she was supposed to be doing. Concentrate. Upstairs. She hefted her overnight bag and gasped as a cramping pain shot through her abdomen. She stopped, pressed her fist against her belly. Nothing to worry about. It was normal. The book had said it was normal to have cramps for several days afterwards.

She picked up her bag again and trudged up the bare wooden stairway. In the upstairs hall, she stared stupidly at the closed doors. Everything was totally foreign to her. Her breasts were aching and damp. She shut her eyes and breathed in deeply, and when she looked again, she saw her own bedroom door in front of her.

Inside, she dropped her luggage and sagged onto the bed. The springs creaked loudly. "Mmmm," came a voice from the other side of the room. "Katie, is that you? Geez, it's late."

"Yeah, Emily," she whispered. "It's me." From across the street, she heard a dog barking and barking. It would go on for an hour or more some nights, a frustrated sheepdog chained to a barren circle of dirt.

"That damn dog," groaned Emily. "Why don't they do it a favor and take it out to the country and let it go?"

"It's not that . . . it's not that . . ." Katie gulped loudly and began to cry.

"Katie, honey, what's wrong?" Emily snapped on a tiny bedside lamp. "Oh sweetie, tell me what's wrong."

Katie shook her head, crying harder. Emily crossed to her bed and sat beside her, hugging her tight. Katie leaned on her shoulder, sobbing open-mouthed, while outside the dog barked and howled into the freezing air.

CHAPTER
THREE

The case clock in St. Alban's meeting room rang twelve slow, ceremonious hours. The donation of a grateful parishioner who had made a fortune carpetbagging in the post–Civil War South and returned to retire in his native eastern New York, it had a place of honor between two enormous diamond-paned windows. Where, Clare reflected, it had undoubtedly sat unmoved since 1882. She was beginning to suspect the congregation of St. Alban's didn't exactly embrace novelty and innovation. Hiring the first female head of a parish in this area may have exhausted their reserves of daring for the next ten years.

Norm Madsen, a basset-faced gentleman in his seventies, tapped the sheet of paper before him reproachfully. "This isn't an agenda, Reverend Fergusson. We always have an agenda for the vestry meetings."

"And the Wednesday lunch meeting is always financials, to get anything ready to pass on to the stewardship committee Thursday night." Terence McKellan, the head of commercial loans at AllBanc— until recently The First Alleghany Farmers and Merchants Bank, he had taken pains to tell her—laced his hands across his commodious middle. "No offense, but articles about unwed mothers ought to go before the activities committee."

"What sort of activity do you want them to take up, Terry?" Robert Corlew snorted with laughter. The wide-shouldered, bull-necked developer had an improbable mass of hair that Clare was sure must be a toupee.

Mrs. Henry Marshall, the only woman on the vestry board, looked quellingly at Corlew. "Since most of the ladies on activities are my age, Bob," she poked a pencil at her silver waves, "I expect they won't be adding to the unwed mother population any time soon. Though most of them are unwed by now," she said thoughtfully.

Clare breathed slowly and deeply. In. Out. "I'm sorry I didn't compile an agenda. I'll be sure to do that next meeting. As for the newspaper article and the figures sheet in front of you," she leaned forward, resting her arms on the massive black oak table that dominated the room, "you all know about the baby found abandoned here Monday night. That inspired me to do some research into what facilites are available to help single teen mothers."

"There's plenty of aid in Millers Kill," Vaughn Fowler said, popping an antacid tablet into his mouth. "Welfare and low-income housing and a Goodwill store. We even support a soup kitchen with the other churches in town." The retired colonel rapped the table with his chunky West Point ring as he enumerated each item.

"That's true, Mr. Fowler. No teenager with a baby is going to starve here. But did you know seventy percent of the girls who get pregnant in their teens drop out of Millers Kill High?"

"Not to sound unsympathetic," Fowler said, "but what makes you think these girls would have finished high school in the first place?"

Clare had seen that question coming since yesterday, when she had woken up with her inspired idea. "If you look to page four, you'll see an article I copied from *The Washington Post*, about a Junior League program I helped with when I was a seminarian."

"Junior League?" Mrs. Marshall adjusted her reading glasses and bent to the paper. "That's always a good recommendation."

"In their area, the League had found that one of two things tended to happen when a girl had a baby. Either she dropped out of high school to care for the child or her mother stopped working, and often went on welfare, to care for the child." Terry McKellan read along, his plump cheeks quivering as he nodded. "Drop-outs were at very high risk for further pregnancies, drug abuse, and domestic abuse. Girls whose mothers gave up work to stay at home with the baby finished high school in higher numbers, but few of them found work afterwards, leading to the same sort of dependencies as their sisters with no diploma."

Corlew frowned. "Couldn't find work? Or didn't look for it?"

"Most of these girls had no experience with or example of combining motherhood and work. That's what the Junior League program did. It partnered girls with mentors, who tutored them in everything from parenting skills to how to interview for a job. It provided free day care for the girls during the school day and a quiet space for them to do homework after school. Girls who went through the program not only had a ninety percent graduation rate, but most of them then went on to either community college or to work."

Fowler rapped the table with his ring. "Funding?"

Clare quelled the urge to respond, "Yes, sir." Colonel Fowler was the double of several commanding officers she had served under, complete with graying brush cut and age-defying figure. He expected her to assess problems, devise solutions, and act. Or at least, that's what he had told her during the interview process for this parish. She flipped open to the last page. "Initial funding came from the League, who paid for the day-care workers, some equipment and baby supplies, and a part-time grant writer to raise money independently. Area churches donated the space. Girls who used the facilities after they had started working paid an hourly fee, adjusted to their income." She looked around the table, meeting the eyes of every man and woman, gathering each vestry member in. "I propose St. Alban's start a similar project here. To be funded out of the general funds, using either the parish hall or the old nursery room for the day care. We could have a powerful effect on the lives of young women and children who otherwise don't have much of a future."

The room was silent for a moment. "You want us to be a home for unwed mothers?" Sterling Sumner raised his bushy eyebrows in disbelief. "Outrageous." He flipped the ends of one of the English-school scarves he always affected.

"How much would this cost us?" Terry McKellan asked, scribbling some notes on the margin.

"What about insurance? State licensing requirements for running a day-care facility? Transportation to and from the school and the girls' homes?" Fowler rapped his ring on every point. "This isn't like opening our nursery for members' children during the Sunday services."

"No, si—no, it's not. All of those are issues that will have to be researched. I don't have a whole, detailed proposal to present yet. But I would like the approval and support of the vestry before I call up a committee or start running down licensing requirements. I'd like to know this project has your support so long as the general fund isn't unduly strained by it." Nervous energy forced her out of her seat to stride around the table. "It's innovative, it's meeting an unmet need in the community, it will open St. Alban's doors to new faces, young faces. It exemplifies Christ's charge to us to be his disciples by serving others." She reached her chair and leaned against the worn green velvet back. "I believe those were some of the things you said you wanted me to accomplish as your priest."

Vaughn Fowler's bright blue eyes seemed to be assessing her for leadership potential. "One of the most important goals we set for you was to grow St. Alban's. Bring in new families. Kids."

"More pledges," Corlew muttered.

Fowler shot him a curt glance. "This . . . unwed mother outreach sounds commendable. But will it attract more of the kind of members we want? Or will it scare some families away?"

Clare went blank. "What?"

"In other words," Sterling Sumner said, "Will the quality families we want to attract stay away because we've filled our landmark Eighteen-fifty Gothic Revival sanctuary with Daisy Mae and Queen Latisha!" He swiped at the table with one end of his scarf, as if wiping away contamination.

"My grandfather would have been more blunt," Clare said, crossing her arms. "He would have come right out and said 'poor white trash' and 'uppity coloreds.' "

Fowler held up one hand. "No name calling. Reverend Clare, please." He gestured, flat-handed, for her to resume her seat. She did so, ungraciously. "Sterling was being melodramatic, as usual. But the core of the thing is a matter of concern. St. Alban's was one of the first Episcopal churches in this area. We've been able to draw members from even beyond the Millers Kill-Cossayaharie-Fort Henry townships because we have traditional worship with wonderful music in a beautiful setting. Many of us," his gesture encompassed the rest of the vestry, "are from families that have been congregants for generations." Clare opened her mouth. "Let me finish. The parish needs to grow. It needs new blood and, realistically, new money. Before you plunge ahead with your teen-mother project, I'd like to see you do something to encourage families in. Something to draw favorable attention to St. Alban's."

Around the table the other vestry members were nodding. Clare folded her hands. "I can handle two assignments simultaneously, si— Mr. Fowler."

His mouth tilted in the suggestion of a smile. "I'm sure you can."

"Perhaps organizing some meet-the-parishioners teas?" Mrs. Marshall said.

"No, no, no." Robert Corlew shook his head. His hair did not move. "We need something that'll get us in the papers. Free advertising."

"Tours of the church? An evening organ concert series!" Sterling Sumner brightened.

"You were inspired, you said, by the baby abandoned at our back door. I suggest you help the Burnses to foster him. That's—" Fowler's ring rapped for emphasis, "the kind of image and publicity that says we're a family-friendly place. Helping a couple become a family by supporting their efforts to adopt."

"But—not that I wouldn't want to focus my time and effort on the Burnses, but isn't that up to the Department of Human Services? And the legal system? And as much as I'm sure we'd all like to see them become parents, I don't see how that will help us attract new members."

"You don't know what this town is like." Terry McKellan laughed. "Word of mouth is a way of life here. Plus, the news about the baby is already in the paper. Why the heck not make sure they say a few nice things about us, huh?"

Clare looked out a leaded-glass window to where snow flurries were spinning through the air. Ideas crowded her mind, far-fetched, practical, too expensive, possible— "We could start by enlisting parish support," she said. She returned her attention to the table. "A letter-writing campaign to the DHS and the governor's office. Get volunteers to help them transition from a couple to foster parents. Hold a Blessing of Adoption and invite the local press. Invite adoption support groups to meet at St. Alban's."

"Good! Excellent! Knew you would be the priest for us," Fowler said.

Clare looked sharply at him. "What about my mother-baby project?"

"You show us you can organize and get results on the Burnses' adoption, and we'll back you to the hilt on day care for unwed teens." Fowler glanced around the table, registering assent from the rest of the vestry. "Agreed? Agreed."

Clare blew out her breath in a puff. "Then let's adjourn." *Before anyone can think of something else to keep out the undesirables,* she thought. Everyone stood, stacking papers and collecting coats.

"I've gotta make it to Fort Henry Ford by one-thirty," Terry Mc-Kellan said, buttoning his wool coat across a wide expanse of midsection. "My daughter blew out the electrical system in her Taurus, so we swapped her my wife's Mazda while she was home for Thanksgiving. Now she wants to keep it. Can you imagine what our insurance is gonna be with her driving in Boston?" He looked at Fowler. "What did you get Wes?"

"A Jeep Wrangler. Good in the snow, appeals to an eighteen-year-old's idea of 'cool.' Unfortunately, it couldn't carry all his stuff down. I'm off to West Point tomorrow with another load. We should have just traded the Expedition with him during the holiday." Clare attempted to edge past the men as they drifted toward the hallway. "And speaking of vehicles, Reverend Clare, that car of yours is totally impractical."

Clare had already heard several people's opinion of her bright red '92 MG. She smiled brightly. "Your son goes to West Point? And you're a graduate, too. You must be very proud."

Terry McKellan roared with laughter. "It was a disappointment to them when he couldn't get into the Culinary Institute . . ."

Vaughn Fowler ignored the witticism. "He's the fifth generation of Fowlers to be an Academy man. Edie and I are very proud, yes."

Clare touched his arm. "Wonderful." She glanced at her watch. "Oh, look at the time. Gentlemen, I've got to run." She waved to the remaining vestry members and quick-stepped down the hall before the subject of her car could come up again.

She ducked into the parish office and caught her secretary, Lois, with a mouthful of nonfat yogurt and raw bran. Lois looked like a strawberry-blond Nancy Reagan, and she kept her size-two figure, as near as Clare could tell, by eating less than any other human being she had ever seen.

"Mmph!" Lois put down the yogurt and waved her hands.

"I'm escaping comments about my car," Clare explained.

"Mmmm," Lois said, swallowing. "It's too tiny. A Lincoln Town Car, that's comfort and styling. And if you have blond hair, you can get the leather seats to match."

Clare made a face. "I'm a dirty blond. I'd have to have dirty seats. Besides, I'm too young for a Town Car."

Lois made a noncommittal noise.

Clare poked at the Rolodex next to Lois' white-and-pink book of message slips. "The vestry says they'll support my young mother's out-reach project if I can help the Burnses successfully adopt Cody."

Lois sniffed.

"Now I just have to figure out how to influence New York State's Department of Human Services."

Lois' eyebrows arched.

"I think I'm going to need some help on this one."

"I think you might," Lois agreed.

Her desk chair creaked as Clare tilted back, looking out the window. Flurries swirled through the air outside, making tiny ticking noises as they hit the glass. The only help she could think of was Chief Van Alstyne. Whom she had already impositioned for a ride from the hospital and bulldozed into offering to take her along on his Friday-night patrol. He was going to think she was only ever after him for something at this rate. Which was a shame, because she had really liked him. He was good people, as grandmother Fergusson would say. He reminded her of friends she had in the army, friends who could always see her, no matter what uniform she was wearing at the time.

Okay. She could ask how the search for Cody's birth mother was going. Find out what was happening with DHS—surely he'd be up to date on that. And if she gave him a chance to change his mind about Friday night, it would probably be the right thing to do. She should do that. Well. Maybe. She picked up the receiver in one hand and the Millers Kill directory in the other.

· · ·

Russ was having one of those days that, if it were on video, you'd fast-forward through until you got to a good part. One of his officers had called in with a suspiciously early-in-the-season flu that was probably being treated with shots of cherry brandy and a long ride on a snowmobile. When Russ had taken a break from patrolling and shown up for an unexpected lunch at home, Linda had been too busy sewing up another order of curtains to eat with him. And she had asked him to drop off her loan application at the bank, when she knew he hated running personal errands in uniform. He always ran into somebody who would make some crack about how he was using the taxpayer's dime.

He had a mountain of paperwork covering his ugly gray metal desk, stuff he'd been putting off and putting off until it had become a full day's job. When he'd bitched about it to Harlene, she told him if he'd worked at it a little at a time, he wouldn't be staring down the barrel now, which he already knew, which made him even more pissy.

And now this little gem. Circled in red in the *Post-Star* courtesy of Officer Pollack, who always brought in his copy before his shift. Russ had been expecting the article about the baby, of course. He'd given the beat reporter an interview, explaining what the police were doing to find the mother, saying the boy had been found "outside an area church" and omitting all mention of the note tucked in the box with the baby. She had gotten the resident from the hospital to describe the overall good health of the child. And a line from the Department of Human Services confirming the baby was being placed with an experienced foster mother.

The usual stuff. What was making him grip his coffee mug to keep from throwing it across the room was the paragraph devoted to the Burnses. How the hell the reporter had found out about them he didn't know, but there it all was, in glorious black and white: Saint Alban's, the note, Burns complaining about DHS, and a plea to the mother to contact the couple directly. "We only want to help," Karen Burns was quoted. "We believe what the mother did was courageous, not criminal."

He looked out his window, almost lost between the bulletins and WANTED posters and advisories taped up all over his wall, and watched the hard, dry snow spitting through the air. Temperature dropping, cold night tonight. He thought about Cody-No-Last-Name, thought about what might have happened if Reverend Fergusson hadn't been heading out for a run that night. Maybe whoever had left the baby had been nearby, watching and waiting for someone to discover the box. Maybe not. Courageous. Yeah.

The phone rang. Through the frosted glass window in his door, he could see Harlene's outline as she crossed the office to pick it up. A moment later his line buzzed. "Hey, Harlene, can you get me some more coffee while I take this?" he yelled. He couldn't hear her reply distinctly, but he thought it was something about being the dispatcher, not a geisha girl. He lifted the receiver.

"Chief Van Alstyne? Clare Fergusson. I hope I'm not calling at a bad time."

"No, no," he said, "Not at all. I'm staring at about a thousand state and county reports I'm supposed to have filled out sometime in November and I'm contemplating whether I can throw Geoff Burns in jail for interfering with an investigation. I can use a break."

"You're contemplating what?"

"I take it you haven't read today's paper. The article about the abandoned baby."

"No. It's here somewhere . . ." There was a rustling and a thumping sound. "Got it. Where is it?"

"Right on page three. Take a look at where Geoff Burns offers his protection and free legal services to the mother!"

There was silence on the other end of the line. "Holy crow," Clare said after a moment.

"Yeah. After I had deliberately left out the note and the location where Cody was found. It'll serve that little weasel right when he starts getting crank calls from half the teenagers in the county, claiming to be the baby's mother."

"Is that what you mean by interfering with an investigation? Because, you know, if the reporter had come to me, I wouldn't have known I wasn't supposed to say anything about the note."

"It's not just that, Reverend . . . Clare. This crap about protecting the mother from misguided officials. Burns might as well come right out and say 'Come to us, and we'll see the police never lay a hand on you.' What are they gonna do, give her ten thousand and ship her off to

Bolivia? Geez, that really frosts my cookies." There was a strangled sound from the other end of the line. After a moment, he realized Clare was trying not to laugh. "Well, it does."

"I'm sorry, it's really not funny." She snickered. " 'Frosts my cookies'?"

"Now you know one of our quaint local expressions." The sound of her muffled laughter took the edge off his anger. He sighed.

"Okay. Do you really think that Karen and Geoff might make contact with the mother and not tell you?"

"Yes."

Now she sighed. "Me, too. Is there anything you can do now the information about where Cody was found is out in the open? You can't really mean to arrest the Burnses."

"I'd like to. At least, I'd like to arrest Geoff Burns. Jesus Christ, what an arrogant little snot. Sorry." Russ held the newspaper out at arm's length to reread the paragraph. "But no, I don't have any grounds. As much as he's pushing the line, he hasn't gone over it. There's nothing illegal about giving your opinion on what the mother did or in offering free legal aid."

"So you can't put the proverbial cat back in the bag. That leaves the problem of the mother turning to the Burnses for help instead of turning herself in to the police."

"There is that problem, yes."

"What if you offered to help them get the baby?"

"What?"

"They want to be Cody's foster parents now. Think about it. That way, they not only have the note in their favor, they also will have bonded with Cody. They'll be able to argue it's in his best interests to stay with them."

"Yeah, but . . ."

"I think they'll be less anxious about who finds the mother first if they have Cody already. You can offer to use your influence with the Department of Human Services to get the baby assigned to them. In exchange, they promise to let you know right away if the mother contacts them."

"My influence with DHS, huh?"

"Oh, c'mon. You must know a few people." Her slight Southern drawl was more noticable over the phone, he thought. "I'll tell you, I'm under the gun here, too. My vestry wants St. Alban's to pitch in and help the Burnses. I've decided to get a letter-writing campaign going among the parishioners. All the well-heeled Republicans here? There must be a few who've donated enough to make some politicians sit up and listen when they ask for a little consideration for this deserving couple, who have waited so patiently for so long to be a family."

He whistled. "You're good. You ever think of running for office?"

She snorted. "Preachers and politicians are kissin' cousins, didn't you know that?"

"I guess it's worth a try. Anything's better than waiting for Geoff Burns to get ahold of some scared kid and wave money in her face to make her disappear. When were you planning to enlist your letter-writing troops?"

"Putting it into my sermon this Sunday would be the simplest thing. Dang, and I was going to preach on what I saw going on patrol with you this Friday. Maybe I can work them both in . . ." There was a pause. "Um . . . you haven't changed your mind, have you? About taking me?"

"If I had, I've been effectively wangled into taking you now, huh?"

Clare groaned. "I didn't mean it that way . . ."

Russ laughed. "Guess I'd better keep my end of the bargain, or you might get your parishioners to write to the aldermen and have me tossed out on my ear. What time can I pick you up?"

"Evening Prayer's at five-fifteen, so I'll be free by six."

"Six is good. Wear a coat this time, okay? And some heavy boots."

"I'll bring two pair of mittens and electric socks. I'm really looking forward to seeing the authentic Millers Kill, Chief. Thank you."

"It's Russ, remember? And don't thank me until the night's over. You may be so bored, collecting stacks of letters might seem like a big thrill."

Standing behind the patrol car's open door, Clare banged her knees together and kicked her feet against the front tire, hoping to keep her circulation going. Wishing she were in her office, writing letters.

"I didn't do nuthin'! Get your hands off me!" In front of a large video arcade, Russ was toe to toe with an angry, drunken young man.

The kid was several inches over six feet, as tall as the police chief, and beefy. Clare glanced at the radio. On television cop shows, people were always calling for backup. Was she supposed to do that? How? She stomped her feet a few more times. If she had stayed home, she could be sitting down to the ten o'clock news with a cup of hot chocolate right now.

Teens were crowded along the sidewalk outside the arcade. Its huge picture windows blazed with neon signs and the hypnotic flash of the cruiser's red lights, giving the place a cinematic, high-tech look that jarred badly with the no-nonsense blue-collar bars and the depressed little shops that were its neighbors. The chief was leaning forward, talking to the kid in low tones. Not touching him, but ready to move if he had to. She couldn't hear what he was saying over the insistent bass thumping from the inside of the arcade.

Clare scanned the crowd, looking for any sign of someone else willing to take on trouble. She shivered inside the roomy police parka that Russ had loaned her. When she had stepped out of the church in her leather bomber jacket, he had laughed at it. Sure enough, within an hour she was begging for something warmer. At the station house, where they dropped off a drunk driver Russ had arrested, Harlene dug through the lockers and emerged with a regulation brown parka large enough to fit a moose. Or the young man who had been brawling in the arcade.

Russ leaned back, said something, crossed his arms. The kid hung his head, and for the first time, Clare could see an oversized boy instead of a threat. From the crowd, another boy sporting several piercings said something she couldn't make out. The kids around him laughed. Russ snapped his head around and pointed a finger at them, bellowing, "You damn well bet he is. And that's what's gonna keep him alive past seventeen. How about you, mister?" The boys in the group visibly shrank back. "I don't want to hear any more from you, got it?" A few nods.

Russ beckoned to two teens who had been hovering near him during the confrontation. Clare couldn't make out his words, but it looked as if he was putting the troublemaker in their care. One of the boys clapped an arm around his inebriated friend. Russ pinned the big kid with a glare, raising his voice so everyone could hear. "If I have to come here again tonight, I'm arresting anybody involved. Got it?" There was a shuffle-footed assent from the crowd. "Good. Now get inside or go home. It's too damn cold to be hanging out here on the sidewalk."

Russ trudged through the slush at the curbside and tugged open his door. He looked wearily across the roof at Clare, the whirling lights emphasizing the lines in his face. He seemed older than he had at the start of the night's patrol. "Idiot kids," he muttered, sliding behind the wheel. Clare gently kicked against her door, knocking snow off her boots before joining him inside the car.

"You're not going to arrest the boy who was fighting?"

"Ethan? Naw. He didn't hurt anybody." Russ reached for the radio. "Ten-fifty, this is Ten-fifty-seven."

"Come in, Ten-fifty-seven."

"Harlene, will you call the Stoners and tell them to pick up Ethan at Videotek? And tell 'em he missed a drunk and disorderly by the skin of his teeth."

"Will do, Chief."

"We're headed out to the kill. See if there are any other kids out tonight making fools of themselves. Ten-fifty-seven out."

"At the kill. Ten-fifty out."

He hung up the microphone and fastened his seatbelt.

"You have got to tell me something." Clare buckled herself in. "What, exactly, is the kill?"

"Huh?" He glanced at her. "You mean, like in Millers Kill?"

"Yeah. What is it?"

"Kill's the old Dutch name for a shallow river or a big creek. Lotta towns around upstate have 'kill' in their names—Fishes Kill, Eddys Kill . . . our kill runs from the Hudson to the Mohawk Canal."

"A big creek? I've crossed over it a few times and it looks more like a full-fledged river."

"It was dredged out during the building of the canal system in the early eighteen hundreds. Between the river traffic and the mills, it made the town. Geez, you're gonna live here, you need to learn some geography and history. I'll see if I can find you a few books to read."

He shifted and pulled into traffic. They headed west, cruising slowly down the strip, past bars, a liquor store, a tightly shuttered pawn shop. No candy canes and reindeer hanging from the battered old light poles here.

"Why didn't you take the boy in?" she asked.

"I know the Stoners. His dad has a thirty-five, forty acre dairy farm that barely supports the family. Ethan's not a bad kid." Russ signaled, turned down a narrow street, and drove past two dark, boarded-up warehouses. Another turn took them into the parking lots behind the buildings. The headlights picked out churned-up snow and tire tracks crisscrossing randomly. "He's just like a hundred other kids in this area. They drink, they do drugs, they get into car wrecks and fights because they've got nothing to do with their lives."

Russ swung the cruiser slowly out of the shadowy parking lot. The rear of the car slid in the snow, and he eased into the skid. "Nothing around here for average kids with high school diplomas and no money for college." Back on Mill Street, the cruiser turned west again. Clare watched through the window as the commercial buildings gave way to shabby-genteel houses. Homemade signs hammered into snow-covered lawns gave mute testimony to the struggle to make ends meet: LITTLE LAMBS DAY CARE. DOLLHOUSES BUILT TO ORDER. PLOWING AND HAULING. DEER DRESSED OUT.

"Thirty years ago, that boy could have gone straight into one of the textile mills and made a good wage. Or gone to work for one of the big dairy farms in the area, saved up his money to buy land of his own. Or gone into the army." Russ pinched the bridge of his nose beneath his glasses. "Voluntarily or not, it gave a guy a chance to learn a trade or get money for college."

The houses were fewer and farther apart. They drove past the last streetlight into the darkness. "This is Route One-Thirty-Seven. We call it the Cossayaharie Road," he said. The pines and alders crowded in along the road, and beyond the trees, the Adirondack piedmont closed the horizon around them. The dark bulk of the hills looked like breaching whales outlined in starlight, old and powerful.

The car cocooned them in warmth, made them fellow travelers into the wilderness. Clare unzipped her parka and stretched her legs. The glow from the dashboard picked out Russ's large, blunt hands, securely controlling the steering wheel. "Thirty years ago, you could get married and buy a house and have a family once you got out of school. And you didn't have to leave the area to do it. But nowadays, there's nothing for Ethan Stoner to do when he graduates next spring except maybe flip burgers part time. So he drives his old beater too fast and gets into fights and goes down to Albany to party with his buddies who've already left for good."

He turned the cruiser into a narrow lane overhung with snowy branches. The road was noticeably bumpier. They were silent, Russ peering forward to negotiate the barely-plowed road, Clare considering Ethan Stoner. They came to a dead end in a clearing marked by a few tire tracks.

She stared into the snow and darkness. "Where are we?"

Russ opened the door. Cold air rushed around the unzipped edges of her parka. "This is the lot for Payson's Park," he said, reaching behind her seat for two long, heavy flashlights. "In the summertime, the town puts out picnic benches and grills, and somebody always ties a few tire swings to the big branches overhanging the kill. It's real nice."

She accepted a flashlight and got out. "There aren't any cars here," she pointed out. "Don't tell me your young lovers are rolling in the snow somewhere. I know teenagers are hot-blooded, but . . ."

Russ walked through the beams from the headlight toward the edge of the clearing. "There's a trail that runs along the river for several miles. When I was a kid, you went on foot or you didn't go at all, but nowadays everybody's got four-wheel drive. And here we are, tire tracks."

He aimed the light into the woods and Clare could see where the trail ran past the open picnic area and over a rise. They tromped forward, following the tire tracks marring the otherwise untouched snow.

"Half a mile upstream there's an abandoned railroad bridge that crosses over the kill. That's another spot we like to keep an eye on, for drinking or doing drugs. There's a sheer slate embankment from the old train bed to underneath the bridge. A lot of people would rather get there by driving the trail instead of risking the climb down."

"I can't help think there must be more comfortable places to have a drink," she said. Her breath hung in the air, glowing in the reflected light of her flashlight.

"Oh, yeah," he said, ducking to avoid a snow-heavy branch. "But Napoli's Discount Liquors and the infamous Dew Drop Inn are less than a mile up the road, offering a last crack at booze before you cross the town line into Cossayaharie. Which is one of the last dry towns in New York State."

"So the good people of Cossayaharie drink here in the park instead?"

"Don't know if I'd say the *good* people, but—"

Clare slipped where the trail took a downward turn, and Russ caught her arm, steadying her. She added boots with serious treads to her growing list of things to buy.

"Watch it," he said, pointing his light to the left. The land sloped steeply down to the half-frozen edge of the river, visible between tangled bushes and slim stands of trees. "You don't want to fall in in this weather." She nodded and walked more slowly, staying between the tire tracks, emulating Russ's steady tread. "I remember last year, some idiot came out here to jack deer, fell in the kill instead, and nearly died from the hypothermia. 'Course, it didn't help that he'd been keeping himself entertained with blackberry brandy."

"Jack deer?" She caught a flash of something dark and gleaming near the water. A deer? She aimed her flashlight toward the thicket it might be hiding in.

"Poaching. At night. If you shine a light into a deer's eyes you can freeze it long enough to shoot."

The gleam looked funny, familiar but out of place. She moved the beam of light to the right. And saw a hand, barely distinguishable from the snow it rested on. The dark gleam, that was hair. That was someone's long, dark—

"Russ," she said.

"What?"

"Russ," she repeated. She pointed, part of her amazed at how steadily she was holding the flashlight. "Down there."

"Oh my God!" he said. He scrambled down the slope, falling and sliding and catching at trees. "Oh Jesus, oh God, oh Jesus, no." He yanked a bush almost out of the ground, stopping his headlong descent before he plunged into the water. Clare held her light tightly. She wasn't sure if she could move it at this point. Russ squatted in the snow and bent over the . . . her mind tried to slide over the word "body."

"Oh no. Oh, Jesus, oh no." He hunkered down for a moment. She could see him backlit by the glow of his flashlight, shaking his head over and over. Then he straightened, wiped his face. Turned toward her. "It's a girl. She's dead."

CHAPTER
FOUR

Clare pressed her gloved fist against her mouth. Her flashlight never wavered. Russ pointed his light up at her, making her eyes sting and blink. "Clare? Are you okay?"

She nodded. She couldn't see him, but she could feel him looking at her, realized he might not see the small movement.

"Yes. I'm okay," she said. "What do you want me to do?"

"Can you make it back up the trail to the car and call for help? I'm going to have to secure the area now, see if I can find anything before—before they get here to take her out."

"Turn on the radio and ask for Harlene?"

"Yeah. Tell her we've found a body off the trail, about a quarter mile upstream from Payson's Park. Can you do that?" She nodded again. "Good girl," he said.

Clare couldn't stop herself from looking at that hand once more, so pale and still it might have been carved out of snow. Snow on snow, the old hymn went. Snow on snow. She could make out some kind of sleeve, disappearing into the tangled brush. Whoever it was must be half in the water. Did she jump? Had she changed her mind and tried to crawl out? Clare blinked the blurriness out of her eyes and filled her lungs with sharp, dry air. She headed up the trail, jogging as quickly as she could in the snow. The trees crowded in against the path. She slipped and slid, trying to keep her footing and not break her pace. There was an explosion of snow from her left. She yelped and almost dropped her flashlight. A doe leaped into the beam of light and vanished again in another shower of snow. Clare staggered, her heart about to hammer its way out of her chest.

She made it to the cruiser finally, her knees aching from several falls, sweaty and hot under her borrowed parka. She slid into the car and flicked on the radio, and when she heard the dispatcher's hail she keyed the mike and said exactly what Russ had told her. Harlene put her on hold for what seemed like an eternity.

"Okay, Reverend, I've got an ambulance on the way and I've notified Doctor Dvorak. He'll be waiting at the county morgue. Officer Flynn is headed out to lend a hand, and the state troopers are sending a technician along with a crime scene van. Can you sit tight and lead them to the chief when they get there?"

Clare keyed the mike again. "Yes, I'll be here."

"Are you okay, Reverend?"

"Yeah, Harlene. Thanks for asking. I'll be fine."

"Good girl. Dispatch out."

Clare stripped off her gloves and blew on her fingers. She could remember the time when she would have torn into anyone who called her a girl. At thirty-five she was finally mellowing. Had Russ seen a woman down there in the snow and ice? Or was it really a girl? She yanked her coat around her, her exercise-induced heat seeping away in the chill of the car. As cold and as still as the grave.

Clare leaned her cheek against the rigid vinyl of the car seat. She shut her eyes very tightly, trying to put the sight of that white hand, that dark hair somewhere she could bear it. Did something drive that woman out here to end her own life? Something inside her so dark and cold that the moonless night and the icy water seemed preferable? Merciful God. That was the start of the collect she would pray tomorrow, looking at the comfortable, satisfied faces of her congregation. Merciful God, who sent your messengers the prophets to preach repentance and prepare the way for our salvation: Give us grace . . . Give us Grace . . . she felt hot tears behind her eyelids. Give us grace to heed their warnings and forsake our sins . . .

• • •

She was exhausted, numb and sleepy when the squad car and ambulance pulled into the lot. The flare of red lights against her closed eyes jerked her into alertness and prodded her out of the car before her mind had caught up with her body. She shuffled through the snow, waving to a uniformed man who must have been Officer Flynn levering himself from his squad car. Next to the car, two paramedics in bulky snowsuits jumped from the ambulance. Clare slogged over to the officer.

"Ma'am," Flynn greeted her. "I'm awful sorry you had to see something like this." She echoed the sentiment silently. The doors to the ambulance clanged open. The EMTs hauled a rescue pallet off the van bed.

"If you follow me, I can take you to the chief," she said. Her voice seemed unnaturally loud in the still, cold air. Flynn opened the trunk of his car and hefted a canvas bag over his shoulder. As they began their slippery processional, he fished into the bag and retrieved a self-starting flare. He yanked the tab and the clearing lit up with a harsh chemical glare. Flynn stuck the flare butt-end into the snow beside the trail.

The EMTs balanced the pallet between them, picking their way through snow as they pushed on toward the water. Every few yards Flynn lit another flare. The trail resembled a nightmare version of a garden walkway illuminated by torches for the benefit of evening strollers. Clare kept her eyes on the tracks as they walked, tire marks crisscrossing at the edges of the trail, two sets of boot prints leading downward, small, deep holes left by deer hooves, and blurry disturbances where she had fallen in her headlong rush to get back to the cruiser.

"There," she said, pointing down the steep slope where a single flashlight beam appeared and disappeared through the pines.

"Chief?" yelled Officer Flynn. Clare pointed her flashlight toward the water.

"Yeah!"

She shifted her light toward his voice and nailed him straight on with the light. Russ threw his hand in front of his face. "I'll come up! Don't anybody climb down until we've gotten some photographs of the tracks."

Flynn pulled the tab on another flare. The trail sprang into high relief. The trees cast hard, dark shadows downslope, concealing and revealing glimpses of Russ's brown parka as he clambered back up the hill. Clare could hear him grunting with effort. By the time he reached them, he was breathing hard.

"Are you all right?" she asked, peering up into his face.

He leaned against a birch tree, panting. "Been up and down this damn stretch of ground about six times already," he said. "Jesus, I'm getting too old for this kind of thing. Sorry, Clare." He sketched a wave to the two paramedics. "Guys, you can retrieve the body just as soon as the state crime lab gets here."

Flynn stared down at the water's edge, craning his neck for a better view. "What's it look like, Chief? Not a jumper moved downstream?"

Russ tilted his head toward Clare. "Every once in a while somebody decides to check out by jumping off the old railroad bridge," he explained. He turned away from the officer and shone his flashlight a couple of yards up the trail. Clare could see where the tire tracks they had been following came to an end. "Somebody drove in to this point and then backed up again." He shifted the light to the edge of the trail closest to the water.

"What's that?" Clare asked. The snow was heavily churned.

"That is where the girl slid all the way down the slope." Russ sounded worn down. "I followed the trail she left back up to the car tracks. Looks just like when little kids roll themselves down a hill."

Flynn whistled, a high, excited sound. Russ glared at him. "Sorry, Chief," the young officer replied. "Just . . . I haven't done a homicide yet."

"Homicide?" Clare looked down toward the water. "Someone killed her?"

"Looks that way," Russ said.

Clare touched Russ's arm, heavy glove over thick parka. "Any clear tracks from whoever drove the car away?" she said.

He shook his head. "Nope. Could be whoever it was threw her body down the hill, hoping she'd land in the kill and disappear for a while. Or it could be she and the driver got into a fight while they were standing here, he hauls off and clips her one, and she falls down the hill. He panics and drives away."

Clare shook her head. "Dear God." She shivered. "Imagine lying there hurt, unable to move or help yourself, and seeing the car lights disappearing . . ."

"Don't. Don't think about it too much," Russ broke in. "We won't know anything until the coroner's report. Don't start speculating or you'll make yourself crazy."

She looked up at him. "The voice of experience?"

"The voice of experience," he agreed. They both looked into the darkness at the creek's edge. Impossible to tell, from here, what was rock and what was shadow and what was water. "There's something else," Russ said.

"What?"

"I think this murder may be connected to the baby you found."

"What? Why on earth would you—"

"Because I have two unusual, unexplainable events happening back to back. A girl abandons a baby. Now a girl shows up dead. This isn't New York City, where kids are stuffed into trash cans and Jane Does turn up twice a week. This is my town. This sort of thing doesn't happen in my town." She cocked an eye at him. He swung his arms wide in frustration. "I mean, of course it happens, obviously it has, but it sure as hell makes the back of my neck crawl. Which is my brain's way of telling me to keep my eyes open."

A halloo echoed further up the trail. A state trooper, bundled up to his ears and wearing his distinctive hat over a knit balaclava, heaved into view around the bend, lugging a chest. "Chief Van Alstyne?" he shouted.

"Yeah, here," Russ called. "Kevin, go on and help him with that." Flynn loped back up the trail and took one end of the box. When they reached the chief, they dropped the chest, stenciled PROPERTY NYSP CRIME SCENE UNIT and the trooper pulled off a glove to shake hands with Russ.

"Sergeant Hayes," he said. "How can I help you, Chief?"

"We need photos, mostly, starting here, where the tire tracks terminate," Russ led the technician toward the site of the disturbance, careful to put his feet into his old boot prints, "and here, where she fell, or they fought, and the slope . . ." he pointed down toward where the body lay hidden. Hayes nodded. "And then let's get her in situ as quickly as we can, so these fellows can take her over to the morgue and our doctor can take a look at her."

They backtracked to the others. Hayes opened the crime-scene chest and began digging out lights and camera parts. Russ pulled Clare to one side. "Why don't you take my keys and go back to the car," he said. "At least one of us can stay warm. I'd have Kevin drive you back, but I may need him here . . ."

Clare shook her head. "I'd rather stay. At least until you bring her up. I'll walk with her back to the ambulance."

"You don't have to do that."

"I know I don't have to. I need to."

He looked at her for a long moment. The reddish lights from the flares were like the last glorious minutes of a sunset falling across his face.

He smiled faintly. "I think I like the way you work, Reverend." Clare shrugged one shoulder and looked away, embarrassed at getting extra credit for just doing the right thing. "Okay," he said. "Stay back out of the way and don't let your feet get numb."

By the time Sergeant Hayes had photographed every mark in the snow, and the chief and Officer Flynn had gone over every branch and every tree for hairs and fibers, Clare had stomped a circle of snow into packed ice. No wonder cop shows never portrayed this part of the job. It was mind-alteringly dull to watch. If she hadn't had to keep moving in order not to freeze, she might have fallen asleep. Hard to keep that edge of horror over the death of another human being when it was surrounded by so much tedious scutwork.

The paramedics, who had waited a lot more comfortably thanks to their arctic-weight snowsuits, skidded down the slope in a zigzag pattern, dragging the pallet behind them. Clare watched as they conferred with the police officers at the water's edge.

"Okay," someone said, "let's do it."

"One . . . two . . . three . . ." said another voice. There was a cracking sound. Someone grunted.

"Watch the water, watch the water!"

"Got 'er. Okay, okay, let go now."

Russ detached himself from the group and hiked up the slope to Clare. The paramedics followed, with Hayes and Flynn behind them in case they slipped. The figure strapped onto the pallet looked like something out of a fairy tale, white skin and dark hair, a train of servants and attendants. The flares' glow gave the scene an otherworldly cast.

When they reached the trail, the paramedics came close to tipping the pallet as they slipped carrying harnesses over their shoulders. "Be careful with her," Russ snapped. Clare had been bracing herself for a disfigured death, but the body was more like a statue of a pretty, round-faced girl, asleep with her head fallen to one side. There were leaves frozen into her long hair. Clare looked at Russ. "May I touch her?" she asked.

He nodded. "Carefully. Don't move her." Clare made the sign of the cross on the girl's marble forehead.

Hayes leaned over toward Russ. "Thought you said she wasn't related to the decedent," he whispered too loudly.

"She's a priest," Russ whispered back.

The state trooper looked at Clare, startled. "Ma'am?" he said. "I mean, Reverend." Clare closed her eyes for a moment. She really, really didn't want to do her song and dance about women priests at this point. "I'm a Christian, ma'am," he continued, "and I'd be glad to join you in prayer."

She looked up to meet Russ's gaze straight on. She wasn't going to ask permission. Their eyes locked for a moment before he nodded almost imperceptibly. "Thank you, Sergeant Hayes," she said. She spread her arms wide across the girl's body. "Let us pray," she said. The men bowed their heads. "Depart, O soul, out of this world; in the name of the Creator who first made you; in the name of the Redeemer who ransomed you; in the name of the Sustainer who sanctifies you." She laid her hand across the girl's icy chest. "May your rest this day be in peace, and your dwelling place in the Paradise of God."

There was a ragged chorus of "Amens." Russ reached past one of the EMTs and pulled a blanket free from the foot of the pallet.

"Chief?" Flynn said.

Russ shook out the blanket and laid it over the girl. "Okay," he said. "Let's all get out of here." Clare let Hayes and Flynn take the lead up the trail, following behind the paramedics and their burden. Russ fell into step beside her. "Don't believe in God, you know," he said.

"Mmmm hmmm," she said.

"Never saw any use for organized religion, either," he said.

"No," she said.

"But I do believe that everybody deserves a basic respect as a human being."

"Even the dead."

They trudged on silently. "Maybe especially the dead," Russ said at last.

Clare nodded. "I like the way you pray," she said. Russ shook his head, smiling faintly. "The last thing any of us can do for the dead is to show respect."

"No. The last thing any of us can do for the dead is give them justice."

She breathed in sharply and scrubbed the back of her glove against the sudden prickle of tears stinging her eyes. "Yes," she said, after she knew her voice would be steady. "You're right. We owe the dead justice."

CHAPTER FIVE

The Burnses' Range Rover was already parked in the lot across the street by the time Clare arrived to unlock the parish hall for their nine o'clock meeting. Fumbling with the heavy chain of keys, she paused to check her watch. She knew she was running behind, but even so, she prided herself on always being prompt. Her old steel Seiko, hanging from its olive-twill strap, read 8:55. The Burnses must not have wanted to linger around the house this morning. Well, neither had she.

Last night, Clare had slept badly, dreaming of Grace for the first time in seven or eight months. When she dragged herself out of bed, still aching with weariness, she went for a long run along Route 51, the river running slow and wide to the old mills on her left, the mountains in front of her, shell-pink and cotton-candy blue in the first light. She ran herself hard in an attempt to outpace the images of angry teenagers, surly drunks, and most of all, the snow-white face of the dead girl. Later, in her shower, she let the hot water soak into her bones, trying to quiet her mind enough to hear the small, inward voice that would tell her which way to go. What to do. In her experience, hard knowledge, painful knowledge, was a gift. God's way of pushing aside the distractions, the self-centeredness, leaving the right way clear, open, marked for travel.

The heavy chunk of the Range Rover doors brought her back to the moment. The Burnses headed across the parking lot toward the back of the church. In their casual coats, jeans, and sweaters, they looked perfectly turned out for a Saturday morning, like models on the cover of a J. Crew catalogue. Younger, and more vulnerable than they seemed in their weekday suits or Sunday clothes. Clare succeeded in unlocking the medieval-looking door and bumped it open with her hip.

"Good morning," she said, juggling her thermos to shake hands.

The Burnses returned her greeting, looking at her attire curiously. "Reverend Clare," Karen asked, "are you moonlighting with the police department?"

Clare plucked at the large brown parka she was wearing. "Oh. This. Chief Van Alstyne loaned this to me last night. I forgot to return it. I have to confess, it's so much warmer than any of the coats I brought with me, I'm tempted to permanently forget to return it."

Karen nodded. "You used to have to go into Saratoga to get anything to wear," she said, "but in the past few years some wonderful stores have moved into Millers Kill. I'd be happy to take you shopping some time if you like."

Clare looked at the lawyer's beautifully-made felt coat, which appeared to have been hand-appliqued by Austrian nuns. Probably the same nuns who did the detailed knitting on her designer sweater. Clare had the feeling she couldn't afford Karen's wonderful little stores.

"Shall we go inside?" Geoff asked. "Ladies?" he tacked on a moment later. They scuffed their boots on the protective mats that reached six feet into the parish hall.

"I brought some breakfast pastries," Karen said, holding up a neatly folded white bag. "There's a place on Main Street called 'In the Dough' that does the most wonderful croissants. Not to mention real bagels."

Clare thought of the donut shop Russ had insisted on taking her to last night. "You can't be a cop if you don't eat donuts," he had said, ushering her into the Kreemie Kakes Diner. He had spun out an elaborate theory that people's personalities could be revealed by the type of donuts they ate. That the choice of jelly donut versus French cruller could unveil the secrets of a person's soul. She had laughed at the time, but watching Karen pull an exquisitely puffed mini-muffin out of the bag, she wondered if he might not be on to something after all. She opened her door and let the Burnses precede her into her office.

"Oh, my," Karen said. They both stopped inside the doorway and looked around slowly. "It certainly is different from when Father Hames was here."

"Yes," Clare agreed, thinking of the unrelieved English-country style that had been her predecessor's office. "It's a nice space to display some of my collections." Over the fireplace that dominated the wall opposite the door, she had hung an intricately carved fragment from a Spanish rood screen, brightly colored Southwestern santos, olivewood bas-reliefs from the Middle East, and Pacific Island fabric-printing blocks. A pair of leather chairs that had originally furnished the admiral's wardroom of a World War Two destroyer—her most spectacular military surplus find ever—were pulled up cozily in front of the fireplace. The large Victorian desk against the far wall was a hand-me-down from Father Hames, but Clare had replaced his oil paintings of stags and spaniels with aeronautical sectional charts and aircraft design blueprints. They shared space on the wall opposite the fireplace with several gilt-framed flea-market mirrors. Clare was very pleased with that touch, since they reflected the light from the west-facing windows flanking the chimneypiece and made the whole room glow at sunset.

"Huh," Geoff Burns said.

"How unique," Karen added quickly.

To the left of the door, a slightly saggy love seat faced the leather chairs. It was a donation Clare suspected hadn't moved at the church's last rummage sale. "Please, sit down," she said, hanging her borrowed parka on the coatrack behind the door. The Burnses followed suit.

Clare dropped her bag on her desk and unscrewed the top from her thermos. In front of the built-in bookcase, Geoff Burns was staring at an Apache helicopter clock her brother Brian had given her for a gag, and Karen was peering at a photo of Clare in T-shirt and camouflage pants. "Is this . . . you?" she asked.

Clare smoothly pushed a mug decorated with a flying rattlesnake and the logo: DEATH FROM THE SKY! out of sight and poured her coffee into a Virginia Seminary mug instead. "That was me," she said. "Several years ago." She sat in a leather chair. "Let's talk about this idea Chief Van Alstyne had for getting Cody into your foster care."

Geoff took the love seat. "Van Alstyne's idea? When he called me, it sounded like your idea. He made it pretty clear that the only reason he was behind it was to make sure we would let him know if Cody's mother contacted us."

"We were both thinking along the same lines, then."

Karen sat down in the other leather chair. "I talked to Chief Van Alstyne, too, and I'll tell you what I told him. There's nothing wrong, or illegal, about Geoff and me helping out Cody's birth mother."

"I'm not suggesting there is. You two want Cody. From all we know, the mother—the birth mother—wants you to have Cody. And we all want to ensure that Cody has a good home with loving parents and that the girl who gave birth to him gets whatever help she needs, whether it be medical, or legal, or counseling. It would be an untruth to say we can guarantee a win-win situation—"

"Of course not!" Geoff interrupted. "What's to prevent a scatter-brained teenager who put him in a box in the first place from deciding, on a whim, that she wants him back? You've never dealt with DHS, Reverend Clare. You have no idea what those people are like. They act as if genetics were sacred destiny. If they get their hands on the birth mother, they'll do everything in their power to persuade her to hang onto the baby. It doesn't matter to them if she's underaged, if she lives in a dump, if she's going to be a welfare breeder all her life. In their book, providing the egg and sperm for a child is more important than providing him with a good life. I'm sick of it."

Clare sat back, blinking.

"Geoff is so right," Karen said. "We've been up one side and down another with them." She opened her arms, encompassing herself and her husband. "Just as a logical starting point, wouldn't you say we were better parent prospects than a girl who would leave a baby out in the cold on the back steps to the church kitchen?"

Clare nodded. "As a logical starting point. Yes." She took a sip of her coffee. "Why do you think DHS hasn't given you Cody to foster at this time?"

"Because we've put up a stink before," Geoff said. "When they re-turned that baby girl we told you about to her abusive mother, we went to the press, we took them to court—"

"It was a nightmare," Karen said.

"If you kowtow to DHS, they might throw you a bone now and again, but if you stand up to their fascist bureaucracy and let others know what they're doing wrong, you get on their enemies' list."

"We knew a couple, the Baldaccis, who ran a home for pregnant teens, a wonderful, caring place. They'd help these girls adopt out or find help for them if they wanted to keep their babies. A few years ago, they fostered a very troubled girl who kept her baby after it was born. She got into trouble later, DHS took the child away, and then, after one of their so-called parental re-education courses, they reunited mother and child. The Baldaccis wrote the caseworker and called her, they sent letters to everyone they knew in DHS warning them that the girl was unstable and the baby would be in danger. Six weeks after what DHS deemed a successful reunification, she murdered the baby."

"Oh, my God. How horrible!"

"Yes, but that's not the end of it. The Baldaccis were so outraged at this utterly needless death, they went public with the whole story. Despite the fact that they were the only home for pregnant teens in Washington county, DHS yanked their license and shut them down."

"That's outrageous," Clare said.

"So you can see why we're not eager for them to get their hands on the birth mother," Geoff said.

"We've already filed suit requesting temporary custody of Cody," Karen said, "but we talked it over, and we think it might be helpful to have members of the congregation write letters in our favor to DHS."

"Especially if anyone knows someone personally they can write to, or call. A state senator, or a member of the governor's staff, or someone on the board of governors for Human Services." Geoff braced his elbows on his knees and cracked his knuckles. "You know, Reverend, when we first started trying to have a baby, I swore we'd do it ourselves, with no help from anybody, doctor or adoption agency. But now?" He scowled. "What the hell. Let's get everyone involved. Maybe someone in the congregation has a friend of a friend who knows Senator Schumer. Whatever it takes to get the baby into our home as soon as possible."

"Okay," Clare said. "At the end of my sermon tomorrow, I'll ask the congregation for help. We'll need some sort of directory, something that gives addresses that people can write to." She reached for one of the croissants Karen had laid out on the flattened bag. "We can just squeak it into the December newsletter if you can get the information to Lois by Monday." She bit off a chunk of croissant, showering her lap with buttery flakes. Her eyes widened at the taste.

"Wonderful," Karen said. For a moment, Clare didn't know if she was talking about the bread or the plan. "I have a good feeling about this. I think having the backing of the whole congregation will make this time different."

Clare devoured the rest of the croissant and brushed the flakes off her lap. "I'd like to talk about the other half of this matter. The part that Chief Van Alstyne brought up with you. Have you thought about what happens when Cody's mother shows up? From what I understand, the mothers in this sort of abandonment case are almost always caught, or turn themselves in."

"That's why we need custody now," Geoff said. "We'll need to be able to argue that the baby has bonded with us, that she is an unfit mother, and that the child's best interests will be served by remaining with us."

"That's a little harsh, isn't it?"

"Reverend, finding a healthy white infant in this country is a harsh business. It's not for the squeamish, or for people who aren't willing to play hardball."

"And besides, maybe the mother won't turn up." Geoff and Clare both looked at Karen.

"That's an unrealistic attitude to take, Kar. We have to position ourselves strategically to win against her, not cross our fingers and hope she's disappeared for good."

There was one more croissant left, and Clare snagged it, wondering what it said about her personality.

"Of course. You're right. It's just I believe that Cody is the one. I just know he's meant to be ours." Karen beamed. Clare hoped that all their focus and intensity wouldn't end in disappointment. Who could say? If passion and commitment made for good parents, the Burnses would be the best thing that could happen to Cody.

"Then we'd better be prepared to do what we have to to ensure that he stays ours," Geoff said.

. . .

Russ resignedly contemplated the old glass-fronted vending machine in the hallway between the coroner's office and the mortuary, where he was reluctantly spending his Saturday afternoon. EAT-A-TERIA it proclaimed in vintage fifties lettering. HOT—COLD—TASTY—CONVENIENT! For a buck in change, you could get one of several sandwiches alleged to be turkey, ham, or cheese, and for fifty cents more you could make your meal complete with chicken soup, which poured out of a spout to the right of the sandwiches.

Everything tasted as if it had been made sometime last summer and had been left in the machine since then. The idea of a limp mystery-meat sandwich and soup with more salt than chicken in it was pretty damn unappealing, but it was closing in on one o'clock, and if he didn't get some food in him he was going to collapse. He was thinking longingly of lunch at his mom's place when Dr. Dvorak came through the heavy wooden doors of the mortuary.

"Don't tell me you're actually going to consume some of that swill," the M.E. said.

Russ snorted. "It's your machine."

Dvorak shrugged off his lab coat and slung it over his arm. "It's the county's machine, my friend, probably put there to ensure a steady supply of customers to the hospital." He headed up the short hallway to his office. Russ fell into step alongside him. "I tell you, Chief, in seven years I don't think I've ever actually seen anyone refill that thing." Dvorak opened his door, solid wood and frosted glass, just like the one to Russ's office. "You didn't need to come here, you know. Right now all I have is my preliminary report. We'll have to wait on the state lab for toxicology."

Dvorak sat down at a desk considerably neater than Russ's. The preliminary report, already color-coded, went on top of a thin stack of similar files, squared to the edge of the desk. A large desktop calendar was filled with precisely lettered notes and reminders, its edges held down with a pencil cup of identically sharpened pencils and a marble-based pen set from the New York State Association of Medical Examiners. The leather cup matched the framed photo of Dvorak, the heavyset, bearded man who was his partner, and their two border collies.

The coroner, who also worked as a pathologist at the county hospital, was a compact man in his fifties, with close-cropped, grizzled hair and pale blue eyes that peered at Russ over the top of his trifocals.

"Of course I needed to stay," Russ said. "A Jane Doe that's a possible murder? You're lucky I didn't sit in on the autopsy."

Dvorak looked askance. "Mmmm. As I recall, the last time you did that you—"

"Don't remind me. What do you know?"

"The basics. From her teeth, she's somewhere between sixteen and twenty-four. She was hit with a heavy, blunt object at the base of her skull, crushing in part of her medulla and causing swelling and hemorrhaging in her brain. It would have rendered her unconscious, and could have led to her death eventually."

"Eventually?"

"My guess is she died of exposure. Based on her lividity, she hadn't been dead more than four hours before you found her. But the body temperature taken by the paramedics was very low, the sort of thing you see a day or so after death. There's no sign of frostbite, which means she was dead before any damage to the skin could occur."

Russ nodded. "Her killer whacked her and then dumped her. And she froze to death."

"In the vernacular, yes."

Russ remembered Clare's voice, shaky with horror, asking what it would be like, watching the car drive away, leaving you alone in the cold and the dark. "Did she ever regain consciousness?"

"No."

He wondered if Clare would think this a mercy from her God. He rubbed his eyes underneath his glasses. "Anything else?"

"No other injuries. No distinguishing marks. The lab work from the state should be back by Monday afternoon, Tuesday at the latest. Then I can let you know if there were any alcohol or drugs involved." The pathologist opened the folder he had carried from the mortuary and slid a paper across the desktop to Russ. "Here are her prints." A set of X-rays. "Her dental profile." A few Polaroids followed. "Pictures for identification purposes. I hope for her family's sake you find out who she was quickly." Russ turned the photos over in his hands, trying to lay the color and expression of life over the pale, fixed mask of death. "She had a baby recently, poor thing."

"What?" Russ jerked his attention back to the doctor. "God damn. I was right. You sure?"

Dvorak gave him a quelling look. "Am I sure? Of course I'm sure. She's about a week, ten days post-partum. Why?"

"Because six days ago we found an abandoned infant we've been trying to place ever since. And when Jane Doe turned up, I had this feeling . . . You got her blood type?"

The doctor looked at his sheet. "AB positive."

"Hot damn. The baby is AB negative. That means she could be its mother, right?"

"Sure. It simply means the father would have to have a negative blood type." Dr. Dvorak steepled his fingers together. "I take it this wasn't a hospital birth?"

"Not that we can track down, no."

"Well, then, if this girl gave birth to a baby with a different rhesus factor, and she didn't receive an antigen shot afterwards, she'll have Rh antibodies swimming in her blood. I can test for that."

"Do it." Russ stood, anxious to get to the station and put her prints into the database. "Would you give me a call when you have the results?"

The pathologist stood as well. "Of course." They shook hands.

Russ glanced back at the report. "Damn. We really don't have a whole hell of a lot here, do we?"

Dvorak shrugged. "She could have been killed by almost anything: a baseball bat, a small log, a tire iron, the leg off a barstool . . ." he opened his hands apologetically. "And the injury could have been done by almost any healthy adult. Sorry I can't make it any easier for you."

"It would be nice if you could have told me it was 'a left-handed man under five-feet-six who pumps iron, wielding a barbell,' but I'll work with whatever you give me."

"You don't want a pathologist, you want a game of Clue. It was Miss Scarlet, in the Conservatory, with the candlestick."

Russ scooped up the photographs, the X-rays, and the print sheet and put them into the empty folder Dvorak proffered him. The two men walked down the short hallway to the waiting room.

"You think there's a connection between this girl having a baby and being murdered?" Dvorak patted his pockets absentmindedly, searching for the keys to unlock the door to the public area of the morgue. "Seems hard to imagine in this day and age."

"I know. What's the big deal about an unmarried girl having a baby these days? Not like when we were young." Russ shook his head as the pathologist ushered him through the empty waiting room to the entrance.

"There are a lot of people willing to kill to get rid of an unwanted baby," Dvorak said, smiling sourly. "It's called abortion, and it's perfectly legal."

Russ did not want to go down that road. "What I need to know is who would be willing to kill to get rid of an unwanted mother." Bright sunshine spilled over the buffed wooden floorboards when he opened the door. "Warmed up. Must be over forty."

"Nice," the pathologist agreed. "As long as you don't count on it lasting."

CHAPTER
SIX

Dvorak was right, Russ thought. As soon as the sun dropped behind the mountains, the mercury plummeted. Turning onto Church Street, he could see the time and temperature sign outside of Farmer's and Merchant's Savings and Loan. Twenty-one degrees, and with the air so clear it was bound to keep on dropping overnight. At least they were done with snow for awhile. Hell of a lot of snow for the beginning of December. Lousy for driving, but good for all the bed-and-breakfasts catering to skiers.

At a red light, his gaze dropped to the folder on the seat beside him. He'd spent the rest of his Saturday afternoon showing the X-rays to all three dentists in town, with no results. He didn't want to consider the possibility that she might have been a tourist. Somebody who had come up to Millers Kill for antiquing or leaf-peeping or skiing and decided it would be the ideal place to drop her baby. If she was an out-of-towner, he might never be able to get an I.D. on her.

He drove past St. Alban's, onto Elm, and pulled into Clare's driveway. The connection to the church. That was the key, his best lead so far. Either the dead girl or the man who had impregnated her had some tie to St. Alban's, and he needed the priest's help to find out what it was. He killed the engine and sat for a moment, looking at the glow of lights through the windows, the intermittent puffs of smoke from the stone chimney. Admitted to himself that he wanted to check up on Clare, too. Not that she'd appreciate the idea. Russ got out of the car and crunched his way across her snow-covered lawn. The Dutch-Colonial house had a deep-hipped roof and a wide porch supported by four plain columns. He swept his boot back and forth as he climbed the stone steps up to the porch, clearing off a little of the snow. There must be another doorway out back by the ramshackle garage that she'd been using. Kind of a shame, because the double front door, with its small, stained-glass windows, was one fine piece of woodworking. He loved old houses.

He tried the wrought-iron door handles. They turned easily. After what she had seen, she still wasn't locking her door. He sighed, rang the bell. From inside, he could hear a muffled lumping, then a faint "Coming!"

The left door opened wide, framing Clare in a swirl of smoke. She coughed. "Russ!" she said. "I didn't expect you. Do you know anything about fires?" He followed her into a roomy foyer, wiping his boots on a worse-for-wear rag rug stretched out in front of the door. The air was acrid, making his eyes sting.

"Holy cow, Clare. What're you doing, burning wet leaves?"

She reached for his coat. "I tried to get a fire going in the fireplace in the living room. But something went wrong." He shrugged out of the bulky nylon parka and she hung it on an old coatrack.

On either side of the door were broad archways. From the size of the brass chandelier hanging in the room to his left, Russ guessed it was meant to be a dining room, although it looked more like a warehouse at the moment, with boxes and mismatched wooden chairs taking up most of the space. He bit back a smile. Evidently even the prospect of living out of cardboard hadn't made the Reverend any more receptive to the idea of the church ladies swarming through her things, doing up the house for her.

Through the right arch, he could see the source of the problem. The Colonial-style brick fireplace in the center of the wall held a pile of overly-large logs that were sputtering flames. Smoke curled under the mantel and filled the room. Since he didn't hear anything, he guessed the quaint rectory had never been fitted out with anything as modern and useful as smoke alarms. "Let me see what I can do," he said. "You open a few windows."

The first thing he saw once he was on his knees on the flagstone hearth was that the flue was closed. He pulled its handle forward, opening it. The air rushed up the chimney with a sucking sound, drawing the smoke with it. There was an iron woodbox to the left of the fireplace and a wrought iron carrier holding kindling. "You got a newspaper handy?" he asked. She scooped yesterday's *Post-Star* off a pine coffee table. He knocked the slightly singed logs to one side and replaced them with crumpled wads of paper, then laid on several small pieces of kindling and a quarter-split log. She had one of those silly brass canisters with foot-long match sticks on the mantelpiece.

"You're supposed to use newspaper?" she asked, as the fire caught cleanly and began to burn. "I didn't know that."

"Where did you learn to make a fire?" Russ asked.

"Survival training," she admitted. "You know, using pine needles, branches, a gum wrapper . . ."

"Do yourself a favor," he said, grinning. "Use paper instead. And start small. Don't pile on the big logs until you've got a roaring fire going."

"I did have a roaring fire going!" she said. "For a minute or two."

"What, when the pinecones caught on fire?" Russ laughed.

"The smoke's cleared out," she said with dignity. "I'll close the windows."

Russ took in the room while Clare cranked the casement windows shut. There was an overstuffed sofa and a few fat chairs with faded chintz covers grouped in front of the fireplace, and a needlepoint rug over the floorboards. The low built-in bookcases on either side of the fireplace were piled with haphazardly arranged books, pictures, and plants, and topped by two narrow clerestory windows.

"So what brings you here? Besides saving my bacon from getting smoked."

"Wanted to talk about the case."

"Ah," she said. "Then why don't I get us some coffee first? Make yourself at home."

"Coffee would be great. This is quite a place you have here. Do you know when it was built?"

She disappeared through a swinging door in the back of the room, but her voice floated out to him. "Nineteen-twelve. It's very Arts-and-Crafts, isn't it?"

"Oh, yeah." He walked back to the foyer and pulled off his wet boots. "Linda and I have an eighteenth-century farmhouse out near Fort Henry. No closets, eleven rooms and not a level wall or floor in any of them."

"Must take a lot of work," Clare shouted from the kitchen.

"Yeah, but I like it. Pretending I'm Bob Vila is a hobby of mine."

She had set up a square chest on legs under the big front window and put it to work as the bar. Nice decanters. Russ uncorked one and took a sniff of Scotch. The smell was enough to make his mouth water. Sighing, he replaced the top. The little cane-seat chairs on either side didn't look as if they could hold his weight, but he liked the plain, bare window, showing off the small panes of glass that ran along the edges. That was the one thing that drove him nuts about his wife's custom curtain business—every window in his house was swagged and draped and ruffled with about fifty-seven yards of fabric.

Two standing lamps flanked a folded gateleg table behind the sofa. There was an assortment of family pictures, some in fancy silver frames, others in good-quality wood. He picked up the largest photo, taken on a beach somewhere. An older couple who must be Clare's parents sitting on a driftwood log. A younger Clare in shorts and cotton sweater, her arm around a similarly-dressed blond girl of eye-catching good looks. Two blond guys flanking them, not much taller than the girls but broad-shouldered and big. Which would explain the two separate photos of men in UVA football uniforms.

A smaller picture in an elaborate frame caught his eye. Mom and Dad dressed like one of those rich couples in a Cadillac ad, and Clare, who was decked out in a heavily-embroidered robe, smiling and teary-eyed. Inside a church somewhere, from the looks of it. The two beefy brothers were accompanied by two cheerleader types, one of whom held a baby.

"Here you go," Clare announced, backing through the door at the rear of the room. She lowered a tray containing two plain crockery mugs and a sugar bowl onto the coffee table. The smell was incredible.

"Damn, that is one good-smelling coffee. 'Scuse my French."

She sat in one of the plump chairs and picked up a mug. "Why thank you. I grind my own mix. Jamaican Blue roast, Colombian . . . I put in a little ground hazelnut and cinnamon . . ." She smiled, the smile of a really good cook attempting without success to look modest. "The secret is to use fresh-roasted beans and fresh spices, and to grind 'em yourself. Don't bother with the stuff in the supermarket that's been sitting around in a bag for who knows how long."

Russ took the other chair. "I'll keep that in mind. Next time I have a spare half hour to make a cup of coffee."

She laughed. "I didn't know how you take it, so . . ." she said, waving a hand over the sugar bowl, packets of artificial sweetener, and creamer.

"I should probably be a macho guy and say I drink it black, but the truth is, I like it real sweet."

"Oh, yeah. I drink mine sweet, too, but I'm always a little embarrassed by it. I used to stash sugar in my pockets and slip it in on the sly at briefings. Hey. Do you think how people drink their coffee reveals their personality?"

Russ stirred sugar into his mug and took a sip. He closed his eyes. "This is good. I needed this." He opened his eyes and looked at Clare. "No. How you drink your coffee while you're eating donuts, that reveals your personality." She was wearing a woolly turtleneck tucked into a pair of khakis and what looked like some New York designer's idea of army boots. She was curvier than he had thought when he had seen her in baggy sweats and thick outdoors clothes. "You run today?" he asked.

She nodded. "Six miles. I needed it, too, after last night."

"Yeah. I've seen my share of dead bodies, and I've never gotten used to it. To tell you the truth, I hope I never do. Seeing someone who's been murdered . . . that should make you lose sleep at night."

Clare sat up a little straighter. "She was definitely murdered? It wasn't a suicide?"

"Oh, no, it was murder, all right." He told her Dr. Dvorak's findings. When he got to the part about giving birth recently, her eyes went wide.

"Cody's mother," she said. "Good Lord. I have to admit, when you said it was too much of a coincidence last night, I chalked it down to, um . . . paranoia."

"Thanks a lot. If I were a woman, you'd have called it intuition." She made a face at him. He continued, "Dvorak is going to send DNA samples to Albany, along with some of Cody's, to make sure. Of course, that will take up to four months."

"That poor girl. I can't imagine . . ." Clare looked into the fire. "I wish she could have known Cody was settled with the couple she had picked out for him. Before she died. Was killed."

He got up and laid another two logs on the fire. "Don't be wishing that so quick. As far as I'm concerned, Geoff Burns is my number one suspect. With Karen Burns following close behind."

"You must be joking! The Burnses? You're just saying that because you don't like Geoff."

"I admit that. I don't like Geoff Burns. He's an arrogant, self-important, humorless pain in the butt." He sat down on the edge of his chair, leaning across the table. "But think about it, Clare. Who else has a better motive? The father of the baby? He's gonna kill to avoid a few bucks child support a month? Or the Burnses, who have been trying for years to get a child, and are running out of resources and time and have no friends at DHS?"

She crossed her feet under her, tailor style. "You know nothing about this girl. What if Cody's father was a married man, with a family, and she was going to blackmail him? Or what if her boyfriend killed her because Cody wasn't his? Or . . . or . . ."

"Or what if she was a hit-woman for the Mafia and they rubbed her out before she could testify to the Feds?"

"Don't be smart. You see what I'm saying, here. You can't pin a murder on the Burnses without doing a lot more legwork. Just because they're convenient."

"Legwork?"

"Well . . . that's what they say on TV."

"I'm not going to cut the investigation short, no. In fact, I want you to help us with something."

She shifted forward in her chair. "Yeah?"

"The one thing we do know about the girl is that she knew the Burnses were looking for a baby, and that she left Cody at the church."

"Or she agreed to let someone leave him at the church."

"Right. Somewhere, there's a connection. She was either a member of your congregation, or she worked there, or the father of the baby did, or she had friends there."

"You think someone in my parish will be able to identify her?"

"Yeah." He leaned back into his chair. "How would you feel about arranging for people to take a look at some photos tomorrow?"

She tucked a strand of hair behind her ear and bit her lip. In the warm light, her hair was the color of honey and molasses. Russ looked into his coffee.

"What do you mean by 'arranging' for people to look at the photographs? Flash them in front of every member of the congregation as they leave the church?"

"Well . . . yeah."

"I can't do that, Russ. Even if I were inclined to try to order them to do something, I'm their priest, not their commanding officer. Besides, you ever hear of a little thing called 'separation of church and state'?"

"Oh, c'mon, Clare, I'm not asking you to march 'em all past a lineup at gunpoint. There are how many members of St. Alban's?"

"Around two hundred families. We'll get maybe a hundred folks at the ten o'clock service, and thirty or so at seven-thirty."

"I've got an eight-man force that has to cover three towns as well as investigate this murder. Can you imagine what going door-to-door with every member of St. Alban's will cost us in lost hours? I can't spare the time this case will take me as it is. You know domestics, drunk driving, and shoplifting all increase around Christmas. Gimme a break. Help me out." She crossed her arms and worried her lower lip. He pressed his point. "Neither of us wants to see something preventable happen because my officers were canvassing your congregation."

She rolled her eyes. "Spare me. Next you'll be trotting out a poor orphan boy and his sick dog. Just because I wear a collar doesn't mean I'm a soft touch."

"Okay, okay, scratch the last. Please. I'll go by your rules, Clare, whatever you say. I need your help."

She crossed her ankle over her knee, like a guy, and rested her mug on her leg. "This is what I can do. I'll explain that your Jane Doe may have had some connection to the church. I'll offer anyone who's willing to help the chance to look at the photographs." She looked into the fire.

"I'll remind them that somewhere she's got parents, or brothers and sisters, who don't know where she is or what's happened to her." She paused for a moment, then looked back at him. "You can take down the names of anyone who views the pictures, and I'll have Lois give you a copy of our membership directory." She smiled a one-sided smile. "The rest, I'm afraid, will have to be legwork."

"You really like that word, don't you?"

"Yes, I do."

"Okay. Thank you. I know this is a lot to throw on you, this being your, what, third week? Thank you. For everything."

"Oh, lord. My sermon was going to be on Cody, and then the announcement about the Burnses' attempt to have him fostered with them. Do I have to tell everyone we think this girl is his mother? Not that I want to sweep it under the rug, far from it, but it will make things sound awfully odd. 'Here's the baby, here are the adoptive parents, and, oh, by the way, will you all look at pictures of the dead mother?' "

"No. As a matter of fact, I'd rather play that piece of information close to my vest. Let's just say I have reason to believe the dead girl had some connection to St. Alban's and leave it at that."

Clare leaned forward, resting her elbows on her knees. "I'm still going ahead with my announcement after the sermon, asking the congregation to write letters in support of the Burnses. I cannot believe they had anything to do with that girl's death." She shook her head. "Oh, for heaven's sake, I hope you can find out her name soon. It sounds so callous to keep calling her 'that girl.' "

He nodded. "I know. I want you to ask yourself if you can't believe the Burnses might have done it because they really haven't ever given you any cause to think they might be capable of such a thing, or if you can't believe it because you've met them, they belong to your church, and they're 'nice people.' "

She frowned, bit her lower lip again. "They're very intense, very focused on getting Cody. But anyone who's been trying to have a baby for so long would be that way, I think. And they strike me more as the types who would throw money or the force of law at a problem and expect it to go away." She looked at Russ. "I met with them just this morning, did I mention that?"

"Last night you told me you had an appointment with them. How did it go?"

"Fine. Karen was all bubbly and hopeful, and Geoff was . . . his usual self. They certainly didn't behave like a couple who committed murder the night before."

"Have you ever seen anyone after they committed murder?"

"Um." She looked into the fireplace.

"Um?"

"I've seen people after they've killed. How's that?"

Russ retreated from the sharpness in her voice. "I didn't mean to be flip. What I'm saying is that you can't always tell by someone's behavior afterwards."

She waved a hand. "No, no, I'm sorry. Sensitive area. You're right." She looked into his eyes. "I do recognize that part of me doesn't want anyone from my parish to be involved. That I can't believe that one of my . . ."

"Nice, white-collar Episcopalians?"

She smiled ruefully. "One of my nice Episcopalians could do something so brutal. Now, if someone had been murdered with poisoned sherry . . ."

"Or clubbed to death with a nine-iron . . ."

"Or strangled with a shetland sweater from Talbots . . ." They both laughed. Clare smiled at him. "I'm really glad you came over." She pushed her hair back with one hand. "Finding her has been weighing on my mind all day, but there was no one I could talk with about it."

Russ removed his glasses and rubbed them on his shirt. "Yeah. You need to talk to someone who's been there. That's why cops tend to go off-duty straight to the nearest bar instead of going home. It's not any different than coming off patrol someplace, you and your buddies getting together to drink too much and tell lousy jokes and talk about what happened over and over again."

"Because nobody else will understand."

"Yeah." They looked at each other in agreement, then she turned to the fire. He rolled the mug between his palms, watching the play of firelight over the many textures in the room. They sat for awhile, the fire hissing and popping occasionally, comfortable with not talking. Russ finished off his coffee and smiled to himself. It was so many years since he had made a new friend, he'd forgotten how enjoyable it could be, getting to know someone whose mind was both fresh and familiar.

"What?" Clare asked.

He hadn't realized he had been smiling at her. "Oh, just that you remind me of myself. Cops and priests have a lot in common, don't you think? Confessions, sin, helping folks no one else wants to help . . ."

"Funny uniforms, working odd hours, lousy pay . . ."

He grinned. "Laughing at things no one else could laugh at . . ."

"Heck," she said, "it's just like the army, except without free medical coverage."

Russ groaned and pulled himself out of his chair. "Speaking of odd hours, I'd better head home before Linda decides I'm out on a call and puts my dinner back in the freezer." He glanced at the fire, burning bright and clean. "Make sure you bank that fire before you go to bed. You don't want to have the volunteer fire department out here in the middle of the night."

"I promise." Clare got up and headed for the foyer. "So, I'll see you tomorrow at church?"

He snorted. "Maybe not for the whole service. That might blow a gasket on this old unbeliever." She handed him his parka. "What's the best way to make sure everyone has the chance to look at the photos?"

"Hmmm. If you station an officer near the main door of the church, and you take the parish hall, we should be able to ensure anyone who wants to help out will be able to get ahold of a picture." She looked up at him while he shrugged on his coat. "Can we try to keep this as low-key as possible? There will be little kids there, you realize."

Russ paused from tugging on his heavy boots. "I realize that. I'll take care to be as unobtrusive as possible. I promise."

"Just promise me you'll look into every possibility, and not just focus on the Burnses." She touched his arm briefly. "As far as we know, the last thing she wanted in life was for her baby to be settled with them. I'd really like to see that happen."

"I promise I'll conduct a thorough investigation. Don't worry, my own theory won't stop me from chasing down any other leads. It's not so much that I want to nail Geoff Burns, Clare, it's that I want to catch whoever did this. Do you realize that if I'd started Friday night's patrol at the kill instead of ending up there, that girl would be alive today?" He kept his eyes on his gloves as he pulled them over his hands.

She rested her hand on his arm again, saying nothing, looking at him with those clear, bright eyes. They were more brown than green tonight. He shook his head sharply.

"Oh, shit, I know I can't stop bad things from happening. But I don't have to like it. Excuse my French. This is my town. My home, where I grew up. They could have hired anybody to do my job, but they gave it to me, and sometimes I get the feeling, Clare, I tell you, like when I first held my sister's newborn, like I had been given something amazing and valuable, and it was up to me to guard her and protect her." He let out his breath explosively. "Am I making any sense at all?"

Clare nodded. "Yes."

"Sorry. I didn't mean to . . . I'm not the sort to usually get melodramatic."

She shook her head. "Telling the truth isn't melodramatic. And I certainly don't think taking your responsibilities seriously is melodramatic." She smiled up at him, a small, thoughtful smile. "Sounds to me like you have a vocation, Russ. You're called to your profession."

"Huh." He thrust his hands in his pockets. "If that's a calling, it's a damned uncomfortable feeling."

"It can be, at times. Other times, it carries you on like nothing else in the world, because you're doing what you know you're meant to do."

He grinned at her. "Are you going to bring God into it, now?"

She crossed her arms. "No, you'll have to wait for tomorrow for that. And don't forget something for the collection plate."

He laughed. "I'll be there." He held his hand out, and she shook it in her firm, no-nonsense way. "See you in church, Reverend."

"Police work in the parish hall. It should make for an interesting Sunday."

CHAPTER
SEVEN

Waiting her turn to recess down the center aisle behind the choir, Clare inspected the crowd, taking the emotional temperature of her flock. The Right Reverend Malcom Steptoe, one of her teachers, had pounded in the importance of seeing the congregation as a whole. "You'll meet with individuals and small groups all the time," he would say. "Once a week, you have a chance to see the whole family of communicants together. Are they peaceable? Satisfied? Discontent? Angry? You must know!"

Right now, at the end of the Eucharist, several of her family looked entirely disapproving. It wasn't from her homily on Cody, she knew. That had been a tight piece of writing, comparing the baby to the infant Jesus, and his waiting for a family to the Christian waiting for the advent of Christ on Earth. It segued nicely into her plea for help for the Burnses. And it was under fifteen minutes long, always a plus for a sermon.

The last of the choir crossed the chancel. Nathan Andernach, the deacon, lined up shoulder to shoulder with Sabrina Campbell, today's reader, and Clare took her place at the end of the line. "The king shall come when morning dawns," the choir and congregation thundered, "and earth's dark night is past." The three trod slowly down the steps, past the alter rail, into the aisle. "O haste the rising of that morn, the day that aye shall last." From her unquestioned place in the front pew, Mrs. Marshall gave Clare a look that said, "This is *not* the way we do, things, young lady."

No, this was definitely about the two police officers in the back of the church. During announcements, in between calls for donations to the soup kitchen and volunteers for the Christmas Eve greening of the church, she had outlined the situation as briefly as possible and asked for everyone's cooperation with Chief Van Alstyne, who had risen from his seat in the last pew and nodded soberly to the crowd. There had been a buzz of conversation, cut short by the offertory and the celebration of the Eucharist. "And let the endless bliss begin, by weary saints foretold," the congregation sang. Sterling Sumner tugged the end of his scarf around his throat and glared at her as she marched past his pew. "When right shall triumph over wrong, and truth shall be extolled." Vaughn Fowler was scanning the congregation, frowning slightly. Probably picking out who was going to be most disturbed by looking at pictures of a dead body.

The choir fanned out in two lines against the back of the church. "The king shall come when morning dawns, and light and beauty brings." Their harmony soared above the congregation's melody. Russ Van Alstyne was singing along, his finger tracing across the hymnal, following the words. Now that was a surprise. Nice baritone too, from what she could hear with the choir reverberating only a few feet away. "Hail, Christ the Lord! Thy people pray, come quickly, King of kings."

Clare held the heavily-embroidered floor-length cope—a literal mantle of priestly authority—out with one arm so she could turn without tangling. She drew a deep breath, letting the words come from a place deep inside herself. "Go in peace, to love and serve the Lord," she said, projecting her voice so that it echoed back enthusiastically from the stone walls. "Alleluia, alleluia!"

"Thanks be to God," the congregation responded, "Alleluia, alleluia!" It was an immensely satisfying moment, even if all hell was about to break loose. A polite, Episcopalian sort of hell, of course. She grinned.

The choir members headed back up the aisles in groups of two or three. Parishioners were rising from their seats, drifting toward the parish hall, putting on coats, collecting squirming children. The din of voices made it hard to hear, so she nearly jumped when Russ spoke quietly in her ear.

"Nice sermon. In fact, the whole thing was pretty cool. Very ritualistic."

"Isn't it? Come for one of the big feast days. You'll get to see me cense the altar."

"Uh huh. Sounds interesting."

"Colorful natives practicing their quaint rituals in their natural habitat."

"Speaking of colorful natives, where should I . . . ?"

"I have to stay here and greet everyone leaving now. You head back to the parish hall, right through those doors there," she pointed to the front of the church, "down the hall to the right." The officer Russ had brought with him slipped through the inner doorway into the vestibule. He carried a plain manila folder. "Do me a favor," she said to Russ, "give people a chance to grab a cup of coffee and have a cookie before you start flashing the photos, okay?"

"Okay." He tapped his own folder and pushed his way through the crowded center aisle, apparently not noticing the round-eyed glances directed at him. It must be hard, being a cop, she thought. Always either a hero or a bad guy to the public, never just another human being.

"Reverend Fergusson!" Mr. Sumner's preemptory tone jerked her away from her thoughts. "Don't you think asking the congregation to view pictures of murdered women in the sanctity of their own church is the height of poor taste?"

Clare's spine stiffened. It was going to be a long Sunday.

"No, I don't think we'll be called upon to help the investigation again, Mr. Fitzpatrick. That would mean the Millers Kill police couldn't find the killer, and I'm sure that won't happen."

"Wouldn't count on that. When I was an alderman, I told 'em we needed another trained investigator. Too many people coming up from the cities these days! It's getting so you can't walk down Main Street without tripping over some newcomer from New York or Albany." The octogenarian wheezed indignantly. Clare laid a steadying hand on his arm, and he responded by seizing her hand and pumping it in time to his words. "Told 'em we'd be needing more investigators, but they wanted to save money, so what do they do? Hire a detective as chief and send one of the boys off to the state troopers for the summer. I blame Harold Collins, that cheapskate. You haven't met Harold Collins, yet, have you? You know how he voted when we had that water treatment problem?"

"I really have to get back to the parish hall, Mr. Fitzpatrick. It's been great talking with you, and I hope that bursitis calms down soon. How about I plan on making a visit later this week? I'll give you a call Monday. Take care!" Clare deftly pried her hand from the former alderman's clutches and trotted down the aisle as fast as her dignity and her flapping alb would allow. She made it to the sacristy without having to speak to anyone else. She unknotted the cincture around her waist, a rope-like belt symbolizing her vows, and removed her stole, kissing the embroidered cross at its center with a hasty reverence. During the four years she had served the church as a deacon, she had worn the rectangular scarf across her chest, and it still thrilled her to feel it in the ordained priest's position, hanging squarely around her neck, falling over both shoulders. She yanked the alb over her head in a billow of white linen, shook it with a snap she hoped would take out most of the wrinkles, and hung it. On a wire hanger. Her conscience pricked her. It didn't make much of a symbol of purity with one sleeve inside out, ready to slip to the floor at any moment. She pulled it off and rehung it on its own wooden hanger.

In one of her less-mottled mirrors, she was amazed to see herself so collected. Not a hair was out of place in her French twist. After listening to complaints and denials and gasps of horror and agreeing over and over and over again that yes, it was a terrible shame, and no, the police didn't suspect anyone in their congregation, and what was the world coming to, she felt her hair should be standing away from her scalp in a frizzled heap, the ends smoking.

There was a knock on the door. Clare sighed. *Not another round of questions, please.* The door cracked open, admitting a hand holding a very full, very enticing sherry glass.

Lois sidled into the room. "I asked the refreshment ladies to bring up the sherry from the kitchen. I thought you might need it."

Clare held the glass to her nose and sniffed deeply. "Ahhhh . . ." She took a larger-than-recommended swallow. "God bless you, Lois."

"Is that official?"

"You bet. How's it going in there?"

"I heard a few comments about priests overstepping the bounds, but so far no one's used the phrase 'meddling woman.' "

"Oh. Great."

"Chief Van Alstyne is being quite charming. He hasn't started waving eight-by-ten glossies of murder victims around, so people are feeling a tad more relaxed."

"Encouraged by the sherry?"

"I brought up the second bottle myself. I thought the chief might like some as well, but he turned me down. No drinking on duty, I suppose." Clare finished off her glass and sighed again, this time with contentment. The secretary went on. "He's really quite attractive, don't you think?"

"Who?"

"Chief Van Alstyne. All that tousled hair and those sexy lines at the corners of his eyes. He has that rugged, all-American look, like the kind Ralph Lauren puts in his ads, except his models always have this slightly gay edge to them. The chief is very . . . heterosexual."

Clare laughed. "The chief is also very married, Lois. Just how much of the sherry have you had?"

"Don't worry," Lois said, floating back into the hall. Clare followed her. "I'm sure there's enough left to rustle up another glass for you."

In the large, sunlit parish hall, things did seem almost normal. Clare worked her way back to the white-draped refreshment table, greeting the people she knew by name and smiling at those she didn't know yet. Mae Bristol, as plump and pale as an over-risen bun, was serving up coffee and tea from the church's silver service. She always wore a printed silk dress with a matching hat—this Sunday it was cabbages in shades of blue. The sherry bottles were between the creamer and the coffee cups. They looked seriously depleted.

"This is stupid, Miss Bristol. My parents let me drink wine at home!" A slim girl in a fashionably skinny velvet-and-patchwork dress leaned across the white tablecloth. Her hair was perfectly retro-seventies, straight and shining and parted in the middle. She reminded Clare of the girls at her old high school whose outfits always looked like they were straight off the pages of *Seventeen* magazine and whose hair was always blown dry to frothy perfection. She could still remember feeling angular and underdeveloped and unfeminine next to them, a jock whose clothes never looked right off the basketball court or the track, a girl whose fingernails were always lined with grease because she'd been helping her dad with airplane maintenance. It had been—what?— seventeen or eighteen years since she graduated? Funny how the individuals changed, but the type remained. There would always be girls who had been blessed by the gods of adolescence, and girls like Clare. She reached around the latest version of the homecoming queen and snagged one of the sherry bottles. Age, thank heavens, most definitely hath its privileges. The girl flashed her a well-polished look of teenage disdain.

"Then your mother can come over here and get a glass for you, Alyson. I'm not giving you any sherry until then, and that's final." The girl flipped her dazzling hair in annoyance and flounced away as well as she could in her high-heeled platform boots.

"The difficult age," Clare said, filling her glass to the top and handing the bottle back to Miss Bristol.

The elderly lady fixed Clare with her black-currant eyes. "That girl is spoiled rotten," she said. "I had her in my fourth-grade class, and she was spoiled then. Alyson will always be at the difficult age, whether she's seventeen or seventy."

"Ah," Clare said. "Well."

"Oh, don't mind me, Reverend. I never felt I could speak my mind when I was teaching, so now that I'm retired, I'm making up for lost time. Which reminds me. Some of those men who believe they run the church undoubtedly want to let you know their opinions about this police business. You stand your ground. I think you're doing a splendid job."

"Goodness," Clare said. "Thank you, Miss Bristol." She turned away, feeling as if she'd been given a sticker for good behavior from an otherwise strict teacher. She took a sip of her sherry, spotting Russ standing by the door to the street. Casual, not obviously blocking it, but making it impossible to get past him without at least making an excuse. He really was tall, several inches above anyone else in the room. It was more noticeable in a group. She wended her way toward him through the crowd, careful not to spill any of her drink on the faded rose-patterned carpet. As she nodded and smiled at her congregants, Vaughn Fowler fell in beside her.

"Any luck with identifying the victim?" he asked.

"At the church door? No,—no." She had to forcibly restrain herself from adding "sir" every time she spoke to Colonel Fowler. Mr. Fowler.

"Let's hope someone here will be able to help the police, then. Speaking as a vestry member, I don't like it. The sooner we get this off church property the better. You do realize there could be a question of liability for St. Alban's?"

"Liability? For a murder? I don't see how."

"If there was some connection. Do the police have a suspect yet? If it's a member of our congregation, we may need to consult the diocesan attorney to ensure that the church, as a corporate entity, has no responsibility."

"Ah . . . as far as I know, Chief Van Alstyne hasn't singled out any one person as a suspect. After all, finding out who she was is a very preliminary step."

"I'm thinking about the next step. Suppose he arrests someone from St. Alban's. It's in the *Post-Star*. It's on the news. Then the real murderer turns up. That leaves us wide open to a lawsuit. Contributing to defamation of character or some such. Lawyers. You have to think of the ramifications of everything you do these days."

Millers Kill's chief of police was smiling reassuringly to a young couple wrestling their two little girls into snowsuits. "Mama," the older child said, "is that Officer Friendly?"

"I was wondering when you'd get over here. I wanted to wait for you before I started showing the pictures around." Russ reached behind him and swept the folder off an unused *prie-dieu* standing beside the door. He looked keenly at Mr. Fowler. Clare introduced the two men.

"I recall reading about you in the *Post-Star* around the time you were appointed police chief, Van Alstyne. You were in the Eighty-ninth MP brigade weren't you? I was chief of staff at Fort Hood during their deployment there in 'eighty-seven."

The chief blinked and straightened slightly. "Yes, sir, I was in the Eighty-ninth." Clare bit back a smile. Evidently she wasn't the only one to have a hard time treating the colonel as a civilian. "I'm surprised you'd remember something like that," Russ went on.

"Military service is something I always look for. It's what makes a man." He frowned. "Or woman." Clare felt her cheeks flush. Fowler pointed to the folder. "You ready to start this, Chief?"

"Yessir," Russ said.

"Then I might as well be the first. Set an example, let everyone know what's expected of them. Nothing to be afraid of, after all." Russ looked at Clare. She nodded. He flipped open the folder. Clare had avoided looking at the photographs when she had been saying good-bye to parishioners at the front door, but now she took a long, steady look at the face of the unknown. Four shots, face front, profiles, and full body, covered with an institutional green sheet. She was struck by how much less real the girl looked, laid out on a steel table, lit by fluorescents and flashbulbs. Not at all like the sleeping princess, leaves frozen into her long hair, that she had stood over on the bank of the creek.

"Sorry," Fowler said. "Don't know her." He frowned. "Where did you say it happened?"

"I didn't," Russ said. "We found her body just upstream from Payson's Park."

The colonel glanced at Russ. "Kids still go there to get away from their parents?" He shook his head. "I used to skinny dip in the river there. Jump off the old trestle bridge and swim downstream. It was a more innocent time. . . . Sorry I can't be of any help."

"Thank you anyway," Russ said.

Fowler nodded, slipping on his overcoat. "Reverend, I'll be seeing you at the next vestry meeting. Chief Van Alstyne, good to meet you." When he opened the door, the sunlight and snowlight flooded the parish hall, drawing glances from the rest of the room.

Clare held up her hands. "May I have your attention, please? For those of you willing to help with the police investigation, Chief Van Alstyne is ready to have you look at the photographs. If you could give him your name before leaving, he'll be able to keep track of which members of our congregation have seen the pictures. I know it's an unpleasant task, but it's important that we all do our part to help the police catch whoever is responsible for this crime. Thank you."

There was a surge of bodies toward them. "Good heavens." Clare murmured. "They don't seem to be too horrified at the prospect of autopsy shots, do they?"

"Reality TV," Russ whispered. "If you've seen all those specials on serial killers, this is pretty tame." He raised his voice. "If you could form a line there, we can get you all out of here quickly."

It was a repeat of the earlier scene in the vestibule of the church, with more people. The same exclamations, expressions of sympathy, philosophical mutterings. No one recognized her. There was a moment of excitement when Mae Bristol's turn came up. She held two of the photos in her hands, looking slowly from one to the other. "I feel as if I should know her," she said. "I just can't place her. But I'm sure I've seen her before." She shook her head and smiled apologetically at Russ and Clare. "Too many years of too many young people, I suppose."

The tedium of the whole process reminded Clare of how she had felt waiting on the trail for the evidence to be photographed. Police work was a lot like combat, she decided, hours and days of boredom punctuated by moments of sheer terror.

"Oh! My! God!" The squeal brought her mind back to the scene at hand. Alyson what's-her-name stood in front of Russ, flanked by two well-dressed adults who were presumably the parents who had spoiled her. "I know her! That's Katie McWhorter! I know her!"

CHAPTER

EIGHT

Clare had offered her office to the Shatthams, figuring it would be a comfortable spot for their daughter to talk with the police chief, but they were insistent that Clare be there for Alyson's statement, so the five of them wound up clustered at one end of the massive oak table in the vestry meeting room. Clare wasn't sure what role the Shatthams wanted her to play. Counsel? Witness? Maybe they hoped she would put the fear of God into Alyson, who, after her first emotional out-burst, had reassumed her pose of pseudo-sophistication and contempt. Clare was out to sea when it came to adolescents, which she'd freely admit if anyone both-ered to ask. The only teens she had known in recent years had been in the army, and she didn't think telling Alyson to keep her weapon grounded and her hands inside the bird would be useful in this situation.

The girl sat in a chair facing away from one of the windows, her hair a blond nimbus, her face shadowed. Her parents had dithered for a few moments before taking up seats on either side of her. Russ sized up his choices and sat down directly opposite Alyson, leaving the chair at the head of the table for Clare. She took it, wishing she had brought her glass of sherry along, wondering how Russ could let the seconds roll on by without demanding Alyson tell them everything she knew.

He flipped open the folder again, arranged the pho-tos against the creamy manila, and slid it across the table to Alyson. The teen's eyes flickered to the pictures and then returned to the chief. Russ reached inside his shirt pocket, removed a pair of sunglasses, and swapped his glasses for the shades. They were mirrored. Clare rested a finger against her lips to keep from making a crack about Cool Hand Luke.

"Katie McWhorter," he said. "What can you tell me about her, Alyson?"

"She was just a girl who went to school with me, that's all. She graduated last year."

"Did she stay in town after she graduated? Or did she move away?"

The girl shifted slightly in her seat. "She went off to college. Somewhere. I'm not sure. It's not like we were friends or anything."

"No?"

"No. She was like, living somewhere around Depot Street? My parents sure don't want me going there. And she didn't exactly hang out at Smoky Joe's drinking cappucino."

"Who did she hang with, Alyson? Before she went to college."

"Nobody much. She was a brainiac, really smart, so she knew a lot of the geeks. I know she had a job at the Infirmary." She paused, frowning. "She had a boyfriend."

Clare wanted to yell, "Yes! Now we're getting somewhere!" Russ didn't twitch. "A boyfriend?" he asked, with no particular emphasis.

"Yeah. Ethan Stoner. They were like, a weird combination, what with her being a brain and him being a head." The unintentional pun made Alyson smile at her own wit. "I think they knew each other from way back, like in grade school or something. He was held back a year someplace, otherwise he would have graduated last year with Katie. They were a pretty hot and heavy item."

"Had you seen her since she went away to school?"

"Had I seen her? What do you mean?" Clare wished there was more light on Alyson's face. She couldn't tell if her voice was strained because it was finally sinking in that an acquaintance, someone her own age, was dead, or if she knew more than she was letting on. Or if she was just hostile to Russ's authority.

"Did you see her back in Millers Kill at any time?"

"No. But like I said, we weren't friends. So if she came back to visit Ethan, I wouldn't have known about it."

"Or her parents."

"Huh?"

"She might have come back to visit her parents."

"Oh. Yeah." Alyson looked at her own parents at this. "Can I go now? I really don't know anything else."

"Can you think of any reason, anything at all, why someone might have wanted Katie dead?"

"God, no. I think it must be one of those random violence things, don't you? Some stranger coming into town and raping and murdering the first girl he can lure into his car?" She shuddered visibly and dramatically.

Her mother whimpered. "Chief Van Alstyne, do we need to be worried about the safety of our daughter?"

"My God, what if it's one of those serial killers, like the one over in Rochester a few years back?" Mr. Shattham put his arm around his daughter's thin shoulders.

"Dad-dy . . ." she said, her voice rising in a whine.

"I can't rule out a stranger killing in this case," Russ said, "but I doubt that's what we have here. And Katie was never raped." He folded his fingers together and leaned his chin on his hands. "She had recently had a baby, though."

Alyson's mouth dropped open. Dust motes rose through the air on thermals caused by the sunlight puddling on the floor and the table. "What?" she finally choked out. "She was pregnant?" It was the first genuine emotion Clare had seen from the girl since she laid eyes on the photos of Katie's body.

"She had been pregnant. The doctor who autopsied her says she gave birth within the last two weeks."

"Pregnant. Holy shit."

"Alyson!"

"Oh, Mummy, don't have a cow." Alyson's shaded face stilled, only a small frown marring the blankness of hard thought. "It must have been Ethan," she said finally. "He knocked her up and then killed her. It must have been Ethan."

"Why do you say that?" Russ leaned back in his chair.

"Like, who else would it be? He was seriously in love with her. Aren't most women murdered by their husbands or boyfriends? I remember discussing that in my health class."

Clare thought back to health class at Hopewell High School. The only thing dangerous she had discussed was venereal disease, which over 50 percent of the male population was afflicted with, according to her teacher.

"Maybe he wanted her to, like, have an abortion and she wouldn't. Or maybe he wanted her to marry him and she wouldn't. Whatever."

"Whatever," Clare said under her breath.

"Wow. Ethan and Katie. And I know both of them. That's like, creepy."

"Alyson," Russ asked, "do you remember Katie's parents' address? Was it on Depot Street?"

"No. I don't know her parents' names. Oh, whoa, she has a big sister, though. She was a senior when I was a freshman. Kristen. She works at Fleet Bank as a teller."

"The branch here in town?"

"Yeah. I know because that's our bank."

"Okay, Alyson." Russ gathered up the photos and closed the folder. "Thank you for your cooperation. You've been a big help."

"I can go? I'm done?"

"That's right. I don't need a formal statement from you, there's no need to go to the station." He pulled off his shades and stared into her eyes. "Remember that we're just gathering information at this point. I appreciate your, ah, insight into Katie's relationship with Ethan Stoner, but none of us can draw any conclusions from that." The girl gaped, a blank expression on her beautiful face. Russ sighed. "Don't go telling everyone you meet that Katie's dead and Ethan murdered her. Got it?" He turned to Alyson's parents. "Mr. and Mrs. Shattham, thank you."

"You will let us know if you come to suspect this was the work of some . . . some . . ."

"Wandering serial killer? I certainly will, Mr. Shattham."

Russ and the Shatthams looked at Clare. She rose from her seat, gesturing toward the door. "Let me walk you out," she said to the Shatthams. They got up, taking coats off the other chairs, and preceded her into the hall. Somehow, she assumed Russ would remain behind, sitting in the sunlight, thinking. Probably the same way he was assuming she'd come back as soon as she had seen the Shatthams off, to talk things over with him.

This time, she did bring her glass, as well as the remaining bottle. "Want a slug?" she asked, brandishing the cream sherry in her fist.

"I don't think you can have a slug of sherry," Russ said. "No, thank you."

Clare sat down in the seat she had vacated, thought for a moment, then moved to where Alyson had been sitting, turning that chair sideways to catch more of the sun. "Lord, it gets cold in this room," she said, pouring herself a measure of sherry. "I must say, though, the sun makes it almost bearable."

"You've got thin Southern blood, that's your problem. Keep your thermostat set at sixty and always wear no more than two layers of clothing. That'll toughen you up."

"Ugh." She took a sip of sherry. "My mamma would call this a little tot." She drawled the expression. "Every drink to my mamma is either a little tot or a splash. A tot of wine. A splash of bourbon." She took another small sip. "So. What do you think?"

"What do you think?" Russ countered.

"I think Alyson's not being entirely honest. I can't say why. It's not as if I know her or her family. It was just . . . something off."

"Mmmm. I agree. You notice that we still don't know what Katie's connection to St. Alban's is. Alyson only mentioned knowing her from school. Maybe that's what she's hiding."

"Why, though? I mean, if you consider Alyson as a suspect, which I find very difficult to do, what possible motive could she have?"

"Jealousy? Rivalry?"

"They moved in entirely different circles, it sounds like. I remember Ethan Stoner from that fight you broke up on Friday. I realize he wasn't showing at his best, but I find it hard to believe that even cleaned up and sober, he'd appeal to Alyson."

"Hmmm mmmm. Ethan Stoner. I hate to think he could do something as bad as this. He was awful edgy and upset that night, wasn't he?" Abstracted by thought, his upstate accent thickened, so that "wasn't he" came out "wun't he?" "Maybe he had real reason to be so upset."

"Are you going to go out and talk to him this afternoon?"

"No. If I'm going to move him onto the list of possibles, I want more information first. There's a good piece of advice about interrogating suspects: never ask a question you don't already know the answer to. Not that you ever know all the answers. But if I haul Ethan in now, I'll be working in the dark. No, I'm going to find Katie's parents first, if I can, or her sister. Get a handle on who she was, what she was about."

"What do you mean, find her parents if you can? There can't be that many McWhorters on or around Depot Street."

"You haven't seen the area. It's our own quaint, rural version of a rat-infested slum. Mostly six- or eight- or ten-unit apartment buildings, falling down around the tenant's ears. Not that most of 'em would notice if a place came down. Half the residents of that area don't have telephones. They have twenty-four inch TVs and satellite reception, but no phones."

"Being poor doesn't make a person bad, Russ. Just as being rich doesn't make a person good."

"I don't blame anyone for being poor. Hell, my mother was poor after my father passed on. I blame people who could change their condition but are too lazy or too attached to drugs or booze or who just plain don't care that they live like pigs and suck off the public teat."

Clare dropped her glass to the table and stared at him incredulously. "Maybe, if instead of being angry at them, you got angry at the forces that shaped their lives, you might find yourself an instrument of change, rather than just a complainer. Maybe if you tried seeing individuals instead of some amorphous 'them,' you'd see people with problems, not just people who are problems."

"Of all the—'scuse me for being blunt, Clare, but that's naive."

"No, it's not. Reaching out to people who may not even realize what sort of help they need is hard, thankless work. I've met men and women who've dedicated their lives to it, and they're some of the toughest, least starry-eyed people I know."

"I notice you're not doing that inner city thing, though."

She threw up her hands. "I think you've pretty well proved that Millers Kill has the full compliment of modern problems, even without an 'inner city.' Part of my work here is going to be to lead my congregation into service. To get them to open their eyes and see the need all around them."

"And do what?"

Clare tucked a strand fallen from her French twist behind her ear. "To start, I want us to reach out to girls like Katie McWhorter, girls whose pregnancies would otherwise mean a lifetime sentence of dependancy and bad relationships. Help them to stay in school. Teach them how to find a job, be a better mother. Mentor them so they know there are other ways they have value besides producing babies. Support them in changing their lives."

"You haven't seen the ingrained pockets of country poverty yet, Clare. Folks who've never held a job, or lived in a house where some man wasn't beating on a woman, or gotten through a day without pounding down enough booze to make 'em forget their hardscrabble life. I've been there, and I've seen it all and cleaned up after the messes, and I'm here to tell you, you're gonna break your heart if you try to change people like that."

She smiled at him. Maybe not such a hard case after all. "I don't have a choice, Russ. We're all called to see the Christ in all people. Even a down and dirty atheist like you must have heard of 'Love thy neighbor as thyself.' "

"Oh. Well, hell, if you're gonna bring God into it . . ."

"You know, I like that about you."

"What?"

"You've just seen me celebrate the Eucharist, I'm sitting here in my cassock and collar, and you still manage to forget that I'm a priest. You argue with me like I'm . . . just me. I like that."

Russ shifted in his chair. "No big deal. I'm just too ignorant to know there's a way I'm supposed to treat a priest, that's all."

Clare smiled into her sherry. Russ spun the manila folder around on the tabletop.

"Katie McWhorter."

"Yes." Clare dropped her glass on the table and rose from her chair. "We can check right now to see if there are any McWhorters listed in the phone book. C'mon into my office."

Russ studied Clare's eclectic decor while she paged through the Millers Kill directory. "No McWhorters listed for Depot Street. Or for South Street or Beale Avenue. No Kristen McWhorter, no K. McWhorter." She flopped the book shut. "Now what?"

"Now, tomorrow morning I go to the bank and see if I can find the sister. The best way to a positive I.D. will be to have a family member identify her at the morgue. Failing that, I'll head for the high school. They should still have Katie's records."

"Would you like me to come along to the bank? Or to the morgue? To be there when you break the news to Katie's sister?"

"To what, comfort her in her hour of need? We don't know if she's religious or not, Clare. Maybe she wouldn't want a priest hanging around."

"Maybe not. But I'll bet she'll want to speak to the woman who was there when her sister's body was recovered. And you'd be better off having someone from St. Alban's there when you ask her about Katie's connection to the church."

"I will, huh? And this wouldn't have anything to do with you wanting to be in on the investigation?"

"I'm already in on the investigation," Clare pointed out. "This simply saves some time and lets me hear what she has to say firsthand. And if you'd like, I could help you tell her what happened to her sister. I'm . . . I took a course in grief work at the seminary."

"Well, I never took any course. But I've broken this kind of news enough times to know what to do. The trick is to not leave 'em hanging. Get to the worst of it fast."

Get to the worst of it fast, Russ reminded himself. He arrived Monday morning right at nine o'clock, opening time. He found the branch manager first off and filled her in on the situation. She expressed sympathy, and welcomed him to use her office when he told Kristen the bad news. She left for the service counter and came back with a young woman in tow.

"Kristen McWhorter?" Russ asked. The branch manager silently shut the door behind herself on the way out.

"Yes . . ." Kristen said, frowning. She was pretty, in a milkmaid sort of way that even her ink-dark punk hairstyle and thick black eyeliner couldn't conceal. "Did my father do something?" she asked.

"Your father? No. I have some very bad news for you, Kristen. This past Friday we discovered your sister Katie's body near the kill, about a quarter-mile upstream from Payson's Park. She had been murdered."

Kristen stood perfectly still, blinking. "No," she said. "You're mistaken. Katie's in Albany. She's a freshman at SUNY-Albany, and she hasn't been home since school started. She's in Albany."

"She was identified in a photograph by someone who knew her in high school. We'd like you or your parents to view the body to make a positive identification."

"I'll go. I'll go right now. It's not Katie. She's in Albany. I'll get my coat right now. You have the wrong person. Oh, no, I'm starting my shift right now. I have to talk with Rosaline about getting off."

Russ gestured through the glass walls at the manager. "I've already spoken with your boss, Kristen. Everything's set."

The manager came in carrying a heavy coat and a purse. "I brought these from the break room. They're Kristen's."

Kristen grabbed at the purse and started scrabbling through it. "Wait! Wait! I can prove to you it isn't Katie. I can call her house. I have her number. I have it here." She dug through the purse like a small, desperate animal digging for shelter. She fished out a plastic address book the size of a box of cigarettes. "Here. Her number's here. I can call her, she's in Albany." She looked around the office, frowning. "It's a long distance number, though. Can I use your phone to make a long distance call, Rosaline?"

"Of course you can," the manager said. She took Kristen by the shoulders and steered her to the phone on the laminate desk. "Go right ahead, Kristen." She looked behind the girl's back at Russ, asking him wordlessly for guidance. Kristen hammered out the number.

Russ made a smoothing gesture with his hands to let the manager know she was doing fine. "C'mon, c'mon . . ." Kristen said. "Pick up." Her face brightened. "Emily!" she said. "It's Kristen, Katie's sister. Can I speak to Katie?" There was a pause. "Is she in class?" There was an even longer pause. Kristen's eyes filled with tears and she pressed her palm against her mouth. She looked up at Russ. "She says Katie took a bus to Millers Kill on Friday morning. She hasn't seen her since." She blinked and the tears spilled over her cheeks. "Oh God, oh God . . ."

Russ held out his hand for the receiver. "Let me talk with her," he said. Kristen surrendered the phone. "Hello, this is Russ Van Alstyne, Millers Kill Police. Who is this, please?"

"I'm Emily Colbaum. Katie's housemate." The voice on the other end of the line was shaky. "Has something happened to Katie?"

"I'm sorry, Miss Colbaum. We believe she was killed Friday night. Can I ask you a few—"

The sound of wailing cut him off. He waited. Kristen was leaning against the branch manager, mopping her eyes with a wad of damp tissues. She had black makeup smeared on her cheeks and her dried-blood-red lipstick had come off entirely. "Emily? Miss Colbaum?" he tried again. He was answered with more sobbing. He put his hand over the receiver. "Kristen, will you come over to the morgue with me now? Or do you need more time?"

She shook her head. "No," she whispered. "If it's her, I want to know. Let's go."

He tried the phone again. "Miss Colbaum? Emily, do you think you can talk with me? Or do you need some time to get yourself together?" She sobbed out something about feeling light-headed. "Emily, listen to me. Are you listening? Is there anyone else there at the house with you? Another roommate?"

There was a confusing sentence about Heather, who had missed an organic chemistry final.

"Good. I want you to give her a yell—" he held the phone away from his ear as she did just that. "Uh . . . good girl. You make sure she stays with you until you're feeling calmer, okay? If you need to, you go on over to the university clinic and tell 'em what happened. There'll be someone you can talk with there, maybe fix you up with a sedative if you need one." Wet, weepy snuffles. "I'm going to give you the number of the police station here in Millers Kill. You got a pen and paper? Good girl." He told her his direct office line. "I'll be calling you to talk later, Emily, but in the meanwhile, if you think of anything, anything at all, call that number. If I'm not there, you can talk to our dispatcher, Harlene."

Emily blubbed a watery thank you and hung up, promising to call with any information she might have.

Kristen was gamely struggling her way into her long black coat, crying soundlessly, mopping her face with the ineffectual tissues. "Would you like me to come with her?" the manager asked, her face creased with what Russ judged to be equal parts worry over her employee and the prospect of leaving the bank unattended on a Monday morning.

"No, I have a, um, grief specialist waiting for us at the morgue. We'll make sure Miss McWhorter's taken care of."

He held the office door open for the women. "Kristen, don't worry about coming in to work tomorrow," the manager said. "I'll make sure your shifts are covered. Take all the time you need, honey." She hugged the girl awkwardly.

Outside, it was another bitterly cold and clear day. Kristen rubbed her gloved hands over her cheeks as they drove. The heater wheezed and complained and started warming the car minutes before they reached the county morgue's parking lot. Clare was already there, waiting in an older-model cherry-red MG that was going to give her more trouble than she could imagine on the winter roads. She got out as he parked the cruiser.

"Let's get inside before we do introductions," he yelled across the lot. She nodded and disappeared into the building, climbing the steps two at a time. He held Kristen's arm to steady her until they got into the waiting room, then released her to help her out of her enormous coat. She had stopped crying and was looking around her with the same absorption she would have shown watching a fascinating movie. Not that there was anything fascinating about the dun-colored walls that someone had attempted to brighten with scenic travel posters. He had seen that look before, many times. It was the look you got when the bottom fell out of your world, and your own life seemed as distant and unreal as any big-screen fantasy.

"Kristen?" Clare took the girl's coat from Russ and tossed it on a chair next to her own. "I'm Clare Fergusson." She held out a hand to Kristen, who took it mechanically. "I was there when your sister's body was discovered." Kristen's lips flexed and quivered. "I'm also a priest." Given the clerical collar peeking out from underneath her black sweater, Russ thought that was pretty self-evident. He went to the window separating the waiting room from records storage. Tapping the bell three times brought the morgue assistant, who took in the scene in the waiting room and went to unlock the inner doors without a word. "Would you like me to come with you?" Clare went on, gently leading Kristen to the hallway. "Sometimes, it can make it less scary to be with someone else."

Kristen stopped, looked into Clare's face. "I've never seen a body before," she said. "Isn't that strange?"

"No, not strange at all," Clare said, linking her arm through the girl's. "It's not bad, like you might think. Death looks different from life, from sleeping, but it's not ugly."

Russ had seen more than a few ugly deaths in his time, but he knew enough to keep his mouth shut. The attendant paused at a small desk outside of the body storage room. "We're here to identify the Jane Doe," Russ said quietly.

The attendant made a note in the log book. "She's in number three," he said, looking at Kristen's black-smeared face. "You can go in alone, miss, or I could come with you, or . . . ?"

She shook her head at the young man and tightened her hold on Clare's arm. "Will you come?" she asked. "I forgot your name."

"I'm Clare. Yes, I'll come with you."

The attendant opened the dull metal door. Russ caught a glimpse of white tile and harsh florescent lighting before the door closed again, Clare and Kristen on the other side. It was a lousy place for a person to end up, laid out naked in a stainless steel drawer. Of course, there were worse ways to finish it. Zippered inside a body bag and hustled into a refrigerated cargo hold, for instance. He shut his hand reflexively. At times like these, he could still feel the material they made those bags from. He stilled his breathing, forcing himself not to get impatient to leave Death's waiting room. What the hell was taking them so long?

Clare pushed the door open, letting Kristen pass through first. The girl looked into Russ's eyes, her own dazed, full of clouds. "It's her. It's my sister." She bit down hard on her lip. "I thought . . . I thought she'd finally be safe once she was in Albany. Once she was away. Why did she come back?" Fresh tears rose in her eyes. "Why did she come back?"

"Kristen, what did you mean when you said you thought your sister would be safe once she was away at school?" Russ handed Kristen black coffee in a mug decorated with fat country sheep and geese, part of a set his sister had given them one Christmas that he and Linda had agreed were too damn cutesie-poo to keep at home. He hated Styrofoam cups: too small, too fragile, and too wasteful.

Kristen bent over the mug until her face was almost obscured by ink-colored hair and steam. "Nothing. I don't know. I don't know what I was thinking."

He dumped three teaspoons of sugar into another mug and handed it to Clare. She was sitting kitty-corner to Kristen, a Millers Kill P.D. tape recorder at her left hand. After Kristen had identified her sister's body, the girl couldn't get out of the morgue fast enough. She had agreed to give her statement at the police station, where Harlene, in full mother-hen mode, had fussed over her, fetching coffee and strudel from the dispatch room, opening the shades in the briefing room to let in the sunlight.

"You know, sometimes, the first thing that comes to mind is the right thing, no matter how bizarre or improbable it seems," Clare said. "It could be your intuition was trying to tell you something. What was it, Kristen?"

The young woman put down her mug and smoothed her hands over her face. She had washed up in the station's unisex bathroom—unisex by virtue of having both urinals and a tampon machine—and without her black and purple and red makeup, she looked like one of the pretty country girls from up the hills past Cossayaharie. Katie must have borne a strong resemblance to her sister before her death.

"Can you tell me how she died?"

Russ sat down in a red leatherette chair, cradling his coffee to warm his hands. "She was hit in the back of the head by something heavy and blunt, hard enough to make her unconscious. Then she was rolled off the trail downhill, to the edge of the kill. The medical examiner believes she died of hypothermia, that she never woke up."

"How did she get out there? Do you know?"

"Only that it was a four-wheel-drive vehicle with all-weather tires. The wheel width indicates a truck or a sports-utility vehicle. We don't know if your sister was conscious when she reached the trail, or if her killer drove her there after she had been knocked out."

Kristen closed her hands over her face again for a moment. "What a weird thing to say," she said. "Her killer. Like, her sister, her teacher, her boyfriend. Her killer. Somebody with a relationship to her." She frowned. "Was she molested? Had she been, you know . . ."

"No," Russ said. He glanced at Clare.

"What? What is it?" Kristen's gaze flickered between the two of them. He tilted his head, passing the job of telling about the baby to the one who had found him.

"There is something else, Kristen," Clare said. "According to the medical report, Katie had a baby within the past two weeks. We have strong reason to believe that she, or someone, left the baby on the back steps of St. Alban's church a week ago. He's in foster care right now."

"He?"

"A little boy, yes. She left a note, naming him Cody."

Kristen's face contorted. "Oh . . . she always loved that name. She used to say if she had a boy, she'd name him Cody, and if she had a girl, she'd name her Corinne." She squeezed her nose and eyes, trying to stifle more tears. "I can't believe Katie would give her baby away. I just can't believe it. Unless he made her!"

"Who made her, Kristen?"

She was crying openly now, shaking her head. "Our father."

Clare and Russ looked at each other. "Your father would've made her give up her child because she wasn't married?" Clare asked.

"No, no . . ." Kristen blew her nose on one of the paper napkins Harlene had piled next to the strudel. She took a shaky breath. "My father would have forced her to give up a baby if he was its father."

Russ felt as if someone had thrown a bucket of the kill's icy water over him. Clare was pale, but calm. "Kristen, what are you saying? Did your father sexually abuse Katie?"

Kristen pushed her hands through her short hair. "I don't know. I really don't know. But he used to do it to me."

"Jesus," Russ exclaimed, under his breath.

"Can you tell us, Kristen?"

The girl looked at Clare, indecision and grief warring on her features. "It's hard. It's hard to talk about."

"Listen, Kristen," Russ said, "You don't have to be afraid of your father. Give me his name and address and he'll be in the county jail before five o'clock," With maybe an unscheduled stop on the way, where the bastard could fall down a few flights of stairs by accident. Nobody at the jail would make a comment.

"No, please!" Kristen said. "I don't want to press charges. I got away, and that's all I wanted. I thought Katie had escaped, too . . ."

"Tell us, Kristen. You don't have to sign out a complaint against your father if you don't want to." Clare forestalled Russ's complaint with a swift glance that said, "Back off."

"I . . . I . . ."

Clare held out her hand, flat on the tabletop. "Take my hand and tell me. If it gets too hard, just squeeze as tightly as you can."

The girl tentatively placed her hand in the priest's. She took another breath heavy with unshed tears. "Okay. I'll try." She shut her eyes. "My father started in on me when I was around fourteen or so. Katie would have been twelve. I wasn't dumb, I knew that what he was doing was wrong. But I was afraid to tell anyone, because without him, how would we live? He had his business—and he's got disability and social security money. Mom was useless. Worse than useless. She would have denied he was fooling with me up one side and down another. Besides, she would have fallen apart without him. So I just . . . hung on. I knew girls who dropped out of school, or got pregnant to get a boy or the state to take care of them, but I wanted something more than that. I knew that if I could just last until I finished high school, I could get a decent job, make enough money to live on. So that's what I did."

"For four years?" Clare asked quietly.

"Uh huh."

Russ felt sick. His muscles shook from the effort of sitting still and not pacing around the room, pounding on the walls.

"I started working at the bank the day after I graduated, and as soon as I had my first paycheck, I was out of there. I begged Katie to come with me, but she wouldn't. She said Mom needed her." She bit down on her lip. "I think she was worried that it would be too much, me trying to support the two of us until Katie finished high school. And she was really ambitious, too. She was so smart, her teachers all said she could get a scholarship. She wanted a college degree more than any-thing."

"That's how she got to the State University at Albany? A scholar-ship?"

"For her tuition, yeah. She's been covering her room and board with student loans, and working for her book and spending money." Russ could see Kristen's hand tighten over Clare's. "I didn't know—before I left home, he never touched her. And she didn't mention anything to me. But maybe she wouldn't have. She was, I don't know, sort of distant her last semester in high school. We didn't get together as much. But I knew she was busy, working at the Infirmary and studying and all that." She looked at Russ, pleading. "I mean, she would have told me if he was, was after her, wouldn't she?"

"You never saw any signs of her pregnancy?" he asked.

She shook her head. "She went to Albany in June, right after she graduated. The university had given her a work-study job in the com-puter center, and they needed her there for the summer. At least, that's what she told me. We talked on the phone at least once a week. She sounded so good! I never guessed. I never would have guessed." She released Clare's hand to pick up her coffee.

"The girl who first identified Katie for us said she's had a boyfriend, Ethan Stoner. Is there any possibility that he could be Cody's father?"

"Ethan? Geez, that's hard to imagine. They did go out for a long time in high school, but Katie broke it off senior year."

"She broke it off? How did Ethan take that?"

"I don't know. Probably not too well. Katie was . . ." she gestured widely, ". . . more than anything else he had in his life. I know she didn't break up with him over any bad feelings. She just felt they had really grown apart over the years."

"She was college-bound, and Ethan was going to wind up on a dairy farm, is that it?" Clare asked.

"Yeah. Plus, Katie is really smart. She used to like to talk about books and poetry and stuff like that. Ethan wasn't much of a talker, and what he did have to say was usually about some TV show or the Nine Inch Nails. You know what I mean?"

Clare nodded. "Did she have any other boyfriends, then? Maybe someone more like her?"

"No. It was hard for Katie. She didn't fit in very well. She didn't have new clothes and money for fun things like the other college-track kids in school, but she didn't have anything in common with the grounders, either."

"The grounders?"

"You know, like Ethan. The kids who are hanging on 'til they graduate and then get married right off the bat and go to work for a gas station."

Russ got up. "Anyone want some more?" he asked. The women both declined. "Kristen," he said, his eyes on the hot coffee flowing out of the pot, "why do you think it was your father who got Katie pregnant, and not Ethan?"

She swiveled around to where she could see him. "I . . . I guess one is as likely as the other. She never said anything to me about sleeping with anyone. As far as I knew, she was still a virgin." She pushed her fingers through her hair. "I guess that's a pretty naive thing to say, isn't it? But I'll tell you something. I can't imagine Ethan getting violent with Katie. But I sure as hell can picture my father doing it. He's an evil man. An evil man. He could have killed Katie and gone home the same night and slept . . . and slept like a baby."

The chief of police stared up at the windows of number 162 South Street from the relative warmth of his car. He had been to this address many times before, though never to the fourth floor apartment of Darrell McWhorter. Unlike his neighbors, who drank and partied and beat each other up where everybody could see, Darrell McWhorter did his law-breaking in private.

Russ opened the door, wincing as the cold pinched his nostrils shut and stung his eyes. From the second floor, a curtain flapped aside for a moment and then fell. Cops were not welcome to this flat-faced yellow building, and he wondered how many baggies were being flushed down the john even as he crossed the sidewalk, opened the chain-link gate, and walked up the sagging steps to the front door. He ran his finger down a double row of tarnished door buzzers. MCWHORTER: 3D. He pressed the bell and waited.

"What is it?" a voice crackled indistinctly over the intercom.

"Mr. McWhorter? Chief Van Alstyne, Millers Kill Police. I need to speak with you, please."

Russ looked at a small plastic slide and trike half-buried under the snow covering what passed for a yard in this place. On the sidewalk, a pair of teenage girls with teased-up hair were smoking and gabbing despite the cold, while two toddlers in snowsuits waited, ignored. One of them stared at Russ, slack-faced and runny-nosed. How could anyone believe in a God who let some kids grow up with everything, and other kids live out their whole lives in poverty and neglect? Or worse.

"What do you want?"

"We don't want to discuss this over the intercom, sir. It's about your daughter Katie."

"Katie?" The voice, as distorted as it was, sounded surprised. The buzzer sounded, cracking the front door open. Russ climbed the stairs to the fourth floor, not holding the banister because he was resting his hand on his holster. Habit. Not a bad one.

The door was open when he reached the fourth floor landing. "What is it about Katie?" Darrell McWhorter was no more than five-ten, squared off, with the look of a high school jock run to flab. His dark hair was pretty well thinned out on top, and he had it combed over in what Linda would describe as a spider-holding-a-billiard-ball style. He looked unthreatening and unremarkable, a cigarette smouldering between his fingers, the kind of guy you'd pass a hundred times in the A&P and never think, "That one's screwing his own daughter."

Russ tamped down the heat behind his eyes. Kristen had emphatically refused to swear out a complaint against her father when she gave his name and address. Until he had something linking the sonofabitch to Katie's death, Russ couldn't touch him. Officially, he was here to break the bad news to Mr. and Mrs. McWhorter. Unofficially, he was here to see if he could shake something loose.

"May I come in?" he asked.

"Sure, sure, come on in," McWhorter said, stepping aside. The apartment reeked of cigarette smoke, but it was well kept, especially compared to the dumps some other tenants inhabited. The furniture was mostly old, too big and too dark for the living room. It had the look of family hand-me-downs rather than Goodwill. The TV in the corner was a built-in in a blond wood cabinet, pure Danish Modern circa 1965. His mom had had one just like it. The picture was surprisingly good for something that old. He could count every tooth in the oversized smile of the game show hostess twirling around a shiny new car.

"Great, innit?" McWhorter thumbed toward the set. "That's what I do, TVs and small electronics. My wife says she wants one of those big-screen jobs, but I figure, as long as I can keep this one running cherry . . ." He took a last drag on his cigarette and stabbed it out in a pedestal ashtray.

Russ turned to face McWhorter. "Is your wife here, Mr. McWhorter?"

"Yeah, yeah, she's in the bedroom. Brenda!" he yelled down the darkened hallway between the living room and the gallery kitchen. "Get out here! There's a cop here with news about Katie."

"About Katie?" An enormous woman lumbered up the hall. "What about my little girl?" She looked like her daughters, blown up to Macy's parade size, their rounded cheeks and soft chins expanded into a fleshy mask through which once-pretty eyes peered at him suspiciously.

Get to the worst of it fast, he thought. "I have very bad news for you folks. Your daughter, Katie McWhorter, was found dead out past Payson's Park last Friday night." Darrell McWhorter stared at him blankly. Brenda McWhorter screamed.

"My baby! My baby!" She staggered around like an elephant with a tranquillizer dart before slipping to the floor. Her husband caught her under her arms and hefted her onto an elaborately-carved Victorian sofa.

A man would have to be pretty damn strong to help get that woman up. Russ wondered what sort of disability kept him from working.

"How did it happen?" Darrell McWhorter asked.

Russ recounted what the coroner had found out about Katie's death. Brenda McWhorter continued wailing, punctuating her cries with, "My poor baby! My poor little girl!" Her husband listened without comment, frowning.

"There's one more important thing I have to tell you," Russ concluded. "Katie had a child within a week or so of her death. DHS has custody of the baby right now."

Brenda's wails cut off abruptly. Darrell looked as if he were trying to get the final *Jeopardy!* answer within thirty seconds. "A baby?" he said.

"A little boy. Did either of you know or suspect she was pregnant?"

Brenda shook her head, her mouth still half open.

"Do either of you know what connection Katie might have had to Saint Alban's church?"

"Saint Alban's?" Darrell still looked as if he wasn't going to make the buzzer before Alex Trebeck called time. "What's that? The fancy looking church across from the old bandstand?"

The small park at the end of Church Street was a popular summer spot. The town still put on dances and concerts there, just like when Russ was a young man. "That's the one."

Darrell thought for a few seconds more. "A baby," he said. Then, "No, I don't know nothing that Katie would of been up to involving a church. How come?"

"Katie, or someone, left the baby on the back steps of St. Alban's, with a note directing that the boy go to the Burnses, a couple from the church that've been looking to adopt for several years. Would you or Katie have known them some other way? They're lawyers here in town."

The McWhorters looked at each other.

"A lawyer?" Brenda said. "We don't know no lawyers. 'Cept that one who settled my dad's estate, but that was ten years back, and he was old then. He wouldn't be looking for no baby."

Darrell reached for a pack of cigarettes lying atop a *Soap Opera Digest* magazine. "These lawyers go to that fancy church?" he asked.

"Yes sir, they do."

"But they don't got the baby yet?"

"No. There are several legal issues to sort out, from what I understand. For instance, we don't know who the father of the child is." Russ fixed Darrell with a level stare. "I had a long talk with her sister this morning, who told me Katie broke up with her boyfriend in her senior year. Kristen hadn't heard of anyone else who might have been going out with Katie."

Darrell lit his cigarette and took a drag. "Can't put much store by what Kristen says. We wouldn't help her out with money she wanted after she was out of school, and since then, she's been bad-mouthing us something awful."

"Never comes to see us," his wife chimed in. "Not in almost two years. It was like we lost her. And now Katie . . ." She started wailing anew.

Russ was tempted, sorely tempted, to ask Darrell to come to the hospital right now for a blood test and cell scraping. But he didn't want anything questioned and possibly thrown out if it went to court.

"Had either of you seen Katie recently?"

"Nope," Darrell said. Brenda shook her head.

"Where were you two last Friday?"

"Why?" Darrell frowned. "You asking if we had anything to do with it?"

Damn right I am, thought Russ. "I'm trying to get a fix on Katie's movements, to see where she might have gone and who she might have seen."

"We went out to that new Long John Silver's at the County Road shopping center," Brenda said. "We had coupons."

"Then we went to the Dew Drop for a few. Met up with some friends. We must of been there until eleven o'clock."

"We come straight home after that. I remember, 'cause it was awful cold and I was worried I had left the bathroom window cracked open and things would start freezing in the bath."

Russ never trusted people who could recall and retell their every movement without having to stop and think about it. Most folks' lives weren't that memorable. On the other hand, first Friday of the month, after the social security check had come in, it might be their big night out.

"You wouldn't happen to remember the names of the friends you were with, would you?" He tried to make his question as inoffensive as possible.

"Sure we do," Darrell said, "It was the Jacksons, Dave and Tessa. They live out to Cossayaharie, where we used to. You wanna phone number so you can check up on them or something?"

"That won't be necessary," Russ said, omitting the "yet." "While I'm here, do you have a sample of Katie's handwriting I could take with me? Printing would be best. I'll send it on to the state lab to see if they can match it to the note that was found with the baby."

"Let me check her room," Brenda said, hoisting herself from the couch.

"Why d'you need that if you know the baby is Katie's?" Darrell said.

"Just another way of making sure. The medical examiner sent a scraping of Katie's genetic material down to Albany for DNA testing. That will prove Cody is her son. That's the baby's name, by the way. Cody."

Darrell rubbed his lips with the edge of his hand. "I heard about that DNA testing on some news report."

"It's one hundred percent accurate. Once we have an idea who the father is, we can do the same thing. It takes a few months to get the lab work back, but there's no way to fudge your DNA. It either matches, or it doesn't." He paused, let that one sink in. "What kind of car do you drive, Mr. McWhorter?"

"Huh? An 'eighty Ford Ranger pickup." He ground the cigarette stub out in the standing ashtray. "Look, Chief, I don't know what Kristen told you and I don't care, I ain't seen Katie since she left for Albany this summer. And neither has my wife."

Brenda hurried into the room, puffing from the exertion. "Here. It's a college application she didn't finish. She printed it, like it says on the form."

Russ took the thin sheaf of papers from Brenda. "Thank you."

"What do you need to find the father for, anyway?" Darrell asked.

"In the first place, the father has rights to the child. Either to take custody of the boy, or to consent to adoption. Understand, we were looking for Cody's parents before we discovered Katie's body. More important, now we're working on the theory that the man who fathered

Katie's child either killed her, or has knowledge that could lead to her murderer."

"And if the father ain't found, we're the closest relatives of the baby, right?" Darrell's eyes lit up with the greatest interest he had shown so far during the interview. The thought of placing a baby with this pair started the acid sizzling along the nerve edges in Russ's stomach. The Burnses would be Parents of the Year material compared to these two.

"Right," he said.

"So, we should get custody of the boy, right?"

At this, Darrell's wife frowned. "Honey, we're kinda old to be having a baby around again."

"Naw, naw, that baby belongs to us. How do we get ahold of the people who got him now?"

Russ pulled one of his cards out of his breast pocket. "I'll write down the number at DHS you can call." He leaned over an oblong table reeking of ashes and dusting spray, fishing for his pen. "The other side of this card has my number on it. Call me if you think of anything that might have slipped your mind. I know it's been a shock." Though they seemed to have recovered mighty quick.

"A shock," Brenda agreed. Darrell took the card, reaching out his hand to Russ, who gritted his teeth and shook hands.

"Thank you for telling us about Katie," Darrell said. "And about our grandson. We'll call DHS right away and see about that little boy."

Russ paused at the door. "DHS hasn't gotten my paperwork yet, identifying Katie as Cody's mother. You may have to wait a day or two." Maybe he could lose it. Not that it would do Cody any good in the long run. Just give him an extra week with the foster mother before Mc-Whorter got his hands on him.

Brenda looked distinctly unhappy. Darrell smiled. "It'll be worth the wait. It'll be just like having a little piece of Katie back with us again."

Clumping down the stairs, Russ was in what his mother would have called "an old cow stew." When a door inched open, revealing a bearded man with spectacularly bad teeth, Russ glared at him with such venom the man nearly caught his facial hair in the frame as he slammed the door shut. Russ toyed with the idea of shouting "Washington County Probation Department!" to see how many residents would cut and run.

It would feel good to do something constructive, even if it did mean filling out packets of forms at the county jail.

What would the McWhorters want with Cody? More accurately, what would Darrell want with Cody? The monthly foster child support check from the state? Jesus Christ, what if Darrell's tastes ran to little boys? It was a stretch, but, still . . . Russ wiped the hand Darrell had shaken on his parka before opening the outside door. Either he convinced Kristen to make a complaint against Darrell McWhorter, or he had better find another candidate as the baby's father right quick. Because if he didn't, Cody would be one of those slack-faced little kids sentenced to poverty and neglect. Or worse.

Russ's wave of determination to help Cody broke apart
on that jagged rock of modern life, the telephone answering machine. He tried to reach Kristen at her
apartment and was met with a blast of unintelligible
music that sounded like jackhammers destroying a gui-
tar shop, followed by a half-screamed order to leave a
name and message. Saint Alban's office had on a machine, too, asking him to call between the hours of
eight-thirty and three. In case of pastoral emergency,
you can reach Reverend Clare Fergusson at the rectory. Except he couldn't. On her message Clare
sounded too enthusiastic to make her apology for not
picking up the phone believable. In case of pastoral
emergency, her pager number was . . . Russ began to
wonder about these pastoral emergencies. What were
they, deathbed confessions? Emergency baptisms?

He weighed the idea of paging her, but decided
against it. Instead, he left a message describing his
meeting with the McWhorters and asked her to call
him back. He slapped his chest and rummaged through
his pockets until he found the paper with Emily Colbaum's number, then sat through a recording featuring
a whole flock of giggling females telling him he had
reached "the girlz in the house!" He left his name and
number and tried the DHS case worker's office next,
only to get caught up in a voicemail system. He tried
following the automated directions—press two, press
the pound sign twice, if you know your party's exten-

sion—and wound up in the mailbox of the educational scheduling department. He banged the receiver down and unloaded a piece of army vocabulary on the person who had first replaced an operator with a machine.

He stomped into the dispatch room, hoping Harlene would ask him what was wrong so he could let loose his opinion of people who were never at the damn phone when you needed them. Harlene wasn't there. He followed her voice into the squad room, a kind of big-city name for a cluster of six desks and a water cooler. Lyle MacAuley and Noble Entwhistle must have just checked in at the end of their shifts, but instead of filling out their incident reports, they were huddled with Harlene over a big red camping cooler.

"Hey, Chief!" Noble said.

"Oh, here he is, you can give it to him now," Harlene said, elbowing Lyle. Lyle dug into the cooler, emerging with a large package neatly wrapped in butcher's paper.

"For you, Chief," he said, grinning. "Steaks and the round. I hit the jackpot with a twelve-point stag the day before season close."

Twelve-point antlers. Russ tried to suppress his pangs of envy. At least Lyle was being liberal with the venison. God damn, a whole deer season come and gone and he had been too busy working to ever get out and—the day before season close? When Lyle had been scheduled on the duty roster? "Weren't you sick with the flu for two days before Thanksgiving?" Russ asked. "What did he do, walk into your yard and have a heart attack?"

Lyle smiled more broadly. "I guess that's the way it happened, Chief."

Russ looked at Harlene and Noble, both of them grinning their fool heads off. Russ pulled himself up to his full height and tucked the package of venison under his arm. "Then I'm sure it will be good and tender, Lyle, seeing as how he died peaceful-like, of natural causes."

Their laughter followed him back to his office where he put on his parka and turned out the lights. At the door, he paused, thinking, before wheeling and scooping up the Katie McWhorter file. He returned to the squad room and laid it on Noble Entwhistle's desk. "Noble, you read the file on our homicide yet?" he asked.

Noble ambled to his desk and flipped open the folder. "Nope," he said.

"Take a look at it tonight before you go home. Tomorrow, I want you to get a life picture of the victim from her sister and start making the rounds of all the motels and bed-and-breakfasts and whatall. See if you can find someone who remembers a pregnant young woman checking in. We're especially interested in any man who might have been with her. Get the bus station, too, see if anyone picked her up when she arrived in town Friday."

The officer ran his finger down the case entry form. "Yup."

"Thanks. Good night, all." Noble was the right man for this job. Unimaginative, not the sharpest pencil in the box, but methodical, with an ability to put people at ease and get them to open up. Russ pulled his knit cap firmly over his head before braving the cold. Outdoors, the temperature had fallen still further. Thank God he had the Ford pickup tonight, with its fast-working heater, and not the old whore. He'd stop at his mother's, give her the venison, and wangle a dinner invitation for later in the week, when Linda was away on her buying trip to the city. Maybe he ought to introduce Mom to Clare. Interesting to see how they'd get along.

It was out of the way to his mother's, but he drove by the rectory just to make sure everything was all right. The lights were all off. Had he left her his number at home so she could reach him? Yeah, he had. His dashboard clock glowed. Geez, he'd better hurry, or he'd miss another dinner.

Clare folded her hands together and bowed her head. "Lord God," she said, "for the blessings of food and fellowship we are about to receive, make us truly thankful. Open our hearts so that in the midst of plenty, we are aware of those who hunger, and in the midst of friends, we remember those who are friendless. Give us a hunger to do your will, and an appetite to see your kingdom, here and in the world to come. We ask this in Jesus' name, Amen."

"Amen," the rest of the room said. The silence was broken by the clatter and ring of utensils and glasses, the scrape of chairs and the sound of eleven voices, all asking to pass this and that at the same time.

The first Monday of the month was the Foyers dinner, an informal gathering of members of the parish, offering a chance to eat and get to know each other outside of the confines of Sunday service or a committee meeting. Tonight's meal was at the home of Chris Ellis and his wife, Anne Vining-Ellis. Anne was a physician practicing in Glens Falls, and everyone, including her own husband, referred to her as Doctor Anne. The Ellises were practically neighbors of Clare's, only three blocks away on Washington Avenue. Their huge Victorian house would have been imposing if it weren't for the obvious wear and tear on the place from their three teenage boys. The formal dining room, where two round tables held tonight's guests, was decorated with a chandelier, a Boaz Persian carpet, several sets of skis propped up in the corner, and a deep gash in the wall, approximately hockey-helmet high. One of the boys, pressed into service as a waiter for the evening, shambled back and forth from the kitchen to the tables on overlarge feet.

Doctor Anne, sitting on her right, passed Clare a bowl of rice. "I recommend starting with this if you plan on having Phoebe's green chile stew," she said. "Hot? I can't begin to describe it. I think she brings it to these things in order to hear people gasping and crying out for water."

"Thanks for the warning," Clare said. "Maybe I should go for that casserole over there instead?"

"Judy Morrison's tuna hot dish," Doctor Anne said. "Judy converted from Lutheranism." She looked meaningfully at the casserole. "After she learned to cook."

"This is a veritable culinary minefield, isn't it? Just waiting for a wrong step. Tell me, am I supposed to take at least a taste of everyone's offering?"

"Only if you want to gain thirty pounds in the next year. I keep trying to get people to bring light dishes to these dinners, but do they listen? Look at Sterling's Swedish meatballs. I happen to know he uses the fattiest ground chuck he can get and then lards it with several eggs before cooking it in a butter-based sauce. Is it a miracle that man's not dead of a heart attack? You be the judge."

Clare laughed. She could feel the tension that had caught in her shoulders dissipating under Doctor Anne's acidic humor. It had been a difficult day all the way around, first in the morgue and the police station, then helping Kristen at Ruyter's Funeral Home. Ignoring the ache of old pain while Kristen ricocheted between anger and bewilderment and grief with the speed of someone fast forwarding through cable channels.

It was good to lean back and listen to the stream of culinary critiques and gossip, and have nothing more taxing to look forward to than a walk home and an early bedtime. "The only thing that could make this any better would be a cold beer," she murmured.

"That's definitely the missing element, isn't it? It would certainly help wash down Phoebe's chili." Doctor Anne passed Clare a basket of rolls. "Sometimes there will be wine at one of these dinners. No one bothers when Chris and I play host, because I'm such a fanatic about drinking and driving I practically give Breathalyzer tests at the door."

"We had sangria at the Foyers dinner I went to in August," Clare said. "A barbecue."

"This was when? During the selection process?"

"Uh huh. And it was about as comfortable a meal as one can get, when you're eating with your prospective employers. I dreaded spilling something and making a horrible stain on myself, so I stuck to smoked turkey on a dry roll." She made a face. "I'm surprised no one concluded I was anorexic."

Doctor Anne laughed. "Where was this?"

"The Fowlers."

"Oh, my lord, and you had to listen to Vaughn speechifying about the charm, intelligence, good looks, and record-breaking success of his kids, did you?" She rolled her eyes. "Me, I figure if the police aren't actively looking for my sons, they're doing okay. Vaughn and Edie, they'll take the family to the beach because they want to see their children walk on water." She laughed. "Oh, come here, darling, say hello to Reverend Fergusson." Doctor Anne snagged her son as he shuffled past with an empty water pitcher. "I was just telling the Reverend how highly accomplished you are. This is my oldest boy, Anderson." The teen ducked his head awkwardly, setting his long blond hair swinging around his face. He mumbled hello. "Anderson's in his last year of school at Millers Kill High. When he's done, we're throwing him out of the house and forcing him to support himself as a karaoke singer in nightclubs."

"Ma!" the boy protested. "She says that because I'm in the drama society. I'm going to Brown. I got my early acceptance," he told Clare.

"Congratulations. That's a great university. It'll be a big change from Millers Kill High School, won't it?" she asked.

"You bet. I can't wait. Hey, they were talking about our church today, did I tell you?" Anderson looked at his mother. "It was all over the place that Ethan Stoner killed his old girlfriend and Alyson Shattham identified her from a picture right in St. Alban's! That was way cool."

"What?" Clare looked from Doctor Anne to her son. "Anderson, there's no evidence that Ethan Stoner killed anyone. The police are looking for anybody who knew Katie McWhorter and who might be able to give some information on the case."

"That's not how I heard it. It sounded like the cops were ready to haul old Ethan into the county jail and charge him with murder. You mean like somebody else might have done it?" He sounded disappointed. "Shoot. If it was Ethan, it would have been the biggest thing to hit the high school since girls' basketball took the state championship."

Of course it would be, in a town of eight thousand. An awful, low, unworthy thought occurred to Clare. What if Geoff Burns *was* guilty of Katie's murder? She could see the headlines in every paper in eastern New York state: SAINT ALBAN'S PARISHIONER SLAYS MOTHER OF ADOPTED SON! And in smaller type: PRIEST SPEARHEADED EFFORT TO PLACE INFANT WITH MURDERER! She shook her head. No. She knew the Geoff Burns type. All the heat and fire came right out, up front, leaving behind nothing more menacing than low-level discontent and grumbling.

"I think we'll have to wait and see what Chief Van Alstyne comes up with in his investigation before we can make any reasonable guesses about Katie's murderer," she said. "Did you know Katie McWhorter, Anderson?"

He draped a gangly arm across the back of his mother's chair. "No, not really. I knew who she was, 'cause she was in Honors track, like me, but she was a year ahead of me."

"Millers Kill High is a big school, too," Doctor Anne said. "It's got the kids from this town, Cossayaharie, and Fort Henry."

"I know most of the other seniors," Anderson said. He pounded his fist against his forehead. "Oh, duh, I should have known Alyson was exaggerating about Ethan. She's, like, 'I'm the center of attention and the rest of you aren't.' I think she's still fried about not getting elected to the student council in September. So now she's like, 'Ethan's O. J. Simpson and I brought him down.' " He looked at his mother. "She never got it that the reason she was in with everyone last year was because she was going out with Wesley. But now, she wants to buddy up with the jocks or the brains—"

"Anderson is a brain-slash-jock," Doctor Anne interrupted.

"—and they're, like, go back to the mall girls, Alyson."

"Do you need that translated?" Doctor Anne smiled wryly.

"I think I got the gist of it," Clare said.

"Wesley is Wesley Fowler, he-who-walks-on-water."

"Ma!"

"Okay, okay, Wes is a perfectly nice boy who helped you a lot last year in the plays you were in together, and the musical, in which he was, of course, the lead." She leaned over in an exaggerated aside to Clare. "I suppose it's not his fault his father made a golden statue of him and put it on his front lawn."

"Ma!"

Doctor Anne laughed. "Me, I practice the traditional Chinese method of child rearing, I never say anything nice about my kids. That way, they avoid the notice of evil spirits." She wrapped an arm around Anderson's waist and hugged him hard.

"Ma, you are so weird," he said. The boy picked up his pitcher and scuffled off toward the kitchen.

"That means, 'I love you,' in seventeen-ese," his mother said.

Clare laughed. "He's a nice kid. You must be very proud of him."

"Very," Doctor Anne said. She leaned toward Clare. "So tell me, Reverend, *do* you have the inside scoop on this murder? Since you've been helping the police?"

Clare shook her head. "I don't know much more than you do," she said. "I'm sure Ethan will be brought in for questioning, but I don't think Chief Van Alstyne is anywhere near to arresting a suspect yet." She took a bite of her roll. "Hard to believe that something like this happened here, isn't it?"

Doctor Anne shook her head. "After thirteen years working the emergency rooms in Washington County and Glens Falls hospitals, I've seen way too much to think we're invulnerable just because we're small.

Small towns have the same evils that big cities do, just in smaller numbers. And instead of some anonymous stranger, the evil is always someone's neighbor or husband or friend. That's the hard part, that you can't blame some 'other' when awful things happen. The 'other' is one of us."

CHAPTER
ELEVEN

When her pager beeped in the middle of one of Mrs. DeWitt's rambling stories about the Depression, Clare expected it to be the hospital. She was chaplain-on-call this Tuesday, responsible for the spiritual needs that might arise in the intersections between health and sickness and birth and death. Clare lowered her teacup gingerly onto the hand-tatted lace of the table runner.

"Mrs. DeWitt? May I use your phone for a moment? I have to see what this is."

"Of course, Reverend," the elderly woman said. "I left it . . . where did I leave it? Try the kitchen table."

Clare would have sworn that not a thing in Mrs. DeWitt's house, other than herself, had been made before 1935, so she almost laughed when she found the latest Toshiba micro-cell phone lying on the metal cherry-painted table. She punched in the number.

"Burns and Burns," a pleasant voice replied.

"Uh . . . this is the Reverend Fergusson. I got a pager message to call here?"

"Oh, let me connect you with Ms. Burns, Reverend." The voice was replaced by a symphonic rendering of "I Can't Get No Satisfaction." The Burnses. Now what? Oh heck, she had tried reaching Russ that morning before setting out on her home visits, but he had already left for the courthouse. Had he found something linking the Burnses to Katie's death?

"Reverend? Karen Burns. Thank you for getting back to me so quickly."

"What's up, Karen?"

"It's complicated." Karen laughed humorlessly. "It's about Cody, so of course it's complicated. Could we meet? As soon as possible?"

"Sure. I'm at Mrs. DeWitt's right now. I have one more home visit to make, and I can keep it brief . . . how about an hour, an hour and a half from now? I can come to your office, that'll be closer than the church."

"Oh, wonderful. Thank you, Reverend. We'll see you in an hour or so."

Clare brought the cell phone back into the living room, her mind caught up in possible scenarios involving Cody.

"Everything all right, Reverend?" Mrs. DeWitt's heavily wrinkled face creased with concern.

"I hope so, ma'am. But I'll have to be going soon."

"Well then," her hostess said, levering herself out of her faded Morris chair with the help of her cane, "before you go, let me show you an idea I had for the church." Mrs. DeWitt braced herself against a Philco radio set as she hobbled toward the hall. "The computer room is right down here."

"The—you have a computer, ma'am?"

"Oh, my, yes. It's the latest Gateway, customized for me. I ordered it over the Internet. Special-ordered cable access for my modem, too. At my age, I can't afford to wait around all day for files to download, can I?" She paused, flicked a bit of dust off a Boston fern sitting on a plant stand. "I've been fooling around with a web site for Saint Alban's, and I want you to tell me what you think."

Russ picked up his receiver. Put it down. Picked it up. Put it down. "What the heck are you doing in there?" Harlene yelled from the dispatch room.

"What are you doing, spying on me?" he yelled back.

"I can see the active light on the phone, you cranky old buzzard," she said, appearing in his doorway.

He tapped the folded legal papers lying next to the crumpled remains of his lunch bag. "Judge Ryswick gave me the warrants."

"For the blood tests on McWhorter and the Stoner boy? Good. Why don't you go on out and serve 'em, then, and leave the phone system to those of us who understand it."

He sighed. "I want to talk to Cody's caseworker at DHS first. If this test clears McWhorter as the baby's father, he and his wife will get Cody faster than you can say 'closest living relative.' I want to try to persuade DHS to keep the baby in his current foster home."

"They'll have to do a home visit," Harlene pointed out. "Maybe they'll find some reason not to place the baby there."

"Aw, Harlene, you have to have shit smeared on the walls to get the state to take a kid out of his home. This place looked . . . respectable. Clean. Probably a fridge full of food and the rent all paid on time."

"So tell them about Kristen."

"I don't know if I can! She won't make a complaint against her father. I can't tell them something she told me in an interview if she won't back it up."

"You know, they encourage citizens to call in and report suspected child abuse."

"Not when the child is twenty and hasn't lived with the parents for two years. Then it becomes our business, not DHS's. Besides, I'm not a citizen. I'm a law enforcement official. An agent of the state."

"Look, Mr. State Representative. Call up. Let them know Grandpa McWhorter is under criminal investigation and that you have a warrant—which means Judge Ryswick thought you had probable cause—to test his blood and see if he's the baby's father. That alone should tell them to put the brakes on changing the baby's custody. You don't need to mention Kristen."

"Damn, Harlene, you're right!"

"Uh huh. Like usual."

"Why don't you leave that switchboard and become an officer, huh?"

"Because you need a mastermind sitting here in this office more than you need another uniform out there, driving around with nothing to do."

"Something to do now," he said, waggling the papers in the air.

"Delivering orders to get a blood test. There's a thrilling day's work. No thanks, I'll stick with the phones." She grimaced. "Besides, I look terrible-bad in brown."

• • •

From the address, Clare had expected the Burnses' office to be in one of the late-nineteenth century brick commercial buildings that gave upper Main Street the genteel air of another century. Instead, she found herself in a brand new post-and-beam construction that looked as if it had been lifted straight from the pages of *Architectural Digest*. Climbing to the second floor law office, she caught disorienting glimpses of the Christmas decorations on the street below through odd, geometric windows.

The reception area was an uneven pentagon, with narrow I-beams crisscrossing the ceiling and large, dramatically colored abstracts on the walls. No wonder Karen and Geoff had goggled at her office. It looked like a curiosity shop next to this place.

"Hello," she said to the receptionist. "I'm the Reverend Clare Fergusson. The Burnses are expecting me."

"Please take a seat, Reverend," the young woman said. "Ms. Burns will be with you in a moment." Clare sat in one of the plump chairs covered in what looked like hand-loomed upholstery and wondered when she'd stop getting the urge to whirl around looking for the real priest whenever she was called "Reverend." When she was a kid, of course, it had always been "Father" Such-and-so, and that title still sounded more . . . authentic to her ear. *Reverend is an adjective after "the," not a title after "hello,"* Grandmother Fergusson sniffed. A proper word for female priests corresponding with "Father" had been on her wish list for years. She supposed they'd think up one right about the time the Roman Catholics began ordaining women.

"Reverend Clare!" Karen strode across the reception floor, her hands outstretched. Clare rose. "I'm so glad you could come on such short notice. Come on into my office, please. Geoff is still stuck in court, I'm afraid."

Karen Burns's office was clean and spare, with more abstract artwork that blended perfectly with the Shaker-style furnishings. Clare sat in a severely-cut chair across from the desk, surprised at how comfortable it was. The lawyer went to the window, then toward the door, then back to her desk.

"Can I get you some coffee? Tea? Water?" Karen was too elegant a woman to actually bustle, but she was close to it now.

"Karen," Clare said. "Sit down. Tell me what's happened."

"Oh, God," Karen exhaled, collapsing in her chair. "We got a call this morning from a man named Darrell McWhorter. He claims to be Cody's grandfather, and said that he had already talked to DHS and was pressing for custody of the baby."

Clare shook her head. "I'm sorry, I should have called you yesterday. Yes, he is Cody's biological grandfather." Should she say anything about Kristen's accusations?

"Presuming that the murdered girl was Cody's mother. That won't be conclusive until the DNA results come in." Karen's shoulders sagged. "That's the law, anyway. Cold comfort. We all know Katie McWhorter gave birth to Cody."

"Why was Mr. McWhorter calling you, Karen?"

The lawyer sat bolt upright. "He wanted us to buy Cody, that's why."

"What!"

"Oh, he didn't come right out and say it. He's smart enough to know that baby selling is against the law. He could land himself in jail for the offense, and lose his chance at custody."

"You didn't . . . you didn't agree, did you?"

"God, no. If it ever got out, it would render any adoption null and void. We'd face jail, the loss of our licenses . . . no." She paused, took a deep breath. "But we did ask him to meet with us on neutral territory, as it were, and see if we could try to work out some sort of . . . accommodation."

Clare frowned. "What sort of accommodation, Karen?"

Karen leaned forward, forearms against her desk. "We need your help. He's agreed to accept you as a mediator if we can get you."

"Get me? Mediating what?"

"We can't pay the man off, not directly. But we can reimburse him for expenses, offer to pay for, say, improvements to his house in order to make it a better place for Cody to visit, things of that nature. And I thought, what if Geoff and I make a large donation to the church, dedicated to helping lower-income residents of Millers Kill? And what if one of the recipients of this aid is McWhorter?"

"What? You're asking me to make the church your money launderer?" Clare stood up, pushing the chair away. "In a scheme that boils down to you paying for another human being. No. I won't do it. It's immoral, even if it is legal." Karen looked up at her, stricken. Clare sat back down. "Karen," she said, more gently, "you can't buy motherhood. I know how much you want that baby. But this . . . this wouldn't work. What's badly begun has a way of turning out badly. Imagine Cody as an older child, finding out that his grandfather had essentially sold him to his parents. Imagine how he would feel about himself."

Karen folded her arms tightly around herself. "Do you think he'd be better off being raised by the man who's willing to sell him?"

Clare shook her head, laid her hands palm up on the desk. "No. I'll do everything I can to help you. Let's go ahead and set up a meeting with McWhorter, see what we can accomplish."

"With what? Earnest entreaties and prayer? Somehow, I don't think he'll respond very well to that."

"Nope. We offer him what assistance you can legally and ethically," Clare emphasized the word, "provide. That's the carrot. Then, we show him the stick."

When Russ turned his cruiser onto Main Street at the end of a long day, his lights picked out Clare's MG half in and half out of the police station's driveway. Grinning, he pulled up behind the little car and gave it a hit of his flashers. The door opened, and the Reverend Clare Fergusson got out, reluctantly turned around, and spread-eagled against the side of her car. Russ was laughing so hard it took him two tries to find his seatbelt latch.

"What are you doing here?" he asked, once he had managed to get out of his cruiser.

"I was dropping by to speak to you between home visits, and my . . . dang . . . car got stuck."

He looked down at the scant two inches of snow and ice the plow had thrown up on the lip of the driveway. "In that? Heck, my niece's trike could drive through that." The old snow had been churned to dirty slush by her spinning tires. "You gotta get yourself a real car for this climate. Not an itty-bitty wind-up toy like that one."

"This car," she told him, "is a marvel of precision engineering. Zero to sixty in five point seven seconds. It handles like a dream, and it can drive a mountain road at sixty miles an hour without a shimmy across the yellow line."

"Yeah? Well if I ever catch it doing that, it can also get impounded. C'mon, I'll help you push it out." He braced himself against the back fender. Clare leaned into the edge of the door, one hand on the wheel. "Okay, push," Russ said. They heaved together. The MG slid over the low snowbank and rolled forward a foot.

"Thanks." Clare looked at the tire marks in the snow, thrown into high relief by the streetlights. "That is an embarrassingly small amount of snow to get stuck in, isn't it?"

"You need something heavy, with front-wheel-drive," Russ said, opening the door to his cruiser. "Four-wheel-drive is better. Until you get that, load up the trunk with bags of kitty litter. It'll give some weight to your rear and if you get stuck, you can always sprinkle some around for traction."

"Great. I can see it now. I'll get my car free just in time to run over some old lady's cat who's come to investigate."

He grinned. "Why don't you park that thing. Let me get the cruiser in, and I'll stand you a cup of coffee."

"Any of Harlene's strudel left?"

"I might be able to rustle something up." She nodded approvingly, slid into her car, and pulled it forward. *A strudel person,* he thought, shifting the cruiser into first. *Should have guessed that.*

In the briefing room, two of the sheep-and-geese mugs at hand and nothing left of the last slice of strudel except crumbs, he told her about delivering the warrant to Darrell McWhorter. "You should have seen him. So cool. The nicest guy about it you could imagine. He drove himself over to the hospital, with me following, thank God, because I sure didn't want to have to make conversation with him in my car. Got his blood drawn and went home."

"That doesn't sound like a man who's afraid the test will show something incriminating."

"AB negative. Same as Katie's."

"And Cody's father has to be Rh positive, doesn't he?"

"You've got it. I'd love to be able to put the sonofabitch away for molesting his daughters, 'scuse my French, but there's no evidence he abused Katie and Kristen still refuses to cooperate. I spoke to a case-worker at DHS and told her about the warrant and everything, but she said after the home study was completed, they could only delay giving

Cody to his grandparents as long as the question of whether McWhorter had been abusing Katie remained open."

"But if he's not Cody's father, there isn't any other evidence of that."

"Right. It'll be a happy family reunion." He licked his finger and picked up a few strudel crumbs.

"I found out why McWhorter is so eager to get his hands on Cody." Russ's eyebrows went up. Clare told him about the offer to the Burnses and the meeting scheduled for tomorrow.

"You really think you can convince this guy to allow the Burnses to adopt the baby?"

"I don't know. I can get him to think twice about taking Cody. It's worth a try."

"Be careful, okay? I don't like the idea of you drawing McWhorter's attention. We don't know what he's capable of."

"He sounds like a bully to me, plain and simple." Clare propped her chin on her fist. "I'm not an easy person to bully. Besides, if the blood tests show nothing, he'll be out of the running as a suspect in the murder, right?"

"Well . . . I'll have to drop him back to third place. I haven't forgotten the Burnses."

Clare waved her hand dismissively. "You don't seriously think they did it. You're thinking it was Ethan."

"Yeah," he admitted.

"Are you going to serve him the warrant to test his blood type tonight?" she asked, glancing out into the darkness.

"No. I have to pick up Linda and get her on the six-fifteen train. There's a big fabric convention or something in New York, and she's buying stock for her curtains." He took a sip of coffee. "I'll drive over to the Stoner's farm tomorrow after school, bring him in then. That'll give me enough time to question him and then decide whether to arrest him or not."

"You're not worried he might take off someplace?"

Russ shook his head. "His whole life's right here. All his family and friends. I'll bet the farthest he's ever traveled has been New York City on the junior class trip. Where's he gonna go?"

CHAPTER

TWELVE

"Mr. McWhorter, Karen and Geoff can't solve your problems for you. But they can help prevent further problems." Clare took a deep breath and thought of the Wednesday Eucharist she would be celebrating a few hours away at noon. The prospect helped her keep her cool. The Burnses shifted on her small office sofa and glowered at her, obviously frustrated and out of temper with McWhorter's continual sad narrative about his financial woes and his declarations of affection for his dear, departed Katie. So far, he had been skirting the outright offering of Cody in exchange for cash, but the implication was clear enough. Karen and Geoff had outlined the benefits they could give Cody; the excellent home, the education, the love and attention, even the puppy dog in the backyard. McWhorter countered with how ashamed the boy would be of his poor grandparents, how he would reject his own flesh and blood, living in a shabby apartment and eating beans and rice at the end of the month when the money ran low.

When Karen asked him if he wanted to bring up Cody in that shabby apartment, he went into a song-and-dance about poor but honest hearts that could have come straight out of *Little Nell*. Clare, who had held Kristen's hand until she thought her bones would grind together while the girl stammered out her story of abuse, kept her peace by picturing herself snapping McWhorter's kneecap with a well-placed kick. It wasn't very Christian, and she wasn't proud of herself, but there it was. They had tried the carrot. Now it was time for the stick.

"What further problems?" McWhorter said.

Clare rose from her admiral's chair. "Are you aware of the average cost of rearing a child these days, Mr. McWhorter?" She retrieved several sheets of paper from her desktop. "I asked a parishioner to do some research for me on the Internet, and she found several articles giving parents the costs for the first year." She handed McWhorter a paper. "Take a look. Diapers. Formula. The medical visits. That's going to be a sizable chunk for a couple living on disability and a pension."

She dropped another paper into his lap. "Here's the monthly stipend you'll be getting as foster parents. Falls a little short of the expenses, doesn't it?"

Clare handed McWhorter more papers. "Unless your pension stretches quite a bit further, I imagine you or your wife will have to go back to work. Child care and baby-sitters are expensive." She gave him another paper. "Here's the average cost of infant care in the tri-county area." She turned to the Burnses. "Mrs. DeWitt did a great job. She's very thorough." The couple were sitting up straight now, staring at her with twin expressions of unconcealed surprise. McWhorter shuffled through the papers, frowning.

"You'll be taking on a big responsibility, Mr. McWhorter. A big, expensive, time-consuming responsibility. And we'll make sure you're doing your job." She smiled blindingly. "We all feel connected to Cody here at Saint Alban's. So we'll be keeping an eye on him. Not just Geoff and Karen, but a whole lot of us. Dropping by to see how he's doing. Talking to the neighbors. Checking him out when he's at the grocery store and the bank and the pediatrician's office." She could hear her voice loosen into a light Virginia drawl. "Chief Van Alstyne is interested, too, and I'll bet he'd be happy to arrange for police drive-bys every day. We'll all be watching out for little Cody. And at the first hint of neglect or abuse one of us will have DHS on you like fleas on a hound."

"Hey!" McWhorter crumpled the paper he was holding. "You saying I'm gonna beat this kid or starve him or something? Where do you get off saying that?"

"I'm not saying what you will or will not do, Mr. McWhorter. I'm telling you what we all are going to do. I'm telling you, realistically, that you are not going to make one dime off that baby. To the contrary, you can look forward to spending a lot more than you're used to on the child. Or, you can authorize the Burnses to take custody of your grandson, and accept their more than generous offer to pay any debts Katie left behind."

"You're threatening me, aren't you? I'm being threatened by a priest and a couple of rich lawyers. For trying to give my grandson a good life and a family he can be proud of."

Clare drank some coffee. She balanced the mug casually in her hand, where McWhorter could see the flying rattlesnake and the motto DEATH FROM THE SKY! She looked at him levelly. "I never threaten, Mr. McWhorter." His eyes flickered from the coffee cup to her face. "You have a chance to save yourself considerable trouble and to do the right thing for your grandson. Why don't you take it?" The Burnses were still staring at her. *Yes*, she thought, *I am a very different priest from Father Hames. Get used to it.*

McWhorter looked at the papers on his lap. He shuffled them together in a messy pile and rolled them up. "I . . ." He looked over to the Burnses, frowning. "Maybe. I'll take this home and show it to my wife. Talk it over with her. She had her heart set on having that baby come live with us, you understand."

"She can visit with Cody as much as she wants," Karen said. "I'll drive her myself if need be."

McWhorter rose, and they all rose with him. "Maybe." He headed into the hallway, Clare and the Burnses close on his heels. "So," he said, eyeing the carpet and the woodwork and the prints hanging from the walls as if he were casing the joint, "Cody would come to this church if he were your kid?"

"That's right," Karen said. "It's a wonderful community. Not many children now, but we expect that to change over the next few years."

McWhorter stopped in front of the parish family bulletin board, looking at the snapshots of congregants and their families. "Hey, here's you." He stabbed a finger at the picture neatly labeled "Geoff Burns and Karen Otis-Burns."

"Many of those pictures were taken during the parish picnic last

June," Karen said, her voice unnaturally cheery and light. "Maybe you and Mrs. McWhorter could come along with Geoff and me next summer. We could all show off Cody together."

McWhorter continued to study the wall of photographs. Clare felt the back of her neck prickle. Something about the way McWhorter was acting didn't fit with a man who had been closed into a corner. "Why don't we all—" she began.

McWhorter shifted to face them. "I don't think so."

"What?" Karen's voice was polite, but shaky.

"I've thought about it, and I can't give him up. He's the only thing I have left of my Katie. He stays with me and my wife."

"What sort of game are you playing, McWhorter?" Geoff Burns crowded the taller man against the wall. "We aren't going to come back with an offer of money, so you can just forget it!"

McWhorter sidled past Geoff and retreated to the parish hall. "No. Sorry. I'm keeping him."

"Wait!" Karen said "Maybe we can work something out! What if we got you a new car, so you could drive over to see Cody?"

She tried to follow after McWhorter, snapping to a halt when her husband jerked back on her upper arm. "Stop it, Karen," he said. "Let him go."

"Wait," she said. "Wait!" McWhorter reached for the doors. "God damn you!" Karen's voice thickened. "God damn you!" Clare put her arm around the other woman. She met Geoff's eyes and tried not to flinch away from the resigned pain she saw there. Together, they held Karen tightly as her body heaved with the effort to expel tears and venom. "I could kill you, you bastard!" she shouted after the vanished man. She laid her head against her husband, weeping with rage. "I could kill him," she whispered. "I could kill him."

A mid-week drive up to Cossayaharie usually relaxed Russ. Although Millers Kill policed the rural township, he seldom patrolled the mountain roads and tiny village himself. So his associations with the area were mostly good ones: visits to his sister's farm, fishing up at the lake, hiking into the hills, or picnicking in the Muster Field, where militiamen had gathered during the French and Indian War and the Revolution after that. Returning from Cossayaharie you could drive through almost every war the men from this area had taken part in. There were the crumbling granite stones in the Muster Field, and then a big marble obelisk at the front of the old Cossayaharie cemetery, a memorial for two brothers who had drowned in the War of 1812. Before you reached Millers Kill, you passed by its cemetery, guarded by a droopy-mustached Union soldier holding a rifle and forever looking South to where his fallen brothers lay. Then over the bridge, stone cairns carrying brass plaques dedicating it to the sacred memory of those who fell in the Great War, and on into town, where a four-sided plinth listed the names of those who had served in each branch of the armed forces during World War Two. If you finished your journey at the post office, you could run your fingers over the bronze plaque memorializing men who had died on the Korean peninsula while he had been in diapers.

There was nothing marking his war. He didn't know how he felt about that, and he didn't want to think about it long enough to make up his mind one way or the other. There had been what his mother described as one almighty patriotic hot flash over Desert Storm, and since then, there had been talk on and off of putting up something for the rest of the veterans. He stayed away from it. He didn't want to become one of those big-bellied guys down at the American Legion, droning on about their war adventures as if they had forgotten what it was really like. Probably file clerks and car-pool mechanics, anyway. The ones who knew what it was really like hardly ever talked about it, not in the Legion Hall bar and not in front of some committee to erect a monument.

He passed the obelisk to the brothers who had died in the waters of Lake Erie and took the next right turn. A dense stand of spruce and hemlock crowded in on either side of the road. As it wound its way into the hills, the evergreens petered out and the scenery opened up onto sprawling, uneven grazing fields bordered by bare-branched hardwoods. The road dipped and twisted, past sheltered hayfields, farmhouses, and an occasional trailer. For a mile or so, a stony creek ran alongside the road, black water barely visible under the heavy banks of snow. He drove past sleeping orchards of dwarf apple trees, modern feed silos, and century-old barns. At Jock Montgomery's place, he saw two of the kids making a snowman in the front yard, and he slowed down, tooted, and waved.

The Stoner's farm was a mile past the Montgomerys'. He crunched into the drive, parking next to Mindy's Chevelle. He was relieved to see Ethan's old pickup by the road leading up the hill toward the cow barn.

Mindy Stoner came out on the porch, wiping her hands on a dishcloth. "Russ," she said. "What brings you up this way?" She was a tall, raw-boned woman, whose square, strong features had looked almost homely back when she was a schoolgirl. Time had refined her so that now, in her forties, she had the spare beauty of a mountaintop blown clean of snow.

He held up the folded paper. "I'm afraid I'm here on business, Mindy. Can I come in?"

She looked back toward the kitchen, then opened the door. "You might as well. No need to freeze out here in the dooryard." Russ scraped the slush off his boots and followed her through the mudroom into the kitchen, a large room of wooden cupboards, blue-and-white dish towel fabrics, and children's papers and artwork tacked up everywhere. The woodstove between the mudroom and the pantry was throwing off heat, and the overhead lamp had been lit in preparation for the four o'clock twilight. Their thirteen-year-old—her name escaped him for the moment—was sitting at the round, oilcloth-covered table, doing homework. "Hannah," Mindy said, "run up to the barn and tell your father Chief Van Alstyne's here and needs to speak with him."

The girl gaped, her too-large eyes widening with a mix of excitement and apprehension. "Is Daddy in trouble?"

Russ shook his head. "No. But I am going to have to speak with Ethan, too."

"He's out in the barn with Wayne, hooking up for the milking. Hannah, fetch 'em both in."

At the mention of her brother's name, the girl had relaxed. "Oh, Ethan," she said, heading for the mudroom. "That figures."

Her mother sighed. "What's he gone and done now, Russ?"

He laid the papers on the kitchen table. "Have you heard about the girl found murdered by the kill last week?"

"Of course. It was on the news. Unidentified body fished out of the kill, that's not something you see everyday around here." Mindy's eyes widened as she listened to herself. She clapped her hands over her stomach. "God in heaven, don't tell me you think my boy had something to do with that!"

"Calm down, Mindy, I'm not here to arrest him for murder. This is a warrant for a blood test. The murdered girl had a baby about a week before she was killed, and I have reason to suspect that Ethan may be the father."

Mindy sank into a ladderback chair. "Dear Lord," she said. "Dear Lord." She looked up at him. "Who . . . ?"

"It was Katie McWhorter."

Mindy pressed her hands more tightly to her stomach. "Oh. No. Oh, no. That sweet girl." She shook her head back and forth. "That sweet girl . . ." She covered her eyes with one hand, screening any tears from his view. Russ's hands twitched, caught between maintaining some sort of professional detachment and reaching out to comfort this woman he had known since his high school days.

She slapped her hand on the oilcloth suddenly, startling Russ into stepping back. "As far as I knew, Ethan broke up with Katie last year. If he was sneaking around without us knowing, and got her pregnant, we'll have the truth out. And he'll take responsibility for it." She rose slowly from her chair, glaring at Russ. "But you listen to me, Russ Van Alstyne. My boy didn't have anything to do with killing anybody, least of all Katie McWhorter."

"What's going on?" Wayne Stoner stood in the mudroom door, prying off his boots with the jack. "Russ?" Wayne had the round reddened cheeks and the ice-pale blue eyes that marked so many people of Dutch descent in the county. He reached out and shook Russ' hand firmly before he crossed to his wife's side. "What's that boy gotten into now?"

"Russ wants to take Ethan for a blood test," Mindy said. "Seems Katie McWhorter had a baby a few weeks back and Ethan might be responsible."

"Aw, Christ," Wayne said, pulling off his hat and slapping it onto the table. "What a damn fool thing to do. Jesus, you can practically buy condoms at the feed store nowadays!"

Hannah had slipped in and was watching round-eyed from beside the woodstove. "Did Ethan get some girl pregnant?" she asked. "Whoa. No wonder he's been acting so weird."

"There's more," Mindy said to her husband, ignoring her daughter. "Katie is the girl they found dead down by the kill. The one that was in the news?"

Wayne shook his head as if he were checking it for loose wiring. He shook it again. He squinted at Russ. "You think Ethan had something to do with that?"

Russ spread his hands. "Wayne, I don't know. First step is to get this blood test and see if he could be the baby's father. Then we'll take if from there."

"I'm calling our lawyer," Wayne said. "I don't want Ethan leaving this property until I've talked to him." He pivoted to the phone table between the two windows looking out onto the dooryard. Russ heard the slap of the phone book opening.

"Wait a minute," Mindy said, "wasn't she killed on Friday? Isn't that what it said on the news? You saw Ethan on Friday. Remember? We had to come pick him up from that video game place. He couldn't possibly have . . . he didn't kill Katie."

"The girl died sometime after sundown, Mindy. I didn't see Ethan until well after ten o'clock." He looked out the windows. The sky was darkening, blue to lavender, masses of pink clouds floating on the icy air. He turned to Hannah, who had lost the gloating look of a younger sister seeing her big brother about to get it from the grown-ups. It was sinking in that Ethan might be in a whole lot more trouble than she had ever imagined. "Hannah, did you tell Ethan I was here when you got your father?"

She nodded. "He said he'd be right down."

Russ looked up to the barn. It wasn't dark enough yet to need lights on, but it would be in half an hour or so. He wanted to get this over with. "I guess I'd better walk up there myself."

"I'll come with you," Mindy said, pulling on her jacket. Outside, they crossed the path separating the barn drive from the house driveway and tramped up the well-plowed gravel road. To the northwest, the clouds were dark blue and heavy, rising from behind the mountains in a solid mass. Snow later tonight or tomorrow.

"You can't tell for sure from a blood test if Ethan's the father," Mindy said.

"No. It's more in the way of eliminating or confirming him as a possibility. If he has the right blood type, they'll send his sample down to a lab in Albany that can compare his DNA to the baby's."

Mindy opened the cattle gate to the barnyard. "If he has the right blood type, what are you going to do?"

"Ask him some questions. He can have a lawyer present. Depending on what he tells me, we'll go from there." He stepped carefully, avoiding half-frozen cow patties.

"Ethan!" Mindy called. The road ended at the gaping two-story-high entrance to the old barn. Even in the antiseptic winter air, the smell of manure and hay and machine oil was strong. "Ethan!"

"Maybe you ought to stay out here," he said.

"Don't be ridiculous. This is my son we're talking about." Inside, the barn was warm with animal heat. The cows on the left-hand stalls had all been hooked up to their milkers, while the ones on the right waited their turn with bovine patience. The machinery was silent, however, and Ethan was nowhere in sight. The low ceiling was punctuated by four trap doors that Russ could see, leading up to the huge hayloft. The back of his neck felt hot and prickly. Something in the situation read wrong, very wrong.

"Where's that lead to?" He pointed to the door at the opposite end of the barn.

"The tank room. See where the tubing goes in through the collars on the wall?"

"Anything after that?"

"Storage. We have a machinery shed for our tractors and such, but that's not connected to the barn. Ethan must be having some problem in the tank room. The pressure valves have been acting up lately. Ethan!"

The tank room door bounced open. Ethan stood framed in the doorway, a big, scared young man with a shotgun pointed straight at Russ.

Russ shoved Mindy into a stall and dove in beside her. "Ethan!" she screamed. The cow sharing the space tried to turn her head around to see what was going on, but her bit chains held her to the feed trough. Mindy jumped up. "Ethan, what are you doing?!?"

Russ yanked her down so hard she hit the floor and lost her breath for a moment. "Shut up, Mindy," he hissed.

"Get out of here, Mom!"

"Ethan?" Russ said, projecting a calm he didn't feel into his voice. "Your mother is going to get out of this stall and walk out of the barn. She'll be alone. Then you and I can talk. Is that okay?"

"I'm not leaving!" Mindy whispered.

"Both of you get out of here!"

"You get out and run to the house and call nine-one-one. Tell them what's happened. Then keep Wayne and your girl away from here. Let me handle this."

"You'll shoot him! You'll shoot him!"

"What are you doing?" Ethan shouted.

"Mindy, I haven't fired my gun off the range in over four years, and I don't intend to start now. Let me talk to the boy." He raised his voice. "Ethan? Your mom's coming out of the stall now. Don't shoot." He hauled Mindy to the edge of the wooden wall. "Go, goddamnit."

She stood shakily. "Ethan, please, don't do this."

"Get out, Mom. This doesn't have anything to do with you." Mindy looked back at Russ.

"Go!" he hissed. "Go, go!" She stumbled back a few steps, moving to the doorway while still facing her son. Russ nodded encouragement. Even when you trust someone, it takes a steel sphincter to turn your back on a loaded weapon pointed at you. When she disappeared into the barnyard, he rested his forehead against the low wooden wall for a few seconds worth of sheer relief.

"Ethan? How about you and me talk now? Okay? Let's work this out."

Mindy Stoner was scrambling up her porch steps two at a time when she heard the shot fired.

CHAPTER THIRTEEN

Mark Durkee had his head in between two half-unscrewed pipes when the phone rang. "Daddy, issa phone," Madeline said helpfully.

"Yeah, cupcake, Daddy hears it." He backed out from under the kitchen sink carefully. The phone kept ringing as he wiped off his hands and moved his tool-box out of Maddy's reach. He hoped it wasn't Rachel with more car problems. He'd have to leave an hour early if he wanted to fetch her home from work and still make his shift on time.

"Yeah," he answered. Maddy was trying to pick up some of the washers he had left on the floor. Were those big enough for her to swallow?

"Mark, it's Harlene. Listen, we've got an officer in distress in Cossayaharie and I want you there."

His first thought was that it must be some sort of prank. Except Harlene sounded dead serious. "What's going on?" He'd have to get Maddy into her snowsuit. Where could he leave her until Rachel got home?

"The Chief went to Wayne Stoner's to serve a war-rant on his boy, Ethan. Ethan's holding the chief in the barn with one of their hunting rifles. At least one shot has been fired."

"Shit! The chief?"

"We don't know. The state troopers are sending a squad there, and I've called Lyle and Ed off patrol, but you're closest."

He was. Maybe a ten-minute drive from the

Stoner's farm. He knew from experience that it would take the troopers at least thirty minutes or more to reach Cossayaharie. A man who'd been rifle shot could bleed to death in fifteen minutes. Less.

"Harlene, I'm gonna drop Maddy off with the Slingers, next door. Will you call my wife and let her know? I'll call you on the situation when I get there."

"Be careful. You know what Russ would say. Don't try to be a hero, okay?"

"Yeah." He hung up. No squad car, no shotgun, no spray, no vest. Shit. He scooped up Maddy, who squealed in delight. "Come on, cupcake. Daddy's going to work early tonight."

Old instinct had sent Russ flat into the straw and the cowshit when Ethan's shotgun went off. A second later, he was back up, crouching against the wall, where he had a chance of keeping the terrified Holstein from crushing him. Throughout the barn, he could hear disturbed lowing and thuds and clanks as the agitated cows tried to flee their stalls.

Ethan couldn't reach him from that tank room door. The boy would have to shoot directly into the stall, opening himself up to Russ's fire. So as long as they both stayed put, they were safe. The cow's white-rimmed eye rolled back and fixed on him. She kicked ineffectually, then tried to rid herself of the intruder by leaning against the wall. Russ rolled into a ball and went underneath her, hitting his head on her udder. She bellowed and stamped, narrowly missing taking the fingers off his left hand. He imagined his obituary in tomorrow's *Post-Star:* POLICE CHIEF SLAIN BY COW. He rolled out the other side of her and stood up as far as he could without exposing himself to Ethan's fire. He hit the cow hard with the flat of his hand, as he'd seen his brother-in-law do when his stock got unruly.

She bellowed again, but it seemed to settle her. "Good girl," he said, thumping her a few more times for good measure. "Ethan!" He raised his voice to be heard down the dimming length of the barn. "I'm willing to say that gun went off by accident. Right now, you're facing resisting arrest and threatening a police officer. Don't make it attempted murder. Put the shotgun down and walk out of the barn with your hands on top of your head."

"Don't jerk with me! I know you came here to arrest me for Katie's murder! I didn't do it!" Ethan's voice had the shaky, defiant sound young men get when they're half-wild with fear and half-drunk on the power of the weapon in their hands. Russ had heard it in jungles and in Third World cities and in squad cars and coming from his own mouth.

"If you say you didn't do it, Ethan, I'll believe you. I came here to ask you to take a blood test, to see if Katie's baby was yours."

"You lie! Everybody thinks I did it! I didn't! I could never hurt her! I loved her!"

"Then let's go to someplace more comfortable than this, and you can clear everything up for me. If you loved Katie, help me find who did kill her."

"I can't clear anything up, you asshole! I was drinking alone in my car before I went to Videotek that night. I know I don't have any damn alibi. Nobody saw me, I got no one who can say I didn't do it. You don't give two shits about who really killed her. You just want to arrest someone, and I'm the easy suspect. You think I'm just a punk anyway."

"I think you're a guy who's in trouble and who needs someone to listen to him seriously. Look, Ethan, you know me. I don't come off like Joe Friday." Jesus, had this kid ever heard of Joe Friday? "I cut you a break last week, when I knew you'd been drinking. Because I'm not interested in an arrest record. I want to help people keep out of trouble. Let me help you now."

"You can help me by getting the hell out of here and leaving me alone! I didn't kill her!"

Russ spread his hands against the cow's warm flank. Somewhere, there was a magic combination of words that would get the kid to lay down his gun and walk out with no one hurt. All he had to do was find them. "Ethan, I'm not gonna tell you what to do. I am going to give you the facts, so that you can make an informed decision. Fact. You picked up a shotgun and fired on a peace officer. That's not going to go away. Fact. Right now, there are cops from the town and the sheriff's department and the state all converging on your farm. Some of them aren't gonna be too particular if you leave this barn walking or feet-first. Fact. I will listen to anything you have to say about Katie and the night she died with an open mind, and I will pursue this investigation until I'm satisfied we have the real killer. Fact. You've got the power, right here and now, to stop this thing. You can put down your weapon, walk out of here, and make your parents the happiest people alive tonight. Or you can choose to shoot it out with a state SWAT team. What do you think the outcome of that will be?"

The cows lowed. Chains rattled. Somewhere, water dripped from a faucet.

"This is Officer Durkee of the Millers Kill Police," a voice shouted from outside the barn.

"Mark! This is Russ! I'm okay!" Now. Now was the moment to take a chance. He eased his 9mm Glock out of its holster. The click of a round chambering sounded as loud as a gunshot in his ears. Keeping the weapon down by his side, he straightened to his full height, shoulders and head above the cow's broad back. In the fading twilight, he could see Ethan's outline at the back of the barn. "Stay where you are, Mark," he shouted. "I think Ethan's going to put down his gun and come out." He ignored the feeling like ants crawling up his neck and through his hair. Ethan could blow his head off before he'd be able to get his piece up past the cow. "Aren't you, Ethan?"

The boy was a space of stillness in the dark. Hay rustled. A cow kicked against her stall with a loud thump. "Yeah," Ethan said.

Russ hadn't realized he was holding his breath until he let it out in a whoosh. "Okay. Put the gun on the floor, then lace your fingers together and put your hands on top of your head. We want to make sure everyone can see you're unarmed when you leave the barn."

When Ethan walked past him, hands on head, Russ slipped from the stall and fell in behind him. He holstered his gun, but left it unfastened. Just in case.

Mark Durkee was beside the barn door. He leveled his gun at Ethan. "Ethan Stoner, you're under arrest," he said. His glance flickered to Russ. "Chief?"

"I'm fine, Mark. Take Ethan to the car while I go talk to his parents, please." He let himself through the cattle gate while Mark read the boy his rights. A Millers Kill squad car flashed its red lights at the base of the driveway. Lyle and Ed were getting out. On the porch, Wayne and Mindy stood with their arms wrapped around each other, straining to see the barnyard in the twilight. Far down the road, he could hear another siren approaching. Russ felt flushed and shaky, his legs almost too heavy to carry him down the barn drive and across the dooryard. The bite of the December air, the dazzle of the house lights on the snow, the sound of people's voices all flooded his senses. It was good to be alive. He forced a smile to his face and began the long, long climb up the porch steps.

Clare smiled when she saw that the driveway to the police station had been thoroughly plowed. She eased her car over the sidewalk and into a parking space. She really was going to need a vehicle that wouldn't get stuck if someone threw a snowball under its tires. Problem was, the only way she could afford a new car was to sell the old one. The thought of which sent her into a blue funk. This MG was the closest she had ever gotten to flying on the ground. She thought of the dark, mid-sized anonymous American cars so many of her teachers at the seminary had driven. Clergymobiles. "Baby, climb inside my car," she sang as she strolled up the sidewalk. A municipal employee leaving City Hall next door looked pointedly at her collar and frowned. Probably a Baptist. Clare winked at him before charging up the steps to the police station.

Inside, she shucked off her jacket. "Harlene?" she said, approaching the dispatch room. "Has the chief left yet? I was hoping to—" She shut up when she saw Harlene's face. "What is it?"

"I really shouldn't talk to civilians yet," Harlene said, her crumpled expression at odds with her formal words.

"Harlene, is anyone hurt? Please . . ."

The dispatcher pushed her headset further back over her springy gray curls. "The chief went to bring Ethan Stoner in for his blood test and the boy pulled a shotgun on him."

The rest of the room faded to a blur, and Harlene's face came into exquisite focus. Clare could see every mole, every hair, the wrinkles around her lips as she pursed them together, the light on her lashes as she blinked quickly, over and over again.

"What happened?" Clare's voice was even.

"I don't know. They're both in the barn. Mindy Stoner heard a gunshot, but I haven't had any news since then."

Clare nodded. She kept nodding as the possibilities flitted through her mind. "Harlene," she said, "I'd be grateful if you'd let me stay. I'd like to find out if . . . if anything has happened."

Harlene held her hand out toward an old office chair next to the filing cabinet. "You just sit right down. I'd be glad for the company, to tell the truth." Clare tossed her coat under the chair and sat. The two women looked at each other.

"Who has—" Clare began.

"Do you—" Harlene said. They smiled weakly at one another. "Go on," said Harlene.

"Who has been sent out to help? With the situation?"

"Three of our own officers. The sheriff's department is sending a car or two, and the state troopers are mustering their SWAT team." She worried at the inside of her cheek. "And an ambulance."

"Oh. Of course." Clare looked at her hands. "What was it you were going to say?"

Harlene looked embarrassed. "I was going to ask if you believe praying can really help at a time like this."

Clare folded her hands together and pressed them to her lips. She paused. "I believe that prayer focuses our human thoughts and energies, sends them to the people we're praying for. I believe that helps, in ways we can't yet understand." Harlene looked surprised. She had probably expected a quick yes. Followed by an exhortation to the Almighty to keep everyone safe. "I believe that God hears our prayers, and cherishes them. I believe He answers by sending us His spirit, giving us strength, and peace, and insight. I don't think He responds by turning away bullets and curing cancer. Though sometimes that does happen."

Harlene frowned. "In other words, sometimes, the answer is no?"

"No. Sometimes the answer is 'This is life, in all its variety. Make your way through it with grace, and never forget that I love you.' "

Harlene creaked back in her wheeled dispatcher's chair. "You're not one of those strict fundamentalist preachers, are you?"

Clare laughed. The phone rang. Harlene had it off the hook before the sound died away. "Millers Kill Police," she said. There was a pause. Her face crinkled up into a huge smile. "Oh, it's good to hear your voice, too."

"Is it him?" Clare whispered. "Is he okay? Is the boy all right?"

Harlene nodded. "No, no, he's absolutely right. You let them handle the arrest and the initial report. You go home!" Another pause. "Then go to your mother's house. I don't care. If you show up here, I'll chase you off myself." She laughed, then listened for awhile. "Are you really okay? You sound kinda funny." Harlene glanced over at Clare again. "Hold on, there's somebody who's been waiting here to find out how you are. Do you feel like speaking to Reverend Fergusson?" She nodded to the phone and held it out to Clare.

"Hello," she said, feeling unaccountably shy.

"Hi," Russ said.

"Remember when you warned me Millers Kill wasn't a sleepy little town? I believe you now."

He laughed. "Good."

"So, it sounds like you're under strict orders not to come into the office."

He sighed. "I guess I should go home. Linda's out of town. And my mother . . . she doesn't need to hear about this just yet. I'm still . . ." he drifted off.

"I know."

"You know?" He sounded surprised.

"I know that you're still . . ." She let her voice trail off, echoing his. "Meet me for a drink somewhere. We can talk."

"Oh, God. I don't think I can handle going out in public right now. Besides, I smell like cowshit and the scared-cold sweats."

"Then tell me where you'll be, and I'll come to you."

"Do you think . . . would my place be okay? I could shower and change, rustle up some burgers or something. Would that be, um, unpriestly or anything?"

She laughed softly. "I think what would be unpriestly would be to let a friend sit at home all alone with no one to talk to. Give me directions and tell me when to be there. Preferably after you no longer smell like cowshit, et cetera."

He laughed. After she had his address, she handed the phone back to Harlene, who said into it, "You gonna confess your sins to Reverend Fergusson? Make sure she has a few hours." She listened, snorted at something he said. "Okay. Yes, I will. Yes, I promise. Don't you trust me? Wait, don't answer that." Harlene laughed. "Good. I hope you feel good about this, Chief. You just captured Katie's killer." There was a pause. Her smile faded. "Well . . .'Bye then. See you tomorrow." She hung up.

"What did he say?" Clare asked.

"Said he didn't know about that. He didn't know what he had just done."

CHAPTER
FOURTEEN

When Russ opened the door to her knock, he looked
... different. It was ... it was ... the jeans and a
sweater. "You're in civvies!" she said. "I was beginning
to think of you like the sheriff of Mayberry, you know,
always dressed in brown poly."

He laughed. "You obviously didn't watch enough.
He had a plaid shirt and jeans he wore fishing." He
looked over her shoulder. "Where's your car?"

She grimaced. "I didn't want to risk getting stuck,
so I left it parked at the base of the drive and walked
up."

He moved out of the way and let her enter the
mudroom. "In that leather jacket and your oh-so-
practical boots, too." She looked down at her soggy,
salt-stained suede half-boots. "Talk about unprepared
for the weather. You're worse than a little kid. I'm
gonna get you a pair of mittens with a string attached,
so at least your hands will stay warm."

"I remembered the important stuff," she said, holding up a six-pack of micro-brewed beer. She dropped
it with a thud and bent to remove her boots. "And I
could have worn my warm parka. Unfortunately, it actually belongs to the police, and I'm afraid if you see
it, you'll confiscate it." She handed him her jacket.

"Stolen property." He hung it up on one of the
many hooks running along the wall.

"I prefer to think of it as permanently on loan."

"Situational ethics." He opened the door to the kitchen.

"Oh. A wood cooking-stove!" she said. "I always wanted one of those. They're supposed to be great for baking bread."

"I hate to disillusion you, but the only thing we make on that stove is hot water." He unhooked a bottle of beer from the cardboard container and opened a paneled pine cabinet to get a couple of glasses.

"I thought your house was two hundred years old," Clare said as Russ retrieved a liter bottle of soda from the fridge. "This kitchen looks kind of forties." The floor was an old linoleum patterned with big flowers, the walls and floor-to-ceiling cupboards warm, glowing pine. The windows over the sink and in front of the table were hung with layer after layer of fruit and flower prints that reminded Clare of the old dish towels in her grandmother Avery's kitchen. Matching fabric-covered balls hung from the evergreen ropes swagged along the cornice.

"You have a good eye," Russ said, pouring their drinks. "The first modern kitchen was built here in the mid-forties. Before that, there was just the summer kitchen, which is on the other side of the mudroom, and a keeping room. I put in the brick wall and hearth for the wood stove, but other than that, we just peeled away the so-called improvements the last owners had made to get to this." He handed her her beer. "You should have seen it. Vinyl flooring and all the woodwork painted in southwestern colors. Took me three months to get down to the pine."

She sat at the round oak table and touched a finger to the tiny Christmas tree serving as a centerpiece. "I like it like this. It's like a bright, warm quilt keeping out the cold."

"Huh." He sat opposite her. "I'll pass that on to Linda. She does the decorating. I'm just the hired help." He drank from a tall glass of soda. She propped her chin in her hand and studied him. He had a fit, outdoors look to him, still slightly tan from last summer, his dark brown hair picked out with gold and copper. She'd have to disagree with Lois, his nose was too big and his lips were too nonexistent to call him handsome. But he looked like a man who had lived comfortably within his skin for the past forty-odd years.

"So," she said.

"So," he agreed. His eyes were Fourth-of-July blue, high and bright with the snap of a flag in the wind. But behind them she could see something moving, like pages turning in a book no one was allowed to read.

"How do you feel?" she asked.

He took another sip of soda. "Fine. No one got hurt, and Ethan's in jail. I count it as a victory for the good guys."

"Have you called your wife yet? To let her know what happened?"

He shook his head emphatically. "No."

"Don't want to scare her?"

"No, it's my mother who gets scared." He smiled wryly. "I figured something might be on the news by tonight, so I called my sister Janet and asked her to talk to Mom. I'll still have to face one of her 'Why can't you get into some other line of work' lectures, but I can duck it for a few days until she's cooled off."

"Uh huh. And you didn't talk to Linda because . . ."

He frowned. She kept her face open, waiting. He glanced around the kitchen, shifted in his chair, cleared his throat. She sat still, her hand lying palm up on the table. "So this is like PTSD counseling?" He laughed a little. She tilted her head a fraction of an inch. Listening. No threat. "Okay. Linda and I have been married sixteen years now. So she's been with me through a lot of shit. Armed deployments, police work, bullets flying, the whole nine yards. And, I don't know if she started out like this or if she cultivated it, but she thinks I'm invulnerable. I've learned that I can't go to her and say, 'I was frightened out of my wits today,' because she won't understand why. What I do, what I've done in the past, is like an action-adventure movie or a television show to her. Nothing's quite real, so why should it bother me?" He flicked a tiny calico ornament on the tabletop tree, then looked at Clare and smiled slightly. "Did I just do an elaborate version of 'my wife doesn't understand me'?"

She smiled. "Uh huh. But you don't have your shirt unbuttoned halfway down your chest to show off your gold chains, so it's legitimate."

"Oh, God save me from male menopause." He laughed a little, shaking his head.

She leaned forward, crossing her arms on the table. "You know, it's not unusual, being unable to share that kind of thing with your wife or your family. I used to see a lot of that, guys who had spent time in very intense, very dangerous situations, couldn't talk about it with their wives.

Couldn't admit to being scared to their buddies, of course, except when it's a joke. It builds up after a while, all that stuff inside and no way to let it out. I think that's why there's so much drinking and wild-ass behavior in some units." She dropped her glance to his glass. "Are you an alcoholic?"

He choked on a mouthful of soda. "Holy shit! You don't beat around the bush, do you? 'Scuse my French."

She looked at him mildly. "You don't need to be handled with kid gloves. Answer me."

"Christ on a crutch. Yes, I'm a recovering alcoholic. I've been dry for five years now. What the hell does that have to do with anything?"

"I'm just wondering, if you can't talk about it with your wife, and you can't pour it into a bottle, who do you talk with? Where do you go?"

He crossed his arms against his chest and leaned back in his chair, looking up toward the ceiling. "I don't, I guess," he said, finally. He looked at her. "But let's face it, it's not like I'm a homicide detective in the city. I'm not looking at dead bodies week after week, or having guns pointed at me on a regular basis. I'm just the chief of an eight-man police force in little ol' Millers Kill. Hell, the entire three town area we're responsible for doesn't have more than twelve thousand people, tops."

"Twelve thousand people for whom you feel personally responsible." She pointed one blunt-nailed finger at him. "Tell me, what feels the worst about what happened today? Being scared you might die?"

"No." He braced his elbows on the table. "Only an idiot isn't scared when somebody pulls a gun on him. I'm not ashamed of it. Not inclined to think about it too much afterwards."

"The rush you get when you walk away and you haven't died? Do you like that?"

"No! I mean, yes, I like walking away, but no, I'm not an adrenaline junkie. I'd be perfectly happy if the most action I ever saw was being dunked at the police booth during the county fair, believe me."

"Is it the fact that you should have known that Ethan was on edge and ready to blow? That if you had handled the situation differently, he never would have picked up that shotgun?"

He dropped back into his chair, his face paling. "Holy shit! Do you believe that?"

"Do you?" She leaned farther across the table, crowding him against the truth.

"When you put it that way . . . shit." He swallowed. "Yeah, I do feel responsible. It was a stupid situation to get into. I kept thinking, what a piss-awful waste it would be if Ethan didn't make it, because I hadn't taken the time to find out the kids in his school already had him tried and convicted and on death row. Instead, I waltzed in there with my patrol car and my service piece and my warrant. Not even a phone call ahead of time so his parents could set him straight about what would happen. That's just plain careless. Careless and lazy and stupid." He clenched the edge of the table tightly.

"I knew about what the kids were saying at the high school. Heard about it on Monday night. I didn't do anything about it."

He scowled at her. "That's different."

She scowled back. "Why? Because it's not my job to know everything about everybody? Because I'm not personally responsible every time one of the citizens of Millers Kill falls off the straight and narrow? Because I shouldn't do all I can to . . . to . . . to protect and to serve?"

He laughed quietly. "That's the LAPD, not Millers Kill."

"No, that's you." She took a drink of her beer. "The angel at the gate with the flaming sword, that's you. Guarding your own little paradise from the evil of a fallen world."

He closed his hand around air as if he were holding something in front of him. "A flaming sword, huh?"

"Yep."

"So you think I should—what? Stop caring so much?"

She slid her elbow next to her glass and leaned her cheek on her hand. "No. Not at all. I think it's a fine thing that you bring such dedication and passion to your work. But I think you should stop beating yourself up when you fall short of some imagined standard of perfection." She smiled lopsided at him. "Come talk to me next time, instead. I'd be happy to point out the flaws in your image of yourself."

"As opposed to pointing out my actual flaws."

"I think I need to know you better before I start in on those."

He smiled at her. "Seems like you already know me a little too well for comfort."

She shook her head, smiling, dropping her gaze to the table. She traced meaningless designs on the tabletop with the water condensation that had dripped from her glass. There was a muffled mechanical roar as the furnace kicked in. The thermostat must have been set high, because the kitchen was plenty warm already. A clock ticked in the next room.

"Would you—" he began.

"Now we've—" she said at the same time. They both laughed.

"You first," he said.

"I was going to say, now we've solved all your problems, how about that burger I was promised?"

"And I was going to ask you if you'd like dinner. Another example of great minds thinking alike."

"More like hungry stomachs rumbling in unison, but, yeah."

Russ made what Clare always thought of as he-man burgers, the same three-inch thick monstrosities her brothers would put together at family cookouts. She asked to be made useful, and he put her to work on a salad, although when she started rummaging through the pantry, pulling out cans of artichoke hearts and mandarin oranges, he looked as if he might have regretted not limiting her to setting the table. They talked about cooking as a chore and as a means of expression, and argued about which state had the greatest barbecue, and agreed that vinegar-and-salt potato chips were better with burgers than home fries, and a lot faster, too.

She would have pegged him as a paper-plate-and-napkin guy when his wife wasn't around, but he surprised her by laying out beautifully pieced place mats and huge cloth napkins, along with old ironware that could have come from the earliest years of the kitchen. As they ate, he listened very patiently when she got carried away describing all her gadgets from Williams-Sonoma, only laughing once, when she told him about her latest acquisition, a shrimp de-veiner. She asked him plainly if he ever missed wine with a meal, and he raised his eyebrow at her and said he had never been a wine drinker, but he sometimes missed a bottle of whisky after.

"You mean a glass," she said.

"I mean a bottle," he corrected. Afterwards, he washed and she dried. She made several pointed comments about historical authenticity nuts who wouldn't have a dishwasher because it didn't fit with the kitchen's time period. He smiled serenely and reminded her not to leave any water spots on the glasses. When the kitchen had been restored to its pristine state—she could hardly believe it looked like this all the time, since hers wasn't as immaculate even when it had been scrubbed for company—she grabbed another bottle of beer and he gave her the grand tour.

It was a jewel-box of a house, small and beautifully crafted. Russ told her funny stories about all the mistakes he made and had to redo when he first began its restoration. She oohed and aahed over the elaborate draperies and slipcovers and pillows, so he took her upstairs to where he had built an enormous workroom for Linda out of the old under-the-eaves space. He showed her the half finished bathroom that was his latest project, and complained about his inability to find a tub anywhere near long enough for him.

She told him about her father, whose mechanical expertise began and ended with aircraft, and who persisted in do-it-yourself projects that had become family legends. Or horror stories. That led to a discussion on the workshop as a sacred place for the American male, and he trotted her all the way down to the cellar, where his impressive collection of power tools looked like high-tech instruments of torture hanging on metal gridwork over the original hewn-rock foundation. Just like her dad's, Russ's workshop had a TV and a suspiciously comfortable chair, although it lacked the dozens of model planes that hung from her father's ceiling.

"How come I've never seen any pinups in one of these workrooms?" she asked. "I'd think that would be the perfect place for a little cheese-cake."

"Introducing the feminine would disrupt the whole Iron Male, sweat lodge, men's-only aspect of the space, though," he said. "For instance, what kind of calendar does your dad have in his workshop?"

"Uh . . . World War Two nose art."

"Nose art?"

"Paintings on the noses of planes. Please don't ask me to explain."

Russ opened one of the cabinet doors. Inside was a glossy calendar showing a man in blaze orange creeping up on a twelve-point stag, who seemed to be waiting patiently to meet his fate. "See? All male, all the time."

Clare laughed. "Okay, I get it. Do you have to blow smoke around the room when I leave, to purify it?"

"No, but if you reveal any of our secrets, the Society of Masks comes to your house in the middle of the night and plays 'Louie, Louie' until you repent."

"Society of Masks?"

"Iroquois ceremonial group. Don't tell me you don't know anything about the Iroquois?" She went back upstairs to a lecture on Iroquois history. She snagged another beer while hearing about their political structure and made herself comfortable on the Chippendale sofa in the living room while learning about their culture, past and present. When she confessed to her abysmal ignorance on anything that had happened in the Adirondack region before, say, last March, Russ rummaged about making disapproving noises until he came up with five books she had to read, to get a grounding in her new home.

"History! That's what it's all about," he said.

"I guess so," she said, craning her neck to look at all the history titles jammed into the bookcase.

"I see a lot of police work as a kind of history," he said, flopping into a high-backed Martha Washington chair.

"Really?" she said, her attention drawn away from the books he had handed her. "How so?"

He propped his sock-clad feet on a footstool. "First, you have to recreate the history of the crime. Who did it, when, where, all that. Then, it's usually the history of the individuals involved that helps you to understand why. This guy was molested as a kid, so he, in turn, molests other kids once he's grown."

Clare made a face. "Like Darrell McWhorter, you mean? I don't get it. I can see where knowing his history would help if he were in counseling. But what effect does it have on your ability to put him behind bars?"

"If you know a person's history, you can use it to help predict what that person might do. A person's history can be the key to understanding his motivation for committing a crime. For instance, in Katie's murder." Russ leaned forward, feet hitting the floor, elbows on his knees. "We know Ethan may be Cody's father. But why would he kill Katie? Is there something in his past or in their history together that would make him likely to do it? What about McWhorter? Apparently, he'd be willing to kill Katie to cover up his molestation of her. But it looks damn sure that the baby isn't his. What's in his history that makes him a suspect?"

"A need to control his daughters?" she suggested. "Katie demonstrated her control of her own body by having another man's child, so he killed her in a rage?"

"Maybe. But compare that to the Burnses' history. A couple tries for years to get a baby, stressing their marriage and their financial resources in the meanwhile, and then a kid falls in their laps. But, the mother shows up and says it was all a mistake, she wants Cody back now. I think that's damn good motive for murder."

"Except for one thing." Clare scooted to the edge of the loveseat and skewered the air with her finger. "If Katie had wanted Cody back, she could have just gone to DHS. She's the birth mother, she doesn't need to deal with the Burnses to get him back."

"Okay, she doesn't want him back. She wants money to stay away."

"Now you're ignoring history. Does that sound like the Katie McWhorter we've been hearing about? And anyway, the Burnses wouldn't pay to get Cody. This morning they—"

The phone rang, cutting her off. "I gotta get this." Russ vaulted out of his chair. "I'm expecting word on the blood test results and how Ethan's interrogation went." He glanced at his watch. "Geez, it's almost ten o'clock! Where did the evening go?"

She rose and followed him into the kitchen. "I'll take that as a compliment on my ability to be a distraction."

He grinned. "You are that," he said, picking up the receiver. "Hello?"

Clare went into the chilly mudroom to retrieve her boots and jacket. She looked glumly out the window. When had it started to snow? *Please God, let the plows be out and the roads clear.* She didn't relish the idea of getting stuck between here and the town. She carried her things back into the kitchen. "Russ?" she asked.

He waved her off, still holding the phone. "Okay," he said. "Okay. I'll be there. Half an hour, forty-five minutes at the most." He hung up the phone and leaned on it, shaking his head.

"I was going to impose on you for a ride into town, since it's really coming down out there. But I can see it's a bad time . . ." She bit her lower lip, unsure if she should ask what was wrong or not.

He passed a hand over his face. "That was the night dispatch out of Glens Falls. A motorist called in what he thought was a deer beside the road. It was a body. Durkee and Flynn went to check it out. Wallet was in the guy's pants." He looked at her. "It's Darrell McWhorter. He's been shot to death."

CHAPTER
FIFTEEN

If Katie McWhorter had resembled a frozen story-book princess in death, her father looked like roadkill. Russ tried to summon some basic human identity with the corpse, but the only emotion he could come up with was irritation that Darrell had died before Russ had had a chance to dig any more information out of him. That, and the conviction that the world—or at least his small corner of it—was a slightly cleaner place tonight.

He and Clare had been the last to arrive at the scene on the old Schuylerville Road. Durkee and Flynn had done a good job securing the area, with tape and flares and cones to redirect the infrequent traffic to the other side of the road. The state crime scene unit was already in place. Two technicians this time, since it wasn't a matter of humping the equipment a half-mile into the woods. They were working as fast as they could, racing the snow that had already covered up tire tracks and footprints, turning Darrell into a blurred heap. Russ turned his collar up against the thick flakes melting along the back of his neck, and wished he had stopped to get his hat. The snow was wetting his unprotected glasses, turning the scene into a kaleidoscope of splashing red lights and a blur of white.

Darrell had died from a single gunshot at the back of his head, delivered only inches away. He had died with his coat on, unzipped, falling face forward onto the narrow pull-off, just missing the guardrail. He had died with a half-smoked cigarette in his fingers. The soggy butt was in a plastic baggy in the evidence box right now.

"Whaddya think?" Mark Durkee swung his flashlight in the direction of the state trooper who was methodically combing through the snow between the body and the road.

"I think he has a better chance of finding the winning lottery ticket than finding a shell casing in all that," Russ said. "We'll just have to cross our fingers and hope Dvorak can give us ballistics information from the autopsy."

"Actually, I meant, what do you think happened?"

Russ glanced down the road, past the ambulance with its anonymous, snow-suited paramedics, past his pickup, where Clare sat steaming at his orders not to leave the cab. "He was in a car," Russ said, recreating the scene in his mind. "Not his car. The killer was driving. McWhorter wants a smoke. They're going someplace . . . not local. He doesn't want to wait for his nic fix until they get there. The killer says, no smoking in my car. But I'll pull off up ahead, you can get out, have one there. McWhorter gets out. The killer gets out, maybe to brush snow off the rear window or snap the wiper blades. There aren't any cars going by. It's an opening, and the killer takes it. Bang, he does McWhorter, gets back in the car, and drives off. Anybody hears the gunshot, they'd think it was backfire, or someone jacking deer." He looked past the guardrail, where a few stunted sumacs thinned out as the land fell away into a sloping valley. On the opposite hillside, a mile or so away, he could see the lights of two or three farms. "It's been coming down hard. If the killer had been a little luckier, Darrell here would have been a mound of snow covered up by the plows when they came through."

"That's somebody very cool. Somebody who can put it all together fast."

"Yeah. Or somebody who has fantasized about killing McWhorter so often that when the opportunity arose, she was ready to snatch it."

"She?"

"Sure. Don't be a sexist, Mark. You think only men can kill?"

"Hell, no. I'm a married man."

Russ laughed. The technician waved at them. "We've got all we're going to get," he shouted. "Tell the medics they can bag him." Durkee nodded and trudged off through the growing drifts toward the ambulance.

A van was coming up the road, slowing down, then pulling in past the crime scene. CHANNEL 7: LIVE! LATE BREAKING! Russ read on its side. He knew it was fashionable to bash the press, but publicity could be a big assist in a case. There was a reason the FBI fought to keep *America's Most Wanted* on the air. He watched a burly guy unload a hand-held camera. He'd have to give them the usual speech about not releasing the identity until the family had been notified. Would anything be likely to shake loose if he mentioned the probable connection to the previous murder and the abandoned baby?

He waved Durkee over again. "Mark, as soon as you can wrap this up, I want you to head over to Geoffrey and Karen Burnses' house and find out where they've been this evening. Do they own a gun, all that. Ask to see the inside of their cars. If they give you any problems, call me. We'll get a warrant tonight, if necessary."

"Okay. Want me to bring them in for questioning?"

"Go with your gut. You get a reasonable suspicion, go ahead. But remember, these two are the sort to sue the department for false arrest, so make sure you cross your T's and dot your I's."

"Will do, Chief."

"As soon as I'm done with the TV crew, I'm going to pay a visit to McWhorter's daughter Kristen. See if after two years, she finally agreed to meet with her dear old dad tonight."

"I've been thinking," Clare announced when Russ climbed into his truck.

"Congratulations," he said, tossing his parka in the back. The cab was almost too warm, undoubtedly the result of leaving Clare in possession of the keys.

"I'm going to come with you when you go to talk with Kristen."

Russ buckled his seatbelt and shifted the pickup into gear. "No, you're not. I said I'd drop you home, and I will. I didn't say anything about making you junior deputy. And what makes you think I'm going to talk with Kristen anyway?"

"She's a logical suspect, isn't she?"

"So are the Burnses." He cautiously pulled into the road. The slap of the wipers barely kept up with the pelting snow. "As a matter of fact, they're the only ones I can think of who had reason to kill both Katie and her father. McWhorter did say he wouldn't let them have custody of Cody this morning, right?"

Silence. He risked letting his eyes leave the road and glanced over at Clare. She was limned by the dashboard light, arms wrapped around herself, frowning. "What?" he said.

She hummed in the back of her throat.

"What, Clare?"

Out of the corner of his eye, he could see her turn toward him. "I've been debating telling you something. I'm not sure if it's covered by pastoral confidence or not, since it was kind of in a public place. Heck, for all I know, Lois could have overheard it."

"What?"

"This morning, things seemed to be going well at first. I thought we had convinced McWhorter to release Cody to the Burnses. But then, just like that, he changed his mind. Karen went absolutely wild. She was yelling, 'I could kill you' at McWhorter." Clare hunched her shoulders and sighed.

"They do start to look more and more like couple number one, don't they?"

"Was McWhorter killed and then dumped?" she asked abruptly.

"Nope. He got out of the car and was shot there on the side of the road." Flashing yellow lights up ahead. Plows and sanders were out, trying to keep up with the relentless accumulation of snow.

"Why would he be in a car with the Burnses? Where does this road go?"

"Away from town, it heads toward Schuylerville and Saratoga and the Northway. As for why he'd be in the car with them, I'd guess they were making a payoff."

Clare shook her head. "No. Even if they were going to exchange money for the baby, which would be a complete turnaround from their earlier position, why would they be heading out of town together? McWhorter was . . . not smart, exactly, but crafty. Looking out for himself as well as the main chance. Why agree to go off on a lonely road with someone who'd been screaming she was going to kill him this morning?"

He tried to come up with a reason that made sense. The frustrating feeling that this case was getting more complicated rather than less was creeping up like a fog around his head. It had been a long, hard day, and he wanted to go home and tumble into bed and forget half-frozen corpses and bloody snow and shotgun-toting teens and sisters who cried until their cheeks ran black.

"The Northway—that's the highway that runs the length of the state, right?"

"Route Eighty-Seven, right."

"That's how you get to Albany."

"Yeah . . ." he nodded. His head was working slowly, but it was working. "Katie's things. McWhorter and whoever killed him could have been headed for Albany to get something from the house she lived in."

"You haven't been there, yet, have you?"

"No, the Albany P.D. is supposed to cover that." His numb brain finally sparked the right connections. "Shee—it!" he said, snatching at the radio. "Do you remember the address?"

Clare spread her hands helplessly. Russ clicked on the mike. "Dispatch, this is Chief Van Alstyne of the Millers Kill P.D. Can you connect me direct to cruiser Fifty-seven-fifteen?"

There was a blare of static and then Kevin Flynn's voice from the speaker. "Fifty-seven-fifteen. Go ahead."

"Kevin? This is the chief. Cancel the Burnses. I want you and Mark to go to the station, get the Katie McWhorter file, and find the address of her student digs in Albany. Then get on the horn to Albany and have them send someone there immediately. I think whoever killed McWhorter may be headed for that house."

"Ten-four, Chief. Fifty-seven-fifteen out."

Clare looked out the window at the snow-blotched roadway. "You think they might catch the killer?"

"Maybe. The paramedics weren't sure about the time of death, 'cause the cold and the snow do funny things to body temperature. But McWhorter wasn't killed much more than three hours ago, I'll bet. If the snow slowed his killer down enough, and if he takes his time at Katie's house, maybe the Albany P.D. will walk in on him. Worth a shot."

"What are you going to do now?"

"Now? Now I'm going to drop you off at the rectory. What do you think, you've got a free pass to tag along every step of the way?"

Evidently, she did. It wasn't that her arguments for coming with him were irrefutable. She didn't actually refuse to get out of the truck. But somehow, she was still there when he cruised past the Burnses, noting the lit windows and the two vehicles in the driveway. "That doesn't mean they're not involved," he said to her smug smile. "It just means they aren't in Albany right now." He put another call through to the station, asking Durkee and Flynn to head over to the Burnses after they had gotten hold of the Albany police. "And for god's sake make sure someone in Albany calls me if they manage to collar anyone!" he concluded.

Clare's smile disappeared when they drove up to the tiny rental park where Kristen McWhorter lived. "What's she drive?" Russ asked as they cruised slowly along a row of tightly packed, two-story town houses.

"An 'eighty-nine Honda Civic," she said, rubbing condensation off the window, trying to spot Kristen's car somewhere in the parking lot. "Black."

"I don't see it."

They parked in the first available space and waited. After a while, he turned on the truck's radio and fiddled until he had the all-talk station. A gravelly-voiced man was dispensing investment and business advice to callers who identified themselves with names like "Randy from Salt Lake City" and who started each conversation with "I have an extra thirty thousand dollars in convertible debentures to invest . . ." The show broke frequently for mutual fund advertisements and the local weather, which could be summed up as deep and getting deeper.

"I can't believe Kristen had something to do with her father's death." Clare's voice broke in on a guy complaining about his wife sheltering her income in off-shore banks.

"I think you can't imagine people you like doing bad things, that's what I think," Russ said. "You said the same thing about Karen and Geoff and Ethan."

"I never said I liked Geoff Burns," she said, grinning.

"Too bad it wasn't McWhorter," he said. "He made such a satisfying heavy." She nodded. "Too bad it isn't like ninety percent of murders," he continued, "where the husband or the wife or the friend is standing there with the weapon in hand when the cops arrive, saying, 'But I didn't mean to do it!' "

Headlights gleamed at the entrance to the parking lot. A small car crept in, tires churning against the snow. The black Honda Civic pulled in a few spaces away from the pickup. Its interior light flashed weakly as someone opened and shut the door. Russ could barely make out the figure struggling up the sidewalk through the screen of heavy snow, something sizable clutched in her arms. He and Clare both opened their doors, the contrast between the almost too-warm cab and the bone-chilling wind taking his breath away for a moment. He could hear the noise Clare made as her stupid little indoor boots sank into five inches of fresh snow.

"Kristen?" he called.

She whirled, bringing her fist up. Her keys stuck up between her fingers like stubby claws. She held a bulky knapsack against her chest.

Russ raised his hands. "It's me, Chief Van Alstyne. Reverend Fergusson is with me."

"What? What's going on? Is it Katie's baby?"

"We need to talk to you. May we come in?"

Under her black knit cap, Kristen looked at them suspiciously. "Okay." She waded through the snow drifting across her walkway and unlocked the town house door. She kicked her boots against the side of the door to knock off the snow. Russ and Clare followed suit. Inside, they all crammed together on a tiny patch of tile, trying to wrestle off jackets and tug off boots without spreading any more snow than necessary onto the pale green wall-to-wall carpet.

Kristen's place was not what he'd expected from her all-black wardrobe and gothic hair. Instead of vinyl upholstery and posters of thrash groups on the walls, she had import-shop bamboo furniture in white with flowery pastel fabric. Reproductions of gauzy paintings of ballerinas hung over shelves filled with thin paperbacks and stuffed animals. The room of a young girl. One more thing Darrell McWhorter had taken away from her.

"What are you doing out here so late?" Kristen asked, dropping the knapsack on a glass-topped coffee table. "Is there news on Katie's case?"

Clare looked at him as if to say, okay, how do you do this? Damned if he knew. *Your father's had his brains blown out tonight. And by the way, did you do it?* If she didn't have anything to do with McWhorter's murder, he was going to start to look like her personal angel of death. First her sister, then her dad. "Where've you been for the last few hours, Kristen?" he asked.

She raked her hand through her ink-black hair, ruffling it upwards. "I went out for some 'za with my friends tonight after class. I'm studying for my CPA at WCCC." At Clare's raised eyebrows, she explained, "The community college." Russ suspected Clare had been reacting to the idea of Kristen as an accountant rather than puzzling over the acronym. "Look," Kristen said, "Will you please tell me what all this is about?"

The college class and the pizza joint should be easy to check out. "How long did it take you from the time you left the pizza place to the time you arrived here?" he said.

Her face shifted, from annoyed and curious to alarmed and cautious. "Maybe half an hour," she said. "Has something happened?"

Clare stepped close to Kristen and laid a hand on the girl's arm. "Kristen, your father was found dead tonight. He's been murdered. If you know anything about it, please tell us." She cut to the chase as quick as any cop he'd ever seen. Somehow, he'd thought a priest would be more . . . euphemistic.

Kristen gaped. "He's *dead*?" she asked in a shrill voice. Then she burst into tears.

CHAPTER
SIXTEEN

Russ felt like he was in a rerun of a bad television show. Kristen, sobbing and bleeding out her makeup, Clare holding the girl's hand . . . if he wasn't so goddamn tired he'd swear it was Monday morning instead of the middle of Wednesday night.

"Why's she broken up over this guy?" he half-whispered to Clare.

She glared at him from over Kristen's shoulder. "She's not broken up like she was for Katie, for heaven's sake. She's angry."

Kristen wailed. "Now I'll never get a chance to tell him what I thought of him!" She sucked air in great noisy gulps. "Now I'll never know about Katie!"

"If your father killed her, Kristen, he's already paid for it. And if he didn't, we'll find who did. I promise you." He watched Clare rock the girl in her arms and wondered if she would come to distance herself more from the people she wanted to help. She was going to crash and burn in a few years if she kept wading right in and feeling all this personally.

She met his gaze and he saw how tired she was, smudgy dark circles under her eyes, the fine lines on either side of her mouth noticeable. "Kristen," she said, "do you have any idea who your father was meeting tonight? Do you have any ideas who might have killed him?" Russ wasn't entirely convinced Kristen was innocent, for all that her tears might be real. But until her alibi checked out one way or another, he'd go with it.

Kristen shook her head. "I told you, I haven't spoken to him since I left home. I got an unlisted number so he can't call me. I was working up the nerve to call him and Mom about Katie's funeral." She jerked her head up, blinking swollen eyes at Clare. "Oh, God, now I'm going to have to make arrangements for him, too! Mom won't be able to handle it." She closed her hands over her face and wept, frustrated, angry tears that even Russ, who had learned to ignore crying from witnesses, could recognize.

"I can help you," Clare said, rubbing her hands briskly along Kristen's upper arms. "I can help."

Kristen shook her head, dumb animal grief, over and over. "All I wanted was some peace to bury my sister in. Now he's even taken that, the bastard. Why couldn't he leave me and my sister alone. My sisterrrr . . ."

Russ mumbled his excuses and went into the kitchen to look for a telephone and to escape the pain and anger ricocheting through the living room. He suppressed a twinge of guilt at letting Clare take on all the burden of dealing with the girl. There wasn't anything useful to be had out of her, not tonight, and maybe a priest was what she needed now, anyway.

He dialed the station first, and when the message to dial 911 clicked on, he hung up and called the Glens Falls dispatcher. She had the number of the detective in Albany who had been sent out with the black and white to Katie's former home. In Albany, they got cell phones. Better pension plans, too, he'd bet.

Two rings and a brisk, feminine voice answered, "Ramirez here."

"Uh . . . Detective Ramirez?"

"The one and only."

"Detective, this is Chief Van Alstyne, from Millers Kill. I understand you're assisting with a murder we've had up here."

"Chief Van Alstyne. Yeah, I spoke with your man, what's his name? Doofee?"

"Durkee," he said. She owed him that for his obvious surprise at hearing a woman's voice.

"We got a unit here right after we got your message, but your man had already been and gone."

Russ slapped the receiver against his thigh and swore quietly. He jerked the phone back up to his ear in time to hear Detective Ramirez say, ". . . identified himself to the girl as your decedent's father."

"There's a witness?"

"For what it's worth. We've got her downtown with an artist right now, but I wouldn't hold your breath. She's eighteen, she'd had a few beers earlier in the evening, and she thinks everyone over the age of twenty-eight is, and I quote, a wrinkly."

Russ laughed in spite of himself.

"The description we have so far is average height, average weight, no discernible identifying features except for a bushy mustache, which may be fake, and that he was one of the previously mentioned 'wrinklies.'"

Geoff Burns was what, forty? forty-two? Certainly would look like a wrinkly to Emily Colbaum or one of her housemates. And "average" would describe him to a T, until he opened his mouth. Russ sighed. "So, what did the perp do at the house?"

"According to the witness, there had been a call earlier from someone identifying himself as the murder victim's father. Said he was coming down to get some of the girl's things. This guy shows up around nine-thirty, goes to her room, and comes back out ten or fifteen minutes later with a backpack. It's hard to tell at this point if the room was left messy or if he tossed it. We're hoping for prints, of course."

"I know this is a long shot, but do you have any idea what he took from the room?"

"Something that could fit into a student backpack?" Ramirez snorted. "Sorry, Chief. Could be almost anything. Was your girl into drugs?"

"Not that we know," he said. "Was there anything pregnancy-related there?"

"Yeah, there was, as a matter of fact. Couple of books stashed under the bed. *What To Expect When You're Expecting*, that sort of thing. Some used feminine napkins in the wastebasket, but that could have been her period. Look, give me your fax number, and I'll have the complete report and the artist's sketch to you by tomorrow morning. Uh, make that later this morning."

Russ looked at his watch. Christ, it was after twelve. He was going to have to switch shifts with Lyle MacAuley. No way he could be working this case and still be alert enough to pull Friday night patrol tomorrow. He told Detective Ramirez the station's fax number, thanked her for her help, and hung up.

In the living room, Kristen was sitting quietly, her head dropped back against the top of her flowery love seat, staring vacantly at the ceiling. Clare, in the bamboo chair next to her, looked up as he walked in. She asked a question with her eyebrows.

He shrugged. "Someone showed up at Katie's house tonight claiming to be her father. He took something out of her room in a knapsack. One of her housemates was there, she's talking to a police artist right now, trying to give us a description."

Clare glanced at Kristen, who didn't move. "Any chance it was Darrell?" she asked.

"Doesn't sound it. Supposedly an older man with a mustache. I'm not discounting the idea that it might have been a disguise."

Clare looked skeptical. "Who the heck could it be? Ethan? He's in jail."

"Kristen," he said, then again, louder, "Kristen?" She rolled her head to face him without stirring from her position on the love seat. "I've asked you this before, but was there anyone else your sister might have been seeing? Maybe an older man?"

"I told you," she said, her voice raw and tired. "If she was seeing someone else, she never let on to me."

He glanced over to Clare. "The detective in Albany asked if Katie might have been into drugs. Maybe we're on the wrong track, thinking her murder had something to do with the baby. Maybe she got on the wrong side of some bad people."

Clare opened her mouth to respond, but she was cut off by Kristen. "My sister didn't do drugs! Or kiddie porn or illegal adoptions or passing bad checks or anything else! She was a good person. A good person! If you weren't such a cluck-ass small town cop you might have caught the man who did this to her by now!" She lurched upright in the middle of her tirade and stood pointing a shaking finger at Russ.

"Kristen!" Clare jumped to her feet. "That's not fair."

Kristen jerked her head around to face the priest. "What do you know about it! My sister is dead! And the best this guy can do is come here and ask me if I know any reason why she might deserve it? Oh, and by the way, did you kill your father tonight? Well, Chief Van Alstyne," she made his name an insult, "if my sister's murder didn't have anything to do with her baby, maybe some nut case is out to kill off all the McWhorters! Who's gonna be next? Me? Cody?"

"That's enough, Kristen." Clare's voice cut through the air like a helicopter blade, sharp and no-nonsense. "You're exhausted and upset and not thinking." She moved to the door, pulling her coat off the rack and finding her boots with her feet, her eyes never leaving the angry young woman twisting her hands back and forth in front of the loveseat. "You call me tomorrow if you want any help with the arrangements."

She waved a hand at Russ, who was still standing, stocking-footed and wool-headed, in the doorway between the kitchen and the living room. He switched into motion, getting his coat and boots while Clare continued. "Chief Van Alstyne will let you know as soon as he finds out anything about the murders." She laid her hands on Kristen's shoulders and shook her once, like a mother cat settling a kitten. "In the meanwhile, I want you to get yourself something hot to drink and go straight to bed. Try to get a good night's sleep and make sure you eat something in the morning. You have my number." Kristen nodded. "Then we'll say good night." Her voice softened. "I'm sorry, Kristen. About everything." Clare opened the door and jerked her head at Russ. "Time to go." He kept himself from saying, "Ma'am, yes ma'am," but he hustled out the door just the same.

"Good night, Kristen. We'll talk tomorrow." She shut the town house door and hunched her shoulders against the pelting snow, high-stepping past him to the truck in a futile effort to keep her boots from getting even more wet. She was inside, brushing off her jacket, by the time he climbed up into the cab, wincing a little at the ache in his hip. Definitely too long a day. He fired up the engine and sat for a moment, too wiped out to shift into gear and begin the long, slow ride back home. He rubbed his forehead with the palm of his hand. Back to the rectory, that was. Had to take Clare home first. On the radio, a psychiatrist was incredulously quizzing her caller who had fallen in love with her sister's husband. "Reality Check!" Dr. Adele barked like a drill instructor.

He smiled as he reversed out of the parking space, his four-wheel drive chugging against the accumulated snow. "So you really were an officer," he said.

"Sorry if I rolled over you in there, but I—"

"No, no, I appreciate it, really. I never know the right way to handle these scenes. Try to comfort someone and you're just as likely to get an ashtray over the head. Hang tough and be professional, and next thing you know you've got a reputation as a heartless monster or worse, there's a suit for police brutality on your desk."

"Mmmm." She turned her face away from him and leaned against the window.

He concentrated on the road, turning the defroster on full to clear the steam from his windshield. The snow came at him horizontally as he drove, as if nature were trying to sandblast his truck with the icy flakes. Traction was bad, even with his weight and the four-wheel drive. It had been a hell of a night. Thank god he hadn't let Clare drive home in that ridiculous little mosquito of hers.

Between the roar of the heater and the annoying jingle for an auto dealership on the radio—"Fort Henry Ford for Quick Credit Cash Back Cars!"—he missed the first two or three muffled gulps from the other side of the cab. He risked taking his eyes off the road for a moment. Clare was twisted so he couldn't see her face, her arms wrapped tightly around her midsection. He heard her again, the sound of something noisy being swallowed.

"Clare?" For a selfish second, he thought please, please, not another distressed woman. I can't handle any more today. "Are you okay?" The back of her head jerked up and down. He saw the bank of yellow lights ahead and coasted to a slow stop well before the oddly angled intersection of Route 39 and Tanco Road. He had once waited here while the Millers Kill fire department used the jaws of life to remove three mangled bodies from a station wagon that had tried to beat the light in bad weather. The driver had been a guy his age. "Clare," he said, turning toward her, "if you're okay, will you please look at me?"

The back of her head jerked back and forth. "Clare?" He thought back to how he felt earlier this evening, the weight and tension dropping off of him as he sat across from her at the kitchen table, talking. "Clare, who do you talk to? You asked me that, remember? Who do you talk to, Clare?"

Her voice was thick and tight. "I'll be all right. It's just been a long—" she couldn't continue. The lights turned green. He didn't move. "It's just—" she tried again. "She makes me think of my sister," she finally got out.

"Your sister," he said. "The blond girl in those pictures on your table? What about your sister?"

She turned to him, her eyes bright, her face drawn and pinched. "She died. Five years ago this Thanksgiving." She scrubbed her face with her open hands.

In the mirror, he could see distant lights headed up Route 39. He shifted the truck into gear and carefully drove on through the icy intersection. "Tell me," he said, wondering as he said it why he was asking. He respected people's privacy more than most, and this was clearly a private pain. "What was her name?"

"Grace. She was . . ." She coughed. "She was like a beautiful decoration on a Christmas tree. Funny and loving and frivolous. She was the sweet little sister and I was the tomboy know-it-all big sister. She was the beautiful one and I was the smart one." One side of her mouth crooked up. "She was always trying to get me more interested in clothes and makeup and dating and all that girl stuff that came so naturally to her." She plucked at the leather sleeve of her coat. "She gave me this jacket when I made first lieutenant, because she thought it looked like something a dashing aviatrix would wear."

"She sounds like a very special person," he said quietly.

"She was to us," Clare said. "She never did anything that would make you stand up and take notice. She worked for our parents' aviation company, secretarial work and bookkeeping. Enough to make minimum payments on her credit cards, she used to say. Mostly, she wanted to get married and have lots of kids. She would have, too. She had guys left, right, and center." Clare smiled, a small, inward smile. "She volunteered at the local hospital because she wanted to meet a doctor."

Russ didn't want to hear more. He hated the dread creeping along the edges of his nerves, knowing how the story ended. He wanted the details left off, so he wouldn't have to feel the ache under his sternum that had already begun. Aching for Clare, who had dried her eyes and was speaking in a low, thick voice.

"She was four years younger than me. Twenty-five when she—when it happened. She had had this pain on and off in her abdomen, thought it was indigestion or gas. It finally got bad enough for her to have it checked out." She closed her eyes. "It was colo-rectal cancer, well advanced. She didn't suspect. No one suspected. No one in our family had ever had cancer. She went in for a checkup in the morning and by that evening she was under a death sentence. In one day."

He made the left-hand turn onto Main Street, the truck's rear fishtailing gently before he got it straightened out. The shop lights were almost invisible in the snowy haze.

"I was stationed at Fort Bragg at the time, about four hours from home, so I didn't ask for compassionate leave. Grace moved back into our parents' house and I visited them every weekend. For awhile, I really thought she was going to get better. They treated it very, very aggressively, and I thought, she's twenty-five, she's under the best medical care possible, she has people all over the country praying for her, writing her letters, of course she can't die. Of course she can't die." She folded her hands and pressed them to her mouth as if she were pushing a prayer back into her throat. "Four months. After four months, 'she can't die' became the problem, not the expectation. Do you know anything about colo-rectal cancer?"

He shook his head.

"She was in agony. She was half-dead from the chemo and the half of her that was alive was suffering every day, all day. The fact that she was young and strong became a . . . a curse, because her body hung on, and hung on . . ." She rested her chin on her tightly clasped hands. "There was an intern she had dated, a friend of hers. Harry Jussawala. He would visit her, sometimes stay with her during treatments in the hospital." She breathed deeply. "He came for Thanksgiving dinner. My folks always have friends as well as family for Thanksgiving. Their house is always open. I wasn't there, I was on duty so one of the married guys could be at home with his family. Anyway, while the rest of them were in the kitchen or outside, Harry went into Grace's room and gave her fifty crushed Valium pills suspended in a solution of cranberry juice and vodka." She looked at Russ. "Does that sound stiff? That's how I always think of it, you know, because that's how I first heard about it from the investigators." Her mouth quirked. "It was a Cape Codder, get it? Her favorite drink. She died within a half hour. She was dead when my mom went in to check on her."

He didn't know what to say. His heart hurt for her. "Oh, Clare. I'm so sorry."

"Harry was never arrested. They talked about murder, then about manslaughter, but in the end, no one could prove anything except that he had brought the crushed Valium to her room. His medical license was revoked. I still don't know, to this day, if it was really her idea to kill herself or if he acted out of his own sense of compassion. She didn't leave a note or anything." Her face crumpled at last. "I never got to say good-bye to her." She furiously blinked back tears. "And you know what's awful? To this day, I don't know whether to curse him or bless him. She was suffering, I know that, and it was going to end in her death. But she was alive! To be put down like a hurting dog . . ." she shook her head sharply, her lips closing tightly over her grief. She rubbed her face again, hard, and sniffled wetly. "I'm sorry. I never talk about this, I don't know what got into me."

He turned onto Church Street, swerving to one side to let a snow plow get by in the other lane. "It's late and you're tired," he said. "Fatigue is like a truth drug, you know. Makes you do and say things you ordinarily wouldn't consider." He stopped at a red light and looked at her. "I think with all this stuff about Kristen and her sister, you needed to talk about Grace, and you needed a friend. I like to think I qualify there."

She wiped a finger under her nose, smiling a little at him. "You do. You surely do. Thanks."

He drove forward, past the park, past St. Alban's, onto Elm Street. Over her protests about not trying to make it into her driveway, he shifted into second and churned a path up to her kitchen door. He was damned if he'd make her walk any farther than she had to in those skimpy boots she had on.

The truck idled quietly. "The guys on the graveyard shift always swing by my place around dawn," he said. "Give me your key. I'll radio them tonight before I turn in, ask if one of them will drive your car back into town if the roads are plowed by then." She nodded, rubbing her eyes once more before fishing a key chain out of her pocket. She looked like a little kid at the end of an overlong day, all flushed cheeks and exhausted, tear-bright eyes. She pulled a key off the ring and handed it to him. "You need me to come in?" he asked.

She shook her head. "I started out this evening hoping I could help you get it all off your chest," she said, smiling. "Didn't expect to be on the receiving end."

He draped his arm over the back of the seat. "Will I embarrass you if I tell you I admire you? The way you listen to people, the way you want to help?"

She smiled more emphatically. "Yes, you will. But thanks. For everything. You're right, you know. I do need a friend." She looked at him seriously. "Thanks. For letting me be just Clare. Instead of the Reverend Fergusson. It's been a long time since I—it's a rare thing to have someone you can just be yourself with, you know. Your whole self."

He was going to make a crack about hanging out with heathens more, but he couldn't, not with her looking at him that way. He shifted his gaze to the dashboard, unable to meet her eyes. "Good night, Clare."

"Good night, Russ." She opened the door and slipped from the cab.

"Clare—" he said. She paused, her hand on the door, the snow swirling around her and into the passenger seat. Her hair stirred in the wind, already hung with feathery snowflakes.

"Nothing," he said. "Talk to you tomorrow." He waited until he had seen her inside the kitchen before he shifted the truck into gear. She waved at him from the window. He pulled out of her snow-drifted driveway and drove away from the rectory at a much faster speed than was safe.

CHAPTER
SEVENTEEN

Clare paused in front of the parish bulletin board, a packing box of Christmas banners propped against one hip. Still woolly-headed from the late night and high emotion, she had tackled the messy, mindless task of digging the church's Christmas decorations out of the undercroft this morning. The Sunday-best of her parishioners' photographs contrasted with her rumpled, sweaty, dusty state and reminded her that she would have to wash and change in order to be presentable. The picture of Karen and Geoffrey Burns caught her eye. They looked so happy and relaxed in the photo, with the kind of sleek contentment that more than enough money brings.

For all of Geoff's raging and Karen's desperation, Clare still couldn't believe that their desire for a child could lead them into murder. She had seen them with that baby in the hospital, seen the instant love and tenderness that was ordinarily lost in the brassy blare of their personalities. Within their small universe of two, they were gentle, caring people. It struck her that perhaps they needed a child most of all so they could show that vulnerable side to another human being.

"Reverend Clare?" Lois's voice broke her concentration. She hoisted the box higher and walked into the secretary's office.

"A few messages for you," Lois said. "Karen Burns called, and Mr. Felton's daughter, to reschedule your visit. He's going in for some tests and he won't be back to the Infirmary until tomorrow."

"Anything serious?"

"She didn't sound too concerned. The last one was Kristen Mc-Whorter. Is she related to the—"

"Her sister. What did she say?"

"She's going to see her mother, and wondered if you'd come along." Lois pushed the pink message memos across her desk. "Her number's there."

"Thanks." Clare dropped the box against the wall and took the paper slips. "Say, Lois, you don't know anyone who could get the mold spots out of these felt banners, do you?"

The church secretary sniffed a few times. "That's what that smell is." She tilted her head so that her perfectly-cut bob swung sideways. "You've come to the right person. Not that I ever have to deal with mold, you understand, but I do know the best dry cleaner in the three-county area."

"Somehow, I knew you would."

In her office, Clare flung herself into her chair with a creak and a snap. She picked up two of the pink papers and held them up, one in each hand, as if weighing Karen Burns against Kristen McWhorter. She looked out the window at the diamond-pieced sky, longing for a four-hour nap. Steam off the smell of moldy old boxes, burrow under her grandmother's guilt, turn her Thelonious Monk CD on low and forget about the world for awhile.

Too bad the inward voice that gently and relentlessly urged her on could find her, even under a Baltimore guilt. And make itself heard even over jazz from the '68 Monmartre session. Heck, God was probably playing at that session. She picked up the phone and dialed.

"Kristen? It's Clare Fergusson. You left a message for me?"

"Yeah. I was hoping . . . I have to go see my mom today to start sorting things out. I was wondering . . . would you come with me?"

"Are you sure you don't want some privacy with your mother? I mean, if you want to do more than go over the funeral plans with her. You two have some very intense issues to discuss."

Kristen groaned over the phone. "Yeah. The thing is, I think if you were there I'd, you know, be more likely to get to the tough stuff. I know it's asking a lot . . ."

"No, I'd be more than happy to come if I can be helpful, Kristen. It's not asking a lot. I'm glad you thought to call me."

There was a pause. "About last night? I'm sorry I got all weird on you. I was just . . . it was all too much, you know?"

"I know. Believe me, I understand." Clare pulled her oversized agenda toward her. "I've got a counseling session at three, but I'm free until then. Give me the directions to your mother's apartment, and I'll meet you there." She scribbled the address on a piece of scrap paper and wrote KRISTEN: NOON in the agenda. "Okay. See you in about half an hour."

Someone had hung a pair of plastic wreaths on the front doors of 162 South Street. The peeling apartment facades must have been working-man's flats a hundred years ago. Utilitarian and cheap back then, and not improved by the last thirty years of unemployment and neglect. Still, Clare could see evidence of the coming Christmas as she fishtailed slowly down the street. Crayon-colored reindeer taped in windows, strings of fairy lights wrapped around the posts of one battered and sagging porch.

She parked as close to the curb as she could. No sign of Kristen's black Civic. She kept her engine running to ward off the cold and turned up the Top Forty station on her radio. Everything was calm in the afternoon's watery sunlight, but she couldn't be far from where Russ had answered a domestic disturbance call last Friday when she had gone on patrol with him.

A girl with a toddler balanced on her hip trudged past Clare, ignoring the unusual sports car, intent on keeping her cigarette ash from blowing into the child's face. She couldn't have been more than sixteen, and Clare wondered if it was choice or a lack of them that kept her out of school. This was the sort of young woman and child her proposed program could help, if she could only get the vestry behind her. She blew out her breath in frustration.

A slamming door jerked her back to the here and now. Kristen had arrived. Clare killed the engine and slid out of her car. Kristen walked around the MG, her eyes wide, nodding. "This is your car?" she said.

"Yeah."

"Wow. Way cool. I didn't think priests had enough money for this sort of thing."

Clare laughed. "I don't. I've had it for seven years and if something big goes, I'll be in deep pockets. I really ought to sell it and get something more practical."

"Must be lousy in the snow." Kristen opened the passenger-side door and peered in at the leather interior. "But, oh, man, it sure has some style."

Clare caressed the curve of the hood. "It sure does, doesn't it?"

Kristen clicked the lock and slammed the door shut. She pointed to Clare's side. "You oughtta lock up around here." She glanced up at the third story windows while Clare complied.

"Are you ready for this, Kristen?" Clare asked, picking her way over the sidewalk snowbank to keep her boots dry.

"No. I feel kinda sick to my stomach, to tell you the truth. But I'm here, so hey. Let's do it."

Mrs. McWhorter buzzed them up without comment. The stairs were steep and poorly lit, and Clare wondered if this place could pass a municipal safety inspection. Did Millers Kill have safety inspectors?

The door to 4A swung open at Kristen's knock.

"Hello, Ma," she said, her voice forcibly calm. Clare tried to school her shock at the size of the woman who embraced the ramrod-stiff girl.

Brenda McWhorter pulled away from her surviving daughter, her expression a mixture of hurt and frustration. "Aw, Kristen, don't be like that." Her eyes flickered to where Clare stood in the hall. "Aw, now don't tell me you've brought a cop with you. Krissie . . ."

"She's not a cop, Ma, she's a priest. She's the one who was there the night they found Katie's—the night they found Katie. She's been helping me out. This is Reverend Clare Fergusson."

Clare stuck out her hand. "Mrs. McWhorter," she said, rummaging for something to say. "Pleased to meet you" and "Sorry about your husband" seemed grotesquely inappropriate under the circumstances. "I'm so very sorry about your recent losses," she said. "From everything I've heard, Katie was an exceptional girl. She'll be missed." *And as for your husband, good riddance to bad rubbish*, Grandmother Fergusson added.

Brenda McWhorter shook hands and led Kristen and Clare into the apartment. They bunched awkwardly in front of a massive maple sideboard. "Well, go ahead, take your coats off," Mrs. McWhorter said, gesturing toward a row of hooks by the door. "Same place, nothin's changed since you left."

Kristen rolled her eyes but obediently gathered up Clare's bomber jacket and hung it alongside her own bulky coat.

"What interesting pieces you have," Clare said. "They look like antiques."

Brenda surveyed her kingdom. "They were my parents'. Came from the big farmhouse we had out toward Cossayaharie. We had to sell it when my dad passed, but I kept some of the furniture."

Kristen plunked herself into the narrow Victorian settee and crossed her arms. "What are you gonna do now that he's gone, Ma? Move back out to Aunt Pat's? Get a job? What?"

Her mother sat, an operation that required her to lower her center of gravity over a well-used, well-sprung chair and then drop in a controlled fall. "Well, honey, I thought I'd stay right here. I know that we've had some problems in the past, but I figured now your daddy's gone you and I can take up again, get to be friends. I got enough money to keep me . . ."

Clare sat on a cane-seated ladder chair, her face composed and pleasant, wondering how another human being could let herself get that large. She shifted in her chair. No, that wasn't fair. Not everyone grew up in an active family and started off in a career that demanded physical fitness. On the other hand, basic self-respect should get you off the sofa and on your feet—she twitched. She didn't call alcoholism a lack of self-respect. She shouldn't see obesity that way, either. If some people didn't have the discipline to push away from the table after a third helping—her cheeks warmed at her persistent failure of compassion. Dear God, she thought, help me to accept as Christ accepted. Keep my mind on helping, not judging. And remind me to put in a five-mile run this evening.

Kristen was going over her mother's financial situation, asking to look over the pension and insurance documents, quizzing her on any other benefits. Mrs. McWhorter was at best vague about money matters.

"Ma, you're going to have to learn to keep a checkbook now. Come on down to the bank tomorrow and I'll set you up. That way, I can help you balance your account for awhile. You got the information on the CDs and the savings? Can I see it, please?"

Mrs. McWhorter heaved herself up from her chair and waddled

down the hall. "Isn't she smart?" she tossed back to Clare.

Clare turned to Kristen, still sitting back with her arms crossed defensively over her chest. "You are smart about finances," she said.

"Everybody's good about something, they say. I like it. I like numbers."

"So consistent, aren't they? So easy to control." Kristen shot her a look. Clare went on. "It can be a lot easier to throw yourself into your work than to face personal problems, have you noticed that? It's comfortable and distracting."

Kristen shot up from the settee and threaded her way through the heavy furniture to the pass-through kitchen. "You want something to drink? I know Ma's got soda in here."

"I'm fine. Are you going to ask your mother about what she'd like for the funerals?"

Brenda McWhorter lumbered up the hallway, a sheaf of papers and envelopes in her hand. She stopped dead at Clare's words. "Aw, Krissie," she said. "We do gotta talk about that. You're gonna take care of the details, aren't you, honey? You know I'm no good at that sort of thing."

Kristen slammed the refrigerator door with enough force to set the contents rattling. "Yeah, Ma, I'm gonna take care of the details. I know you're no good at that sort of thing." Her voice began to crack. "You don't like to deal with life's crappy little details." She slammed a liter bottle of orange soda on the counter and knocked over two plastic glasses in the drainboard before grabbing hold of one.

"Krissie . . ."

"Ma, I'm the kid here, remember? You're the mom. You're supposed to be taking care of me, not the other way around." The soda slopped over the pebbled sides of the glass. "You were supposed to take care of me and Katie and I gotta tell you, Ma, you did a piss-poor job of it." A barking sob escaped her before she covered her mouth.

"Krissie . . ." Brenda's hands fluttered ineffectually. Clare suddenly saw, very clearly, the small woman inside that bulky disguise. Had she done that to herself? Or was it more of Darrell's handiwork? "I tried . . . you don't understand. You never understood what it was like to need someone." She looked down at the paperwork charting how her and Darrell's money had grown over the years. She looked beseechingly toward Clare. "In a lot of ways, he was a real good husband and father."

Clare clenched her teeth tightly to keep her gorge down.

"Ma, I gotta know. Was he doing Katie? Did he start messing with her after I moved out?"

"Kristen! How can you say that!"

Her daughter leaned over the speckled countertop, hands braced. "I know. We never say that, do we? We none of us ever came right out and said what was happening, did we? Not even Katie and me. Did he, Ma? Did he?"

Brenda dropped her gaze to the carpet and shook her head. "He . . . I dunno if Katie told him something or if it was . . . if it was just you. He was good around Katie." She looked up at her daughter again. "I couldn't lose him, Krissie. I didn't think . . ." She looked at the papers in her hand. "I didn't think about it, that's all. You gotta learn to overlook some things when you're married. He took good care of me, and he loved me." She started to cry.

"Aw, Ma. Jesus, Ma. You didn't think about it." Kristen plodded around the counter and put her arms as far around her mother as she could. "Ma, he used all of us." Her voice cracked, but she went on, "I made myself into the kind of person who will never get used again, and you can, too. It's not too late."

Her mother shook her head. "I ain't tough like you nor smart like Katie. I've always needed somebody to help me get along. I know you hate him, and I can't blame you, you got that right. But I don't know what I'll do without him. God damn him for thinking he could make one last big deal."

Clare stepped forward involuntarily. *What?*

Kristen wiped her eyes and nose with her sleeve. "Geez, him and his big deals . . ."

"Kristen." The girl looked at Clare, red-nosed and blotchy-eyed. "If your father was killed while involved in one last 'big deal,' whoever he was dealing with may have been his killer." Brenda jerked her head off her daughter's shoulder. "It may have been Katie's killer."

Kristen and Clare both looked at Brenda, who stepped back out of her daughter's hold. "No," she said. "I don't wanna borrow trouble, Krissie, and neither do you." She darted a glance at Clare. "I already said my piece to the cops, I don't got anything else to say."

"Ma . . ." Brenda shook her head, backing away another step. Kristen's eyes narrowed. "Ma," she hissed, "if you know something and don't tell me, I'm heading out this door and you can bury Dad in a shoebox by yourself for all the help you'll get from me."

Clare laid a hand on the girl's arm. "I don't think your mother's reluctant so much as she's scared. Is that it, Mrs. McWhorter?"

The woman shifted from foot to foot, her gaze darting from Kristen to Clare to Kristen again, her face a mask of misery. "I don't want no trouble from the police," she said.

"The police will have to know what you tell us," Clare said, "but I don't see that they need to know who told us." She caught Brenda's eyes, wide and white, and made herself still, wiping out everything she already knew about the woman, her whole body open, listening.

Clare held Brenda's gaze until the older woman sighed and quivered in relaxation. "Darrell said he knew who the baby's father was. Said he had surprised Katie and him together last winter, in a car." She looked at the sheaf of papers trembling in her hand. "He said he could get money from the guy. He called him that afternoon, that last afternoon."

"Darrell called someone?"

"Oh my God, Ma, do you know the phone number? Do you know his name?"

Brenda's face quivered. "He didn't tell me none of the details, honey. You know I'm not good—"

"Not good with details. Yeah, I know."

"There was a phone number written down." Clare's heart squeezed with excitement. Now they were getting somewhere. "I thought about doing something with it, but I wound up throwing it into the disposal." Clare couldn't help a small groan of frustration. "I was scared. I figured whoever this man was, he'd killed your father and maybe your sister and who's to say he couldn't kill me, too. I may not be smart, but I know when to keep my mouth shut."

"Mrs. McWhorter, when Darrell told you that he was going to get in touch with this man, did either one of you consider that you were going to be making a deal with the man who probably killed your daughter?" Clare knew she was speaking too sharply, but Brenda's monstrous self-absorption was sucking the patience out of her.

"Well . . ." Brenda looked uncertainly at Clare. "You know, there wasn't nothin' gonna bring Katie back, was there? And maybe Darrell would have turned him in after he'd gotten what he wanted." She opened her hands. "I didn't really . . . think about it."

CHAPTER
EIGHTEEN

Russ was dropping piles of papers on the big scarred-oak table in the briefing room when Mark Durkee strolled in, fifteen minutes early for the evening shift. "Hey, Chief. How y'doing?"

"This goddamn case is giving me a goddamn headache," Russ informed him, slapping down a manila folder next to a reprint of Katie McWhorter's high school photo.

"Actually, I was thinking more like, how are you feeling after that shootout at the Stoner's place yesterday? Everything cool?"

Lyle MacAuley stopped in the doorway, already changed into his civvies. "Yeah, Chief. That post-cow stress disorder can be a killer." Mark laughed. "Maybe you ought to have yourself checked out," Lyle went on helpfully, "make sure you didn't pick up any hoof-and-mouth disease."

Russ gave both of them what he hoped was a killing look.

Mark laughed harder. "Really, Chief, we were worried about you."

Lyle nudged past the younger officer. "Hell, Mark, it'll take a lot more than some pumped-up kid with a twenty-two to take out the chief here. It takes a solid ton of muscle, hide, and milk to make the man sweat." He leaned over the assorted folders and files, his bushy, graying eyebrows rising in interest. "Whatcha got here?"

"I'm drowning in reports on the McWhorter case. I'm sorting everything out, trying to shake something loose." Russ slid a broken stick of chalk across the table to Lyle. "Get up to the board there, Lyle, help me time line this thing out."

Lyle moved to the school-room sized blackboard hanging on the windowless wall of the briefing room.

Russ opened the medical examiner's report on Katie McWhorter. "Friday, December fourth." Lyle chalked the date in the upper left-hand corner. "Sometime between seven and nine o'clock, the killer—no, wait, better make that killer A—bashes Katie's head in and drives off." Underneath the time, Lyle added "A→Katie McW."

"A could be one or both of the Burnses. They have no alibi other than each other for Friday night. It could have been Darrell McWhorter—"

"Those names he gave you checked out, though," Lyle reminded him. "Dave Jackson?" He stepped back to the table and ran his finger over the single-sheeted investigative reports. "Here it is. He was ready to affidavit that he and his wife had been with the McWhorters from seven to eleven that night."

"Yeah, I know. Okay, erase McWhorter. Ethan Stoner could have done it, too. He had the truck, he had the time, and he was mighty riled up about something that night when I saw him around ten or so."

"I took his initial statement," Mark said. "He said his friends would testify that he'd been with them all that evening."

Lyle and Russ looked at each other. "Is it me, or does that boy seem awful young to you?" Lyle asked.

Russ pushed the bridge of his glasses up his nose. "I'm sure his friends would say just that, Mark. And I'm just as sure that five minutes of grilling would bust that story wide open if the Stoner boy hadn't been babysat all night by his buddies."

Lyle wrote down the name.

"Ethan's blood type checks out as the possible father of Katie's baby. But," Russ tapped the hospital's test report, "Noble showed Katie's picture around to the local motel owners and found that the guy who runs the Sleeping Hollow Motor Inn saw Katie with some man who wasn't Ethan Stoner right around Thanksgiving. Had a record of the car and everything. We ran a match on the '86 Nova they were driving. Turns out it's one of Katie's roommate's cars. We haven't been able to match the name and the numbers on the license the guy showed the clerk, which leads me to believe it's a fake I.D. So, Katie and whoever stayed three days, and when they left, they took a blanket with them that's an exact match to one of the blankets the baby was wrapped in."

"So Ethan's not the father?" Mark hitched a hip onto a wide sill and leaned back against the wire mesh covering the lower half of the tall, turn-of-the-century window.

"I don't like Ethan as the father," Russ said. "It doesn't fit with what we know about Katie. She broke up with him clean, and according to her sister, she was nice to him, but not friends with him, after that. She doesn't strike me as a girl who'd have jumped in the sack with her old boyfriend on a whim."

"Doesn't mean Ethan couldn't have killed her when he found out about the baby," Lyle said. "He wouldn't be the first rejected guy to build up a fantasy about getting together with a girl and then turn violent when reality intrudes. And let's face it, we've seen he's capable of picking up a gun and threatening to kill someone."

"I know. That's why I haven't discounted him as her murderer." Russ flipped open the medical examiner's report on Darrell McWhorter. "Let's take a look at the next one. Darrell McWhorter meets with the Burnses on the morning of December eight." Lyle noted the date. "He tells them he and his wife are keeping the baby, because it's the last link to their little girl or some cowpuckie like that. Sometime between eight and ten that night, he's shot to death by the side of the Old Schuylerville Road. Probably while on his way down to Albany. In Albany, some man shows up at Katie's house around ten o'clock, says he's her father and ransacks her room."

"It couldn't have been Ethan Stoner, because he was sitting in the county jail in Glens Falls at the time," Mark reminded him.

Lyle tapped the chalk stick against the Burnses' names. "How 'bout these two?"

"How 'bout them?" Russ said. "Again, no alibi except each other. Reverend Fergusson and I drove past their place at eleven-thirty that night, and both cars were in the drive."

"It only takes an hour to get to Albany," Lyle said. "An hour and a half in bad weather."

"Was the Northway speed limit reduced to forty-five last night?" Russ asked.

"Nope. Snow wasn't that bad, the plows kept up with it."

"So it'd be tight, but possible."

"Maybe they have a winter rat," Mark said.

Lyle and Russ looked at each other again. Lyle nodded thoughtfully. It was a common practice for people to protect their good cars from the ravages of rock salt, potholes, and cycles of freezing and thawing water by garaging them between December and March and driving a winter rat instead; any junky old heap with a heater and a defroster that worked.

"If they did," Mark went on, "One of them could have taken it out while the other one stayed home, parking the cars in the drive, turning on the lights, maybe even making phone calls to establish an alibi."

"Is it just me, or does that boy seem awfully smart to you?" Russ asked. Lyle grinned. "Okay, Mark," Russ continued, "run with it. Get into the DMV records and find out how many vehicles are registered to Mr. and Mrs. Burns. Don't forget to check any that might be under her maiden name. Or registered to their law practice instead of to them as individuals."

"If it was Geoff Burns who tossed the student apartment in Albany," Lyle said, "what was he after?"

"Maybe there was something there that would tie him to Katie's murder," Russ said. "A letter, a note she wrote to herself—something." He leaned one-handed against the table and tapped the folder containing the Burnses' statements. "The way I see it, during the negotiations with the Burnses, Darrell thinks of whatever it is that could prove Geoff Burns killed his daughter. So he calls everything off. Tightens the screws, makes the Burnses see he's going to play hardball. Then he calls Burns later, tells him about the evidence or whatever, and arranges the meeting. On the way to Albany, Burns shoots him."

"Burns shoots him because . . ."

"Hell, I don't know. To cover up the blackmail? Because Darrell pissed him off bad enough? Geoff Burns has a temper like a bantam rooster, and believe me, Darrell McWhorter was the kind of guy you could easily get pissed off at."

Lyle took aim at Mark with a half-cocked finger. "Did you ask 'em about owning any firearms when you spoke with 'em last night?"

"She's got a nine-millimeter Smith and Wesson registered in her name. Said she keeps it in the trunk of her car for when she's travelling long distances alone. I didn't even ask to see it at the time. It was late, and the chief had said to go real carefully."

Russ nodded. "We're gonna need a warrant to be able to test that weapon, sure enough."

Lyle crossed his arms over his flannel shirt and looked at the worn-down green chalkboard, where abbreviations and arrows connected the Burnses to Katie and Darrell McWhorter. "You think you got enough to convince Judge Ryswick to let you take a look at that gun? These are a couple of lawyers, remember. People like him. Not the usual type to get hauled up on a murder charge."

Russ sighed. "Dunno. Maybe." He pointed at the three events Lyle had written down and circled. "We've got an abandoned baby. We've got a dead mother and a dead grandfather. So, do we have three separate suspects, one who fathered the baby, one who killed Katie, and one who killed Darrell?"

"Too complicated. I don't like it," Lyle said.

"So maybe we have one suspect. The same man who was at the motel with Katie when her baby was presumably born, later killed her and her father. It's a lot neater, but we've got squat evidence." He rapped his knuckles on Katie McWhorter's autopsy report. "Or we have one man, identity unknown, who is Cody's father, and one other suspect who did both the McWhorters." He smiled one-sided at Mark, who squinted up at the blackboard's crisscrossing lines. "Maybe I should take the chalk-board in with me to Ryswick, you think?"

"I think finding another car will help." Lyle dropped the chalk into Russ's hand and headed for the door. "Maybe we'll luck out and find a bloody baseball bat locked in the trunk."

"Oh, yeah," Russ said. "A signed confession, too. Get out of here, stop bucking for overtime."

Lyle rounded the corner, waving good-bye. Over the sound of his boots clumping down the wooden stairs, Russ could hear him mooing.

"That guy," he said to Mark. "Tell you what, you do the run-down on the Burnses' registration, and I'll cover your patrol time until you're done. I'll just drive the squad car home afterwards if I'm not near the station."

"You don't have to be home?"

"Nope. I'm batching it until Linda gets back on Saturday."

"You got a deal."

The streets had been plowed clear early in the morning, and the day's sun, though intermittant, had warmed things up enough to dry up the slush. It was a pleasure to drive without having to pay too much attention to the condition of the road. Russ headed south, where the scenery opened up into long valleys between easy, rolling hills. The lights of farmhouses and barnyards scattered across the landscape, familiar and comforting. To the west, and behind him, to the north, the Piedmont rose in wave after rounded wave. The great hills broke the sky into two darknesses, the one above glittering with stars, the one below glowing, here and there, with snow.

He loved this part of the world more than any other, loved the sight of those old hills surrounding him. There was something unknowable about them, a mystery that had been there when the first Dutch and Scottish settlers had carved farms for themselves along the rivers running out of the vast wilderness. With the dark hills looming and the lights few and far between, it was easy to imagine what it had been like nearly three hundred years ago. The Adirondacks were still a wild and sometimes dangerous place, sparsely settled, with few roads in and out of the great Adirondack Park, a wilderness stretching thousands of square miles over ten counties. Every year, a few unprepared or incautious people went into these mountains and never came out.

He thought about that fight he had had with Linda their first winter here, when she was planning on driving up to Gore Mountain to consult on a curtain order for somebody's chalet. He had insisted she pack the car with a blanket, a self-heater, a flare, and even rations. She couldn't believe a stalled engine or a car in a snow-covered ditch could be fatal. He had won that one, and was rewarded, when she got back, by her casual observation that the chalet hadn't had another neighbor within twenty miles. Twenty steep, single-lane, hardly-plowed miles.

"Ten-fifty to Ten-fifty-seven, over." The crackle of the radio brought him back to his squad car.

"Ten-fifty-seven, go," he said.

"Mark's all done, Chief," Harlene said, "and he says to tell you he hit the jackpot. There is another car."

"Yes!" He pumped the radio receiver in truimph. "Give that man a kiss, Harlene."

"Well, if I gotta . . ."

"I'll sign off and take this unit back to my house if he's ready to roll."

"Okay, I'll log you off duty. You had a phone call a while back. Reverend Fergusson."

"Clare called?"

"Ayeh. Said she wanted to talk with you about the McWhorter case."

"Oh. That all?"

"Yes, that's all. She's a smart girl, she knows better than to waste a police dispatcher's time with a lot of chit-chat."

"Uh huh. Don't forget who signs your paychecks, honey."

"The town clerk. I won't."

He laughed. "Okay, thanks, Harlene. I'll see you tomorrow." He realized a second after he clicked the unit off that he didn't have Clare's number on him. He thought about calling Harlene back and getting it, but it was only fifteen, twenty minutes into town. He'd feel better if he could check up on her, make sure she was doing okay after everything that had happened last night. And while he was there, it would be worth-while checking that MG of hers, making sure she was prepared for a winter breakdown. He swung the squad car across lanes and headed back north, toward the ancient hills half-hiding the winter stars.

St. Alban's was dark when he swung past it from Church Street onto Elm. For a moment, he thought the rectory was dark, too, until he saw the lights shining out the back of the house. Of course, it was seven o'clock. She was probably making dinner. Nothing like showing up un-invited and unexpected at suppertime. He parked behind her car and trudged along the beaten-down snow. Didn't she have anyone to plow for her? He kicked his boots against the lowest stairstep before mounting to the door.

The kitchen door was as uncurtained as the rest of the house, and Russ could see the rector of St. Alban's sipping red wine and cooking up a storm on her gas stove. She was wearing jeans and a University of Virginia sweatshirt hacked off around the waist. From the bulk of the sleeves pushed up her arms, it must have belonged to one of her hulking brothers at one point. He could hear music through the glass, the pounding of the bass vibrating throught his palm when he touched it. Some group from the 'eighties, Sons of the West or something, singing, "Live it up, live it up, Ronnie's got a new gun," and as he watched, smiling helplessly, Clare shimmied back and forth shaking some sort of dried herb from a little glass bottle into an enamelled pot on the stove. He started laughing at the point where the music blasted, "You can take all your flags and march 'em up and down," because she did just that, swinging her hips and jabbing a wooden spoon in the air. Russ knocked loudly on the door before he could scare her by suddenly appearing in her window when she turned around.

He startled her anyway. She spun at the sound, dropping the spoon, her stockinged feet slipping on the floor. She didn't screech, but she did clap a hand dramatically to her chest as she reached for the door. "Holy cow, you nearly gave me a heart attack," she said, standing in the door-way.

"Sorry." He retreated down a step, so her eyes were almost level with his. Coming over in person suddenly seemed intrusive. "I'm sorry, I should have just called."

"I tried to reach you at the station," she said, crossing her arms around herself against the cold. A gust of wind stirred her hair. "Good lord, it's freezing out here. Please, come in."

He paused. "Just for a minute." He stomped more snow off on the top step. There was a wide rubber mat inside the door and beside it, a cardboard moving box held rubber rain-boots and a pair of wet running shoes. A coat tree tilted precariously toward the telephone, weighed down by the Millers Kill police-issue parka she still hadn't returned.

She shut the door behind him. Her arms were still crossed, the wooden spoon clenched in one fist. "Please. Take your things off. Can I—oh, dang!" A dollop of tomato sauce had dripped off the spoon onto the worn white linoleum. Clare grabbed a rag and swiped at it while Russ shucked off his parka and hung it on the opposite side of the tree. There was a calendar thumbtacked into the wall next to the phone, picturing a stained glass window. There were saints listed in most of the days, and each Sunday was highlighted in red.

Clare tossed the rag into a bland, stainless steel sink, and replaced the spoon in the pot. She leaned one hip against the counter, her arms crossed again, while Russ rocked back and forth in his boots, reluctant to tread muck all over her floor, hesitant about taking them off.

"Oh, take off your boots and sit a spell," Clare said, as if he were a book she could read. Bent over unlacing, he could hear her deep breath. "I wanted to apologize for last night," she said. "I never just break down like that. It was inappropriate and poorly timed and I'm sorry." It sounded as if she had practiced the speech.

Russ straightened, sliding his boots off heel by heel. "Never? You never break down and cry?"

A flush rose in her cheeks. "Okay, almost never. Certainly not with someone I haven't known for very long." She clapped her hands to her cheeks. "Oh, this is embarrassing."

He sat in one of the four wooden chairs clustered around the kitchen table. "Funny. It doesn't feel as if we haven't known each other for very long. Does it?"

She blinked. "Honestly? No. It doesn't."

He spread his hands. "Remember what you asked me last night? 'Who do you go to when you feel this way?' "

She smiled faintly, then laughed, a breathing out kind of laugh. "You're doing me, aren't you? That's supposed to be me. Okay, okay, you're right. I guess I don't need to apologize for dumping on you."

"I bet you'd call it 'sharing' or 'venting' if somebody did it to you."

"Hmmmm." She turned to the stove to transfer sauteed mushrooms from an iron skillet to the sauce pot.

The rectory kitchen was a faded white, with a dull and unpolished white linoleum floor, unornamented white cupboard doors, a serviceable white refrigerator, and a matching dishwasher next to the sink. The whole room had been turned out as cheaply and inoffensively as possible around fifteen or twenty years ago, he guessed. Reminded him of army housing.

Clare had evidently dealt with the blandness by littering the refrigerator door with photos, clippings, and cartoons, and hanging up a series of framed prints, each one featuring a single vegetable: an improbably wide carrot, a voluptuous eggplant, an aggressive tomato.

Crimson and yellow canisters marched across the white and gray-veined countertops, accompanied by thick glass jars filled with exotically-shaped pastas. The sauce pot she was vigorously stirring was a startling cobalt blue, and whatever was in it, it smelled to him like he had died and gone to Provence.

She turned back to him in time to see the expression on his face. She laughed. "Hungry? Why don't you stay for supper?"

"Oh, no. No, I couldn't," he said, as unconvincingly as possible.

She opened the refrigerator door, retrieved a wedge of cheese and plunked it on a cutting board in front of him. "You can grate the Parmesan," she said. She rummaged in one of the drawers a moment before handing him what looked like the top of an egg beater with no beaters attached. "Just stick a chunk of cheese in that opening there and turn the handle," she said, pointing. "It does all the work. Grates hazelnuts, too."

She opened the oven door, releasing a cloud of bread-flavored steam. His stomach rumbled at the smell like a dog whining to be fed. "Almost done," she said, shutting the door and retrieving her wine glass. She leaned against the counter. "I went with Kristen McWhorter today to her parent's apartment."

"That dump? Jesus, you—sorry—you shouldn't be wandering around that neighborhood by yourself. And for God's sake, stay away from that family until we've closed on whoever killed McWhorter."

"For God's sake? For God's sake I should stay away?" She grinned at him hugely. He shook his head, pushed his glasses up his nose and applied himself to the overcomplicated grating gadget she had stuck him with.

"As I was saying, I met Brenda McWhorter, and she told me that between the time I saw him at St. Alban's and the time he showed up dead, Darrell McWhorter got in touch with the man he said was Cody's father. Evidently, he had seen the two of them together some time before Katie left for college, although Brenda didn't know anything about it. Obviously, he thought he could get money out of the guy by threatening to reveal his identity."

"What?" He let the grater drop to the cutting board, a pungent chunk of Parmesan still stuck in its basket. "He made a call to Cody's father? Was she sure? It couldn't have been to Katie's killer? Darrell knew who had killed her and was preparing to blackmail him?"

She tucked her hair behind her ears. "He told Brenda he knew who had fathered Katie's baby. She didn't know his name or their plans for meeting." She grimaced. "The woman was so self-absorbed, it was scary. She hadn't even been bothered that Darrell was going to cut a deal with the man who might very well be her daughter's killer."

He picked up the grater and pressed the cheese further into the opening. "That's assuming we're dealing with one person. That Katie's lover was also her killer. And Darrell's."

She sipped her wine. "It certainly indicates they were one and the same."

He finally jammed the Parmesan in and slid the cover shut. He cranked hard, nearly wrenching the gadget from his hand. He gripped it more tightly and tried again. The nutty-sweet smell of Parmesan burst from the grater as he showered the cutting board with fine shavings. "I was going with this scenario: Geoff Burns killed Katie, Darrell had something that linked Burns to her murder and threatened him, Burns met with Darrell and iced him. Literally."

"But if Darrell was blackmailing the father of the baby, and not Geoff Burns . . ."

"Maybe he was working both of them. There's no guarantee whoever it was met with Darrell, after all. Maybe he had the wrong guy, anyway. What if he was thinking of some boy she walked home from school with, or went to the sock hop with?"

Clare pulled a chair from under the table and straddled it backwards, still holding her wine glass. "Listen to you. Have you ever heard of Occam's Razor?"

"No. What is it, like a Columbian necktie?"

"It's a principle of logic that says that the simplest theory is usually the right one. Which is simpler, that Geoff Burns killed Katie, negotiated with Darrell, was blackmailed by Darrell who also and at the same time was blackmailing Cody's biological father, and shot him? Oh, also rifling Katie's student digs and returning home in time for us to see both their cars in their driveway at eleven thirty?" She pointed a finger at him. "Or is it simpler to say there's one man, who fathered Katie's child, and in a panic to cover it up, killed both Katie and her dad, the only two people who could reveal his identity?"

"Murder isn't something you can apply principals of logic to, Clare. Bad guys kill people for reasons that are too stupid to believe."

"I'm not saying his reasoning was logical. I'm saying we need to be logical."

"We do?" He shook a last few flakes of Parmesan free and laid the grater on the board. "We?"

She pushed back her chair and took the cutting board to the counter. "You know what I mean." She pointed to one of the cupboards. "Plates are in there."

Dinner was a lamb stew thick with winter vegetables, garnished with Parmesan. He went through half the loaf of golden-crusted bread sopping up the sauce. "Where'd you learn to cook like this?" he asked between mouthfuls.

"My grandmother Fergusson. We went to live with her and Paw-paw when I was seven. I was a handful. A tomboy in a household of Southern ladies and mad at the world to boot. One day she caught me dropping eggs off the veranda to see what would happen to 'em. She marched me into the kitchen and tied about an acre of apron around me and said, 'I'm going to teach you to put those eggs to better use, missy.'" She smiled. "First thing she taught me to make was meringue. Talk about starting at the top."

He grinned. "I can just see you. You must have been a cute kid."

"Lord, no. I was a homely little girl. My sister got the looks."

He shook his head. "There isn't such a thing as a homely little girl." He tore off another hunk of bread. "And I've seen pictures of your sister. She was pretty, yeah, but pretty like hundreds of other girls. You," he dabbed the bread in the air as if sketching her, "you're . . . memorable. Who you are just shines through your face." He popped the bread in his mouth and watched, amused, as she blushed bright red. "You're one fine-looking woman, Reverend." She clapped her hands over her cheeks. He laughed.

She snorted loudly and jumped up from the table to ladle more stew into her bowl. "I should have you meet my mother. She loooves," she drawled out the word, "a flatterin' man." She turned and batted her eyelashes hard enough to create a breeze. "More stew, Chief?"

He surrendered his bowl. "Yeah. Sounds like you miss your family."

"Sometimes." She put his stew in front of him and sat down. "Sometimes I'm glad we have some distance between us. My decision to enter the priesthood, coming on the heels of Grace's death, was hard for them. It wasn't what they had wanted for me."

"You can't blame them. It's a lot to give up." He blew on a spoonful of stew. "All parents want their kids to have the same things they had. Marriage and a family. I know my mom regrets that Linda and I never had any children."

She leaned back in her chair, her head cocked. "Marriage and a family?"

"You know, giving that up to be a priest."

She grinned, then quickly covered her smile with her hand. "I think you're under some misapprehension here. Episcopalian priests don't take a vow of chastity. We can get married, have kids, the whole nine yards."

"What?" He dropped his spoon into the bowl and stared at her. "But the old priest, the one you replaced, he was there forever and he never—"

"Some priests choose to remain celibate. But it's just that, a choice. Not an obligation."

"Huh. If that don't beat all." He watched as she devoured a wad of sauce-soaked bread. He felt unsettled and annoyed, as if she had deliberately kept the truth from him. He tried to picture her going out for a night on the town with a man and his mind drew a blank. "You'd think they'd just call you ministers, then, instead of all this priest business and the white collar and all."

She sighed, pushed her chair back and headed for the living room. "Hang on," she said. She reemerged a minute later to hand him a large paperback.

"*The History and Customs of the Episcopal Church in America*," he read. "Sounds like a real page turner."

"If I can read up on the Iroquois Nation, you can read up on my church. Now, finish that stew up and you can have some pumpkin roll for dessert."

He declined dessert on behalf of his waistband, which had a tendency to shrink in the wash when he ate too much. She turned down his offer to help wash the pots and pans, but she did let him load the dishwasher.

"Would you like some coffee?"

"No, I'd better get going. It's late." He climbed back into his boots and parka. "Thanks for the dinner."

"It was my pleasure. Company makes the meal, Grandmother Fergusson used to say."

He stuck out his hand just as she wrapped her arms around herself. Like an idiot, he shoved his hands into his pockets just as she reached out to shake. Finally, he slapped his hand around hers and pumped her arm like he was at a Rotary Club Meeting. Over the lingering odors of dinner, he could smell her, fresh and green, like new-mown hay in his brother-in-law's field. "Night, now," he said, and yanked open the door so hard he could hear the hinges bite into wood. They both looked at the door frame. He turned to her, frowning. "And for God's sake, lock your doors."

The squad car was freezing. He cursed the heater, cursed the weather, cursed the drive back to a dark and empty house. Why the hell had Linda gone on this fabric-buying trip anyway? He wanted her home. Only two more days. Then he'd feel better.

CHAPTER
NINETEEN

Clare knew she ought to be more interested in the boiler. She flexed her chilly fingers together and glanced at the papers on the black oak table, listening for the telltale hiss and rattle of the radiators. She seemed to be the only one who noticed that the meeting room—the entire parish hall—never warmed up, so Robert Corlew's projections on repairing the aging water heater ought to have her spellbound. Contractors, unfortunately, rarely made compelling speakers.

"—rests directly on blocks, so that the insulation can be applied—"

She needed to be getting more sleep. Through diamond-paned windows, she could see the front corner of St. Alban's, its stone walls massed like a storm front against the wan December light. So little daylight on a Friday afternoon, she thought, already noon and only four more hours 'til sunset. A month or more until she could see longer days. She flexed her shoulders back, stretching the neckline of her thick wool sweater, causing her collar to tug against her throat. She turned her attention back to the table, where Vaughn Fowler was calling the vote.

"Aye," she said, copying the rest of the votes. Had she just agreed to replacing the hot water heater with a nuclear powered furnace?

"All right, then, we're agreed to hold off replacing Old Bessy until the replacement prices go down this summer."

Serves you right, missy, she could hear her grandmother Fergusson say. *If you're cold, put on another sweater.*

Terence McKellan and Mrs. Marshall pushed their high-backed chairs away from the table. "Before you go," Clare said, "I'd like to update you on the Burnses' situation. The letter-writing campaign is going very well, with lots of participation. The police have a strong lead on the identity of Cody's father, and as soon as he's identified, we're going to try to persuade him to sign adoption papers naming the Burnses as parents." At least she hoped someone would be able to get the paperwork in front of him before Russ hauled him off to jail. "With that in mind, I have some more facts and figures about the mother-and-baby outreach project that I intend to present at our next meeting."

Sterling Sumner harrumphed, but the rest of the board managed at least polite expressions of interest. The meeting adjourned. Clare headed straight for the coffee machine. She poured herself a cup, yawning convulsively.

"Tired?" Terry McKellan grinned. His coat's moulton collar, the same color as his moustache, made his fat, friendly face look like Mr. Badger in *Wind in the Willows*.

Clare nodded. "You'd think with sixteen hours of night, I'd be getting more sleep, wouldn't you?"

He grinned. "Only if you're not up on police business."

Clare started. She hadn't told anyone about chasing down Darrell McWhorter's murder scene or questioning Kristen. "What? I'm sorry, I don't . . . ?"

"I understand there was a cop car in your driveway last night." He winked. "And your car was at the police chief's all night Wednesday. Small town, Reverend Clare."

She gaped. "Good heavens." Gossip had simply never occured to her. Especially when the whole thing was so innocent.

McKellan grinned again, wiggling his badger-colored eyebrows for effect. "May be time to trade that MG of yours for something less conspicuious. Come to my bank, I'll make sure you get a great rate on a loan."

"Mr. McKellan! Chief Van Alstyne is a married man!"

"So?"

She sighed with exasperation. "He had been in an armed confrontation earlier that day. I was at his place Wednesday for counseling." *Stretch the truth too far, missy, and it'll snap back to hit you in the nose,* her grandmother said. She ignored the waspish voice. "It was snowing hard by the time I left, so he drove me home instead of me taking my car, which, as everyone keeps pointing out, is terrible in winter driving conditions."

McKellan looked disappointed.

"Last night, he stopped by around dinner and I invited him to share a little stew with me while we discussed the Burnses and the baby." It really had been entirely innocent. She had never done or said anything to Russ that she couldn't have done or said in front of the entire vestry. So why did she feel like she was lying to Terry McKellan?

He squeezed her sweatered arm. "I'm suitably chastized. Next person I hear talking about it, I'll set him straight."

"Thank you."

"You should still come in and see me about a car loan, though."

In the parish office, Clare hitched one hip onto the unnaturally neat desk. "Lois, have you heard any gossip about—" she looked at the secretary's disdainful expression. "Never mind."

Lois tore off a pink memo slip and handed it to the priest. "Gossip." She sniffed. "Never listen to it, never repeat it."

Clare glanced at Lois's Parker-penmanship writing. "The Department of Human Services? For me? How did—" she looked at the memo again, "—Ms. Dunkling sound?"

"Ms. Dunkling sounded just a tad put out."

"Just a tad, huh? Guess that means the letter-writing campaign is having some effect."

Lois lowered her reading glasses and raised her eyebrows. "Uh-huh."

"No sense putting it off. Better beard the lion in her den. Lioness." Clare reversed step in the hall and poked her head back through the door. "And can you speak to Mr. Hadley about getting some wood and kindling into my office? I don't intend to shiver all winter long with a perfectly good fireplace just sitting there."

She pretended to ignore the warning that floated down the hallway after her. "Winter hasn't even begun yet, Reverend . . ."

The radiator was wheezing under its window in a respectable effort to take the chill off. Clare slipped her copy of Mr. Corlew's report in the "Building Maintenance" file, which already took up an entire desk drawer and threatened to spill over into a cardboard filing box at any moment. She poured a cup of coffee from her thermos, grimaced at the taste, and abandoned it on the bookshelf cabinet. Her desk chair creaked and snapped as she sat down and reached for the phone. Waiting for Ms. Dunkling to come on the line, she flipped through her calendar. Infirmary visits. Music meeting. Stewardship committee. Marriage counseling. "Yes, hello. Angela Dunkling, please. Clare Fergusson." She frowned and jotted down a note to call Kristen McWhorter about the funerals. "Ms. Dunkling? This is Clare Fergusson of St. Alban's."

"Yes, Ms. Fergusson. I called you about these letters I've been getting from your membership." The voice on the other end of the line sounded nasal and inflectionless, like someone who had long ago memorized her speech and could recite it without thought or effort. "DHS is not an organization you can lobby, Ms. Fergusson. We have a legislative mandate to answer only to the best interests of the families we serve. Taking time out to read and answer a bunch of letters only results in less time and resources for our vital mission to protect the children of New York."

Clare frowned. "Are you saying that getting information about Cody's prospective adoptive parents isn't an important part of your job?"

Angela Dunkling let out an irritated snort. "Of course it is. Believe me, we have considerable information on the Burnses already. We don't need to hear from everybody who goes to church with them about what a great couple they are."

Clare tucked a strand of hair behind her ear. If the letters were so ineffective, why was she getting this call from a DHS caseworker? "Why not simply file the letters in with the other information you have, then? Why are you answering them?"

"Let's not pussyfoot around this, okay? Your people are sending us letters, and they're getting their state legislators and senators to send us letters, too. I don't need some House Rep breathing down my neck over this just because some supporter of his has decided the Burnses would make ideal parents. It's our job to determine what living arrangements will serve the best interest of the child. We're still waiting on the police investigation to try to track down the biological parents of the child."

"Parent. His mother is dead."

"Father, then. The child can't be cleared for adoption until we've made a final determination of his status vis-à-vis his father or living relatives."

"So meanwhile, Cody spends his first formative year in a foster home instead of with his future parents?"

"Ms. Fergusson, he's in a perfectly good home with a caring, experienced foster mom. I'll give you her number and you can check her out yourself if you're so concerned." There was a pause, the faint sound of a filofax flipping. "Deborah McDonald. 555-9385. Believe me, we're not running orphanages out of Charles Dickens." Ms. Dunkling sighed exasperatedly. "Do you have any idea how many prospective parents are out there looking for the Great White Baby? There are couples who've been on lists a lot longer than the Burnses. Why should they get to jump line?"

"Because Cody's biological parents left a note saying so?"

"Forget it. Call off your hounds, Ms. Fergusson. We don't need the additional headache and believe me, it's not going to alter our final disposition in the case. If you want to help the Burnses, tell them to settle down and learn to work with the system instead of trying to manipulate it to serve their own purposes. And tell them to stop making unauthorized visits to Mrs. McDonald. They know the rules."

"What—they've been just stopping by to see Cody? That's a problem?"

"Yeah, it is a problem. As prospective adoptive parents, they shouldn't be seeing the child without DHS supervision. Call Mrs. McDonald, she'll tell you. Wednesday, Geoff Burns showed up without so much as a phone call at eight o'clock at night. Believe me, stunts like that aren't going to help their application any."

Clare rested a hand on her open calendar. "This past Wednesday? The eighth?" The night Darrell McWhorter was killed.

"Yeah. Why?"

"No reason. Yes, I'll talk with them about that."

"And you'll stop the letters?"

Clare paused for a fraction of a second. "I'll pass on your comments to my parishioners. I can only suggest, I can't order them to do anything."

The DHS caseworker grunted. "I'll look forward to being able to get back to work without attempts at coercion, then."

Clare rang off quickly. She tapped a finger on the square labeled "Wednesday, 8th." Eight o'clock. Russ said they had told his officers they had been home all night. Perhaps Geoff Burns considered that to be the end of the workday and not the night? Maybe he stopped by Mrs. McDonald's on his way home and hadn't thought to mention it. Maybe he had driven straight home and spent the rest of the night watching TV with his wife. Maybe he had a passenger in his car when he visited Cody. Maybe he killed Darrell McWhorter, drove to Albany, rifled Katie's room and returned to Millers Kill with no one the wiser.

Clare folded her arms against her desk and slid flat until her head was resting on her arms. Dear Lord. She closed her eyes. Please, please don't let me have been wrong about them.

TWENTY

Clare grimaced at the back of the eighteen-wheeler spraying dirty slush over her windshield. The plows had cleared the roads efficiently after Wednesday's snowfall, but the same wet combination of grit and salt that gave her enough traction to navigate through the winding hills to Fort Henry had turned her car's Scarlet Metallic Special Lacquer finish—for which she had paid an extra seven hundred dollars in the days when she was young and flush—into a drab sparrow color identical to every other car she passed. She wondered how Russ and his officers identified vehicles when they all looked as if they'd been spray-painted with industrial waste. He was right, she was going to have to get another car. She could almost hear the salt eating away at the undercarriage as she drove.

She glanced down at the directions Deborah McDonald had given her. "I'd be happy for you to come call, Reverend," the foster mother had told her in their brief phone call. "All the ways I've had babies come into my care, and never by being dropped at a church doorstep. It's a miracle you were there, that's what I believe. A miracle." Clare gripped her steering wheel more tightly and thumbed a spray of blue antifreeze across the windshield.

The McDonald's vinyl-sided garrison looked as if it had been plucked from some densely populated suburb and capriciously planted on a windy hillside surrounded by pasturage. Two life-sized plastic snowmen flanking the front steps and a plyboard Santa-with-reindeer did nothing to ease the loneliness of the house, whose only neighbor was a dairy farm a half mile down the twisting road.

The woman who opened the door to Clare's knock was like her home, a disconcerting blend of bare-bones plainness and cozy domesticity. Angular, unhandsome, with tightly permed hair and coffee colored eyes, wearing double-knit polyester pants and a sweatshirt decorated with puffy bears. Deborah McDonald smiled widely and took both Clare's hands in her own.

"You must be the minister. I'm so glad to meet you. Come in, come in!" Her kitchen was country cute and immaculate. "I was saying to Keith, that's my husband, that of all the babies I took in, there never was one left on the church steps. Thank goodness you were there. Take off your coat! Can I offer you some coffee? Hot cocoa? You have to tell me what to call you. Our minister goes by the name of Mr. Simms— we're Church of Christ—but I know you folks may do differently. We have lady ministers, too, you know. Not here, of course, but other places. I seem to recall reading in the *Evangel* there was one in New Jersey."

Clare accepted the proffered coffee. The geese marching around the rim reminded her of the mugs in Russ' office. "Call me Clare. Please. I appreciate you seeing me, Mrs. McDonald."

"Deborah, call me Deborah. All these years and 'Mrs. McDonald' still sounds like my mother-in-law, though she's eighty and living up at the Infirmary now." She tilted her head toward a bulletin board covered with photographs of infants, children, teens, and young adults. "After all the kids I've had, 'Mom' seems more natural than my own name."

Clare examined the faces on the wall. "Looks like quite a crew. They must have kept you busy."

Deborah laughed. "Still do. I make it my business to knit something for each one of my kids for Christmas. Hats, scarves, mittens, the like. I start in January. I'm down to just three more to go. Four, including Cody. I'm doing up a little hat for him."

Clare, whose only craft accomplishment was refinishing furniture, almost missed the baby's name while contemplating the scope of the foster mother's gift-making project. Cody. Right. "Is the baby asleep?"

"Lord, yes, you'd be able to hear him if he wasn't. He's a noisy boy, that one, always wanting to talk with us." Deborah gestured Clare through the archway leading from the kitchen into the living room. "He gets the cutest expression, too, like he's thinking, 'Who said that?' whenever he makes a noise." She led Clare through a carpeted hallway into a white-walled nursery with two cribs. The windows and cribs were swathed with petticoat fabric, and dancing bears lined the walls like gingerbread men.

Cody sprawled in the middle of one of the cribs, his round tummy pushing out his fuzzy blue sleeper. "Gosh. He's gotten bigger. I can't believe it's only been ten days since I saw him last." Clare found it hard to connect this fat and contented infant with the bundle she had unwrapped that night in the parish kitchen.

"He's close to ten pounds. The doctor's very pleased."

Ten pounds must be good. "Shouldn't he be sleeping on his stomach?"

"Oh, no. Only on the back, we know that these days. Cuts down on the instances of crib death." Deborah smiled at Cody, the chocolate-sundae smile people get around babies. "We don't want anything happening to this little guy."

Clare reached inside the crib. "May I?"

"Touch him? Go ahead, until he's hungry again nothing's going to wake him up."

Clare settled her whole hand over Cody's head and blessed him with an inarticulate surge of tenderness and amazement that the most helpless of creatures were caught and held by God. As she signed the cross on his forehead, Deborah nudged her arm and pointed to a needlepoint hanging near the window. HE KEEPS HIS EYE ON THE SPARROW it read. "Yes," Clare said. "Yes, he does."

In the living room, Clare admired more pictures of graduations and proms and weddings before getting to the point. "I understand the Burnses have been visiting Cody. Did Ms. Dunkling from DHS tell you about the note that was left with Cody?"

"Ayuh, she did, she's kept me up to date on everything about Cody. She's wonderful that way."

"Is it true Mr. Burns was here this past Wednesday? In the evening?"

"Ayuh, though that's not the only time it's happened. Mrs. Burns showed up at the pediatrician's office when I took Cody in for his checkup. And they came 'round unsupervised a day or two after I got him, although to be fair, there hadn't been much time to arrange a proper visitation and they did call first."

"Did Mr. Burns call before he stopped by that night?"

Deborah crossed her legs, a slither of polyester. "No, he didn't, and to tell you the truth, the whole visit made me nervous. I won't say he was drunk, because he wasn't, but he smelled like he had definitely dropped off at the Dew Drop Inn for a few after work."

Clare shook her head. "After work?"

"I figured he must have left his office, gone out for a beer or two and then hit on the bright idea to visit Cody. He was still in his coat and tie. Really, I don't like to complain. I understand how hard it is for the adoptive parents to wait, and I'm not against a few visits. I like the company, and it's good for the kids and the parents. But, Lord!" She threw her hands in the air. "I can't have folks showing up here at eight o'clock at night, sulking all over my living room and disturbing the baby's routine."

"Geoff Burns seemed sulky?"

"I guess angry would be a better word. He showed up without so much as a by-your-leave, invited himself in just as I was getting ready for Cody's eight o'clock feeding, and acted mad at the whole world. Insisted on holding the baby, but he was so mad or tense or something that he got Cody all riled up and the poor thing wouldn't settle down to his bottle for over half an hour." She leaned forward. "Babies can sense people's moods very well in their body language, you know."

Clare took a drink of coffee. The newspaper headline she envisioned, PRIEST SUPPORTS MURDERER'S ATTEMPT TO ADOPT VICTIM'S CHILD had been joined by a subsidiary lead: DIOCESE SUED BY DEPARTMENT OF HUMAN SERVICES.

"Deborah," she said, "how long does it take to get to the Old Schuylerville Road from here?"

"Hmmm? Are you heading that way next? Let's see, if you take the turn at Power's Corners and then use old Route eleven, you can reach it in about ten minutes."

"Ten minutes." Long enough to get to the spot where Darrell McWhorter's body had been dumped, take off for Albany, and still be home in time to meet the Millers Kill police at his front door. Clare had a sudden urge to drive to the Burnses' office right that minute. She wanted the truth from them, no matter how wrong it might prove her instincts.

She put her coffee on a needlepoint coaster. "Deborah, thank you so much for having me over to take a look at Cody and chat." She stood. "I'd like to stop by and see him again sometime, if you wouldn't mind."

Deborah McDonald stood, gathering the mugs in one hand. "Not at all. I'm glad of the company, like I said."

The two women walked to the kitchen. "I promise you I'll talk to the Burnses and mention your concerns."

The foster mother unhooked Clare's coat from the rack. "I appreciate the chance to let 'em know without having to go through DHS and making it all official. I'm sure they're perfectly nice people. Just terrible eager for their baby by this point, I imagine. I've seen it before. Waiting on a baby when you can't have one of your own makes folks a little crazy at times."

Clare had to drive around the block three times before a parking space opened up. It looked as if the boutique owners at this end of Main Street would have a merry Christmas. She could have found a space more readily a few blocks away, but she still hadn't gotten around to shopping for new boots and her low suede ones had already seen more than enough snow and salt.

The Burnses' receptionist looked up, startled, when Clare came through the stairwell door.

"Ummm . . . can I help you?"

"Yes. I'm Clare Fergusson. I need to see Mr. Burns right away. Or Mrs. Burns, if he's unavailable." Clare unzipped her coat and let it drop onto the asymmetrically striped sofa.

"I'm sorry, Mr. Burns is in court all afternoon and Mrs. Burns is working out of her home today. I could make you an appointment for tomorrow . . . ?"

"Oh—" Clare bit down hard on what she had been about to say, "— gosh darn." She snatched up her coat again. "No, thanks. I'll try to get Mrs. Burns at home."

On the drive to the Burnses' house, Clare tried out what she might say. Karen, did your husband shoot Darrell McWhorter? Or how about,

Karen, did your husband father a child and try to cover it up with this abandoned-at-the-church-doorstep scheme and when that fell through, did he start killing everyone else involved? "Oh, shoot me now," Clare groaned.

The Burnses' house was a brick Italianate revival with five-foot-high windows and a cupola that must have given them a view of the entire town. Wreaths decorated with wooden fruits hung from the deeply-paneled front doors, which had the look of an unused entrance. Down the long drive, by the separate garage at the corner of the house, Clare found the back door.

Karen Burns opened at the second ring. "Reverend Fergusson? What brings you out here?"

"Well, I—" Clare stamped her boots on the welcome mat.

"Please, come on in. No need to stand in the cold to talk."

Clare pushed into the narrow hall lined with hanging coats, boots, shelves of hats and gloves. She left her coat, following Karen into the kitchen.

"Is this about the letter-writing campaign? I've gotten some wonderfully supportive notes and phone calls from people, you know. Mrs. Strathclyde told me she actually called our congressman's office to complain. Can you believe it?" Karen led Clare through a high-ceilinged, granite-countered kitchen into a small den done up in burgundy and hunter green. Karen waved at the glass-fronted barrister's bookcases and the computer centered on a wide mahogany desk. "My home office. I work here about seventy-five percent of the time, now. When we adopt Cody, I'll be able to switch to a twenty-hour-a-week schedule without making any drastic changes." She gestured toward a tapestry-covered love seat.

Clare sat. She took a steadying breath. "Karen, I didn't come to discuss the letters."

Karen sank gracefully into a green leather chair. "You didn't."

"I know that the police have been asking you about the night Darrell McWhorter was killed. I know you both claim to have come straight home from work."

"Claim?"

Clare leaned forward, trying to meet the other woman's eyes. Karen tilted her head, examining her hands. Her fingernail polish matched the study's rug. "I know Geoff wasn't at home at eight o'clock that night. He was at Cody's foster mother's house. Wearing a suit and tie, as if he'd come straight from work, and smelling as if he'd had a drink or two."

The lawyer looked straight at Clare, her beautiful face calm. "What are you suggesting?"

"It looks bad, that's what I'm suggesting! Karen, you two have got to tell the police the truth. What happened that night?"

Karen looked toward the bookcase. "Nothing." She compressed her lips into a tight line. "I don't know."

Clare slid to the end of the love seat until their knees almost touched. "Tell me what you do know."

The other woman continued staring at the bookcase. Clare touched her arm. "Please, Karen. I want to help you. And Geoff. But you have to be honest with me."

There was a pause. Slowly, Karen turned her head to face the priest. "We had a horrible fight that afternoon in the office. We had been arguing about what approach to take with McWhorter all day long and we got . . . it just . . . anyway, I told him what he could do, and took off. I was so angry with him I wanted to . . ." She blew out a breath. "I did a little shopping, I called my mother, I fixed some stir fry for dinner— you know, working the mad off." She laced her fingers together. "Dinnertime came and went, with no Geoff, and no phone call. I started to get worried. I mean, really worried; the weather was bad and he was driving the little Honda Civic. Finally, finally he showed up around ten or so." She shook her head. "I didn't know whether to kill him or kiss him. Turns out he'd been out at the Dew Drop Inn most of the night. I don't know how he managed to get himself home, he was in no condition to drive. I was horrified! He could have killed himself. Not to mention the damage to his reputation if he had been picked up. The last thing we need is a morals censure from the Bar Association or a D.U.I. conviction on his record."

Clare pressed her forefingers against her mouth to refrain from mentioning that Geoff could just as well have killed other people out on the roads that night. "Does this sort of thing happen often?" she asked, her voice neutral.

"God, no. Geoff's idea of a blowout indulgence is a bottle of Nouveaux Beaujolais the week it hits the stores. So you can imagine how I felt when those two officers showed up at the door asking where we had been that evening! All I could think of was Geoff being hauled in for questioning. So I told them we'd been home all night, having a few drinks and watching TV." She sagged back into her chair. "Geoff just went along with my story." Her gaze went to the ceiling, as if looking for the Fates lurking there. "Yesterday, when we learned that Mc-Whorter had been killed, it was too damn late to recant. There wasn't anyone except a few anonymous bar patrons to say he'd been at the Dew Drop instead of . . ."

"Instead of taking Darrell McWhorter on his last drive to Albany?"

"Yes. We had already lied to the police. As you said, it looks bad."

Clare tilted her head back, closing her eyes. Did she believe Karen Burns? Yes? The question was, did she believe Geoff Burns told the truth to his wife? "You've got to tell this to the police. You and Geoff."

"No!"

"Do you believe your husband's story about what happened Wednesday night?"

"Yes, of course. He would never lie to me."

"Then tell Chief Van Alstyne. Geoff's absence that night is going to come out sooner or later. If you wait until the police find out on their own, the two of you are going to look guilty as sin. Go to Van Alstyne's office, tell him what you've just told me, admit that you were both royal idiots to lie about it, and offer to enroll Geoff in one of those driver education courses. Voluntarily."

"What? There's no way they can prove drunk driving after the fact—"

"We're not talking about legalities, Karen, we're talking about admitting you did something wrong and setting it right. Confession and repentance." She braced her elbows on her knees. "Because on a moral and emotional level, you aren't going to be able to continue on with this lie weighing you down. And because on a practical level, if you don't cop to the drinking and driving and lying, your husband's going to look like a murderer when the police do find out."

Karen pressed the palm of her hand to her forehead, half-shielding her face from Clare's direct stare. "There's a good chance they won't find out," she said, trying the idea on for size.

Clare exploded out of the love seat. "There's no chance Chief Van Alstyne won't find out, Karen, because if you don't tell him, I will!"

"You can't do that!"

"I can't tell him anything of this conversation we're having right now, no. I can certainly tell him Ms. Dunkling of the Department of Human Services called me to complain that your husband was at Cody's foster mother's house Wednesday night. And I can tell him Deborah Mc-Donald confirmed Geoff was upset and smelled like he'd been drinking."

Clare collapsed back into the love seat. "I'll do everything I can to help you talk to the police. I'll do everything I can to help you become Cody's parents. But I won't compromise the truth for you. I won't help you stand in the way of finding Katie McWhorter's killer. We owe her that. We all owe her that."

"You're lucky he's in. Five minutes more and you would have missed him." Harlene punched the intercom button on her heavy, licorice-colored telephone. "Chief? Reverend Clare's here to see you. And Karen Burns."

The door to his office banged open and the chief of police strode out. His gaze flicked between Clare and Karen, back to Clare, finally settling on Mrs. Burns. "What can I do for you ladies?"

Clare tucked a strand of hair behind her ear, suddenly aware of the effortless chic of the woman standing beside her. She looked like a badly-tailored crow next to Karen's drapey wool separates and hundred-dollar haircut. Which was ridiculous. Appearance was not what was important here. She tugged her bulky, faded sweater down, revealing more of her clerical collar.

"Mrs. Burns?" Russ said. "Reverend Fergusson?"

Karen looked uneasily at Clare. "I . . . uh . . . was going to wait for my husband, but he's being held over in a deposition . . ."

Russ tilted his head a little to the side. His eyes narrowed thoughtfully. "Why don't you come into the interview room with me. We can be more private there."

Karen nodded. "Clare, will you stay with me?"

"Of course."

Russ looked at her hard while pulling out a chair for Karen, asking what was going on as clearly as if he'd said it. Clare raised her eyebrows, radiating encouragement. He rolled his eyes at her before crossing the room and taking a seat opposite Karen. Clare seated herself.

"Mind if I tape this? I hate to have misunderstandings later on because we're remembering different things." He rested his hand easily on a cheap portable tape recorder.

Karen frowned. "As long as you make it clear I'm speaking without an attorney."

"Oh? Do you need one?"

Karen flushed. "As you say, I'd just hate to have misunderstandings later on."

He nodded, turning on the tape machine. "This is Chief Van Alstyne, interviewing Karen Burns." He glanced at Clare. "Accompanied by her priest, Reverend Clare Fergusson. Ms. Burns is unrepresented by legal counsel." He looked at Karen. She nodded. "The date is Friday, December tenth, and the time is . . ." he glanced at his watch, "six P.M."

Karen took a deep breath and began. Clare listened to her voice, calm and orderly. Her recounting of the events of Wednesday night was organized, yet compelling. Clare propped her chin in her hand, struck by Karen's poise. She must make a dynamic advocate in court. Russ, on the other hand, looked less than impressed. He sat with one hand resting on the tape recorder and the other splayed across a pad of paper. Clare supposed his expression could qualify as neutral, but she could see something underneath. Disapproval? Skepticism? She bit her lower lip. It was important that he treat Karen right. How else could he encourage this kind of honesty?

When she concluded her story, Karen folded her hands, as if waiting for comment. Russ chewed the inside of his cheek for a moment. He tapped the tape machine a few times. "Your husband was driving a Honda Civic that night?"

"That's correct. He uses it instead of his Saab when the roads are salty."

"Has he driven it anywhere since that night?"

"Yes . . . he's got it today. He likes me to keep the Land Rover, in case I need the four-wheel-drive. Why?"

"Was he drinking at the Dew Drop Inn before he went to Mrs. McDonald's?"

"No, that's in the opposite direction from our office and her house. Um . . . he didn't actually say, but I assumed he'd gone to the Sign of the Musket after work. That's where we usually go for Happy Hour."

"Mrs. Burns, when you spoke to Officer Entwhistle Wednesday night, you said you own a nine millimeter Smith and Wesson, registered to yourself, and that you keep it in your Land Rover for times when you're on the road by yourself."

"That's . . . correct. I have clients spread out between Albany and Plattsburgh, and a woman traveling alone can be vulnerable. What relevance does this have, Chief?"

"Is that gun still in your Land Rover?"

"Yes."

"You sure?"

"Yes!"

Russ nodded. He popped the tape from the machine and rose from the table. "Will you wait here for a moment? I'll be right back." He closed the door on his way out.

Karen jerked around in her seat. "Clare, I don't like this. I do not like this at all."

Clare rested her hand on the other woman's forearm. "Karen, we knew he'd be suspicious. After all, you did lie before. I'm sure Chief Van Alstyne wants to check with someone at the, what was it? Sign of the Musket? And at the Dew Drop Inn."

"You're right." Karen sighed. "He's going to want to talk to Geoff, too. Oh, God, I should have just waited for him to get back from that damn deposition. We could have done this tomorrow."

By which time, Geoff could have argued her out of talking to the police. Clare patted Karen's arm and tried not to doubt Geoff Burns when she hadn't even had the chance to talk with him.

The women sat in silence as the minutes crawled by. Clare got up and checked the coffeemaker, but it was cold and dry. The plate beside it was empty. No homemade strudel today.

"What on earth is taking him so long?" Karen demanded. She pushed her chair back and stood. "I'm going to find a phone. I want to call the office and see if Geoff's there yet."

"Maybe you should wait until you hear what Chief Van Alstyne has to—"

The door opened. Russ and Officer Durkee walked in. The young man smiled discreetly at Clare, who waggled her fingers at him. He'd been good company at the hospital the night she'd found Cody.

Russ cleared his throat. Officer Durkee fell in, his face serious. Russ held up a curling sheet of fax paper. "Karen Burns," he began formally. "I have here a copy of a warrant executed by Judge Ryswick granting us permission to search your cars and to confiscate any firearms in your or your husband's possession for testing. We are also warranted to search your house for any materials possibly related to the deaths of Katie McWhorter and Darrell McWhorter." He folded the piece of paper carefully, creasing it with finger and thumb pressed tightly together. "Judge Ryswick thought our new information was sufficient to issue a separate warrant for your husband's arrest."

Karen's posture went rigid, and her arm, still holding the back of the chair, trembled slightly. She made no other sign or sound.

"However, I won't execute the arrest if Geoff presents himself to the station for questioning within the next two hours. I've sent someone to your office to let him know. If he comes home first, of course, we'll have someone there," Russ said. "Officer Durkee will accompany you to your vehicle. If you'll hand over your keys?"

"I want to call my lawyer. Now."

"There's a phone at the main desk. Mark, will you escort Mrs. Burns to the phone?"

Karen shot Clare a venomous glance. "Confession and repentance?" Her voice hissed like caustic lye. She turned and swept out of the interview room, Officer Durkee close on her heels.

Clare faced Russ. "This is absolutely outrageous!"

"Stay out of it, Clare."

"Stay out of it? I'm the one who persuaded her to come in her and tell you the truth! How you can twist that around in order to search her car and her house. . . . Are you going to arrest Geoff Burns?"

"Depends on whether he shows up or not. What he says in the interview. I may very well hold him overnight while we test the gun."

Clare clenched her teeth to keep her voice from rising. "*I* brought Karen Burns in here. *I* persuaded her to come clean with you. *I* assured her you would listen to her. I thought—"

"No, you didn't think. You just jumped in feet first without looking where you were going or considering the consequences. I'm a cop, Clare! What the hell did you expect me to do when a woman I suspect is an accessory to two murders walks in and tells me her husband was drunk and unaccounted for during the time Darrell McWhorter was killed? Shake her hand and give her a good citizenship badge? Get real!"

Clare pressed her hands flat against the table to keep them from shaking. "I was trying to help—"

"You were trying to help the Burnses, yeah, I know. And you're trying to help Kristen McWhorter, and the baby, and the unwed mothers of the world, and every damn soul you come across. That's why you're a priest, Clare. I, on the other hand, am a cop. The only thing I'm trying to do is catch the sonofabitch who killed Katie McWhorter and her father and send him to the chair. And I will do anything—anything within the law—if it means getting closer to that arrest." He spread his legs slightly and hooked his thumbs into his belt, an archetype of law enforcement authority. "If that interferes with your agenda, I'm sorry. But don't act the outraged innocent with me when I'm doing my job."

Clare flushed hotly. "You! Can kiss my ass!"

"Oh, very nice. They teach you that in seminary?"

She spun on her heel and stalked out of the room, past an embarrassed-looking Harlene, past the abandoned main desk. Behind her, she could hear Russ's voice, exasperated, angry. "Clare. Clare!"

She took the stairs two at a time and burst out into the icy night air. She interlaced her fingers tightly and took a deep breath. The cold, dry air made her cough. She clattered down the front steps, almost losing her footing, and swung around the corner into the station parking lot.

Karen was standing next to her Range Rover, arms folded. Officer Durkee was inside, his flashlight bouncing off the windows and mirrors. Karen's lips pinched together when she saw Clare. "I'm not going be able to give you a lift back to my place. My vehicle's going to be out of commission for awhile. And I have to wait for our lawyer to get here." She glanced at Durkee's shadowy form. "I've asked him to try to get a stay on the warrant."

"Karen," Clare began. "I'm so sorry . . ."

The other woman pulled a knit hat from her coat pocket and twisted her hair underneath it. Automatically, she pulled a few loose curls down here and there, framing her face. "I'm sure you are. And I'm sure that when this is all over, I'll be able to listen to your apology. But right now, I'd rather you just leave me and my husband alone."

Clare dropped her arms to her sides. She could feel a hot pricking behind her eyes. "Of course. I'm . . . I'm so sorry. I didn't think . . ." Karen's scornful look told her it was obvious she hadn't thought. Clare bobbed her head and left the parking lot as fast as she could, wanting nothing so much as to put the fiasco behind her. What had she been thinking? Her mind drew a blank. She had been dismayed that the Burnses had lied to the police. She had been hopeful that Karen's confession would finally clear them in the investigation. She had been . . . pleased with herself, bringing a new piece of information to Russ, like some attention-starved dog showing off a trick. She jammed her hands deep into her pockets in disgust. She hadn't been thinking, just feeling. And reacting.

She stopped at an intersection and waited for cars to pass. Damn, it was cold. Her ears already ached and it was another mile at least to the Burnses house, where her car was parked. Why hadn't she worn a hat? *A stitch in time saves nine*, her grandmother said. *Proper prior planning prevents piss-poor performance*. That voice belonged to the warrant officer who had taught her survival course. They were evidently in agreement with Russ.

The light turned green and she crossed. But, dammit, he was so focused on the Burnses he couldn't consider any other possibility. Why would Karen have told her about Geoff's absence the night Darrell was murdered if it wasn't to exculpate him? It was so obvious! But Russ couldn't entertain the notion that he might be wrong. Him and his 'Me cop, you priest' routine. Patronizing jerk.

The flash of red lights and brief blurp of a siren jerked her attention to the road. A cruiser was pacing her, its passenger-side window unrolled.

"Get in, I'll drive you."

"No," she told the car.

"For God's sake, Clare, just because you were wrong about the Burnses doesn't mean you have to sulk like a little kid. It's a long walk to their house."

"I can use the exercise."

"Clare, get in the goddamn car!"

"No."

"I won't ask again!"

She remained silent, facing in the direction she was walking, her eyes fixed on the building across the next intersection.

"Fine, dammit. Be that way!" The cruiser picked up speed and drove off.

In the fading rumble of its engine and the accelerating swish swish swish of its tires, she could hear her grandmother Fergusson's voice. *Self-righteousness won't mend any shoe leather, missy, and pride won't put a meal on the table.* Wrapping her arms and her self-righteousness around her, Clare trudged on into the night.

CHAPTER
TWENTY-ONE

Weekends were peak time for the Millers Kill Infirmary. Children and grandchildren and great-grandchildren, busy from Monday through Friday, would come for visits Saturday and Sunday, bringing magazines, photographs, and potted plants that the staff would labor to keep alive. So far, Clare had kept her visits to weekdays, when the corridors were largely quiet and the oldest members of her congregation were happy to see someone from the outside.

But Mr. Howard's niece had asked her to stop by to encourage the old gentleman, who had just gotten back to the Infirmary after a rough bout of pneumonia, so here she was, hoping that by showing up first thing in the morning she could avoid the sullen teenagers and guilty-looking adults who populated the corridors on Saturdays.

Mr. Howard looked weak and washed-out but seemed to be in high spirits. Clare had visited with him once before, and found what he most wanted was an audience for his stories of the Great Depression and his never-ending string of dreadful puns. He didn't acknowledge she was a priest: whether that was from faulty memory or a politely unvoiced disagreement with the ordination of women, she didn't know. They did pray together at the end of her half-hour visit, though. She wondered, leaving him with a promise to say hello to his niece, if the prayers of a man of ninety were somehow more easily heard by God. After that many years, God must seem like just one more old friend living on the other side of the divide.

At the unmanned nurses' station, Clare tucked her brown police parka under her arm and flipped through the roster of residents, finding names she knew, reading the brief notes to see if anyone was doing poorly or heading for the hospital. The sound of muffled crying caught her attention. She dropped the notebook and stepped around the counter into the corridor. An old woman dressed in a heavy floor-length robe leaned against the wall, her fist jammed into her mouth, her eyes wide and frightened.

"Hello," Clare said quietly. "Can I help you?"

"I—I don't know," the woman said. She looked about her. "I don't know where . . ."

Clare held her hand out. "Are you lost? Let me help you find out where your room is." She tucked the woman's arm under her own and craned her neck, looking for a nurse or aide.

"Do you know my husband? I'm looking for my husband." She held tightly to Clare's arm.

"I don't work here, I'm just visiting. Let's find someone who can help us."

"I'm all runny," the woman said, touching her eyes. "I need a . . . a . . ."

Clare tugged a tissue out of its box at the nurses' station. Behind a partial wall, she spotted a door marked DIRECTOR OF NURSING. "Let's try over here. Can you walk this way with me? That's great." She knocked at the door.

Nothing. Clare was about to try the nurses' station on the next floor when the door opened. "Yes?" a deep voice rumbled. The doorway was filled with an enormous bear of a man, tall, broad, well-padded, luxuriously bearded. His gaze immediately fell onto the woman clinging to Clare. "Oh, Mrs. Ausberger. Did you get lost again, dear?" He draped a massive arm around the frail lady's shoulders and guided her back to the nurses' station. He picked up a handset and punched in a number. "Staci? Can you come to three, please? Mrs. Ausberger is here." There was a pause. "Yes, probably."

Mrs. Ausberger patted the man's tweed jacket, visibly calmed by his presence. "Oh, you smell just like my husband. Just like my husband."

The man grinned sheepishly at Clare. "You two caught me smoking a pipe in my office. I know I'm not supposed to, but I hate going outside to puff away on these cold days. Takes all the pleasure out of it, reminds me that it's really just a filthy addiction." He reached out with his right hand. "I'm Paul Foubert. Director of Nursing."

"Clare Fergusson. I'm the new priest at St. Alban's."

"Yep, the collar kind of gives you away. Thanks for rescuing Mrs. Ausberger. She's been known to wander pretty far afield. Hey, Staci, great."

A cute young woman barely out of her teens clattered down the corridor. "Sorry, Paul. I was fixing Mrs. Meerkill's hair in the bathroom and didn't realize she had slipped out." She took Mrs. Augsberger's hand. "C'mon, Mrs. A. How 'bout we get you washed up and I'll make your hair pretty."

"My husband likes my hair down."

"You're not going to be seeing your husband today, Mrs. A. But your grandson Nicholas will be visiting with his family. Won't that be nice?" The girl's cheerful voice faded as the pair turned the corner.

Clare looked up at Paul Foubert. "Her husband?"

"Dead ten years." They both looked down the empty corridor. Foubert idly slapped his hands against his coat pockets. "Damn. Left my lighter in the office. Why don't you come in for a minute or two?"

The director of nursing's office was appropriately den-like in brick and wood. Tall shelves crammed with books and memorabilia lined one wall, facing a collection of obviously amateur artwork, undoubtedly done by residents of the Infirmary. Foubert gestured to one of the comfortable chairs facing his generously cluttered desk before settling himself into a well-sprung leather armchair.

"So, how long have you been at St. Albans?"

Clare propped her leg on the opposite knee. "A little over a month. It's been . . . hectic. I'm still trying to get to the point where I don't have to have a directory to remember my parishioners' names and a map spread over my legs when I go out for a drive."

Foubert picked up a pipe from a lumpy, half-glazed ashtray. "Do you mind?"

"Not at all."

He tamped in fresh tobacco. "What do you think of our Infirmary?"

"It seems like a good facility. The staff members I've met have all been pleasant and helpful. Caring. I imagine the small size helps. I did some work at a nursing home in Virginia while I was at seminary. It was huge. Well-run, but impersonal."

"Mmmm. I've been fortunate to be able to get good people, both staff and volunteers. You're right, being small does help. Makes it more like family. Before we moved here, I was at a large facility in New York City, and Lord, sometimes it felt like a body warehouse."

"You're not from here?"

He lit the pipe. The rich tobacco tang filled the room. "I am, originally. My dad worked in the mill. I escaped to the big city like a lot of kids and didn't return until I was a burnout case, with nowhere else to go. I've been here eight years now."

Clare glanced at the multiple diplomas hanging on the wall opposite the windows. "Some people would say running a nursing home is a burnout job."

"Oh, no. Caring for men struck down in the prime of their lives, watching a dozen of your best friends die, that's burnout." He waved his pipe toward the rest of the Infirmary. "This is much more peaceful. It's—you'll pardon the slightly facist sound of this—the natural order. It's a privilege to help our oldest through the ends of their lives. I try to impress that on everyone who works here, because I've found folks who don't feel that way tend to get depressed and impatient with our residents."

Clare nodded. "I'll consider myself impressed upon." The diploma wall also held a photo collage that stretched a good three feet square. She could pick out shots of parties and Christmas celebrations, elderly residents surrounded by three and four generations of family, doctors in white lab coats and nurses in cheerful-print smocks. A very large Easter Bunny in one picture turned out to be Foubert himself. She laughed.

"My Hall of Fame. Or Shame, as the case may be."

"We have a similar one hanging outside our parish hall. But your pictures are definitely more fun than ours." She opened her mouth soundlessly, struck by a sudden thought. "Are there pictures of all your volunteers here?"

"There sure are. We couldn't run this place without them. I can't afford to hire LPNs to do what they're willing to do for free."

"You must have a photo of Katie McWhorter, then."

Foubert's pleasant expression tightened under his bushy eyebrows. "I read about her in the paper." He looked down at the pipe in his hand. The tobacco smouldered fragrantly. "She was such a wonderful kid. A little too much on the serious side for her age, but a damn hard worker. And smart." He shook his head. "What a waste." He looked up. "You leave the city to get away from that sort of thing, but it's everywhere nowadays, isn't it? There isn't any safe spot anymore." He rose from behind his desk and hunkered down in front of the collage. "Here she is. This was taken last year, at the Christmas party. She was prettier than she photographed. It was her expression, I think."

Clare got out of her chair for a better view.

"The residents loved her. She never got antsy around them, the way some of our teenage volunteers do. She liked being here."

"Who's the boy with his arm around her? He looks sort of . . . have I seen him here during one of my visits?" "

"No, he's off to college as well. That's her sweetheart, Wes Fowler. He was another volunteer." Foubert laughed softly. "They used to take breaks together, go out to his car. Later I'd see them come in all pinked up and grinning. Kids." His smile faded. "What a waste. What a terrible waste. I remember once when—"

Clare sat back in her chair. Foubert's voice seemed to come from far away, as if he were on the radio in another room. Her ears buzzed.

Wes Fowler.

What had Doctor Anne's son said about the boy? Serious, studious, hard working. Just like Katie.

Golden boy. From a family that had everything the McWhorter's didn't. The Fowlers three-thousand-square-foot dream home was maybe ten miles from the apartment on Depot Street, but it could just as well have been on the other side of the planet.

A boy who had everything going for him, including an appointment to West Point and a beautiful girlfriend from a family as well-respected as his own. What would a boy like that do to hide a screwup? A really big, life-altering, won't-go-away-for-the-next-eighteen-years screwup?

Wes Fowler.

The boy Katie didn't want her family to know about. He evidently felt the same way about keeping it secret.

She was going to have to tell Vaughn Fowler and his wife about this. Oh, God.

"—you'd think, wouldn't you? Reverend Fergusson?"

"Huh?"

"Are you okay? You look odd."

"I feel odd. I mean—yes, I'm okay."

She stood up. Foubert rose with her, clasping one huge paw around her arm. "Are you sure?"

"Yes, thank you." She smiled at him, a kind of social grimace. "I do need to be going, though. I just remembered something important."

"Alright, then." He cradled his pipe in the ashtray. "I wish I knew who to send my condolences to about Katie. She never talked about her family."

"She has a sister, Kristen. She's asked me to perform the burial service, as it happens. If you'd like, I'll let you know when and where. She has to wait until the police, um . . ."

"Yeah. I do. I'd like that, please." Foubert plucked a business card off his desk and handed it to her.

Hand halfway to her pocket, Clare stopped. "Paul, could I borrow the photograph of Katie? I'll return it."

He squatted and peeled the picture off the board, balling up sticky gum between his fingers before giving it to Clare.

"Thank you."

He opened the office door and ushered her out. "I'll be hearing from you, then. Stop by the next time you're visiting, will you?"

"I sure will do that, yes." She took off with indecent haste. The photograph of the young couple, projections for the cost of the church roof, Karen Burns's angry face, all jostled for space at the front of her consciousness.

Wes Fowler! My God!

There was a Pathfinder parked next to the Fowler's Explorer at the top of their long, well-plowed drive. Clare pulled in close behind them and killed her engine. The two hulking SUVs could probably four-wheel-drive straight over her windshield and down the back of her car without noticing more than a little bump. She rested her head on the steering wheel for a moment, reaching for the sense of someone outside her and within her, looking for strength, looking for courage. Asking for the right words to come when she needed them.

Gravel and snow crunched underfoot as she walked up to the side porch. The Fowler's home was a modern interpretation of a Georgian house, a sweep of white clapboard frequently broken by double-glazed windows with Palladian arches. At some point, the rolling acreage upon which the house sat must have been a farm, but it was all pleasure land now, the pastures used only for cross-country skiing and snowmobiling. Idyllic spot to be a retired gentleman. Pressing on the bell, Clare felt like the angel with the flaming sword, sent to roust the inhabitants out of their Eden.

"Reverend Fergusson! What brings you out here?"

Edith Fowler was a horsy-looking woman whose extreme slenderness was beginning to look bony with age. Her short brown hair was clipped to a sporty, no-nonsense length and she wore pearls and a shetland sweater over a monogrammed turtleneck. Clare pulled her hat off. *If someone had been strangled with a shetland sweater from Talbots*, she had said to Russ, laughing at the idea of one of her congregants commiting murder.

"Honey? Who is it?" Vaughn Fowler crowded around his wife's shoulder as she was standing back to let Clare in the door. "Clare. This is an unexpected pleasure."

Clare stuffed her gloves into the pockets of her oversized parka and pulled it off. "I apologize for intruding, but I needed to speak with you." Edith Fowler took the coat and hung it in the hall closet. "Both of you."

The couple looked at each other. "We're entertaining right now . . ." Edith said hesitantly.

"It shouldn't take long. It is important."

Vaughn gestured her through the kitchen door. "Of course." Inside the kitchen, preparations for a brunch were obviously in progress. Bowls of batter, a carton of eggs, cutting boards of chopped vegetables. And, sipping what looked like mimosas, were the Shatthams. Clare smiled feebly. Great. They were probably getting ready to toast Wes and Alyson's engagement or something.

The Shatthams greeted her warmly, which made her feel even guiltier for what she was about to lay on the Fowlers. "Clare needs to speak with me and Edith for a few minutes," Vaughn said. "I know you two can entertain yourselves."

"Barb, give a quick poke to the sausages, will you?" Edith asked.

"In here's my study. Right next to the kitchen in case I get a snack attack while working." Vaughn let Clare and his wife enter the room, then shut the door behind them. The study was a monument to Fowler's family and military career. Photos and maps and trophies and a few threadbare battalion flags.

"Working?" Clare asked, temporizing the moment of truth.

"On a history of Washington county." He waved toward a pigeonholed desk, where an electric Remington typewriter sat next to several hardbound books. "It's going to fill in the gaps other histories leave out." Clare bent down to examine a black-and-white photograph of a lean young man in fatigues standing next to a general with a whole salad of ribbons on his chest. Both men were squinting into the sun, smiling stiffly.

"Sir. Is that you?"

"With my father. 1965. Day before I shipped to Vietnam."

"You look just like him." Clare straightened. Edith Fowler looked at her husband, who cocked his head toward Clare.

"You needed to speak with us about . . ."

She took a deep breath. "Sir . . . Vaughn . . . you recall when Chief Van Alstyne was showing the photographs of the dead girl in the parish hall? You said you'd never seen her before."

"Of course I remember. That's not the sort of everyday Sunday you're likely to forget."

"We know the girl's identity now."

"Yes, I know. Mitch and Barb told us all about it. Alyson identified her as one of her classmates."

"Yes, sir. Her name was Katie McWhorter." Clare clasped her hands behind her back. "Did your son ever mention that name?"

Fowler looked at his wife. "No," she said. "What on earth does this have to do with Wes?"

"Today I discovered your son was seeing Katie McWhorter secretly. They were volunteers at the Infirmary together, as well as being in the same class at the high school. The director of nursing told me he used to see them sneaking off to neck. Whatever it was, it probably started in the fall, when Katie broke up with her boyfriend. It was certainly going on at Christmastime last year."

"Wait a minute," Fowler said, turning toward his wife again. "Wasn't he going out with Alyson last year?"

"Of course he was." Edith Fowler frowned at Clare. "If you had to speak with us about our son cheating on his girlfriend, Reverend Fergusson, I'm afraid I don't see the point. Nor do I see that it's any business of yours."

Clare bit the tip of her tongue. "Katie McWhorter had a baby just a week or so before she was killed. So far, the police haven't been able to identify the baby's father."

"So far? Are you suggesting—"

"Calm down, Edie. Clare, you don't know our son. If anything, he's overly responsible. And devoted to Alyson. Maybe he did have a little romance with this girl, but there's no way he'd be so thoughtless as to risk a pregnancy."

"This is ridiculous. How do you know it's not some other boy anyway?"

"I have a photograph of them taken at the Infirmary Christmas party last year. It's—" she reached into her pants pockets, coming up with nothing more than a fistful of change and a wadded tissue. "I left it in my coat pocket." She let her hands drop. "I'm not saying that your son is involved in Katie McWhorter's murder. I'm suggesting that he may have fathered her child. We know she had a boyfriend that she didn't want her family to know about. Somebody accompanied her to a local motel around Thanksgiving and stayed with her while she had the baby. She named him Cody, wrote a note asking that he be adopted by Geoff and Karen Burns, and left him on the kitchen steps at St. Alban's, despite having no connection to the church." She flipped her hands open. "Don't you see? Wes had a reason to want to stay anonymous. He was home around Thanksgiving, right?"

Vaughn Fowler nodded.

"And he's a member of the church. He would have known about the Burnses looking for a child."

Edith Fowler covered her mouth for a moment. "Oh, dear God. Vaughn, do you think . . . ?"

"I don't know. It's a long chain of supposition from just one link." He looked at the floor, frowning. "Have you been to the police with this, yet?"

"No. Chief Van Alstyne is . . ." she paused, reining in the anger she still felt from yesterday. ". . . anxious to find the killer. He's been frustrated so far, and he's pouncing on possibilities without giving them much thought." Had Geoff Burns been arrested yet? Not that Karen would call and tell her. "I'm afraid that if he hears about the connection between Wes and Katie, he'll leap straight to the conclusion that Wes murdered her. And probably Darrell McWhorter as well." Darrell had looked at the parish bulletin board before changing his mind about giving Cody to the Burnses. He had seen Wes's picture there, with his family. And made a phone call that afternoon. "Does Wes have access to any money?" she asked.

"What?"

"Certainly. He has an account with a bank in West Point."

"Sorry, I was just thinking." A scared kid with his own cash made an easy target for blackmail. She glanced at Mrs. Fowler, leaning against her husband. Maybe their son was a murderer. One way or another, though, she was going to make damn sure she had gathered some evidence before handing the boy over to Russ's tender mercies. "Let me check this out some before we involve the police," she said.

Vaughn nodded. "I want Wes here to answer questions." He looked at his watch. "I can head for West Point later this afternoon and bring him back tomorrow morning first thing."

"Good. I'm going down to Albany. Katie's sister gave me the address yesterday. I'll talk to Katie's housemates, and see what they remember. Do you have a picture of Wes I could borrow?" She looked around the room. All the family photos were framed and hanging on the walls.

"Here, take this." Edith Fowler grabbed a large bound volume off the coffee table. "It's his high school yearbook."

"Thank you. I—"

"I'd like to see that photograph you have," Edith went on. "Just to make sure there's no mix-up."

"Of course."

Vaughn opened the door. In the kitchen, the Shatthams were intently poring over cookbooks. Clare wondered how soundproof the study door was.

"All set. We'll just see Reverend Fergusson out."

In the hall foyer, Edith handed Clare her coat. "Thank you. It's—" Clare yanked her gloves from the pocket and dug inside. "—right here."

The Fowlers examined the Polaroid. Edith made a soft noise.

"It's him, all right," Vaughn said, his voice gravelly. "I'll get him on the phone right away. I want to get to the bottom of this." He shook his head. "May we keep this?"

Clare reached for the picture. "I'd like to take it with me to Albany. I hope it's nothing, but it may need to go to the police." She deposited it back into her pocket.

There was a noise from the kitchen entrance. "We wanted to say good-bye," Mitchell Shattham said hesitantly.

"Edie, are you all right?" his wife asked. Edith Fowler shook her head.

"We'll want to get in touch with you as soon as you're back from Albany," Vaughn said.

"I'll stop by my office. You can leave me a message and I'll call you from there." She tucked the yearbook under her arm and shook hands with the Fowlers. "I'm sorry to lay all this on you this morning. I sincerely hope I'm wrong." She waved to the Shatthams as she stepped off the porch. Before the door closed, she could see Barbara Shattham embracing Edith Fowler.

In her car, Clare let her head drop back against the headrest and closed her eyes, boneless. She opened them again. Through steel and glass, she could hear the familiar flat pulsing of rotors. She pressed her face against the chilly window. There it was, at maybe eight hundred feet, flying northwest. Maybe a skiing trip. She squinted. Looked like a Bell AH-51. Good ship, fast, reliable. Before she left Virginia, she had been trying to talk her dad into replacing his old OH-50.

Shifting, she flipped open the glove compartment and flicked through the maps there. Eastern New York State, with a city map of Albany. She folded the heavy paper into a manageable size and started the engine. She could see the helicopter in the passenger-side window now. As she watched, unable to look away, it heeled its tail rotor up, accelerating toward the Adirondacks. She rubbed a gloved hand over her dry lips. God. She wished she were up there right now.

CHAPTER

TWENTY-TWO

Emily Colbaum was a tiny, fey girl with huge brown eyes and a close-cropped haircut that looked like Audrey Hepburn on speed. She stood in the doorway of the room she had once shared with Katie McWhorter, crossing and uncrossing her arms. "You see, Reverend? I mean, I'm not a complete slob, but it would be hard to know what went missing."

Clare crawled backwards from underneath Katie's bed. "I'm really not so concerned about what the man took. I was hoping maybe there was something left behind. A photograph, a note from a phone message . . . something." She grunted in frustration as she clambered to her feet.

"The cops were pretty thorough. Of course, I think they were thinking, like, drugs, or something bad like that, like the only thing that could get a girl killed was either a rapist or being mixed up in something bad." Emily crossed her arms around herself again. "Katie wasn't like that."

"I know." Clare sat on the bed that had been Katie's. The posters on her half of the room ran heavily to cute kittens with inspirational sayings and landscapes with greeting-card poetry. There was nothing hinting of a secret life in her messy desk and overstuffed bookcase. Clare brushed a piece of a dust bunny off her nose. She was eighteen, and pregnant. Let's say by Wes Fowler. She didn't want anyone to know. Why?

"Emily, did Katie ever talk about what she wanted to do after college?"

"Oh, sure. She wanted to get into computers. Maybe Web designing, SYSOP, she had lots of ideas. She wanted her own business, to work for herself. She could have done it, too. She was just amazingly hardworking. She was like, never partying or blowing off class."

"So getting married or having children right away wasn't in her plan."

"No way. I couldn't believe it when they told me she'd had a baby. I just couldn't believe it."

"Hey, who's here?" A black girl trailing layers of knitwear sidled around Emily into the room. She had multiple earrings and a small stud set in one nostril. "Hi, I'm Ebony."

"Ebony rooms with Sara, across the hall."

"Yeah, the room where you don't have to listen to that nasty dog next door."

"Yeah, but you get the street lamp all night long. This is Reverend Clare, from Katie's hometown. She's kind of helping Katie's sister."

"Hi, Ebony." Clare rose and shook the girl's hand. "I have a picture I already showed Emily, of Katie with a boy. I think he might be the father of her baby." She dug into her pants pocket, grateful she was wearing off-duty khakis and a wool turtleneck instead of her usual garb. "Have you ever seen him?"

Ebony studied the photograph. She shook her head. "No. I'm sorry. I don't think I ever saw any guy with Katie, you know? She was . . . focused. She wanted to hit the ground running."

"I was telling the Rev how I was, like, in disbelief when I heard she had had a baby."

"Oh, yeah," Ebony agreed, handing the photo back to Clare. "I thought she was just putting on weight. We all were complaining about the food, and the freshman fifteen and all that stuff. Most of us eat at the dining halls, and man, that stuff is nasty for your figure."

"I remember," Clare said, smiling a little. "Look, I left a yearbook from Katie's high school downstairs. There are some more pictures of the boy—his name is Wes. Did she ever mention that name?"

Ebony and Emily looked at each other.

"You ever hear that?"

"Nope."

"Me, neither."

"Would you take a look at the yearbook? Just in case?"

The living room of the group house was cheerfully ramshackle, furnished with someone's old family-room sofa, crate-style and director's chairs, an elaborately-carved coffee table that had been the height of Mediterranean chic in 1972, and the ubiquitous cinder-block-and-board shelving. The girls sat on the sofa together. Clare retrieved the yearbook from the coffee table.

"This is his senior picture." Wes was a good-looking boy, square-jawed and athletic, a young version of his father.

"What is this, skinhead hair?"

"No, he's in the U.S. Military Academy."

"And he got an early start on the buzzcut thing. No, I've never seen this guy." Ebony leafed through a few pages. "Here's Katie." She read the script below the photograph. " 'SUNY Albany. Favorite memory of MKHS, the junior trip car wash fund-raiser, and Mr. Delogue's class. Quote: I think I can, I think I can.' " She flipped through a few more pages. "Man, I knew she came from a small town. Look at these folks. What's the matter, they don't allow black people in Millers Kill?"

"Ebony!" Emily squealed.

Clare smiled crookedly. "Let's just say that diversity is not their strong suit."

"No lie. Hey, Em. Isn't this that girl who came to see Katie at the beginning of the year?"

"What? Who?" Clare leaned over the coffee table to see.

"This blonde copping an attitude. Remember her, Em?"

On a page of candid photographs, Ebony had one finger squarely on a *Seventeen* magazine blonde with perfect skin and a form-fitting tie-dyed dress.

"Alyson Shattham was here visiting Katie?" Clare blinked in disbelief.

"It wasn't like, a social call." Emily said. "She was a bitch on wheels."

"She had some sort of problem with Katie. Actually, she had a problem with all of us. Acted like her shit didn't smell." Ebony looked at Clare, biting her lip. "Oh. Sorry, Reverend. I forgot."

"That's okay. Tell me what you remember about Alyson's visit."

"She wanted to speak with Katie. She was, like, very rude. They went into the kitchen to talk and shut the door."

"She was definitely riding Katie. But Katie, she could hold her own. I don't know what they went on about while they were in the kitchen, but blondie flounced out of here like somebody had caught her tail in a crack."

"Did Katie ever tell you what they talked about?"

"No. She was, like, very private with stuff bothering her. She would smile and change the subject if you asked if she was okay. Like, she didn't want to burden anybody."

Ebony nodded in agreement.

"Did either of you ever see Alyson here again? Or did Katie mention she saw her again?"

Ebony and Emily looked at each other.

"You ever see her after that time?"

"Nope."

"Me, neither."

Clare stood up straight and rubbed her forefinger across her lips. Alyson Shattham. Now that was interesting.

Clare picked up the yearbook. "I think I'll show this around at the computer center where Katie worked. Maybe someone there overheard her or saw her with either Wes or Alyson." She glanced out the window. "Then I'd better head back home. I don't want to get caught in any more of this upstate weather. I have a friend who doesn't trust my car in the snow."

Clare checked her rearview mirror, changed lanes, and wedged her soda between her thighs. She adjusted the radio tuner as an eighteen-wheeler passed her. Traffic was light on the Northway this Saturday afternoon.

"WNCR's accu-weather update!" the speakers blared. She turned the volume down. "A low pressure system continues to move in fast from the northeast," the announcer said portentously. "I'm looking for snow to start mid-afternoon, with temperatures falling into the single digits by nightfall and increasing storm intensity. Accumulations from four to six inches along the Hudson Valley areas, higher in the mountains. Get out those skis if you haven't already, because it's prime time at the peaks!" The weather report broke for an ad extolling snowboarding at Hidden Valley Ski Area.

"Wonderful," Clare muttered. She ate a few more french fries. She was a long way from being able to "smell snow" as Russ claimed he could do, but even she could tell the lead-gray clouds darkening the sky to the north meant another snowstorm. Didn't it ever stop snowing up here?

"Is it my imagination, or is this a really snowy December?" the DJ asked.

"It's not your imagination, Lisa, this is the third snowiest December since 1957," the smooth-voiced weatherman said. "And with the storms now forming over the Rockies and the Canadian plains, we may set a new record before the month is over."

Clare groaned.

"So get out and get that Christmas shopping done before you're stuck indoors waiting for the plows, right, Dave?"

"That's right, Lisa!"

"Let's have something seasonal, then!"

Harry Connick, Jr.'s voice filled the car. "I'm dreaming of a white Christmas . . ." Clare picked her bacon burger off the yearbook cover. She might as well have left Albany right after talking with Emily and Ebony, instead of waiting until the afternoon, risking driving into the storm. No one at the university's computer center could recall seeing Katie with Wes or Alyson.

She chewed her rapidly-cooling burger thoughtfully. Alyson had lied straight out to her, Russ, and her parents. Maybe Wes had thrown her over for Katie. Could she have murdered in a fit of jealousy? What could she have said to have lured Katie back to Millers Kill? Had she found out about the baby, somehow?

Keeping her eyes on the highway, Clare groped for a napkin and wiped her mouth. She found it easy to think the worst of Alyson. Something about that girl got under her skin. Who would have guessed she still had unresolved issues from her high-school days as an ugly duckling? She frowned. Maybe Alyson and Wes both did it, like that high-school couple out in Texas, who had murdered a girl who threatened their romance.

She sighed. She was going to have to call Russ and tell him everything she'd found out. The convoluted strands of this case twisted around like bad wiring, an offense to her pilot's sense of order. Maybe he had been right to jump on the Burnses. Not because they had been guilty, but because trying to put together the events of the crime with only pieces of motivation and insight into the human heart was hopeless. Real, physical evidence, that's what pointed the finger at the guilty. Besides, how was she going to get Alyson to talk to her? Russ was . . . was . . . not entirely right. But he was a little right when he told her to leave it to the professionals. Although if he thought she was going to admit that over the phone, he had another think coming.

She pulled into the tiny parking area behind St. Alban's an hour or so before sunset, grateful to have beaten out the storm. She had no illusions about her winter driving skills. She unlocked the back door and made her way up to her office, pausing to plug in the coffeemaker. Lois must have turned down the thermostat when she left at noon, since the parish hall was even colder than usual. Clare could up the setting by a few degrees, but her first good look at the yearly oil bills a few days ago had shown her exactly why the church was rarely warmer than 62 degrees, even in the coldest weather. She sighed. Mr. Hadley would be in at 5:30 tomorrow morning to turn the heat up before the services. She could tough it out for a few hours this afternoon.

She carried her coffee into her office. As if in answer to her virtuous intentions, there was an iron carrier overflowing with split logs and a basket of kindling next to the fireplace. "Mr. Hadley!" she said. "You dear, sweet man!"

She had once read that a fire actually takes warm air out of a room, but you couldn't prove it by her. With flames popping the logs and the iron fire-back radiating heat, she finally felt warm enough to take off her parka. Reaching for the phone, she shook her head in bemusement. Computers and cell phones and nuclear power and space shuttles, and here she was, heating herself like a curate in a Dickens novel.

"Millers Kill Police. May I help you?"

"Harlene? It's Clare Fergusson. Is the chief in?"

"He sure isn't, Clare. But I know he's been trying to get ahold of you. I expect him back within an hour or so. Want to leave a message?"

"He's been trying to reach me? Okay. Yes . . . tell him I called, and that I'll be here at my office for a couple of hours. I need to speak with him about Katie McWhorter's case."

"I'll do that. Have a good one."

"Thanks, Harlene. You, too."

She clunked down the receiver. Tapped a pencil against her lips. May as well get the messages and start returning calls. Maybe the Fowlers had spoken to Wes and persuaded him to tell the truth about his relationship with Katie. And there was Alyson to consider. It was probably a bad idea to talk with the Shatthams before she heard back from Russ.

She retraced her steps to the main office and pressed the messages button on Lois's phone. The first message was from Russ. "Just calling to see how everything's going. Give me a call when you get in." The second was someone asking about early-morning services, the third was from the Cutlers, wanting to know their pledge balance. The forth and fifth were also from Russ. "I've tried calling your home. Are you out, or what? Give me a call when you get this, will you?" The last message was from Edith Fowler. "Reverend Clare? Vaughn and I spoke briefly with Wes this morning. I don't want to go into it over the machine, I'm sure you'll understand. Vaughn called the Commandant and has permission to pick up Wes for the rest of the weekend. If the driving's not too bad, they'll be back late tonight, otherwise he'll stay over and they'll return tomorrow. Can we all meet tomorrow afternoon? Let me know. 555-1903."

Six or seven pink memo slips poked out of her mail cubbie on the wall. She squinted against the growing dimness in the hall, reading them on the way back to her room. Inquiry about a christening. Possible new members. Sterling Sumner wants another meeting about the boiler. Chief Van Alstyne called, no message.

Kristen McWhorter called, left no return number. Most urgent, underscored by Lois's confident pen. Has info re: who killed her father. She and mother are hiding out—here Lois had made a big, black question mark and exclamation—at cousin's hunting cabin. Please come at once. Mother does not trust police. The detailed directions to the cabin covered the rest of the pink slip and continued onto another.

"Lois!" Clare said to her fireplace. "Couldn't you put the 'most urgent' one on top? Holy cow." Too many years as a church secretary undoubtedly gave a person a jaundiced view of others' emergencies. She took a quick gulp of coffee and donned the police parka. She really did need to get her own someday soon. She stuffed the directions into her pocket and pulled on her gloves. Kristen's call had come in just at noon, three and a half hours ago. She must be frantic by now.

Outside, snow was showering down in tiny, dry flakes, freckling her cheeks and nose as she brushed off her windshield. There wasn't that much accumulation yet. If it took her less than an hour to reach the cabin, she shouldn't have too much difficulty with the roads. The MG's engine roared to life reassuringly. Of course, she might not be able to get back out until the storm finished up. She used the last napkin to wipe the melted snow off her face. When she had been young and romantic, she had fantasized about being snowbound in a rustic cabin. But she had for sure never pictured Brenda McWhorter in there with her.

Route 9 North was well-trafficked and easy to drive, even though the plows hadn't been out yet. She exited near Lake Lucerne and took River Road south. To her left, the Hudson River ran high and fast, carrying away clots of snow and ice in its gray waters. Far fewer cars kept her company here. Snakes of snow slithered across the road, obscuring the macadam. She glanced at her directions. The right onto Tenant Mountain Road turned her due west, but there was no sign of impending sunset behind the hills ascending in front of her, only an iron shell of sky and the snow, falling faster and harder against her windshield. Infrequently, she passed houses, their lights glowing through the swirling flakes like figures inside glass snow globes. Beautiful and unreachable. The sense of isolation pricked at her. Skittered. She turned the radio up for its illusion of company.

She spotted Alan's Gas and Grocery, the landmark mentioned in her directions. From here it was two miles to the road leading directly up into the mountains. It was a small general store with lighted signs blazing cheerfully if commercially through the storm. COCA COLA! BUDWEISER! DIESEL, $1.00! She almost pulled over. It would be dry and safe, there would be a phone, she could admit she was too inexperienced to be driving in this weather and call—who? One of the congregation? A taxi?

She gritted her teeth. Russ was the only person she considered enough of a friend to ask for a favor like that. She drove past the entrance to the grocery's tiny parking lot. How could she come begging for a ride like a stranded teenager after yesterday? She blew out a gusty breath. Her inexperience at winter driving, and the unfamiliar landscape, were making her jittery. If she calmed down, drove carefully, and didn't run scared to the nearest big, strong man to save her, she'd be fine. Alan's Gas and Grocery disappeared from her rearview mirror. Two miles to the turnoff. Six miles to the camp road. Less than a mile to the cabin. Even if she had to drop down from her current speed of thirty miles an hour, it shouldn't take her more than twenty minutes. Then she would whap Kristen upside the head for not leaving a phone number where she could be reached.

She slowed as she hit the two-mile mark. Her headlights shone blurrily through the gathering dark, their edges softened by the snowfall, their light swallowed up in the storm. Two large stone cairns marked the otherwise signless road. Hidden under white, they looked like lean and misshapen snowmen, and she was suddenly sorry she had thought Mrs. McDonald's plastic snowmen were tacky. On a night like this, they would be beacons of hospitality, marking the boundary between safety and the storm.

She set the trip odometer to zero, turned, fishtailed, over-compensated, then recovered. The MG pulled steadily along the line of ascent. The trees closed in heavily, shrouding the road, giving some protection against the full force of the snowfall. The twilight turned the sky, the air, the snow shades of underwater blue, as if she were piloting through a drowned world. She downshifted, and the engine growled as her tires churned through the light, dry snow. The headlights picked out a few well-covered tracks, but no one had driven through recently enough to compact the snow, which made it easier for her front wheels to get the traction she needed.

The road wound its way up the mountain, never stretching more than a few car-lengths before disappearing around another bend. There was still light enough to clearly see the outlines of the culverts on either side and Clare kept her speed to a steady twenty-five miles an hour, grateful she wasn't trying to navigate the twisty turns in total darkness. She passed an opening in the trees and realized it must be another camp road. She bit her lip. Kristen had better have been dead-on accurate about the miles to the turnoff, or she was going to be lost but good on this God-forsaken road.

Rounding the next bend, she saw twin lights, small and bright as halogen bulbs, windshield-high in the middle of the road. She slammed on the brakes at the same moment the lights resolved themselves into eyes and her car skidded past harmlessly as a buck bounded off the road into the cover of the brush. She swore out loud for the first time in three weeks and it felt so good she continued to rain down curses on every deer in New York State as she coaxed her car into a straight line and slowly, slowly accelerated.

A mile up the mountain, there was another narrow, unmarked road, barely visible through the encroaching trees. Unplowed, of course. She was beginning to worry about getting through the camp road to Kristen's cousin's cabin. The snow was piling higher with every minute, deep enough to seriously impede her car, deep enough to make the mile walk an unthinkable misery in her lightweight boots. She turned off the radio, the better to hear the sound of her tires slurring through snow. She would just have to chance making it as far as she could toward the cabin, and if she got stuck, she would lay on the horn until Kristen came. Let her bear the burden of finding some decent footwear for slogging through the rest of the way.

The trip odometer crawled toward the six-mile mark. She speeded up the wipers, peering through the curtain of snow for the entrance to the camp road. The light had leached almost entirely away by now. She tried switching her high-beams on, but the dizzying flurry of snowflakes through the field of light and the reflected glare from the snow on the road was disorienting.

Up ahead there was a gap in the wall of trees. She slowed, and unrolled her window for a better look. It was hard to tell, but the faint depressions under the new-fallen snow seemed to be tire tracks from earlier in the day. She rolled the window back up and carefully turned onto the camp road.

Thankfully, it sloped downhill in a gentle, hillside hugging curve. Nothing requiring agile maneuvering from the already-overtaxed car. She glanced at the odometer. Almost there, although between the watery blue darkness and the screen of trees and brush and the snow, she could probably drive into the front door before spotting it. Ahead, the road rose along a lengthy, uneven incline. She groaned. On a clear fall day, that hill would be nothing but a pleasant surge under her tires and the fun of watching the leaves scatter. Now ...

She clutched the steering wheel more firmly, downshifted again, and stepped on the gas. Hard. The back end shimmied, then lurched forward, pulling hard. Clare leaned toward the windshield, as if shifting her body weight could tip the balance in favor of an uphill climb. The engine keened.

"Come on. Come on," Clare hissed between gritted teeth. The car crept upward. "Almost there, almost there . . ." She tromped down on the gas pedal a final time, laughing in triumph as the front wheels dug in, held, and hauled her over the crest of the hill. She instantly surged downhill, the car twisting violently to the left, as if the roadbed were half eaten away. The steering wheel nearly jerked from her grasp. Clare yanked her foot off the gas and slammed on her brakes. The front wheels locked. She skidded downhill, the car swinging sideways, tipping. Clare fought for control, pumping the brakes, steering out of the high-velocity skid.

She shrieked involuntarily as the car's undercarriage slammed into something low and hard, then shrieked again, louder and longer, as she tipped for real this time, crashing and bouncing and crunching over and over.

CHAPTER
TWENTY-THREE

Stillness and dark. She heaved for air, shuddering gasps sounding abnormally loud in the silent aftermath. She hung from her shoulder belt, her left arm pressing against shattered glass and smeared snow. Her car had come to rest on its side. The remains of the driver's side window showed slaggy rock. The windshield was intact, but half popped out of its rubber and chrome frame. Above her, like some crazy-cracked skylight, what had been the passenger-side window was slowly whiting out under the falling snow.

She breathed in deeper and more deeply, feeling for pain in her lungs or ribs. She shifted her legs carefully. Her knees felt like someone had been hammering on them, but all her joints moved and nothing seemed to be grinding or poking out. She reached for the door handle above her. Something twinged nastily in her side. Her gloved hand came short. She swallowed. She had to get out of the car. Hitching her hip up, she fumbled at her seatbelt latch. As she slowly shifted her weight, leading headfirst toward the passenger-side door, the car shivered. Metal screeched. Clare flung herself against the seats, clinging to the leather while the vehicle slid downward another half-foot, stopping with a kidney-bruising crunch. She was canted at an easier angle now, some of the car's weight resting on its upslope side. She pulled at the passenger door latch. It stuck. She braced her boots on the remains of the driver's door and yanked at the latch again, hunching over and throwing her shoulder against the door at the same time. It popped open with the scrape of metal against raw metal. Clare scrambled out.

She balanced unsteadily on a steep field of boulders and jagged rock, halfway down a crevasse that cut through the mountain as far as she could see upslope and down. Five or six yards beneath her it bottomed out in a wide stream, whose black waters ran fast enough to have kept it from icing over despite the past three days of below-freezing temperatures. Above her, the camp road slanted down to two blocky cement pilings and then vanished into thin air. Her car had gouged a scar along the snow, the pilings, the rubble, and scree. Reluctantly, she looked at the MG. She made a small noise in the back of her throat, resolutely turned away, and picked her way uphill slowly, testing each foothold as she climbed. When she reached the cement pilings, she propped her backside against one and rubbed her knees vigorously. Across the gorge, there might have been twin pilings underneath the unmarked snow. Hard to tell. There was certainly more road there. She could see the cleared width of it between the trees. A bridge had been here. Once.

Clare stamped her feet, knocking away some of the snow clinging to her boots. If there was a cabin in the woods over there, no one had gotten to it by this road. Which meant either the directions got garbled between Kristen and Lois, or she had taken a wrong turn somewhere, or . . . she looked again at where the road simply vanished. Or someone had sent her here. Deliberately. The thought made her stomach clench and her skin prickle coldly.

She pushed herself away from the piling and hiked the rest of the way up to the crest of the road. Whichever it was, mistake or malice, she was in a bad way. She was close to ten miles away from the last outpost of civilization she'd seen, and although her parka and sweater were keeping her upper body warm, she could already feel goose bumps beneath her cotton khakis. Her boots were a bigger problem. Even with . heavy woolen socks, her toes ached with cold. How would she feel after one mile in the snow? After five? At what point would she stop hurting and start permanently damaging her flesh?

She pulled the parka hood up and tied it under her chin. The fake fur edging tickled her cheeks. Normally, she could walk a mile easy in fifteen minutes. She started down the road, stepping inside the rapidly filling tire tracks. Fresh snow, packed snow, uneven terrain—say it would take half again as long to go a mile. Twenty-two minutes or so.

Her heel came down on something slippery and loose. She skidded, flailed, and landed hard on her backside, grunting. She picked herself up, beating snow off her pants. Make that twenty-two minutes plus time to fall down and get back up again.

At the side of the road, a dead branch was wedged between the fork of a tree. Clare yanked it loose. It was straight and spar-like, thin enough for her to grasp in one hand and long enough to test the depth of snow a few feet ahead of her. She knocked off the snow crusting its bark and continued on, bracing her steps with the stick.

All right. Ten miles to Alan's Gas and Grocery would take her four to five hours. What about another cabin? She could hike down the mountain until she reached the closest camp road. She had passed one two or three miles before reaching her turnoff. If it was another mile to a cabin it would still be less than half the distance to the store. She could have shelter. Blankets. Probably a fireplace. Maybe even, God willing, a working telephone.

Snow collected on her cheeks and chin. She scrubbed her face with her glove, trying to dry her skin as much as possible. Not heading straight for the Gas and Grocery would be risky, of course. If she couldn't find a place within a mile of the main road, she would have to retrace her steps. She pulled the parka sleeve away from her wrist and lit up her watch. Almost five o'clock. By the time she reached the next camp road, it would be full dark. Could she trust herself to stay on a narrow, unplowed road at night with a heavy snow falling? Already the underwater blueness was thickening, making distance impossible to judge, swallowing the details of the forest only a few yards away.

The thought she had been pushing aside crystalized, unavoidable. *I could die out here.* Her stomach lurched as if she'd dropped a thousand feet of altitude in a few seconds. She could become just one more missing person, her whereabouts a mystery to her family and friends, until some autumn day who-knew-how-many-years in the future, when hunters stumbled over her bones wrapped in a Millers Kill police parka.

"God," she said, her voice very small in the immense quiet of the woods, "I don't want to die. Please help me."

She poked her walking stick into a particularly deep depression one of her tires had spun into the snow. There didn't seem to be much more she could add to that prayer, unless it was, "and let me find the so-and-so who sent me directions to this place so I can throttle him or her." No, that wouldn't do.

. She braced and stepped, braced and stepped. The 139th Psalm. It had been a dim twilight, like this one, the sky dark with rain instead of lit by snow. She had been sitting by Grace's bedside, her sister's hand resting weightlessly in hers because it hurt Grace to be touched firmly. Their father had read the 139th Psalm in his deep, soft voice. "If I say, surely, the darkness shall cover me; even the night shall be light about me. Yea, the darkness hideth not from thee, but the night shineth as the day. The darkness and the light are both alike to thee." It had been the last time they had all been together. In the silence and the dark, so far from where Grace had lived and died, she felt an urgent closeness to her sister, a moment of absolute certainty that death was just a pocket-trick, that the dead were all around her, supporting her, giving her strength, pricking her with warnings to watch the road, watch the road—

A dark shape emerged from the bend in the road before her.

Clare blinked. Her heart thumped once, hard. She tightened her grip on her walking stick, wondering, even as she halted in her tracks, muscles tensing, why she wasn't running forward.

The bulky figure moved ahead another step. It was a person in a jumpsuit, one of those allover padded things they wore snowmobiling around here. Clare eased a fraction and opened her mouth to speak when a flashlight beam suddenly speared her.

"Take off your coat," a voice hissed.

Clare squinted, dazzled by the sudden light, trying to make sense out of this bizarre sequence of events.

"What?"

"Off!" The voice was guttural, deep, like a man's, but as unidentifiable as the figure behind it. The flashlight beam dipped low, as if the person had shifted it in his grasp, and Clare heard the distinctive sound of a round being chambered in an automatic pistol.

Her throat closed. Heat surged through her body. She hurled her walking stick as hard as she could toward the flashlight and dove head-first for the brush at the side of the road.

The gun went off, shattering the stillness like an axe through thin ice, dwarfing a strangled scream of "Goddamnit!" A trio of deer exploded from a thicket of trees, careening into the camp road, the beating of their hooves echoed by wings everywhere overhead, winter birds fleeing in terror.

Sprawled beneath a fir tree, Clare saw the flashlight beam arch crazily into the sky and took off, scrambling hand and foot downslope, away from the sounds of thrashing and swearing. She made it to her feet and ran a yard, two yards, three, before tripping over something buried in the snow and tumbling. She kept her momentum going, rolling forward, regaining her footing, dodging ancient oaks and dense, matted stands of fir, steadying herself on deadwood and saplings. Branches whipped her face. She changed direction, ran until she fell, pawed the snow from her face and shifted direction again. A long-thorned bush scratched and caught at her parka. She plunged through snow up to her thighs, hauled up a slide of scree and branches, her heart pounding and her breath sawing in her ears as loud as jet exhaust.

At a slight rise, she climbed a toppled pine tree and stood, gasping, to get her bearings. She couldn't see any light from where she had come. Where she thought she had come from. She shook her head, disoriented. If, as she thought, her attacker had dropped his flashlight, as soon as he found it he'd be on her trail. Her all-too-obvious trail. She gulped air, turning away from where she'd been, staking out the lay of the land ahead. Somewhere to her left, hopefully not too far, was the mountain road. If she lost that, she was dead, whether the shadowy man in the snowmobile suit caught up with her or not.

She struck out for where she thought the road must be at a diagonal, picking her route more slowly and carefully, jumping from treefall to treefall and squeezing under the thick shelter of hemlocks and firs whenever possible. She couldn't leave a clean trail, but she could put breaks in it, make it hard to follow, slow him down.

If she went straight for the road, it would only make it easier for him to catch her. Even if she could manage to run in the slippery snow, he must have a vehicle somewhere, not too far from where he ran into her, near the junction of the camp road and the mountain road.

He had a gun. He had a flashlight, was dressed for the environment, was bigger and probably heavier than she was. He wanted her dead.

She had . . . a branch of feathery needles whacked Clare in the face.

She spat out the taste of pine tar. She had a head start. She would be able to see his flashlight a long way before he saw her. Her night vision would be sharper, not relying on artificial light. He was carrying something small-caliber, without much stopping power, so he'd have to get right in close to her in order to drop her. And one other advantage: he had underestimated her, and chances were he'd keep on underestimating her. Her survival school instructor at Edgeland AFB, a shiny-headed old warrant officer nicknamed "Hardball" for obvious reasons, told them, "Biggest advantage any woman's got in an escape and evasion situation is the fact that ninety-nine percent of the men she runs into won't look past the fact she's a girl! So don't use your tits for brains!" The first time she had given up in an exercise, he made her do push-ups in the mucky Florida swamp water until she threw up. She had never surrendered again.

She could use some Florida heat right now. Her feet felt like they were being squeezed in an icy vise. She paused near an old hemlock, its trunk studded with dozens of branches starting only a few feet from the ground. She looked up, the snow pelting her eyelashes, blinking furiously. Time for her to locate an ambush site. The only way out of this forest now would be over the body of the man hunting her.

She went up the tree hand over foot, showering down snow and the odd abandoned nest. Small branches broke against her arms, smearing her coat with gummy pine tar. She climbed as high as she could, until the tree trunk shivered beneath her weight, and bent back a heavily needled branch to take in the view.

Through the murky underlight, too close for comfort, she could see the bobbing and twitching of a flashlight. Her St. Elmo's Fire, heralding death and disaster. She shifted another branch, straining to see through the snow and the darkness. She needed to find high ground. Someplace she could lure him up to, bringing him to her, letting him tire himself out.

To her right, at a distance impossible to judge in the gloom, a series of steep little hillocks rose from the general downward slope of the mountain. It would mean heading away from the road, which was a disadvantage, but there were thickets of evergreens mixed in with the birch and maples, perfect for what she had in mind. She clung to the hemlock trunk and swivelled around. If she were quick enough, she could backtrack to the small ridge she had stumbled over and make her trail from there, something big and obvious to lead him to the ambush. And her real route . . . she squinted, willing in that moment to trade a year's pay for a single set of binoculars. The last hillock was cut by a darker gash. She followed it as far as she could with her eyes. It looked as if it might be part of the crevasse that had taken her car. Running water would explain the little hills, harder stone rising from the softer earth of the mountain, eroded away each spring.

She bit her lip. The crevasse it would be. She descended from the hemlock gracelessly, crashing and dropping as fast as possible. If her assailant caught her out in the open, all the clever plans in the world wouldn't amount to a snowball in hell. She retraced her trail to the spot beneath the lip of a ridge where she had stumbled and fallen. From the well-thrashed disturbance in the snow, she set out for her ambush site, trotting in a fast, low shuffle that left a clear path plowed through the snow. She took the most direct route possible, avoiding any cover, arrowing straight for the thickest clump of fir trees at the edge of the first small hill.

It would look, she hoped, as if she had seen a potential hide and bolted. She turned and shuffled back the fifty yards or so to the ridge, more slowly, careful not to stray outside the path she had laid down. She was damp with sweat under her parka, her heart rattling the cage of her ribs from exertion and fear. Back at her starting point, she picked her way downhill, stepping on fallen branches as much as possible, swinging around tree trunks to conceal her footprints from her hunter's view. She wanted him to see nothing but the dense clumps of evergreens, see that she would have picked it as a good hidey-hole, see there were more places to huddle unseen at the top of the hill, where a frightened woman could crouch and pray to be overlooked.

From behind her, she heard a noise. She froze, crouching, her gloved hands folded against her mouth to still her breathing. It came again, a crackling. Then a scrape. She fought the urge to close her eyes like a little kid, hiding from the monsters' sight by refusing to see. There was a rushing, a clap of air, and from the corner of her eye she saw a snowy owl take wing. Her lungs wrung every ounce of oxygen from her body. For a second, she couldn't move while she tried to remember how to breathe.

She headed downhill again, moving faster as she got farther away from her starting point at the ridge, risking obvious footprints in order to gain time.

She hit the crevasse unexpectedly and nearly went headfirst to the bottom when she fell short of the rocky outcrop she had picked for her next foothold. She slid belly-down a few uncomfortable yards before hooking onto an exposed root, breaking her fall. She grimaced at the wide trail she had left. Just like her car. She would simply have to hope he wouldn't track her this way, because she was committed now. No time to make alternative plans. She clambered down the remaining length of the crevasse, wincing at the feel of snow-dampened pants clinging to her legs.

Balanced on a rock edging the black, rushing water, she hesitated for only a heartbeat. She might have been able to make it all the way to the hillocks hopping from stone to stone, never wetting her feet, if she had half an hour. But her time was measured in minutes and seconds now. She stepped in. The water was shallow, rising just over her ankles, but so cold, it brought tears to her eyes. She jogged downstream, slowly at first, picking up speed as she got her footing on the smooth cobbled stones lining the stream. It felt as if she had two great toothaches at the ends of her legs, and every joint in her body throbbed with sympathetic pain.

She kept jogging, her teeth gritted hard against any sounds she might make, her arms held away from her body for balance. On and on she sloshed through the almost-freezing water, unable to think of anything except her misery. It wasn't until she looked up and saw the darker outcropping of heavy stone that she realized she had reached the hillocks. She thrashed her way to the shore and leaped out of the stream, shaking and kicking each foot to expel as much water from her boots as possible.

Between the water and the snow was a tumble of smooth stones, wet but still free of ice, varying in size from hail to small boulders. Clare bent over and picked one up. It hefted well, about five pounds, flat enough so she could hold its edge with one hand if necessary. It was as close as she was going to get to an offensive weapon, unless she could take the gun off the man in the snowmobile suit. She stowed it in one of the parka's cargo pockets, where it banged against her thigh every time she drew her leg up to climb the hillside. The ascent was difficult. She couldn't flex her feet enough to get toeholds, so she had to use the outside edge of her boots and hang on, hoping she wouldn't topple back to the bottom of the crevasse.

At the top of the hill she collapsed beneath the shelter of a pine tree. No light bobbing in the distance, yet. The rush of elation was enough to get her back on her feet. She looked at the hill she had just climbed. This way back would be her escape route if her ambush didn't come off. She could roll down the crevasse within seconds and be headed in either direction quick enough to vanish. For awhile.

She squelched through the snow, keeping to the far side of the slope, her head a handsbreadth above the crest of the hill. She wanted a clear view of that flashlight. She teetered down one hill and trudged up another, looking for the trees she had marked in her mind. Surprisingly, her feet didn't feel so bad. They prickled a little, but she didn't feel the cold as keenly as she had.

By a cluster of tall firs, she went over the top, crawling on her elbows and knees to keep her profile low. The pines she had made a path to were a dozen yards away and almost directly below. He would step around them, careful to keep his gun between himself and the trees, and when he found she wasn't there he would want to head up to the next obvious hidey-hole, the firs near the crest of the hill. On his left, he would see birch growing too thickly together to make an easy route up the hill. So he would go to the left of the firs. She hoped. With no time to create an obstacle to channel him toward her ambush, it would have to be nature or nothing.

She reversed direction, up over the top, backtracking a half-dozen steps. From this spot, she walked, crouching low, taking long steps, leaving as little trace of herself as possible. A little more than halfway between the two clusters of evergreens she spotted what she wanted. A birch sapling, almost branchless, a couple feet taller than her head and slim enough to wrap her hand around. She yanked open the bow beneath her chin and pulled the long drawstring out of the parka's hood. Reaching as high as she could along the sapling, she drew its slender length down, holding hard against its springy recoil. She looped one end of the drawstring around a pair of miniature branches near the top of the sapling's trunk and tied off tightly.

Scarcely two yards away lay the brown remains of a toppled fir, spiky, tangled branches and dead needles rising less than a foot out of the snow. Low cover, enough to keep her out of sight—barely—if she dug down and stayed flat. Low cover her hunter might overlook while he kept his gun and flashlight trained on better hiding places. Only problem was, the drawstring wouldn't reach that far.

In the distance, a light winked. Clare's stomach squeezed. Time. No time. She abandoned the sapling, string dangling, for the nearest shaggy hemlock. She grabbed a flexible, living branch from low near the ground, pulled it taut, and smashed her heel over the juncture where it grew from the trunk. The branch snapped free. Clare teetered for balance. She had scarcely felt the blow with her foot. That had to be a bad sign.

The light flashed again and again in the darkness. She retrieved the loose end of the drawstring and tied it with the feathery tip of the branch in a double knot. She pulled down on her string and branch. It held. She pulled farther, bringing the sapling over in an arch, retreating toward the desiccated corpse of the fir. The branch and the drawstring held. The birch sapling trembled, and Clare twisted the whip-thin fir branch several times around her fist, straining to bring the sapling closer and closer to the ground. One-handed, she tossed the heavy river stone beneath the dead fir and knelt, quickly pawing away some of the snow. She settled down flat on her belly, wiggling herself as far into the painfully sharp needles as she could go.

She pulled on the birch with two hands now, the effort shaking her shoulders, the tension in the branch cutting into her gloves. The sapling was almost buried in the snow now, a few feet of its trunk bowed up into view. It looked, she hoped, like a large fallen branch. Something a tired and angry man wouldn't think twice about stepping over. Or at least stepping near. She couldn't see the light anymore from her hiding place, but he was out there. Close by. On her trail.

She counted her own heartbeats, willing them to slow, disciplining her breath to a deep, even relaxation. She held perfectly still except for an involuntary twitch or shiver, letting herself be covered by a gentle layer of falling snow. The muscles in her arms and shoulders ached from the effort of keeping the springy sapling arched taut. Her feet seemed detached from her legs, which stung and burned from the cold radiating out of the frozen ground. Even the heavy parka wasn't enough to keep her warm, lying motionless in a bed of snow.

Below her, she heard a noise. A slight snagging sound, the liquid slide of nylon dragged over something sharp. She gripped the branch more tightly. Tilting her head a fraction of an inch, she saw the faint glow of the flashlight beam playing over the tops of the fir trees, as if someone were crouched low at the base of the hill, training his light up underneath the first cluster of trees. The light shifted, disappeared.

Clare swallowed. Her heart felt as if it were trying to force sludge through her veins. The light reappeared, clearer now, sweeping across the hillside. It hit the birch trees, canted to the left, and then swung straight across toward her hiding place. She shut her eyes and held her breath. When she dared crack open an eyelid, the light had moved on. The flashlight was rocking, coming closer, the round brightness of it shockingly brilliant in the nighttime darkness. There was no sound of footsteps, no telltale crunch or snap or rustle. The thick, dry snow swallowed everything. He was nearing the kill zone. Cutting a zigzag path up the hill, pausing every few steps, shining his flashlight into the brush and evergreens.

Clare's jaw clenched, excitement and adrenaline warring with fear until her muscles shook. She could make him out behind the light, now, the padded outline of a man, larger than she had thought on the camp road, face concealed behind an enveloping ski mask. He held the flashlight high, over his head, where the reflected light would least impair his own vision. His other arm pointed down, away from his side. Keeping the gun muzzle away from his body. He was cocked and locked then, ready to roll as soon as he caught sight of her.

A few more steps would bring him into range. His caution was the wariness of a hunter afraid of scaring off the game. Underestimating her. She was the hunter here. He had become the game the moment he stepped onto her hill. Everything except her awareness of him faded away, and she watched intently as he moved closer and closer toward the kill. Just a few more steps.

The flashlight beam played over the trees at the top of the hill. He took a step. He took another. Clare squeezed her hands around the branch. Waiting for him to give himself up to her. He shifted the flashlight away from the crest of the hill and scanned the first group of trees again. He paused, searching slowly and carefully with the light. Clare's lungs burned, reminding her to breathe. One. More. Step. One more. Step. One more step. His face still turned downhill, he walked into her trap.

TWENTY-FOUR

Clare let go the draw. She heard, rather than saw, the swish of the sapling, the snap of the draw whipping the air, the shower of displaced snow. She seized the river rock and was on her feet before the full force of the young tree caught her assailant across the shoulders and back. The gun went off with a deafening hammerclap. His yell of pain cut off abruptly as he crashed belly-first into the snow. She launched herself into the air, smashed full-length onto his back, levered herself to a straddle and raised the rock over the back of his wool-covered skull. He bucked hard as she clubbed downward. Her killing blow fell off-center with a sound like rotten wood breaking open. He gurgled and sagged limply beneath her thighs.

She scrambled backwards, off his body, the rock banging and bruising her fingers as she staggered into a standing position. Crouching, she raised the rock again for the strike that would split his skull open. *If you kill him while he's unconscious, you'll be a murderer.* The thought seemed to come from outside herself. The rock trembled between her hands. *If you aren't gonna do him, at least make sure he's not playin' with you,* the old warrant officer drawled in her ear. She drew back one ice-stiffened boot and kicked the sprawling form as hard as she could between his legs. No reaction. He was for sure either dead or unconscious.

She dropped to her knees and shoved both hands underneath him, flipping him with a grunt. She tugged her gloves off with her teeth and unsnapped the big pockets on his thighs, digging frantically for keys to a car, a truck, a snowmobile. At his waist the pockets had zippers with freezing cold tangs that bit into her fingers as she yanked and wiggled and pried them open. Nothing. The zippers on his arms were the same way, sticking tight, either frozen shut or jammed. She gave up trying to open them, instead compressing and sliding the fabric between her fingertips, hoping for something small and metallic. One pocket held a pencil or pen inside that rolled under her thumb, the other was empty.

Clare squatted back on unfeeling heels, her wet pants clinging to her thighs. Whatever he drove, the keys must still be in it. She pulled her gloves back on. She would have to make her way back to the junction of the camp and mountain roads. He had to have parked somewhere within walking distance of where he first assaulted her. He had to. She breathed deeply, striving for calm.

She looked about for the gun. The flashlight was lighting up a snow-bank halfway down the hill, but she didn't see a weapon anywhere. She stood up and circled around her opponent, casting about for a hole in the snow that could hold a firearm. She bounded loosely down the hill, re-trieved the flashlight, and played the light over the snow while she hiked back to the unconscious body. Nothing. She blew out a breath in frustra-tion. She was zero for zero. No, that wasn't true. She was awake, on her feet, and had the flashlight. That put her way on top, for the time being.

She crouched at his head and tugged at the ski mask covering every-thing except his closed eyes. It was a long one, the dark wool disap-pearing into the zippered and snapped neck of his snowmobile suit. It stretched slightly, but stayed on. She tugged harder. It obscured his eyelids as it slid, then pulled up tight against her grasp. It was either caught in the zipper or fastened inside somehow. Clare tugged again, harder, and his head tilted. He moaned.

She leaped to her feet, raising the flashlight as if to club him sense-less again. Except there was no way to ensure that hitting him on the head hard enough to put him out wouldn't also kill him. She didn't want to kill him. She didn't have to kill him. He breathed out, a sigh. All she had to do was make sure she got to his vehicle before he did.

She circled around him and crouched just below his feet. He wore leather and rubber hunting boots, the kind LL Bean made, tucked beneath the elastic opening of his snowmobile suit. Clare pushed the padded nylon up his calf. His boot was laced and knotted tightly to a good five inches above his ankle. She yanked her gloves off again, stuffed them into her pocket, and picked at the double-knotted bow on top. It fell apart under her fingers. She hurriedly unhooked the laces from the endless series of hooks on either side of the tongue, then undid another double-knotted bow. Cradling the heel and toe between her hands, she wrenched the boot off. She wrinkled her nose at the sour smell. He moaned. Louder than the first time.

Clare shoved the other snowmobile suit leg up out of the way and tore at the top knot of his left boot. He moaned again. His leg twitched. She unlaced as quickly as she could down the rows of hooks, her fingers clumsy with tension and cold. She heard his head shift slightly. She scrabbled at the second knot, her fingernails shredding, her heart thumping in her ears. She loosened the knot a few inches before it caught and tightened again. She dug her hands into the boot's tread and yanked, getting her legs under her. She landed on her backside, boot in hand.

Her assailant cried out something unintelligible. Clare dropped the flashlight into one of her cargo pockets, tucked a boot under each arm, and scrambled downhill, slipping and sliding. It took her several seconds to find the false trail she had laid down. Night was no longer imminent, it had arrived, and details that had stood out in the twilight blueness were completely obscured by the darkness and the relentlessly falling snow.

She jogged off at a fast shuffle, headed for the spot beneath the ridge where she had started her ambush trail. If she had kept the relative directions straight in her mind, that ridge should lead toward the mountain road. The flashlight in her pocket banged heavily against her thigh. Useless for finding a way to the mountain road through the trees and the storm. She would use it only as a last resort, if she had to retrace her route all the way from here to the spot on the camp road where the man had tried to shoot her. Otherwise, it would only make her an easy target. She hugged the boots more tightly under her arms. Not that she thought he'd be able to catch up with her now.

From the hillside behind her, she heard an enraged bellow. She skidded to a halt. She turned around, her feet deadened, her legs burning and stinging with cold, her arms cramped and aching. She clutched the boots in her stiff, clumsy hands and shook them over her head.

"Suck wind, you loser! I'm gonna put your boots over my fireplace and laugh at you every time I see 'em!" She spun around and bounded away. Another garbled, angry cry. She could make out, "Bitch!" and "kill you . . ." There was a sound of branches cracking, a deep whumpf as a heavy load of snow slid off an evergreen. Was he coming after her? Clare churned through the snow, blinking away the flakes that landed on her eyelashes, desperate to find that ridge.

She fell onto it, face first, when her nerveless feet rolled over a branch hidden underfoot and sent her sprawling. She swiped at her face, a hopeless gesture of drying, and groped for the boots. Dangling one glove from her teeth, she knotted the laces together and hung them over her shoulder. She went up the ridge soundlessly, listening for any indications that her attacker was on her trail. The huge silence of the forest was disorienting; she had no way of knowing if he had given up on catching her or if the sounds of his pursuit were being muffled by the snow and the trees.

At the top of the ridge, Clare crouched, looking for her old tracks. She finally found a few, frighteningly indiscernable, already vanishing under the falling snow. She stood up, thighs and back complaining, and pressed a gloved thumb hard between her eyes. Risk that the ridge would lead her to the road? Or backtrack along to the camp road, hoping that there was enough of a trail left to follow?

There was a sharp crack followed by a rustle. Impossible to tell how far away. Her heart seized hard, trying to send the icy slurry that was her blood into her frozen extremities. Time to fish or cut bait. She took one last look at the blurred marks she had left climbing up the ridge during her flight from the camp road. She stamped her boots and waded into the virgin snow to her right.

It was slow going. Plodding over branches and around trees, stumbling down one side or another and scrambling back up to the narrow ridge crest, misstepping again and again because she felt as if she were walking on wooden boxes, unable to read the terrain under her feet.

The cold stole inside quietly, implacably. Her legs had gone numb. Beneath her parka, she shivered spasmodically, violent quakes that did nothing to dispel the damp chill of her skin. Her face felt raw, her hands distant and unwieldy. Even her brain seemed stiff with cold. Instead of listening alertly for any noise from her attacker, she found herself drifting, mesmerized by her legs breaking the snow, by the constant movement of the flakes filling the air, by the patterns of the trees she slapped against as she plowed onward. Birch, pine, birch, unknown, fir, fir, hemlock.

With a start, she realized she had run out of ridge. The thin spine of rock had melded seamlessly into the forest floor, no slope on either side of her to keep her headed in one direction. No indication of which way she should continue. Nothing to keep her from wandering in circles until she surrendered to the cold. *They say hypothermia is a happy death*, the old warrant officer observed. Angry, frustrated tears flooded her eyes and spilled over, hot against her raw skin. She took off a glove and wiped them away with the heel of her hand. Breathed in shakily. Okay. She would navigate by line-sighting between trees, even if she could only see a few feet ahead. Tree by tree, she would try to keep to a straight path. If she didn't reach the road within . . . a half hour, she would dig in. Branches and evergreen boughs were sure to provide her with some protection. Snow itself was an insulating material.

She had to force her spine to straighten, her legs to move forward. Her fear had cooled, too, to chilly despair. She sighted a marker tree and stumbled through the snow. When she reached it, she did it again. And again. And again.

When she caught the first flash of light from the corner of her eye, it almost didn't register. It flashed again, and she jerked her head left, her mouth dropping open. It was a flashlight beam, a strong one, casting through the forest from some distance away. She steadied herself against a birch. Either she was saved, or there were two of them. All she had to do was find out which.

She giggled involuntarily. All she had to do was stalk this one, knock him down and whack him with her flashlight. Then she could take his car keys. She giggled again, shrilly, unable to stop herself. *Stress and tension*, the warrant officer drawled. *Screws up your thinkin'.* She swallowed a giggle, hiccuped, giggled some more. Hit herself three times hard in the midsection. When she was silent again, she set out for the light in the distance.

"Dispatch ten-fifteen, this is unit ten-fifty-seven." Russ gingerly picked up the Styrofoam cup of hot cocoa and blew on it.

"Unit ten-fifty-seven, this is dispatch."

"Hey, Harlene. You get ahold of Lyle and Noble yet?"

"I reached Lyle, he said he can come on in. Haven't been able to find Noble yet."

Russ took a sip and swiped whipped cream off his upper lip. His arteries were probably clogging even as he idled in the Kreemie Kakes parking lot, but on a stormy winter afternoon, nothing beat their homemade hot chocolate. He'd do penance later tonight when Linda served up frozen diet dinners. "Keep trying. Two Saturdays before Christmas, nobody's gonna let a snowstorm stop 'em from shopping. I want to make sure we have enough men on the road once folks start plowing into each other."

"That's why I'm doing all my Christmas shopping over the phone this year."

Russ took another sip before keying his mike. "Did you know Linda wants to put out a catalogue?" It was all she could talk about when he had picked her up at the train station noontime.

"Does she? Good for her! Sell enough of those fancy curtains and you can retire a rich man. Let her support you."

"That's the plan." He slid the hot chocolate into a plastic cup holder. The prices she had been quoting for publishing the damn thing would have made his eyes pop out if he hadn't been wearing his glasses, but she was convinced the increased sales would make it worthwhile. Linda knew a damn sight more about the care and feeding of money than he ever would. He hadn't asked if increased sales would make their lives more worthwhile.

"Dispatch, I'm rolling out of Main and Canal, heading for Route forty-seven. Anything else?"

"Reverend Fergusson called a half hour ago. Said she'd be in her office in the church until five thirty or so. Want me to raise her for you?"

He tapped the microphone against his chin. "No," he said, "I'll swing by that way. Let me know if you can't get Noble, we may have to call in one of the part-time guys. It's gonna be a mess out here within a few hours."

The church was dark when Russ pulled into the tiny parking area out back, but he could see lights shining from the attached building that housed the offices and parish hall. The kitchen door was locked tight. He followed the walkway shoveled around the parish hall until he reached the big double doors. Open, of course. He shook his head. It wouldn't occur to her to lock the door behind her.

"Clare? Hey, Clare, it's me. Russ." He brushed snow off his parka. The coffeemaker squatting on the table was on. So were the hall lights. In Clare's office, the remains of a fire burned low on the brick hearth. Her appointment book, a fistful of pink phone message slips and a half-full mug of cold coffee sat on her desk.

"Clare? You here?" Maybe she had run over to the rectory? He backtracked outside, crossed the parking area and craned to see over the tall boxwood hedge separating Clare's driveway from the church grounds. The rectory was dark. No tire tracks or footprints marred the fresh snow on her steps.

Frowning, he returned to her office. What the hell had taken her in such an all-fired hurry she couldn't bank the fire or turn off the coffeemaker? He glanced at her appointment book. Nothing for Saturday except a morning visit to the Infirmary. He flipped through the pink phone message slips. Nothing. He walked down the shadowy hall to the cold, dark church. A single votive candle hung in a red glass container to the left of the altar, washing a carved wooden cabinet with a ruddy glow. "Clare?" he called. His voice echoed back from hard lines of stone.

He slapped his gloves against one thigh, talking himself out of the unease creeping up the base of his skull. She had probably been called away on one of those mysterious "pastoral emergencies." No big deal. There was nothing compelling him to find out what it was. Of course, if he listened to the answering machine, he might be able to figure out where she had gone without making an ass of himself calling around. He stalked back up the hall, annoyed at Clare for being so damn hard to get hold of, annoyed even more at himself for wasting time worrying about it.

The main office was as dark as the church. He snapped on the lights, dropped into the secretary's chair, punched the blinking red button on the answering machine. It beeped and obediently began reciting its messages. Next to the phone was a spiral-bound book for written messages, yellow carbon copies, and unused pink tear-out squares. He sat up straighter. There were carbon records of his calls, that one about the baptism, a meeting, and there, slopping over two spaces, a detailed message he hadn't seen on Clare's desk.

Russ held the memorandum book at arm's length, tilting his head back to make out the words. A meeting with Kristen McWhorter up in the mountains? He closed his eyes, envisioning the route described on the message copy. Somewhere around Tenant or Buck Mountain? West of Lake Lucerne. Wherever this cabin was, it would be one hell of a tough drive for Clare's car. He cut off the recording in the middle of some woman going on about her son and dialed the station. "Harlene? I need you to find a phone number for me. Kristen McWhorter. It'll be in either McWhorter file."

He traced the slashes underlining URGENT! while waiting for Harlene to return with the number. Jumping into that piece of flashy junk and driving into the mountains without stopping to think about the consequences sounded just like Clare. Somebody needed to teach that woman to measure twice and cut once.

"Chief?" Harlene rattled off Kristen's number. "Anything I can help with?"

"Nah. I'm just trying to track down Reverend Fergusson. She's not here at the church. If she happens to call in, make sure you find out how I can reach her."

"You got it."

He hung up and immediately dialed Kristen's apartment. It rang once. Twice. Three times.

"Hello?"

"Kristen? This is Chief Van Alstyne."

"Oh, Christ. What is it now? You find something new?"

"No. Kristen, did you call Reverend Fergusson earlier today and ask her to meet you and your mother at a cousin's cabin? Someplace near Tenant Mountain?"

There was a blank pause. "What? I'm sorry, Chief, my cousins live in trailers, not mountain cabins. I haven't spoken with Clare since the day before yesterday. What's going on?"

The unease Russ had been fending off jelled into a solid icy mass of dread. "I'll get back to you."

"Can you—"

He dropped the receiver in its cradle, rubbing his forehead with his fist. Christ on a bicycle. The question of who had set out to lure Clare into the Adirondack wilds would have to be put on hold. Whatever was waiting for her there was more important.

He tore the yellow carbon sheet out of the memorandum book and left the church office at a fast dogtrot. In his cruiser, he radioed Harlene while firing the engine up and maneuvering out of the tiny parking area. "Ten-fifteen, this is ten-fifty-seven, come in."

"Ten-fifty-seven, this is dispatch, come back."

"Harlene, I want you to call in Tim and Duane for traffic duty. Somebody pretending to be Kristen McWhorter conned Reverend Fergusson into driving up into the mountains." Squinting at the yellow sheet, he read the directions to Harlene. "I'm heading after her. I'm inbound to the station, gonna switch this cruiser for my truck. She'll handle the roads up there better." He slowed to take the left onto Main.

"Do you want me to send backup along?"

He frowned at the snow spattering against his windshield. "No. I have a feeling we're going to be short-handed as it is. I can handle this. Ten-fifty-seven out."

He pulled into the station's parking lot as he hung up his mike. His truck was parked in the rear, already blanketed with snow. He killed the cruiser's engine, got out, unlocked the trunk. From its locked safety box, he removed the rifle and a box of shells. He cracked the magazine. The chambers were loaded.

Russ laid the rifle and the ammunition in the backseat of the pickup before starting it up. It roared to life reassuringly, warming up fast as Russ swept the dry powdery snow off the windows and headlights. By the time he hiked himself up into the cab, warm air was blasting from the vents. He tossed his gloves onto the yellow memorandum sheet, reversed, and rolled out of the lot, the four-wheel-drive gripping tight to the packed-down snow.

He made good time, considering the roads. Traffic was heavy on Route 9, as he had predicted, shoppers heading home to fix dinner passing shoppers just hitting the stores. The evening trade would be starting soon, maybe not dinners-out so much in this storm, but worse, habitual drinkers who spent every Saturday night on a barstool, Christmas party-goers who wouldn't see anything wrong in having just one more cup of rum and eggnog.

The driving was trickier once he had taken the exit to Tenant Road. His truck held well to the road, but it was a bad surface, driven over just enough to be slushy and half-frozen. His windshield wipers beat away steadily at the spitting snow. The sound made him think of Wednesday night, driving through the last storm, Clare in the passenger seat, exhausted and weeping. Paying attention to everyone's feelings except her own, until they snuck up and blindsided her. A single car approached. He squinted to make it out, snorting as it crept past slowly. Some Subaru. God damn, he should have dragged her to the Fort Henry dealership and made her lease something winter-worthy.

He passed a mom-and-pop store. Once its lights had dwindled in his rearview mirror, there was nothing except rising country and snow. His headlights tunneled through the dark, barely reaching two or three truck lengths before vanishing in the storm. The touch of light on each snowflake was as distracting as popping flashbulbs. Long habit helped him ignore the show, concentrating instead on what he could see of the road ahead.

Even so, he overshot the mountain road. The gap in the trees and the blank white roadbed registered a few seconds after he had seen it. He slowed carefully, taking his time before finally stopping and turning the truck around. Too many people forgot four-wheel-drive was meant to help acceleration, not braking. He had cleaned up too many of their accidents to make the same mistake.

His pickup ground slowly up the mountain road. He shook his head, trying to imagine Clare making it up here in her featherweight car. If she had made it. The snow had covered any traces of tire tracks that might show her route up the narrow, twisting road. He checked the trip odometer against the numbers on the directions. He ought to be getting close. If there was no sign of her at the cabin, he didn't know what the hell he was going to do.

The unmistakable sound of a shot made him jerk reflexively, swearing. He slammed on his brakes, sending the truck into an angled skid. Twisted off the heat and killed the engine, rolling down his window clumsily. There was a bump, and the silent truck slid backwards and down slightly, its rear wheels coming to rest in the snow-covered gully at the edge of the road. Russ thrust his head through the window, straining to hear any other noise through the darkness.

CHAPTER
TWENTY-FIVE

The slithery hissing of dry snow meeting snow. Every-thing else was an immense silence. He didn't realize he had been holding his breath until it rushed out of his chest. He opened the glove compartment and re-moved his flashlight, long and heavy, a weapon in itself. Reaching into the backseat, he retrieved the box of shells and the rifle. He poured a good handful of shells into his coat pocket before tugging on his hat and gloves and stepping out of the cab.

He hesitated at the edge of the trees. He didn't dare go more than a dozen yards from the road in the dark with no compass. He tugged his knit hat lower on his forehead. The thought of walking toward an un-known shooter shining a light and calling out made his nuts want to crawl back up inside his body. But if Clare had been—if she couldn't see him, he could search for a week without stumbling over her. He cradled the rifle and thumbed his flashlight on. What the hell. Either the shooter wasn't interested, or he was going to get drilled. Either way, he wasn't walking out of here with-out doing everything he could to bring Clare with him.

He waded into the forest, sweeping his light around in 180 degree arcs, listening for anything that might indicate the presence of another human being. The cold pinched at his face. He thought of Clare, under-dressed for the weather as usual, slogging deeper and deeper into the woods, slowly freezing to death. A hun-dred paces into the trees, he angled back toward the road, traveling downhill. If someone had been shooting, she must be around here. Noise traveled far in the mountains, but that shot had been close. Too damn close. He held up his arm to fend off lashing branches of bittersweet, trying not to picture her lying in a crumpled heap, her blood staining the snow red.

He angled again, away from the road, pushing through pines and hemlock. It was important to be methodical, not to give into the urge to run around yelling. A long zigzag pattern, working his way downhill because that's the direction most lost folks take, his light shining like a beacon.

He heard nothing except his own breathing and the sweep and stretch of snow over the mountain. His throat closed over the fear rising in his gorge. Not the fear that he might get drilled by whoever else was out here with a gun. Fear that Clare was gone for good.

The flashlight beam hit him straight in the eyes, blinding him. He yelped involuntarily, so startled his mind went blank. His body knew how to think for him, though, dropping into the snow and sighting the rifle toward the other light.

"Russ?" Her voice was weak and cracking from the cold.

"Clare?" He scrambled back to his feet, swinging his flashlight in her direction. "Oh, my God. Clare." She staggered toward him. He crossed the distance first, catching her in his arms, the rifle and flashlight clunking together as he picked her up off the ground. "Clare. Jesus, are you all right? Were you hit?"

"My feet . . . I can't feel my feet anymore."

He released her to shine the light over her again. Her face was raw, chapped and scratched. Thank God she had been wearing a departmental parka. It looked as if it were holding up, but her pants were wet up to her thighs and chunks of ice and caked snow were frozen to her flimsy boots. He flashed the light up again.

"What the hell are you doing with hunting boots hung over your shoulder?" She opened her mouth. "No, don't tell me now. My truck's about seventy yards away. I can carry you, but I think we'll be faster and steadier if you can walk."

She nodded. "I can walk," she said.

He looked around them. "The shooter—is he close? Did you get a look at him?"

She shook her head. "I couldn't see his face. He's—" She rubbed her eyes with a snow-clotted glove and blinked hard. "I don't know if he's close by. He's unarmed, though. He lost his gun when I took him out."

He hung the rifle strap on his shoulder and took her arm, shining his flashlight toward the way out of the woods. "You took him out? What do you mean?"

She clutched at his arm, but otherwise walked steadily. "I knocked him down with a sapling tree and bashed him with a rock. I couldn't find his gun, but I took his flashlight and his boots."

He helped her over a fallen log. "You took his flashlight and his boots."

"I wanted to find his car keys but he wasn't carrying them. I was . . ." She gulped air. "I was working my way back to the road. To find his car or whatever. Snowmobile." He tightened his grip on her arm. She gulped again. "But I was going the other way when I saw your light, Russ. I was going the wrong way." Her voice cracked. "I thought I was headed for the road, but I must have gotten turned around. I would have . . . I would have just kept on walking . . ."

Up ahead, he saw a flash where the light caught metal. "Almost there." He couldn't see her face. Only the fur encircling the hood. He forced himself to speak confidently. "You wouldn't have kept on walking, darlin'. You're too smart. You would have dug in, covered yourself up. Probably figured out some way to build a fire. With pine needles and a gum wrapper."

She made a dry sound, halfway between a laugh and a sob. He could see his truck clearly now. "C'mon, let me take you up." He picked her off the ground and settled her against his shoulder, grunting with the effort. "Good God, woman, what are you wearing, lead-lined pants?" She made the sound again, this time more a laugh.

At the truck, he opened the passenger's door first and helped her in. Climbing into the driver's side, he almost laid the rifle in the backseat again, then thought better and slid it bore-down next to the door, within a moment's reach. He fired up the engine and turned on the dome light before rummaging in the back for his two spare blankets. "Okay, darlin', let's get your wet things off."

She nodded jerkily. She pulled off her sodden gloves and dropped them on the floor, but she couldn't manage the snap and zipper at her neck. "My fingers," she said.

He nodded. "We need to take a look at your feet first anyway." He lifted her stiff, ice-encrusted boots into his lap. "What the hell did you do to get these so wet?" The laces were unmanagable. He flipped open the glove compartment and removed his knife.

"I . . . ran through a stream. Only fast way to . . . get to the spot I picked to . . . ambush him." She shivered violently as he sliced her laces away and gently wiggled each boot off. "I'm so cold . . ."

He adjusted the vents to blow on her. The hot air was already blasting at top speed. He carefully peeled away her socks, sucking in his breath at the sight of the blotchy white patches mottling blueish skin. Jesus. How had she hiked through the woods like this? Under his hands the flesh felt like heavy clay that had been stored in a refrigerator. "Oh, darlin'," he said.

"Is it bad?" He looked at her. "Tell me the truth, Russ."

"It doesn't look like frostbite, but we're going to have to soak your feet in cool water and bring 'em up to temperature slowly. Here, let's get those pants off you." He tried to be gentle, but he had to tug and wrestle the stiff, wet khaki off her, each jerk and twist causing her to gasp. "I'm sorry, I'm so sorry, Clare."

She shook her head. "No, it's good. It's burning. That's a good sign, isn't it?"

"Yeah. Means the blood is coming back." The skin on her legs was alarmingly cold and pale, but there were no signs of frostbite there, either. He cocooned her feet and legs in one of the blankets. "It's gonna hurt like a bitch when you get circulation going. Like when your leg falls asleep, but lots worse." He kept her legs resting on his thighs while he went to work on the parka, unbuttoning and unzipping. Underneath, her woolly turtleneck was dry. He wrapped the second blanket around her, chafed her hands between his own. "How do they feel?"

"Cold. Like the rest of me."

"Can you feel this?" He ran his fingertips lightly down her fingers and across her palm.

She looked at him. Her eyes were huge and dark. Her fingers flexed over his. "Yes," she whispered. The hot air roared past him, stirring staticky cobwebs of her hair. He opened his mouth to speak, then shut it again. She raised her free hand as if she would touch his cheek, then let it fall. "I'm so glad you're here," she said. She blinked against the watery light in her eyes. "I was such a jerk last night. I'm sorry, you were right, you were right about everything."

He dropped his gaze to her hand, picked up the other one and began rubbing them vigorously. "Maybe. But I shouldn't have been such a hard ass about it." He smiled at her. "And I wasn't right about everything. Ballistics came back negative on their gun. We're still waiting to hear about the hair and fiber samples from their cars." He looked at her extraordinary face, laced by angry scratches and chafed raw by the snow and cold. He squeezed her hands hard. "I was right about one thing, though. This isn't any business of yours. Jesus, Clare, you could have died out there!"

She smiled waveringly. "Not me. I'm too smart."

He released her hands, swinging her feet to the floor. He reached around her and buckled her in. "Let's get you someplace warm, smart girl."

The truck strained and groaned before lurching from the ditch and turning slowly back down the road. "What about the man who attacked me?" Clare asked.

Russ kept his attention on the road. "What about him?"

"Aren't you going to try to find him? Or at least find his vehicle?"

He spared her a glance. "Do you have any idea where he is? Or where his truck or snowmobile is?"

"No."

"And he doesn't have any boots on?"

"No."

"You said you couldn't see his face?"

"No! He had one of those face masks on, and I tried to get it off, but the damn thing was stuck!" She snorted. "Then he started to wake up and I thought I'd be better served getting the heck out of there."

"Good girl. And the answer is no, I'm not going after him. I could turn out the National Guard and we'd still never find him in this weather. My first priority is to get you thawed out. We can be at the Glens Falls Hospital in half an hour if the county's gotten the plows out."

"No. No hospital. I don't like hospitals."

"You go to hospitals all the time, for Chrissake!"

"Not for myself!" She had an edge of hysteria to her voice. He shut up. "Just take me home, Russ," she said. "Please."

"Okay, darlin'. Home it is." He downshifted in preparation for churning the truck out of the snow and leaf-filled gully. *And then I'm going to get someone to take a look at you if I have to knock you down and sit on you to do it.*

CHAPTER TWENTY-SIX

They didn't talk much on the ride back to Millers Kill. Clare leaned back against the seat, exhausted, her mouth thinning occasionally when they went over a bump. He knew her legs must be hurting. Despite his sensible words, he was sorely tempted to round up as many men as he could and scour the mountain for the sonofabitch who had done this to her. But he had been right, it would be a waste of time at this point. Either the guy had found his way back to his vehicle or he was losing his feet to exposure someplace.

He glanced over at Clare. Knocked him down with a tree and bashed him with a rock. Jesus. He smiled a little.

When they pulled into her driveway, he said, "Keys?"

"I left them in my car. But don't worry, it's—"

"Unlocked. Of course." She didn't argue when he opened her door and picked her up to carry her inside. He grunted as they went up the steps. "Don't make a habit of this, Clare, or I'm going to have to buy a truss."

Inside, he deposited her blanket-wrapped form on the sofa and cranked up the thermostat. "Okay," he said, "You need dry clothes, a tub of tepid water to soak those feet in—" She groaned loudly at the suggestion. "—and something warm to drink. Not coffee, the caffeine's bad for your circulation."

"Hot cocoa?"

"That's fine. Where can I find stuff?"

She gave him directions. Her bedroom was spartan, nothing but bed, dresser, and her Army sweats tossed over some wooden kneeler-prayer-thingy in front of the uncurtained window. He grabbed the sweats and dropped them next to her on the sofa before hitting the kitchen to find the cocoa ingredients. No bags of instant, of course. He put the milk on to heat and rummaged beneath the sink for a plastic tub, which he filled with lukewarm water.

"You decent?" he called from the kitchen.

"Yeah."

He walked slowly, careful not to slosh the water. "Stick your feet in there," he said, settling the tub in front of the sofa. She pulled the legs of her sweatpants up a bit and complied.

"It feels warm." She looked surprised.

"That's because your feet are so damn cold. I don't have to do anything like hand-grate imported bittersweet chocolate and hazelnuts for this hot cocoa, do I?"

She made a face. "Just sugar and cocoa. Oh, and a drop of vanilla extract is nice."

"I have to introduce you to the Kreemie Kakes Diner version of hot chocolate." He found everything quickly. Like her office, her kitchen was orderly and well-organized. She was a woman who had her priorities, no doubt about it.

"Here you go." He put two mugs on the coffee table, then crossed to the front window and tested to see if the tops locked.

She craned her neck to see what he was up to. "What are you doing?"

"Locking you in." He moved to the front door, threw the bolt and latched it at the top. "Who can I call to come and stay with you tonight?"

"Russ!" She sounded scandalized. "I couldn't impose on anyone like that."

He turned to her. "Clare, someone put a lot of effort into killing you tonight. Let's not make it any easier for him to take a second crack at you."

"But he's—"

"We don't know what he is. The guy who attacked you might be a Popsicle right now. Or he might have gotten onto his snowmobile and ridden away. And don't forget whoever that woman was who called the church to get you out there."

She worried her lower lip. "All right. You can make sure the doors and windows are all locked," she said. "But I don't know anyone well enough to ask over. It would be an imposition."

"Your mother teach you that? You sound very Southern when you say 'an imposition.'" He crossed the room to stand in front of her sofa. "You're exhausted and you can barely walk. You think of someone you can 'impose' on right quick like or I'll station one of my officers here." She glared at him. "Which will mean taking someone away from traffic duty during a major storm."

Her face melted into a look of concern. She gnawed on her lower lip again. "Doctor Anne," she said finally. "Anne Vining-Ellis. She lives a couple blocks away."

"She the same Doctor Anne who works the Glens Falls emergency room?" Clare nodded. "I've met her. I'll give her a call." There was a cordless phone on the table behind the sofa. He dialed information, punched in the number and headed for the stairs. "I'm going to check the upstairs windows," he told Clare.

"I can't believe I'm letting you do this," she said.

"Hello, Ellis residence." He jiggled the latches in Clare's bedroom. Locked.

"Hi, is this Dr. Vining-Ellis?"

"Sure is."

Another bedroom was empty except for a Nordictrak exercise machine and a floormat. The windows were locked.

"This is Chief Van Alstyne of the Millers Kill Police Department. We've met a few times before—"

"Over a few drunk drivers. Of course. How can I help you, Chief?"

He sketched out the situation while testing the latches in the next bedroom. It looked as if it had been a guest room for the former priest, and nothing had been removed. He was pretty sure the gun and dog prints and the dark Depression-era furniture weren't Clare's. Doctor Anne was horrified at the story of her priest's ordeal. "Of course I'll come over and stay with her," she said. "It's absolutely no trouble at all. I'll bring my kit and give her a going-over, too, just to make sure she doesn't need to be admitted to the hospital."

He thanked the doctor and rang off. One of the windows in the bathroom was propped open a sliver. A fine line of snow had accumulated on the sill. He shut and locked it. The toilet was running, and he couldn't get it to stop by jiggling the handle. Inside the cistern, the plunging apparatus was falling apart. He frowned. Couldn't her parishioners pay for a plumber, for Chrissakes? Well, he could pick up something at Tim's Hardware, put it in for her next time he was around this way.

"Doctor Anne's on her way over," he announced as he reentered the living room. Clare groaned. "And she said to tell you it was not an imposition." He stuck his hand in the water her feet were soaking in. Cooling. "So, you wanna tell me about what happened?" He headed into the kitchen for more hot water.

"Master Sergeant Ashley 'Hardball' Wright saved my sorry ass," she called after him.

He poked his head through the swinging doors before emerging with a teakettle of hot water. "Hey! I thought I saved your sorry ass."

She smiled faintly. "You helped. You surely did help." She sipped her hot cocoa and dabbled her feet while he poured a thin stream of steaming hot water into the tub. "How on earth did you know I was out there?"

He told her about finding the paper trail at St. Alban's and calling Kristen.

"So she didn't have anything to do with it. Well, I didn't think so, not after that guy took a shot at me." She tipped her head back and closed her eyes. "Although before that, when I drove my car over a cliff, I had my doubts. Maybe she was just really bad at directions."

"You drove your car over a cliff? Christ."

She frowned.

"Sorry."

"Well, maybe it wasn't quite a cliff. A big gorge. My car is totaled." She compressed her lips in an expression he was beginning to recognize. "I loved that car. I don't get attached to many material things, but I really loved that car."

"You have any idea who could have been behind this?"

"How about this? This morning, I found out that Katie's secret lover was Wesley Fowler. His family are members of the congregation. And about as far from the McWhorter's as you can get, socially, culturally, economically . . ."

"How the hell did you get that piece of information?"

She told him about her visit to Paul's office at the Infirmary and the photograph. "It's still in the pocket of my parka. Your parka," she amended. "I visited the Fowlers to see if they knew anything about it, which they didn't, unsurprisingly. Then I went to Albany."

"Albany?"

"I wanted to see if Katie's roommates might recognize Wesley's picture."

He rolled his eyes. "You know, Clare, the Albany PD already questioned at least two of the roommates."

"But they didn't have a picture, and I did. And I had his yearbook." She twisted on the sofa to face him more fully. "Ow! You were right about the hot prickles. Anyway, at first I thought it was a bust, because none of the girls recognized Wes. But then, just by chance, they spotted a picture of Alyson Shattham. And guess what? She had been to see Katie. It was not a cheerful social visit. They had a fight."

"When was this?" He swept the newspaper off one overstuffed armchair and perched on the edge.

"Beginning of the school year. September."

"Huh. Little Alyson Shattam. Who said she hadn't seen Katie since graduation."

"Guess who Alyson's boyfriend was all through last year."

He smiled slowly. "Wesley Fowler."

"Ten points."

"Where is this kid? Still in town?"

"No, he's a plebe at West Point. His father's gone down to bring him back, though. They should be here tomorrow."

He began twisting the sheets of newspaper into kindling. "Want a fire?"

"Please."

He raked the old ashes to one side and laid splitwood from a big basket over the paper. He crossed two small logs over the kindling and struck one of her silly six-inch-long matches. "Alyson and Wes," he said, tossing the match on the fire with five inches left unburnt. "A boy and a girl. Go to the same church. Are their families friends?"

"Oh yes," she said. He sprawled back onto the armchair. "Oh, I feel warmer already. I may become addicted to fires."

"Yeah, the Shattams were with the Fowlers this morning when I went over. I knew about Alyson and Wes before, though. Dr. Anne's son gave me the inside scoop on all the high school gossip this past Monday. Sounded like they were the classic king and queen of the prom pair."

"You sound a tad disenchanted, there."

"Oh . . . that's just an old high school outsider looking in, I suppose. She crossed her arms over her chest. "You've met Alyson. She clearly believes that the world owes it to her to treat her like the princess she is. And from what I've heard of Wes Fowler, he's the same type, a golden boy who's never had anything bad happen to him."

"So what do you think? Did Alyson know Wes was seeing Katie on the side? Maybe she wouldn't put out and Katie would? So she let Katie keep Wesley-boy happy?"

"There's no doubt that Katie did, as you oh-so-tastefully phrased it, 'put out.' But honestly, I can't see Alyson Shattham standing by while her boyfriend gets . . . serviced. She strikes me more as the kind of girl to keep him on as tight a leash as possible."

"Yeah, I know that type. Gets her kicks from making some poor slob jump through hoops for the promise of some—" Clare was looking at him with undisguised interest. He felt the tips of his ears redden. "Never mind. I agree, it's more likely Alyson didn't know that Katie was sleeping with Wes."

"But then, at some point, its more than just sleeping with her. He gets her pregnant. Could he have come running to Alyson then?"

"What for?"

"Help. Advice. Forgiveness. Knowing a little bit about the psychology of teenage boys, I'm willing to bet a non-pregnant girlfriend suddenly looked a lot more appealing to him."

"She looked genuinely surprised to me that morning at your church. Of course, I've been fooled before." He watched Clare twist a strand of hair around her finger and chew her lip. "Okay. Let's say he did tell her. What do the king and queen of the prom do when he's gotten another girl knocked up?"

"They make the problem disappear?"

"Let's say Wesley persuades Katie to give away the baby."

"That could explain Alyson's visit to Albany. Maybe she was the go-between, trying to talk Katie into it."

"But a few days after leaving the baby at your back door, Katie gets back in touch with Wesley. She says she can't stand it, she wants the baby back."

"I don't think Wes Fowler would have been too keen to have it come out that he got a girl from Depot Street pregnant and then abandoned the baby outside St. Alban's on a freezing winter's night. The West Point commandant and the ethics commission take a dim view of that sort of thing."

Russ snorted.

"And there had already been a story in the paper, remember? The day after we found the baby? There wouldn't have been much chance of him keeping it quiet if Katie tried to reclaim Cody."

"So one of them—Wesley or Alyson—decides to stop Katie before she can tell anyone she's the baby's mom. One of them gets her out by the kill and cracks her head open and leaves her there to die."

She swished her feet through the water.

"But then another problem rears its ugly head," he said. "Darrell, who evidently once saw Katie and Wes together."

"He must have seen the Fowlers' family picture on our parish bulletin board Wednesday morning when he met with me and the Burnses. That would explain why he broke off the discussion so quickly, if he had a name to put with a face, finally." She shook her head, silent for a moment.

"If he did, it's not your fault, Clare." She glanced up at him. "You've got your responsible look on," he explained. She gave him a half smile. "We know he called somebody. Maybe he was putting the squeeze on Wesley, and the kid high-tailed it back to town and put a bullet through Darrell's slimy little brain."

"Or Alyson did."

He looked at her, nonplused. She spread her hands. "You think she couldn't? Maybe she's the shooter while Wes went to the house in Albany to collect any incriminating evidence."

"The guy who said he was Katie's father? The roommate described him as older, with a mustache."

"According to Dr. Anne's boy, Wes Fowler was in the Millers Kill High School Drama Society. He appeared in several plays and in the yearly musical. A little left-over gray tint in his hair, a fake moustache . . . it might been enough to fool a couple of freshmen who had had a few too many beers."

Russ slid out of his chair and squatted on the floor in front of her. "Let's have a foot." She lifted one, dripping, out of the water and let him squeeze it. "Need to heat it up a bit," he said. He held a hand against the copper teakettle, checking to make sure it was still warm before pouring a stream of warm water into the tub.

She made a noise in the back of her throat, flexing her toes. "If he did kill Darrell and clean out Katie's room, he must have thought at that point he had covered all the bases. There wasn't anything to link him to Katie except Cody himself, and who would think to ask for Wes Fowler's DNA to test for paternity of poor Katie McWhorter's abandoned child?"

"Nobody, until the Reverend Fergusson got her hands on a photo of the two of them together and immediately rushed over to confront his proud parents with evidence that one plus one makes three." He turned to the fireplace and tossed another log in. "Holy Christ, Clare. You really could have died up on that mountain. You were supposed to have died." He rubbed the back of his neck.

"Would he have had time to get from West Point to here and set up that ambush for me?"

He stood slowly, turning around, scanning the dark corners of the room without meaning to. "I don't see why not. It's a three-hour drive at most, another hour to get himself parked somewhere safe on a camp road on Tenant Mountain. It's not as if he needed to come up with an elaborate way to trap you. All he needed was a good way to get you up to that mountain and someone pretending to be Kristen McWhorter."

"Which brings us back to Alyson."

"She knew you were helping Kristen, didn't she?"

Clare nodded.

"And she must have known you're the sort to charge off to help first, without asking questions until later."

She cocked her head at him. "You make me sound like the Lone Ranger."

"Doesn't make it untrue. The fact that you're impulsive is not a deeply-hidden character trait."

"I prefer to think of it as making decisions quickly."

"I'm sure you do. Prefer to think of it that way."

The doorbell chimed. He headed for the kitchen to admit a snow-dusted Dr. Anne.

"My car's blocking you in, so we'll have to switch," she said, unwinding an immense scarf from her neck. "How is she?"

"I've got her soaking in a tub of lukewarm water that I've been heating up gradually." The doctor stared at him. The tips of his ears reddened. "I mean, her feet. She's soaking her feet. In there." He led Dr. Anne into the living room in time to see Clare standing wobbly-legged, clutching at the back of the sofa. "What the hell do you think you're doing?" he said, more loudly than he intended.

She grinned at him tensely. "I believe it's called 'walking.' It's all the rage of the over-one-year-old set. Hi, Dr. Anne."

"Sit down, you damn fool woman."

She straightened, releasing the sofa. The lines and planes of her face tightened. "I have things to do," she said through gritted teeth. "I have to call Kristen, and Mrs. Fowler. And the deacons, to let them know I may not be able to celebrate seven A.M. Eucharist tomorrow morning."

He reached over the sofa and wrapped his hand around her arm. "You don't need to prove how tough you are. I already know. Clare, please. Sit down."

She looked at him, then sat.

Dr. Anne dropped her medical bag on the sofa next to Clare. "As soon as I've checked you out, I'll help you make those phone calls." She glanced at Russ. "Anything in particular I need to watch out for?"

"You see anything, or hear anything that makes you feel uneasy, call the station. No, give me a call." He scrawled his home number on the scratch pad next to the cordless phone base.

"I will, Chief. Let's move those cars so you can get out."

He looked down at Clare. She smiled crookedly. "Thank you. It seems inadequate, but thank you."

He crossed his arms over his chest. "Just take care of yourself. I'll see you tomorrow. Try not to get into any trouble until then, okay?"

"Okay."

Dr. Anne waited while he pulled on his boots and coat. Outside, snow still fell furiously. His truck was already blanketed again. "I can't thank you enough for coming to stay with her," he said. "She's so damn busy taking care of other people's needs she completely ignores her own."

Dr. Anne smiled knowingly. "Mmmm. Yes, I know the type." She paused, one hip bumped against her car door. "Chief? I don't mean to pry, but I heard Clare's car was parked at the foot of your drive all night Wednesday."

"What? That's ridiculous! I mean, yeah, it was there, but that's because it was snowing and I drove her home."

Dr. Anne raised her hands placatingly. "I'm not trying to imply anything. I just wanted you to know that if I've heard talk, other people have too. It's a small town."

Russ hauled open his truck door. "Christ, isn't that the truth. If folks are so interested in the whereabouts of Clare's car, let's hope somebody saw something that'll tell us who wanted to dump it into a gorge. With her along for the ride."

CHAPTER
TWENTY-SEVEN

Clare looked out at her congregation as the last notes from the communion hymn faded and wondered if one of the people looking back at her wanted her dead. Alyson Shattham and her mother were in their usual spots, but the Fowlers, who usually sat nearby, were missing. As were the Burnses. Sterling Sumner was glaring at her again while Doctor Anne, who last night had argued strenuously against her celebrating the nine o'clock Eucharist, was frowning in concern.

Ronnie Allbright, her acolyte, turned a page in the huge presentation prayer book that lay propped open on the altar. Clare glanced at the text of the post-communion prayer and took a deep, slow breath, focusing on the clear channel of the words. "Almighty God," she began, and the voice of the congregation joined her in a rumble, "We thank you for giving us the most precious body and blood of your son, Jesus Christ . . ." She knew the prayer like she knew the names of her family. It settled and centered her, so that when she raised her hands to bless the congregation, she could feel an honest surge of affection and support for them all.

Martin Burr attacked the organ, pumping out the opening strains of "On Jordan's Bank the Baptist's Cry." The torchbearers and the crucifer assembled in front of the altar to begin the recessional. Clare glanced up from her hymnal just in time to see the inner vestibule door opening at the end of the church.

Russ Van Alstyne slipped inside. Across the length of the nave, his eyes met hers.

The calm and centered feeling she had been nursing vaporized. She joined the recessional, last in line, inadvertently wincing at the ache that intensified every time she put a foot down. She kept her gaze fixed on the hymnal in order to remember a song she had known by heart since childhood. At the conclusion of the hymn, she stood for a beat too long, unable to dredge up the simple words to dismiss the congregation. She could see the back of Alyson Shattham's hair, immaculate and shining. Finally she blurted out, "Go in peace to love and serve the Lord, Alleluia, Alleluia," and bolted toward the door while everyone else was still responding with their own Alleluias.

"What are you doing here?" she hissed at Russ.

"I'm going to talk to Alyson," he said, bending down to keep his voice close to her ear. "What are you doing up and walking around? How do your feet feel?"

"They hurt. But not bad enough to miss the Eucharist. Why here?"

"Because I want her comfortable enough to talk, of course. You'd be amazed at how many people clam up and call for a lawyer when you haul 'em into the station for questioning."

"The whole 'separation of church and state' thing doesn't carry much weight for you, does it?"

"I think the church-as-sanctuary rule went out a few centuries ago."

One of the ushers bumped past them. "Excuse me, Reverend, but I have to get these doors open."

Clare and Russ stepped out of the way. Parishioners clad in bulky winter wools and chain-tread boots jostled each other on the way down the aisle. "I have to do the receiving line," she said. "I want to be there when you talk to her."

"I figured you would."

She pasted on a pleasant expression, shaking hands, exclaiming over bits of news, thanking those who offered to volunteer for the Christmas preparations, all the while watching as Russ intercepted Alyson and her mother in their pew and spoke with them. Alyson shook her head. Russ jerked his thumb toward the door. Alyson said something to her mother, who fluttered her hands like a bird afraid to fly. Russ leaned forward.

When he stepped back, both the Shatthams collected their things and followed him up the side aisle toward the parish hall.

Clare had no idea there were so many people in her congregation. She felt as if she had shaken five hundred hands and listened to at least that many comments about yesterday's storm before the last of them left the vestibule and she could painfully stump her way up the aisle, through the hall, and into the meeting room.

This time, Russ was the one sitting with his back to the window. Brilliant sunshine from a sky swept clean by the storm glowed around him, partially obscuring his face. Alyson slouched in the chair opposite him, twisting a strand of hair around two fingers.

Clare shut the door against the hum of conversation and the clink of coffee cups coming from the parish hall. "Good morning, Alyson, Mrs. Shattham."

"Reverend Clare," Barbara Shattham said, "Chief Van Alstyne says he needs more information about the dead girl. And that we've been waiting for you?"

Russ rose and ceremoniously pulled out a chair. Clare cocked an eyebrow at him. "I know your feet must be hurting you after your ordeal last night," he said.

"Ah." She got it. "Yes, thank you." She hobbled more obviously toward the table and sat down.

"Where's your husband, Mrs. Shattham?"

She frowned. "At home. He's not feeling well. He went cross country skiing yesterday and overdid it."

Clare shot a glance at Russ, but his eyes never left Barbara Shattham's face.

"Did you go with him?"

"It's not a sport I enjoy." She turned to Clare. "Reverend Fergusson—"

"Did he get home early or late?"

"What?"

"From skiing. Did Mr. Shattham get home early or late?"

"I don't know! Early evening. Seven or eight o'clock. What's this all about?"

Now Russ looked at Clare. She bit her lip, thinking. Could Mitch

Shattham have been the man who attacked her? He was about the right height and size, inasmuch as she could tell from a bulky snowsuit. Just how much would he do for his little girl?

"Yesterday evening," she turned toward the Shatthams, "there was a phone message waiting for me when I got back from Albany. I believe you knew I was going to Albany, Mrs. Shattham."

Barbara Shattham blinked, then nodded.

"And you told Alyson about what had happened at the Fowlers. That I discovered Wes and Katie McWhorter had been dating."

"Yes, I did. It concerned her, after all."

Clare looked directly at Alyson. "But you weren't surprised when your mother told you that Wes had had another girlfriend last year, were you? You already knew about him and Katie."

Alyson's fingers twitched at her hair. "No, I didn't." Sweet. Simple. A child who had never been called on cookie-stealing or missing homework.

"Katie has three roommates who have identified you from photographs as having visited her at the beginning of the school year." Russ's voice was calm. "Now, we can have them all come up for a live lineup—"

"A lineup? You mean as in arresting my daughter?"

Alyson's mouth dropped open. Her hair fell from between her fingers.

"She could do the lineup voluntarily. Or, she could do it after we've arrested her." He stared at the girl. "Or, she could tell us what she knows right here."

"I didn't do anything! Mummy, honestly, I didn't hurt anyone!" Her blue eyes swam soft and liquid with tears.

"There, you see?" her mother began.

Russ rose from his seat. "Alyson Shattham, I'm placing you—"

Alyson squealed. Russ sank back into his seat, slowly. The girl glanced at Clare and dropped her eyes. "Okay, I did know Wes was hanging around with Katie. I didn't have anything to do with what happened to her, okay? I only went down to Albany to tell her to lay off because it was like, time for the school-year fling to be over." She turned to her mother. "I mean, can you really see some chunky girl from Depot Street going with Wes to the Academy Ball? She was like, so wrong for him."

Clare leaned into the table. "You didn't know she was pregnant when you fought with her in Albany, did you?"

"God, no! That's so gross!" She raised her eyebrows. "I think Katie must have done it on purpose. Like to get him to marry her. Or for the welfare money. You know what those girls are like."

Clare opened her mouth but Russ stopped her with an upraised hand, shaking his head minutely.

"Why did you lie to us about not having seen Katie, Alyson?"

The girl glanced at her lap. Her shoulders twitched in what might have been a shrug. "I . . . um . . ."

"Where were you yesterday evening?"

"Huh?"

Mrs. Shattham frowned. "She was at home all afternoon and evening."

"Did she receive any phone calls?"

"Are you kidding? Of course she did. If Mitch and I didn't have our own line, we'd never be able to use the phone."

Russ removed a small notepad from his chest pocket. "Can you give me her number, please?"

"Why?"

"It'll make things go faster Monday morning when we contact the phone company for a record of all her outgoing calls."

Clare watched Alyson. She had never seen anyone actually go white before. Barbara Shattham started to protest. Clare laid a hand over her arm, stilling her. "Last night," she said, "a young woman claiming to be Kristen McWhorter called the church and left an urgent message for me to join her." She looked steadily at Alyson. "This young woman left directions for me to drive. I'm not very familiar with this area yet, as you know, so it helps a lot if I have directions. These ones weren't so good, however. They led to a washed-out road crossing a gorge. My car went in. I was fortunate—very fortunate—to walk away. My car was totaled."

"Dear God," Barbara Shattham said. "Are you suggesting my daughter had a hand in this? That's outrageous."

Alyson's gaze darted between Clare and Russ.

"I was stranded on Tenant Mountain with no vehicle and no cold-weather gear," Clare went on. "But that wasn't the worst. The worst was when a man in a snowmobile suit began shooting at me."

Everyone was silent for a moment. Russ clicked his pen and poised it over the notepad. "We can get a list of Alyson's calls first thing tomorrow morning," he said. "We'll be able to see right away if she called the church office yesterday."

Barbara Shattham stood abruptly. "She's not saying anything else until we see our attorney."

Russ leaned back, crossing his arms. "Well, that's certainly your right, ma'am. I was hoping we could sort things out right now, though." He shifted, splaying his hands on the table. "Let me make my position clear. Katie McWhorter and her father are both dead. Your daughter was seen arguing with Katie, who was poaching on her territory with Wes Fowler. She has access to a four-wheel-drive vehicle, she was in town during both murders, and when Reverend Clare found out about Katie and Wes, I believe your daughter sent her off on a wild goose chase designed to get her killed." He pinned Alyson with a level stare. "Either you give up a better suspect, Alyson, or I'll arrest you on two counts of murder and one of attempted murder."

The girl let out a nasal whine. "It wasn't me!"

"Alyson, don't—"

She swung her head violently, her perfect hair cascading everywhere. "I'm not going to jail for Wesley Fucking Fowler, Mother! Not after the way he's blown me off!" She reached across the table toward Russ. "He sent me an e-mail yesterday afternoon. Asked me to call and say I was Kristen. He was all sweet, just like he used to be, you know? It was just, like, a joke, because the Reverend had been poking around. I didn't know anyone was going to be hurt. I swear! I should have known he was yanking my chain. He's been, like, thanks but no thanks ever since he started sneaking around with that bitch."

Barbara Shattham sat down heavily. "Alyson," Clare said, "What about Katie?"

"I didn't have anything to do with that. And you can bet Wes didn't say anything to me. Except for a family get-together around Thanksgiving, he hasn't said shit to me since he left for the Academy."

"Alyson, your language . . ." Mrs. Shattham's voice trailed off.

"When was the last time you saw Katie?" Russ asked. "For real, this time."

"When I went to her house in Albany that time. I didn't know she was pregnant, I swear. I kept thinking, like, how could he prefer her to me? She was like, a size fourteen, for God's sake."

"Did Wesley ever indicate that he was having problems, or that he was troubled about his relationship with Katie?"

"He was weirding out before he went away to the Academy, but when I tried to talk with him, he blew me off. I had already figured it out, him and her, for God's sake. But he goes, 'just don't tell anyone.' Like I would. That's why I went to see her. And that's the last time I saw her. Alive or dead."

Russ and Clare looked at each other. He nodded slowly. "Thank you, Alyson. Mrs. Shattham, I suggest Alyson stay close to home."

"What do you think she's going to do, run to Canada?"

"I'm not worried she's going to flee jurisdiction. I'm worried because she knows something about Katie and Wesley. Just like Clare and Darrell McWhorter did. And look what happened to them."

Barbara Shattham clutched her daughter's sleeve. "Dear God." She glared at Russ. "She's in trouble because she's spoken to you. I expect you to provide us with police protection."

Russ pinched the bridge of his nose beneath his glasses. "Mrs. Shattham, she's in trouble because she's an accomplice to attempted murder. I'm not going to arrest her now. I may not ever arrest her, depending on what the district attorney has to say. I will," he stressed, "take any attempt to get in touch with Wes Fowler as a sign that she's actively assisting him. So take her home and keep an eye on her."

After the Shatthams left in a swirl of silky hair and tearful glares, Russ shook his head. "Girl like that makes me grateful I never had kids. Holy shit. What a self-centered little monster. Excuse my French."

"You wouldn't have a girl like that."

"I can understand why kids from crappy neighborhoods with piss-poor parents get into trouble. But how can kids with every advantage turn out so badly?"

Clare leaned forward. "Because the things you have, and the neighborhood you live in, doesn't have anything to do with what kind of human being you are. As I've said before."

"As you've said before." He smiled slightly. "What do you think? Was she telling the truth?"

"I don't know. She sure sounded pi—peeved at Wesley, though. I'd swear she was genuinely surprised that first time you questioned her, when she found out about Katie being pregnant."

"Well, that shoots my boy-and-girl-did-it-together theory."

"Vaughn Fowler should be back home with Wesley by now."

"That's assuming he wasn't already back home last night, trying to shoot you." From the open door, Clare could hear the sounds of coffee hour. "You probably have to go join your flock."

"Oh, no." She sank back into her seat. "I missed the Christmas cookie sale." At Russ's look she explained, "Fund-raiser for the choir. Everyone brings in cookies and you mix and match what you want to buy. I was going to show the flag by getting two bags' worth." She tried to pile her hair atop her head, but it was already in a French twist. She settled for pushing at the bobby pins. "I guess I may as well bow out entirely and come with you to see the Fowlers. Give me ten minutes to change out of my vestments and say good-bye."

He looked at the ceiling. "Why don't I just deputize you and issue you a gun, while I'm at it?"

Clare rose from the table. "No, thanks. But if there's a paying position as departmental chaplain, I'll take that. I'm going to need some extra money if I ever hope to replace my car."

CHAPTER
TWENTY-EIGHT

It was a short drive from St. Alban's to the Fowlers, but it was long enough for Clare to work up a full head of nerves and excitement. Fortunately, Russ was an easy person to be keyed up with; he listened to her ramble on about her ideas for the mother-and-baby outreach program, interjecting a question every time she stalled out over the realization that they were minutes away from confronting the young man who might be Katie's killer.

As they turned down the long country road that led to the Fowler's house, she confessed, "I'm a little tense about all this."

"Oh? I never would have guessed."

She punched him in the arm.

"Ow!"

"Don't you feel it, too? This may be it! Finally."

"I've done this a few more times than you, Reverend. Questioning someone doesn't get me all worked up." He glanced over to see her scowling. "Of course, it's different if I think the person I want to question is going to start shooting at me. I remember one time, I was working the violent crimes unit at Mannheim, we were investigating a series of rapes. Chief suspect was a ranger who taught hand-to-hand combat. One of these guys who can disable you with his forefinger and kill you with one hand tied behind his back. Walking up to his quarters to question him, I thought I was going to piss my pants, I was so scared."

"What happened?"

"I talked him into coming with me to the M.P. post. That's ninety percent of police work, you know, being able to talk and keep on talking until the problem is defused."

She pointed to a neatly plowed gravel drive. "Here it is." She recognized the Fowlers' Explorer and Volvo sedan. There was also a brand new Jeep Wrangler parked in front of the barn. "That must be Wesley's truck."

Russ parked the patrol car behind the Jeep and took a slow walk alongside it on his way to the door. Clare, staring into the windows, caught sight of herself and quirked her mouth. What did she think she was going to see, the abandoned snowmobile suit and a gun? She stepped lively to catch up with Russ, who had mounted the front steps.

Edith Fowler opened the door. Her deep-set eyes showed stark and white in her narrow face, like a spooked horse trapped in its stall.

"Mrs. Fowler? I'm Chief Van Alstyne. May I come in?"

Her social graces kicked in and her face relaxed. She opened the door widely. "Certainly, Chief. Reverend Clare, I'm glad to see you here as well." In the foyer, she took their coats. "I'm sorry we missed church this morning, but it's been . . . well . . ." She gestured down the hall. "They're in the family room."

Clare stepped out of rubber rainboots, the only foul-weather footwear she owned since trashing her leather boots last night. She was glad she hadn't changed into civvies. Her collar and black blouse created a shield dividing the woman who had slogged through an icy stream from the priest who was here to counsel and support this morning. *You are what you wear*, she could hear her grandmother lecture, stuffing Clare-the-tomboy into a ladylike dress. She plucked a piece of fluff from her ankle-length black wool skirt and followed Russ through the door.

The family room had obviously been a later addition to the old house. Its cathedral ceiling allowed for a Christmas tree that was easily twelve feet high, and the sweep of windows created an unbroken vista of snow and hills. The Fowler men were rising from a cluster of leather-covered love seats and chairs.

"Chief Van Alstyne." Vaughn Fowler didn't sound surprised to see a uniformed officer in his home at eleven o'clock on a Sunday morning.

Wesley looked startlingly like his father: same height, same strong features, same heavily-muscled build. His hair was shorter than even his father's military clip, shaved down to a bare fuzz. His face was strained and weary. He looked older than his eighteen or nineteen years, and Clare thought it entirely possible he could have been the "older man" Katie's roommates had seen.

"This is my son, Wesley."

"Sir." Wesley pumped Russ's hand.

Vaughn waved Clare over. "Wes, I don't think you've had the chance to meet our new priest yet. This is the Reverend Clare Fergusson."

"Ma'am." Clare and Wesley studied each other while shaking hands. He was definitely discomfited to see her. Was it because she was the one who had brought his connection to Katie out in the open? Or because she had brained him with a rock last night? A tough, strong kid like him could have recovered enough from last night's violence to appear this morning as if nothing had happened.

"Let's all sit down." Vaughn gestured Clare to one of the caramel-colored chairs. He was looking the worse for wear, too. As the men took their seats, she wondered if his control of the situation was what was keeping him together. "I've been talking with Wes." Vaughn said, before Russ could speak. "He has something to say to you, Chief."

The young man stood. "Sir, I am—I was Katie's boyfriend. I am the baby's father. There's no need to do a blood test. I'm responsible."

Russ laced his hands across his belt. "Sit down, Wes, you're not on report." The boy sat, spine held straight and away from the back of the love seat. "So you're Cody's father. Were you with her when she had the baby?"

"Yes sir. It was just after Thanksgiving." He glanced at his father. "I told my folks I was spending a few days with a friend. I took Katie to the Sleeping Hollow Motel, and she . . . she had the baby there."

"What happened after Katie gave birth?" Clare said.

"We waited a day to make sure he was, you know, okay, then we left him on the steps at St. Alban's."

She leaned forward. "Why?"

He glanced at her and then focused his gaze at a point two inches to the left of her head. "Ma'am, we agreed with each other to give the baby up. We thought—I thought, with the Burnses looking to adopt for so long, that it would be easy. Make sure they had the baby and then Katie and I could get back to our lives."

Clare steepled her fingers against her lips, holding back her reaction to such raw thoughtlessness.

"I didn't know the police would get involved!" he said. "I didn't know she would—" he caught his breath. "I just found out last week she had been, had been, killed. Alyson called me." Clare noticed a distinct lack of warmth when he mentioned his official girlfriend's name. "She said Ethan had been arrested for the murder."

"Ethan Stoner was arrested for threatening an officer and resisting arrest." Russ said. "He's no longer a suspect in the murders."

Wesley drew a deep breath. "I didn't kill Katie or her father. Sir. I—" his voice broke, a reminder that he was barely more than a boy after all. "I cared for her very much." He looked at Clare, square on. "I guess it was stupid to just leave the baby. But I knew there was a meeting that night, and that somebody would find him quickly. I thought once he was gone everything could be normal again."

His distress caught at Clare. "Pretending nothing happened can't right the world again, though, can it?"

He shook his head. "I want to do the right thing. Even though it's too late for . . . Katie. I'm ready to take care of the baby, to be his father." He glanced at his own father. "I've discussed it with my folks."

"That's a very stirring sentiment from a boy facing a double murder rap," Russ said.

Vaughn laid a hand on Wesley's shoulder. "My son has said he had nothing to do with the murders of the girl or her father, and I believe him. He's a Fowler. He wasn't raised to tell lies."

Russ unlaced his hands. "No offense, Mr. Fowler, but your son has already lied through omission about a lot of things, including his relationship with Katie, his whereabouts, and the fact that he's now a father. You'll understand why I have to take what he says with a grain of salt." He turned to Wesley. "The way I see it, you were desperate to keep the existence of Katie and Cody under wraps. You thought the Burnses would step in and take care of your responsibilities for you. My guess is, sometime between the night you dropped Cody off at the church and the night Katie's body was found, she got in touch with you and said she had changed her mind." The young man's face flinched almost imperceptibly. "Your plan for getting on with your life was about to be royally screwed. So you told Katie to meet you back in Millers Kill, drove her out to Payson's Park to discuss things, brained her with a tire iron, and rolled her down the hill into the river."

"No!"

"It wasn't the blow to the head that killed her, you know. She froze to death."

"No!" Wesley erupted from his chair, lurching toward Russ.

His father moved like an uncoiling spring, seizing his son by the arms. "Stop it, Wes! Stop it."

"This is what we're going to do," Russ said, standing slowly. "Wesley, you and I are going to the station, where we'll have a talk with Mr. Kaminsky of the D.A.'s office. If we decide we have enough to hold you on, we're going to charge you." Russ's gaze flicked from the young man's pale face to that of his father. "Mr. Fowler, I suggest you call your lawyer and meet us at the station."

"You can't question him without the presence of one of his parents."

"He's over eighteen."

"I didn't do it," Wesley said. "I didn't do it." He shook himself free of his father's restraint and turned to the older man. "What if I refuse to go?"

Russ broke in. "I'll arrest you right here."

Vaughn looked at his son for a long moment. "You go with him, Wes." The young man opened his mouth in protest. "It'll be for the best. We'll get a lawyer over there and have you back out by dinnertime."

"I didn't kill her, Dad. I couldn't have."

Vaughn squeezed his son's shoulders. "I know you didn't, Wes."

"Let's get your coat, Wesley." Russ stepped out of the way, keeping behind and to the side of the young man. He looked as if he sorely wanted to use his handcuffs.

"Mr. Fowler," Clare said quietly, "I didn't drive myself here. If you'd like me to, I'd be happy to stay here with you and Mrs. Fowler and come back to town with you. If you think I could be of some help."

Vaughn Fowler looked toward her, his gaze already a thousand yards ahead of him. He shook his head. "Thank you, Reverend, but under the circumstances . . ."

"Of course. The last thing I want to do is be intrusive." She impulsively took one of his hands between hers. "If I can do anything, please. Please give me a call."

From the hallway, Mrs. Fowler wailed. Vaughn Fowler jerked his hand from Clare's grasp and strode toward the sound.

"No, no, no," Wesley's mother said, clutching at her parka-clad son. "You can't take him! You can't take him!"

"Edith!" Vaughn Fowler grasped her upper arms firmly and tugged her away from Wesley. "Edith." He spoke quietly, almost intimately. "I'm calling the lawyer right now. Wes will be back home with us tonight."

"Mom, I'll be okay. Please."

"This can't be happening, not to us, not to our son—" Edith Fowler pressed one hand over her mouth, shuddering. She blinked hard, but no tears fell.

Her husband glared at Russ. "If anything happens to my son while he's in your care, I'll have your job."

Russ bristled. "I don't allow police brutality in my force, Mr. Fowler. Come on, Wesley. Clare, are you riding with me?"

She snatched her coat from the hall closet.

"Don't say anything until our lawyer gets there, Wes. Understand me?" Wesley nodded to his father as Russ led him down the steps toward the squad car.

Clare stood on the threshold. She spread her hands, miserably aware of how much she had contributed to these people's unhappiness and how little she could do to comfort them. "I'm so sorry. At times like these, it's tempting to feel as if you've been abandoned, by God and by your friends. Please remember that's not true."

Edith Fowler blinked again and wiped her eyes. "This whole thing is like a nightmare." She looked at her husband. "My God, Vaughn, do you realize we're grandparents?"

"I guess you're right." His face tightened. "Clare, will we be able to see the child? Or do we have to jump through some bureaucratic hoops now that he's in foster care? Where is he?"

"I don't know what sort of requirements the Department of Human Services will have. I suspect that if you two feel up to it, they'd be happy to have you serve as Cody's foster parents. His caseworker's name is Angela Dunkling, and right now he's fostering with Deborah McDonald, out toward Ft. Henry. I'll call you with their phone numbers as soon as I get back to my office."

Behind her, Russ tapped on the horn. "Meanwhile, I hope you'll reach out for some support and not try to go it alone."

Edith nodded. "I'll call Barb and Mitch. After all, they're involved too, in a way."

Clare opened her mouth and closed it again. If she got into exactly how involved the Shatthams had become last night, she could be here all afternoon. They'd find out their son's latest attempt to get out from under his problem soon enough.

"You do that." She retreated down the steps. "We'll speak soon."

She tugged on the car door, only to find it locked. Russ leaned over and let her in. Sliding into her seat, she glanced through the clear Plexiglas screen at Wesley, sitting perfect-postured in the back. The small sliding door that allowed for communication between front and back was latched shut. Clare reached for it.

Russ shifted the car into gear. "Clare, I'd rather not have any more questions until we get to the station. I want to do this by the book." He backed slowly out of the Fowler's drive. "I want his voluntary statement on the record, not in a car where his lawyer will be able to get it thrown out at trial."

She cast one more look back at the young man. He met her eyes, bleak and hopeless. She had wanted to feel a sense of triumph, of justice, when they caught up with Katie's killer. Instead she felt an ache in the pit of her stomach. So much damage. To so many lives. And it wasn't over yet.

TWENTY-NINE

At the station, Russ escorted Wesley into the interrogation room and latched the door behind him. "I'm going to make a pot of coffee," he said to Clare. "I don't know about you, but I could use a cup right now."

"Please. What happens now?"

"I already talked with Kaminsky last night, so he'll be expecting my call. He's going to be here to listen in to the questioning. I want to charge this kid some bad, but I want it to stick." He squinted into the distance. "We'll need a cross-jurisdiction warrant to search his room at the Academy. And I want his truck . . ."

Clare cut him off. "Can I speak with him now? Not as part of this, but as priest to parishioner?"

Russ frowned. "You just met him this morning. How much of a pastoral relationship can you have?"

"That's not the point, Russ. I want to help him if I can. He's obviously very troubled."

"He's very troubled because he carefully planned and executed two cold-blooded murders and now I've caught his ass, excuse my French. And let's not forget he would have done the same to you if you hadn't escaped him. Jesu—um Crow, Clare, you'd try to make excuses for Charles Manson!"

"I'm not making excuses for anything he may have done." She crossed her arms. "No one is beyond forgiveness, Russ. Or beyond asking for forgiveness. I have to believe that."

He pulled off his glasses and polished them on his shirt front. "I don't even know why you're here. After I speak with Kaminsky, I want you to take my truck and go home." He rapped on the door to the interrogation room. "Wesley? Reverend Clare here would like to speak with you as your—" he glanced at Clare, "—spiritual advisor. You want to talk with her?"

There was a pause. "I guess so. Okay."

Russ unlatched the door. "There's an alarm buzzer on the wall. If he makes any moves on you, use it. I'll be back in a few minutes."

Clare nodded. The room was a smaller version of the meeting room, albeit without windows. Heavy, well-worn wooden table and chairs, tired institutional green walls. She had thought there would be one of those two-way mirrors like in the movies, but it looked like the Millers Kill police department wasn't quite up to cinematic standards yet.

Wesley was standing at the far end of the room, his back against the wall, his eyes shadowed and suspicious. She tugged at a chair. It was bolted to the floor. She sat down and propped her chin in her hand. "I'm the one who found Cody, you know."

Wesley looked at his boots. "Yeah, I know." He darted a glance at her. "My dad says you've been working hard to see that the Burnses get to adopt him."

She nodded. "You could help with that. As his father, you can authorize a legal adoption just by signing over the papers. They wouldn't have to wait and wonder the way they are doing now."

He brushed the speckled vinyl floor with the toe of his boot. "I guess we never realized that you couldn't just give away a baby. I didn't mean to have them wait. We just—it was easier to not think about it. The fact that there was a baby on the way. We never exactly planned any of it."

"What about the motel? The fake I.D.? That must have taken some planning."

"I already had an old I.D. I had doctored up so I could, um, get into bars." He looked at the wall opposite him. "I met her at her school— she had her roommate's car—and we stopped at the first place that was open. We weren't even sure if she was going to have the baby then or not. She'd been having those, you know, fake contractions." He tilted his head back. "It all seemed so unreal. Being there, the baby, everything. I just wanted things to go back to the way they were. Without our parents finding out."

"Why did you leave the baby at the church instead of at the Burnses' house?"

"They weren't home when we drove by. Then I remembered my parents talking about the reception for the new priest that night. We figured somebody would find the baby and read the note and hand him over to the Burnses. Pretty dumb, huh?"

She bit her lower lip. "It wasn't the smartest thing, no."

He glanced at her. "Hey, do you think if I help the Burnses adopt the baby quickly, it'll help me with the cops?"

"I don't think so. It might help you with your own conscience, though."

He dropped into a chair opposite her. "What we're talking about here, you can't tell that to anyone, right?"

"No, I can't. What we say here is just between you and me and God."

"I didn't do it."

"Wesley . . ."

"Reverend, I didn't kill her. Or her rotten father. And it's been driving me crazy, because I don't know who could have done it. She was so . . . she was so special. Sweet. Funny. She didn't like me because of my family or my car. She didn't care if I got into student council or West Point. She liked me because of who I was. Not who I was supposed to be. You know?" He rubbed his hands back and forth against the tabletop. "I didn't want to have a baby. And I didn't want to get married. But it wasn't her, it was just . . . it was too soon. You know what I mean?"

"Yes."

"And I don't think she really wanted to get married and keep the baby, either. She sent me a long e-mail about how she did, after we had both gotten back to school, but I don't think it was something she had thought out. My dad said that after-pregnancy hormones can make a woman kind of crazy, and if I just let it be for awhile, she'd realize that rushing into marriage would be a bad idea."

"Your dad said that?"

"Yeah. I figured, if she really couldn't stand not having the baby, I could transfer from the Academy to SUNY Albany. Forget the whole military thing and go for a business degree, something so I could support them as soon as I graduated. But I didn't know how I'd swing it financially." He looked up at her. "You don't have to pay to go to West Point, you know, so I didn't have anything saved. I didn't know if my parents could help us out. I wanted to talk about it with Dad before I suggested it to Katie."

She took a slow, deep breath to keep her voice even. "You offered to leave West Point? You spoke with your father before Katie was killed?"

"Yeah. I didn't want to let him know how bad I screwed up, but I had to. I mean, if we had taken Cody back and gotten married, Katie would have had to drop out if she joined me at the Academy. Lose her scholarship. That would have been a total waste. She was so smart. God, I can't believe she's actually dead." Wesley buried his face in his hands.

Clare sucked in air and held her breath for a moment. "Wes? This is going to sound strange, but can I touch the back of your head?"

He looked at her as if she had lost her mind. "Uh . . . this isn't some sort of faith-healing thing, is it?"

"No." She rose partway from her chair, extending her arm toward his close-cropped hair. "May I?"

He shrugged. "Sure."

She ran her hand lightly over the crown and back of his skull, then pressed more firmly with her fingers. Nothing. No bump, no swelling, no soft spot. "Does this hurt anywhere?"

"No. What are you doing, Reverend?"

"Feeling my way toward the truth." She sank into her chair again. "You weren't out in the woods last night trying to kill me."

He reared back. "Are you crazy? Of course I wasn't out trying to kill you. I wasn't trying to kill anyone! I was in my dorm room, studying."

"What time did your dad pick you up to bring you home?"

"Early this morning. There must have been a dozen guys who saw me there last night, in my room, in the hall, in the john. You can ask them. I wasn't out trying to kill anyone. I'm not a killer!"

Clare looked at her hands, flat on the table. She flipped them over and studied her palms. "Anyone can be a killer, Wes. All it takes is the right training. And enough motivation." She blew out her breath. "Could your father access your e-mail account?"

"Huh? Not my account at the Academy. He could send stuff from my old address at home, he knew my password for that." Clare stood, wrapping her arms around herself. "Why? What the hell does this have to do with—" his face changed suddenly.

"Your father," she said.

"No," he said.

She felt as if she had just flown into a strong thermal and gained a thousand feet of altitude in a few seconds. Dizzy. Disoriented. From where she was now, everything was the same, but everything looked different. "Your father, Wesley." She looked down at the young man. His face was a mask of absolute denial. "Your father is so proud of you. And so determined that you go to West Point and have a brilliant military career. What wouldn't he do to protect you from 'ruining your life' with some white-trash girl and her baby?"

"No," he said.

"He must have contacted her and invited her to Millers Kill. Maybe he tried to bribe her into forgetting about you and Cody first. But that didn't work. He wouldn't have known that that wouldn't work with someone like Katie. So he got rid of the problem another way."

"No!"

She paced around the table, talking as much to herself as to Wesley. "We assumed that Darrell McWhorter threatened to blackmail Cody's father. But why go to a kid in college when you can tap into so much more money from his dad?" She leaned over the table. "He saw you two together, didn't he? Darrell."

Wesley hesitated, then nodded. "I drove her home from the library late once. She used to have me leave her at the intersection, but it was dark and starting to snow, so I took her right to her apartment house instead. She was always scared that her dad would find out about us. He was just getting back from a bar or something that night, and got a real good look at me." He leaned back in his chair and scrubbed at his face with his hands. "Katie said he asked her a lot of questions about me, but she convinced him I was just a guy in her study group."

"Darrell was smarter than any of us gave him credit for. As soon as he saw your family photo on the parish bulletin board, he put all the pieces together. When he called your father, they must have agreed to ride down to Albany to get any incriminating stuff left in Katie's room as part of the deal. And when your father saw his chance to get rid of Darrell, he acted quickly and decisively." She straightened. "Wesley, your father's been methodically removing every person who might interfere with you becoming the fifth generation of Fowlers to graduate from West Point."

"This is insane. My dad wouldn't kill anybody! And if he's willing to do anything to protect me, why the hell wouldn't he confess instead of letting the cops cart me off to jail?"

"Your dad could kill somebody, Wes. He's done it before, lots of times. It's just not in the line of duty this time." She paused. "Or maybe for him it is." She crossed her arms and blew out a frustrated breath. "But you're right, it doesn't make sense that he'd let you be convicted of—" her stomach clenched into a tight ball. "Oh, my God. The baby."

"What? What do you mean?"

"The baby, Wes, the baby! The one you told him you were ready to raise as a single father? The baby who is the root of all his troubles? Oh, holy God, I told him where to find him. I told him." She slammed her palm against the alarm button, setting off an electronic siren that made the edge of her back teeth ache.

The door rattled and then Russ was inside the room, crouching low, his gun drilled at Wesley. "Down on the floor! Now!" Wesley fell out of his chair, flat and spread-eagled. Russ didn't look away from him. "Clare? Are you okay?"

The siren made it impossible to talk. "Yes!" she shouted. "I just needed to get out of the room!"

"What?" Russ straightened and stalked over to the alarm. He twisted a knob. It fell silent, leaving sound-echos ringing in her ears. "What the hell did you mean, setting off an alarm just to get out? You don't move until I say you do, mister!" He swiveled his gun back toward Wesley, who had levered himself up on his arms.

Clare opened her mouth to tell Russ everything, then shut it again. What we say here is just between you and me and God. Priestly confidence. Her throat and chest felt as if they would burst with her discovery. A discovery she couldn't share with anyone. She groaned.

"Clare?"

"Give me your truck keys. Now."

"What's—"

"Now, Russ!" He fished his keys out of his pocket.

"I'm going to Deborah McDonald's house out on Aubry Road near the intersection of old Route One Hundred." She jabbed a finger at Wesley. "You! Tell the chief everything!" She pelted through the door before Russ could stop her with any more unanswerable questions.

After her speedy little MG, driving Russ's pickup felt like piloting a C1-30 Hercules transport down the runway. She rolled over the corner curb getting out of the parking lot and nearly sideswiped a carload of Christmas shoppers. Fortunately, the route to Deborah McDonald's was mostly through countryside. As soon as she hit the town limits, she tromped on the accelerator. "Let's see how fast you can go, big guy," she said to the speedometer. She knew her way from Millers Kill to both the Fowlers' and the McDonalds', but she had no idea how long it might take Vaughn Fowler to get from his place to Cody's foster mother's. She pressed harder on the gas pedal. Maybe she was wrong, and she'd find the baby napping peacefully. Maybe the McDonalds were out shopping. Maybe Wesley's father was too busy rousting out a lawyer on a Sunday afternoon to think of Cody. Maybe.

Just past the turnoff from old Route 100, she went over the ridge and around the corner way too fast, overcorrected, and would have hit an Explorer heading up the hill if it hadn't slid into the shoulder. Its horn blared as she went past, her heart beating out of her chest. The next corner she took slow and safe, cresting the top carefully until the valley stretched out before her like a Christmas card. Everything looked peaceful in the McDonalds' yard as she pulled in.

As she jumped down from the truck, the front door flew open to reveal Deborah McDonald. Today's sweatshirt pictured two kittens playing with mistletoe. "Oh, my goodness," Deborah said, "you're that lady priest. Are you with the family? Do you know where he's gone?"

Clare's skin prickled. "What's happened, Mrs. McDonald?"

"I just had a visit from Cody's grandfather. At least, he said he was Cody's grandfather. He knew who Angela Dunkling was—"

"What happened?"

"He was with the baby in the living room while I went to get some pictures, and when I came back, they were gone! I wasn't sure what to do. I was about to call the folks at DHS . . ."

Clare took the front steps two at a time. "You need to call the police. Tell them Vaughn Fowler has the baby. What was he driving?"

"A big, blue sports utility truck."

The Explorer! "Tell them he's in a dark blue Ford Explorer. I passed him on the curve before this. I didn't notice the driver." God had better forgive her for being such an idiot, because she wasn't about to. She swung around to dash down the steps again.

"Wait! Where are you going? Where did he take Cody?"

Clare closed her eyes. *Where.* "Let me use your phone for one moment before you call the police," she said.

Deborah McDonald pointed through the door. Clare strode through the living room, snatched up the receiver and dialed Information for the Fowler's number, which she punched in before the electronic voice was finished with the last digit.

The phone rang. And rang. And rang. Clare thought she might scream.

"Hello?" It was Edith Fowler.

"Mrs. Fowler, this is Clare Fergusson. Do you know where your husband is?"

"He's not here, Reverend. He asked me to call our lawyer and left right after you did. Why? Nothing's happened to Wes, has it?"

"No, no. Did Vaughn have his gun with him?"

"His gun?"

"Is there any way to check? Please, it's important."

"Why on earth—"

"Please! It's important."

"Let me look in the gun case . . ." over the phone, Clare could hear the sounds of a door opening and shutting. "I'm right here in his study. His rifles are all here, but his Colt is missing."

Clare would have bet a year's salary the Colt was buried in a snowdrift somewhere on Tenant Mountain. "Listen, Mrs. Fowler. I'm calling from Cody's foster mother's house. Your husband has taken the baby. If he comes back home or contacts you, try to keep him calm and get the baby away from him. Let the police know right away."

It was so silent Clare thought for a moment the line had gone dead. "I understand," Edith Fowler said finally. "I will."

Clare rang off and headed back outside. Vaughn Fowler was unarmed. But she couldn't shake the conviction that he meant to dispose of Cody once and for all.

"Did she know where he went?" Deborah McDonald asked as Clare hauled herself into the truck's cab.

Where would he go? Where, when it was so easy to kill an infant? Clare pressed her fingers to her forehead. *When you are threatened and on the run, you will tend to return to the same base of operations,* "Hardball" Wright drawled. *If not to the same spot, then to the same sort of terrain. Remember that. The enemy will.* She opened her eyes. "I think he's headed for the river. The trail from Payson's Park or the old railroad bridge. I'm going to head there. Let the police know." If Russ had any better ideas, he could chase after them without her. She ground the gears and backed out of the driveway, catching the McDonald's mailbox with the rear bumper and setting it swinging wildly.

Traffic through the north end of town was agonizingly slow, but she didn't know any other way toward where she and Russ had discovered Katie's body. She swung onto the Cossayaharie road, Route 137, driving carefully, tamping down the urge to go faster and faster, afraid she might miss the turnoff to the park.

She nearly did miss it, mistaking the newly-plowed entrance for a driveway. At the last moment, she turned the truck into a frame-shuddering turn and rolled down the lane toward the parking area. The county plow had cleared a large U out of the fresh snow before heading back to the main road. She couldn't tell from where she sat if there were tracks heading down the trail. Leaving the truck running, she jumped from the cab and ran to the edge of the parking lot. Behind the ridge of snow thrown up by the plow, the trail leading down to the kill was unbroken by footprints or tire tracks. "Vaughn Fowler," she hissed from between clenched teeth, "where are you?"

CHAPTER
THIRTY

Clare ranged up and down the edge of the parking lot to make sure Fowler hadn't cut through the woods to join the trail further down. Her rubber boots weren't meant for snow, and the treads slipped and slid as she searched for any sign of the man. Nothing. She muttered obscenities she hadn't allowed herself to use in several years and climbed back into the truck. The engine on, she rested her head against the steering wheel and breathed deeply to calm herself. Could she be wrong about where Fowler was headed? After all, it would be easy to kill a baby anywhere—a story where ancient Romans had disposed of infants by smacking them into walls thrust itself into her consciousness. She wrenched her mind away from the horrific image and concentrated on Vaughn Fowler.

The riverside bank, the rest stop on a remote stretch of highway, an abandoned camp road high on a mountain. Every place he had killed or tried to kill had been isolated, a place where a body could disappear for hours. Or years. She sat up, rubbing at the crease in her forehead left by the wheel. Her instructor from Survival School had been right. Fowler was returning to the same sort of terrain. She had to try the abandoned railroad bridge.

She swung the pickup through the plowed area, turning left when she reached the road. Where was she going to find the thing? Russ had told her it was a half-mile upstream from the trail, but that didn't necessarily translate into a half-mile drive up the road. There must have been train tracks leading straight toward the river, but where were they?

Ahead of her, high-voltage lines crossed Route 137, sparking memories of the times she had navigated small planes by following the clearly-visible paths maintained by electric companies. She slowed the truck, then pulled over onto the shoulder. Metal transmission towers marched in a receding line down a wide right-of-way through the forest. It vanished over a gentle rise that led, if she wasn't mistaken, toward the river. The kill. She couldn't see any train tracks under the snow, but there were clear marks of snowmobiles crisscrossing beneath the towers and there, ahead of her and to the right, tire tracks along what must be the electric company's access road.

She fumbled with a dial on the steering column, engaging the four-wheel-drive. She downshifted and rolled onto the snow, following the other tracks as closely as possible, praying hard that she wasn't chasing after some die-hard fisherman or snowmobiling enthusiast.

The truck growled up the access road, crunching snow beneath its big tires, carrying her forward surely and steadily. As she crested the rise, it struck her that none of the squad cars would be able to follow her. Hot prickles ran up the insides of her arms and she bit her lip. Some of the officers had better have four-wheel-drive vehicles or she was going to be in a world of trouble. She refused to think about the possibility that the police might not be following her at all.

The right-of-way, and the tire tracks, curved gently to the left, disappearing from view in the thick stand of trees. She accelerated slightly, the rear tires whining a complaint. As she rounded the bend, the landscape opened startlingly before her: blue sky, white snow, black water. Dark green bridge. Dark blue Ford Explorer.

She slammed on the brakes, sending the truck into a skid that ended with a jarringly abrupt stop. She almost fell from the cab in her frantic need to get out. She could see him, perhaps halfway along the span of the bridge, silhouetted against the sky. Well-bundled up against the cold, carrying something.

"Mr. Fowler!" she screamed. Running through the snow to the bridge was like running in a nightmare, slipping and dragging and making almost no headway despite the efforts that left sweat running down her spine. "Stop!"

He did. She thrashed through the remaining few feet to the bridge and staggered onto the rails. She saw why he had been walking so slowly: the train track was supported on a huge trestle but open to the air. On either side of the railbed was a riveted steel walkway and parapet, something the rail workers must have crossed on decades ago. Between the scanty patches of snow that hadn't been scoured off by the wind, she could see patches of rust eating away the green-painted metal. She decided to stay right where she was, on the half-foot-wide wooden ties.

Vaughn Fowler was facing her now, cradling a blanket-wrapped bundle with one arm. "I can't say I'm surprised to see you, Reverend," he said, his voice carrying clearly through the cold air. "As president of the vestry, I'm disappointed in your performance so far. Way too much time spent on a situation that is out of your area of concern."

She heard nothing from inside the blanket. Shouldn't the baby be crying after all this? She pressed her lips tightly together. Dear God, don't let him be already dead. "My area of concern? It's the people around me. The McWhorters. The Burnses." She picked her way along another few crossbars, moving closer. "Your son. Your grandson. You." She looked steadily at Fowler, searching his face for something she could reach with her words. "Let me help you."

"Very comforting, coming from a woman who tried to kill me last night." He held out a hand. "Stop there, Reverend."

She stopped, her arms spread for balance. Beneath her feet, she could see the kill, black and glittering in the pale sunlight. Chunks of ice bobbed lazily in the slow current. "Are you going to try to shoot me again?" she asked.

Fowler laughed, a short, coughing sound. "Hardly. I lost my side arm when you ambushed me. Carried that Colt for twenty years, and lost it to a damn woman. A priest to boot. Damn, I liked that piece." He narrowed his eyes. "You were good out there. I'm lucky to have survived with my feet and my balls intact."

"I'm so sorry. I didn't mean to hurt you—"

"Bullshit. You meant to hurt me, and you did. I underestimated you, and I paid the price. Don't apologize for being successful."

"No, sir." The acknowledgment was an automatic response to his tone of voice. She sure wasn't going to reach him by appealing to him as a priest, but maybe she could engage him officer to officer. The longer they kept talking, the more likely it was Russ and his men could find them. "I thought taking your boots and flashlight to keep you from reaching your vehicle was good strategy, but obviously, it didn't work."

"I had a penlight in my snowmobile suit. Always carry backup equipment when you're in the woods. As soon as I'd assessed the situation, I stopped chasing after you and headed straight for my snowmobile."

"But . . . your feet . . ."

"Were damn cold by the time I reached my friend's cabin. However, I was wearing insulated hunting socks. Next time you try to cripple someone, make sure you leave him with bare feet. Better still, just split his head open."

"Sir, my objective was to slow you down, not to kill you."

"Stupid objective. The only way to deal with an enemy is to take him out. Period. Otherwise, you'll never know when he'll jump back up and bite you in the ass."

"Like Darrell McWhorter?"

His face crinkled in disgust. "Slimy bastard. Called me up and said he'd tell the cops about Wesley and his daughter if I didn't pay him off. Ten thousand dollars. He thought Wes had killed her and he was still willing to overlook it for money. What a scumbag."

A raven flew past the bridge, cawing loudly. She took another step along the railroad ties. "How did you persuade him to come with you to Albany, sir?"

"I told him I'd pay if he'd collect any telltale evidence from the girl's apartment and hand it over. I knew he'd jump at the chance to find something more substantial to hold over my head." He gave her a look that invited her to agree that the late Darrell McWhorter was an idiot. "I planned on getting rid of him in Albany; as it happened, a better opportunity presented itself."

"So that was you who rifled through Katie's things."

He tucked his head in assent. "With some of last year's Halloween costume stuck to my face. Crude, but effective."

From below, Clare could hear the flat lapping of the river against its rock-and-snow-covered banks. Would dropping Cody in also qualify as crude, but effective? She glanced at the bundle in Fowler's arm.

"Oh, he's alive. The little bastard fell sound asleep in my truck, can you believe it?"

"What is it you're looking for here, Colonel? What outcome are you after?" She let a note of challenge creep into her voice. "Wesley's already off the hook for the murders. What do you hope to accomplish out here?"

"I'm trying to save my son from himself. He's already fumbled badly, getting that girl pregnant in the first place and then not insisting she have an abortion. He was going to walk away from everything, just because she decided at the last minute she didn't want to give it up. Can you believe that?"

Clare bit her lip. "There's no chance of that now, though, is there? You took care of that."

"You mean the girl? I didn't set out to eliminate her. If she had just taken the money I'd offered—Christ, she could have paid her way through the state school and had a nest egg left over! She was too stupid to do what was best for her."

"Some people might say she was too principled to trade money for her child."

"Bullshit. She saw an opportunity to trap a boy from a decent family who could be counted on to earn a good paycheck." He glared at her. "If Wes had quit school to marry her, if he takes on her—" he glanced at the blankets in his arm, "—kid, he'd regret it for the rest of his life. I'm not going to let that happen." His face tightened. "Wes is still too soft, yet. It's up to me to protect him."

"By killing his son and sending his father to death row? Do you really think that's going to protect him? That he won't regret it for the rest of his life?" She stepped toward Fowler, never taking her eyes off him, feeling out the ties through her boots. "Wesley's ready to sign the boy over to the Burnses. He told me so himself." She balanced on one leg, bumping her other boot against a wooden tie until she had a foothold. "He's a good kid. Sensitive, responsible, caring. You can stop this right here without damaging him any further." She stretched out her arms. "Give me the baby. The other two you . . . eliminated, those were on the spur of the moment, unplanned, right? That's manslaughter. You can plead to diminished capacity or temporary insanity or . . . or . . . something."

She kept her arms open. Her chest and throat ached. From a distance, she could hear the sound of a motor. A snowmobile, maybe. She wanted it to be help. She wasn't up to this. She couldn't do this all by herself.

You aren't all by yourself, the thought came, from inside and outside all at once. She breathed in sharply. "Give me the baby, Colonel. Don't burden the rest of Wesley's life with the knowledge that he was the reason you did this terrible thing."

He frowned, pressing his lips together. Considering. Poised between two ties, she held herself absolutely still, arms burning, reaching.

Behind them, the sound of an engine cut through the air. Fowler looked past her. "Ah. Reinforcements," he said. He hefted the blanket-wrapped parcel higher.

Clare couldn't look back. She heard thudding doors and the faint squawk of a walkie-talkie. "They don't change anything," she said. "This is still your call."

"Vaughn." Russ's voice was measured, temperate. The sound of it was like seeing the landing lights at the end of a long night's flight. "How 'bout I walk onto this bridge and we all try to resolve this situation?"

Fowler raised his bundle higher. From within the blanket, the baby began to cry, short, sharp squalls demanding attention. "Stay where you are, Chief, or I toss this into the kill."

"No!" Clare's hands clutched around empty air. Beneath them, she heard the motor coming closer, a spluttering roar.

"You're not going to walk away from this, Vaughn. That's a police boat covering the water. The state troopers will be moving men in on the other side of the kill, and they're going to be bringing a sharpshooter with them. Give the baby to Clare, and let's all get out of the cold. Your son is waiting to see you. He's worried sick about you."

Fowler shook his head. "I didn't plan to walk away from this, Chief. I knew when I moved decisively to save my son from dropping out and marrying that trailer trash that I would have to be an acceptable loss."

"No. Colonel." Clare moved forward another shaky step. "Think what you'll be doing to your family."

"I have. I'm saving them the embarrassment of a trial and incarceration. Don't you think I considered how this would look? No one understands sacrifice these days. No one appreciates what it is to put your duty to your family or your service first."

In her peripheral vision, Clare caught a glimpse of the boat, motoring slowly upstream toward the bridge. She took another step. Fowler began to unwind the blanket from the wailing infant. She knew, at that moment, he would toss Cody into the kill, no matter what they said or did. She unzipped her parka and peeled it off. "Give me the baby, Colonel," she said, holding out her coat. "You can put him right in here." She balanced on a single tie, feet together, pressing down on the back of one rubber boot. "I promise you, I'll see that the Burnses get him. He won't interfere with Wesley's schooling ever again." Her stockinged foot slid free. She wavered, one-legged, almost losing her balance. She didn't take her eyes off Vaughn Fowler's face.

He looked down at the angry baby kicking in the crook of his arm. "He's such a responsible kid, that's part of the problem." Clare found her footing again. Her toes curled over the edge of the tie as she lifted her other leg and shook the boot free. It hit one of the ties and fell off her foot. A moment later, she heard a splash.

"Give her the baby, Vaughn, and let's get out of here. Your son needs you." Russ's voice sounded much closer now. She could feel him, radiating strength and reassurance, almost close enough to reach back and touch.

Vaughn drew a deep breath, as if savoring the taste of the air. "Wes is the fifth generation of my family to attend West Point, did I tell you that?"

Clare nodded. "Yes, sir, you did."

He looked into her eyes, soberly, measuring. "It's a good thing to live as a soldier." With a shrug and a twist of his arms, he tossed Cody over the parapet.

Russ shouted, "Get down, Clare!" as the parka tumbled from her arms. She went over the side before she had a chance to think about it, her shins scraping the iron, the wind tearing up her eyes and blinding her, and then she was under the water, and it was cold, cold beyond any definition of cold, burning her skin like acid. She followed her bubbles up to the pale sunshine, broke the surface, unable to breathe, the shock of it seizing her lungs. She heard yelling, a motor gunning, shots. It was hard to think, impossible to focus. She couldn't see Cody. She gulped in air with a sob, forcing her chest to work, went under again. The boat motor throbbed through her nerves. Her body felt like one huge tooth ache. She spiraled through the clear water. There was a flash of white ahead, but when she broke surface, it was a clump of snow and ice. Someone was yelling her name. She went under again, the ache intensifying, although she couldn't have imagined it could get any worse.

She saw him. Floating so near the surface his ice-blue sleeper was dappled with sunlight. She stroked through the water, kicking against the drag of her skirt, time slipping past her like bubbles, until she reached the tiny form. She surfaced again, hauling Cody up with her, holding his head out of the water one-handed while she tread in place. "Here!" she screamed. "I've got him! Here!"

The sound of the boat was everywhere, but she was still surprised when she turned and it was there; cutting engines, sliding alongside her. Hands reached out, so many hands, and she held up Cody and let him be whisked out of view. She reached for the side, but she was too weak to hold on. More hands grasped her, grabbed her arms, and she was hauled in like a fish, flopping and twitching on the bottom of the boat until someone tossed a thermal blanket over her and rolled her in it. Through the press of parkas, she saw a man half-dressed in diving gear recussitating Cody, his mouth covering half the baby's face.

"Breathe."

"For Christ's sake, take us over to the shore so we can pick up the chief, he's going to freeze to death."

"Get on that radio to County Hospital, tell 'em we're coming in with possible hypothermias."

"Miss, I have another blanket. Can you get your clothes off under there?"

"What about the perp's body? Are we fishing him out?"

Cody's tiny fist jerked in the air. The diver pulled away, rolling the baby onto his side. Cody coughed, vomited up a stream of water, and began to cry. Everyone cheered except Clare, who squeezed her eyes shut against hot tears.

The boat bumped and scraped against rock. She opened her eyes in time to see Russ wading through the water. The boat tipped hard to one side as he heaved himself in. "Come back here, Chief," the voice beside her said. "I've got a blanket for you. Jeez, you tore the hell out of your pants, didn't you? What the hell were you thinking of? We had them."

Clare focused on the man who had been helping her, and recognized

Kevin Flynn. The engine kicked in again, pulling them steadily away from the shore, gaining speed as they motored downstream.

"Shove it over, Kevin," Russ said, his voice thick. The young officer handed him a blanket and carefully shifted down the bench. Russ wrapped himself from the waist down and sat heavily. "Lyle, you notify the hospital we're coming in?"

"I sure did, Chief."

"Call the staties, let 'em know we're going to need a diving team and a water search to recover Fowler's body."

"What happened?" Clare asked, her teeth clicking together.

"You mean after you did your swan dive? Fowler fired on me."

"Oh, no. Oh no. Were you the one who—"

"No, my gun was still holstered. Mark was my backup. He's a damn good shot." He shook his head. "Fowler was hit. He went between the ties." He looked at her, his eyes so deep she thought she could dive in and touch the bottom of him.

"I'm so sorry," she said.

"For Fowler or for Mark?" He raised a hand. "No, don't tell me. I know. For both of them." He took off his glasses and wiped them on a corner of the blanket. "When I saw you go over the edge like that . . ." He shook his head. "I took the fast route down by sliding down that goddamn slate embankment. My ass is going to feel that one for a month. 'Scuse my French." He threw his arm around Clare and pulled her blanket-wrapped form tightly to his side. "Jesus Christ, Clare, what were you thinking of? Do you have any idea how fast you can die in water that cold? We had a diver standing by, for chrissakes."

"I didn't know it was going to be that cold," she said, shaking uncontrollably against him. She jerked her chin toward the squalling baby. "It was worth it."

He nodded. "Yeah, I guess it was." He smiled a bit. Then he started to laugh softly.

"What?"

"Damn, I sure had you pegged when I said you jumped in feet-first without thinking . . ."

CHAPTER
THIRTY-ONE

At twilight, the small parking area behind St. Alban's was already filled. Well, he should have expected that on Christmas Eve. Russ parked in the lot across the street, collected his package, and trudged across Elm toward the Gothic double doors hung with wreaths. The pavilion in the square was glowing with Christmas lights and the shining windows of the last stores open, and for a moment he could have been back in 1962, when everything in his world was safe and understandable. Where businesses never closed and marriages were forever and no one ever died.

He shook his head at his sentimentality and hauled on one of the elaborately cast bronze door pulls. Inside the church, his glasses fogged over, blinding him. The smell of pine and beeswax filled the shadowy air. From the choir stalls a soloist was singing, then stopping, going back and repeating her phrase.

"Hey. Chief Van Alstyne. Are you here to help, too?"

He popped his glasses back on. A startlingly well-scrubbed Kristen McWhorter faced him, carrying a box of tall white candles.

"Kristen. Hi. I'm surprised to see you here."

She jiggled the box. "Reverend Clare talked me into helping with the decorating. I'm sprigging the candles. Don't ask."

He grinned. "Okay. How is everything?"

"Pretty good. The funerals were hard. Hard to get

through. But knowing what happened to her helped. I still haven't spoken with Wes Fowler. Which I can understand. But I have been seeing Cody." She smiled. "The Burnses have asked me to be a godmother, isn't that cool? He's going to be baptized here in January."

"That's very cool, yeah. I'm glad for you." He glanced around the church. A woman was twining greenery around huge standing candelabras and an elderly man was wedging votive lights into recesses in the windowsills. "Where's the Reverend?"

"I heard her muttering something about coffee. I'd check in her office."

The hallway was dim and quiet. He knocked on her door frame. "Anyone in?"

"Russ! Well, isn't this a nice surprise. If you're here for the seven o'clock service, you're a few hours early." Clare rose from one of her odd-looking admiral's chairs, elegant in a tailored black blouse and long skirt. "Let me get you a cup of coffee." She poured from her thermos into a Virginia Seminary mug. The coffee was hot and sweet and tasted of cinnamon. He dropped his package on the shabby love seat and laid his parka over it before sitting down.

"I meant to call when I saw the notice about Fowler's funeral in the paper."

"I didn't officiate. I asked Clifton Whiting from St. Ann's in Saratoga. I thought my presence would be more of a hurt than a help." She looked into her coffee. "I can't help but think that if I'd been a little more on the ball—"

"You could have stopped Fowler from destroying himself? Someone once told me you can't take responsibility for everyone around you. Seems like a pretty smart observation."

She smiled crookedly at him. "I should have had you around to put in a good word for me when the vestry called me on the carpet to explain what had been going on. I don't know who shocked them more, me or Vaughn Fowler."

He slipped off his glasses and polished them on his scarf. "If you need me to let them know what a genuine help you were—"

"No, no. They just need time to readjust their worldview. I'm taking advantage of the confusion to push forward my young mothers' mentoring program. For which, by the way, I have the support of the Burnses, who have forgiven me for narcing on Geoff's drunk driving episode."

"Let me get my glasses back on. Whenever I think about Geoff as a father, I get a headache."

"It's given him a sense of humor. He told me they were signing Cody up for infant swim classes." Her eyes glinted. "At least, I think he was trying to be funny."

He almost snorted coffee out his nose. He put the mug down. "I'm really here to give you this." He pulled the wide, foil-wrapped package from beneath his coat. "Happy Holidays."

"For me? You shouldn't have!" She tore into the paper eagerly. "Oh, Russ." She started laughing. "Thank you. They're just what I needed." She held up the waterproof, insulated, chain-tread-soled boots. "How did you know?"

He laughed. "Lucky guess?" She turned the boots back and forth, admiring them.

"I love them." She dropped them into the box. "I'll wear them tonight after midnight mass."

"It must get crazy for you on Christmas Eve. Everyone else is having a holiday and you're working your tail off."

"Like a cop."

"Like a cop."

"It easy for me to lose all sense of what I'm here for and turn into this grumpy, harried martinet, obsessing with getting everything done right and on time. That's why I'm hiding out in my office."

"Oh. I didn't mean to interrupt."

"Oh, no, I'm glad you came. I haven't seen you since they hustled you off to get your backside dressed at the hospital." The last light of the sunset was flooding the room, from windows and mirrors. Her hair, caught up in its usual twist, had already come loose, strands the color of gingerbread and fire floating around her face.

"Seems like a long time, yeah."

"I've really missed having you to talk with." Her words hung in the air.

"Me, too." There was a long pause. He had a sudden, lung-constricting conviction that coming here had been a mistake, that he had to leave right away, had to climb back into his truck and go home. "I ought to be going."

"Oh." She looked at the coffee mug in her hand. "Of course." She placed it carefully on the desk. "Thank you. Thank you for my favorite present." They both stood. She reached out and they clasped hands, squeezing hard. She smiled brightly. "Merry Christmas, Russ."

He pulled her to him without conscious thought and she came, settling against him, their arms wrapped around each other. He held her pressed tightly against his heart. "Merry Christmas," he said into her hair. It smelled of beeswax and cinnamon.

She looked up at him. Her eyes were very large.

"Clare," he said.

She swallowed.

"Clare . . ."

She shook her head. "No."

He touched her face. She closed her eyes and for a moment, pressed her cheek into his palm. Then she opened her eyes and stepped backwards, breaking his hold. He reached for her. She threw up both hands, a barricade against him. "Leave. Now. Go home to your wife."

He let his hands drop, heavy and useless. "I wouldn't—"

"Yes, you would. And God help me, so would I. Go. Please."

He nodded, turned, walked away, through the dim hall, through the scent of pine and beeswax, through the haunting voice of the soloist, singing. "Earth stood hard as iron, water like a stone. Snow had fallen, snow on snow, snow on snow. In the bleak midwinter, long ago."

Around the square, the remaining shops were closing, employees chattering down the sidewalks, last-minute shoppers slipping and sliding under the weight of bags and boxes. The fuzzy candy canes and reindeer, the fat lightbulbs, everything the same as it always was, as it always had been. Everything the same. Everything different. Everything.

He climbed into his truck and headed home.